CRISIS IN THE CONGO

ANTHONY C. FABIANO

A FICTION IMPRINT FROM ADDUCENT
WWW.ADDUCENTCREATIVE.COM

Titles Distributed In
North America
United Kingdom
Western Europe
South America
Australia

CRISIS IN THE CONGO

ANTHONY C. FABIANO

Crisis in the Congo

By Anthony C. Fabiano

ISBN 978-1-937592-22-6 (PAPERBACK)

PUBLISHED BY ADDUCENT UNDER ITS ESCRIRE FICTION IMPRINT.

JACKSONVILLE, FLORIDA

WWW.ADDUCENTCREATIVE.COM

PUBLISHED IN THE UNITED STATES OF AMERICA.

Dedication

To my wonderful sons - Christopher and Gabriel - may your life adventures take you to far-off destinations.

CHAPTER 1

Chaos erupted in the Democratic Republic of the Congo and the Director of the Central Intelligence Agency was puzzled by the magnified upswing in violence. He remembered a quote. "All roads in Africa lead to the Congo." The Director could not recall what arcane historical reference that the quote originated from. Decades had passed since he heard the statement. He wondered who paraphrased Africa's most turbulent nation in one masterful quote. Brutal violence, tribal ruthlessness, mineral wealth abuse, government instabilities, and failed colonial transitions allowed despot dictators to cause havoc in the Congo. The Director wondered for a moment if the famed legendary traveler Doctor Livingston made the quote. The seasoned Washington stiff shirt with over thirty years of federal service hurled papers across the table. The table was covered with classified analysis reports; satellite images of a secret uranium mine; MI6 classified reports on Zimbabwe diamond smuggling; village massacre photos; and dossiers on the major players in the newly formed Congo government. Papers landed haphazardly. Frustrated, he tossed the UN select intelligence report on the Congo in the burn bag. The Director was mentally spent. He had just received a four hour brief, so much information - so little time to process. He had thirty minutes to contemplate the shit storm brewing in the Congo before he briefed the President of the United States alone in the Oval Office.

On the other side of the world, the UN Special Envoy to the Democratic Republic of the Congo looked out the window. Armageddon arrived in the city of Kinshasa for the third time within a year. Rebel forces gained a substantial foothold outside the capital city. A paid insurgency, supported by criminal masterminds, had sprouted. Fires cascaded across the skyline. Screams and deep gurgled sounds of pain resonated. Darkened hollowed buildings held many hiding faces.

As the Special Envoy read the daily intelligence report, he shook his head in disbelief. UN troops were ineffective at quelling violent

1

attacks. Over eight thousand UN troops were deployed throughout Kinshasa. Heavily armed soldiers had little impact. Frightened Congolese who resided in the capital city pleaded for protection. Refugees from the interior traveled to the Kinshasa to escape the rebels. Tent cities popped up everywhere. UN forces were spread thin, and rebel leaders freely recruited a new generation of child soldiers. Remote villages became bloodbaths to the utter dismay of the occupants who sought UN protection. Over the year, a huge migration ensued as organized crime syndicates erupted and mercenaries arrived – all holding power with an octopus-vice grip.

As the world watched in horror, the Dark Continent experienced yet another war – now centered in the Congo. Upwards of five million had died in the past nine years. At any one time, thirty-five rebel factions operated freely. The vast wilderness and geographic isolation of the Congo helped conceal large rebel camps. The massive influx of money from illegal diamonds ignited a vast smuggling operation. Conditions became ripe for a major insurgency.

"Nothing is going to stop the rebels now," a frightened tone emitted from the UN Special Envoy as he talked to the UN Secretary-General on the secure phone. He wanted more troops, yet many partner nations were reluctant to offer support. The risk of a bloodbath was too great. "What about the Americans?"

"The President made it quite clear that he would not send any American troops." The Secretary-General replied. The seasoned diplomat was very concise in his comments. He continued. "The Iraq surge has the Americans tied up, and Afghanistan still lingers in unchartered territory." He paused for a moment to collect his thoughts. "Besides, the Americans are scared by memories of Mogadishu." He heard a deep sigh on the other end of the phone. Every UN diplomat knew not to discuss the Somalia carnage with the Americans. The Secretary-General continued. "You will have to work with what you have."

"If the rebels storm my compound," before he could finish, the Secretary-General cut him off.

"You do not have the authority to withdraw forces." The UN Secretary-General stated firmly. "If the Congo fails," his voice inflection rose, "everything we have done in Africa could be jeopardized." After a brief moment, he added. "Our reputation is at stake." The career diplomat understood the magnitude of the situation.

"What about the British?" The UN Special Envoy asked.

"The Prime Minister will send a counterinsurgency expert." The UN Secretary-General knew how to get results by leveraging many nations. He asked for the most experienced soldiers and the British responded with a Colonel who had served many years in Africa and most recently in Liberia. Unbeknownst to UN leadership, the Director, CIA had a plan to send his own special operative with recent African experience with utmost haste.

Meanwhile four thousand miles away from the turmoil that ravaged the Congo, the scene was vastly different. Tom Russell plunged an ice axe into a sheer ice wall. The weight from the lifeless body of an injured hiker forced him to pull with all of his strength. Every muscle in his back ached as he hung in mid-air. The satellite phone attached to the chest harness buzzed loudly, but he was busy – it would have to wait. In a split-second, the ice shelf where he previously stood collapsed from the weight. Chunks of ice descended two hundred feet into open space and revealed a large gaping hole. The summer snowmelt on Mount Rainier evaporated the protective ice layer that he now hung precariously over. As he held a firm grip on the injured hiker, Russell pulled a spare ice screw from his harness and slammed it into the ice wall to anchor their body weight. With every ounce of energy, he dragged his body onto an adjoining ice shelf and set up a rigging station to recover the bruised climber. Russell shifted his weight, pulled the rope taut, and pinned the extra rope loop underneath his leg. The line held the lifeless climber's body secure. He breathed heavy as he escaped death once again.

Russell looked far off to the Seattle skyline and wondered how many more rescues would be needed today. As a volunteer for Seattle's Mountain Rescue Team, he knew the Fourth of July weekend on Mount Rainier would be packed with inexperienced climbers. The last rescue was his fifth one, and he racked up twelve in the past two days. The satellite phone rang yet again. He thought the phone call was from the inbound rescue helicopter. He cued the satellite phone on speaker.

3

"Russell here."

"Tom, this is Colonel Crevace from Africa Command." Russell froze instantly not from the cold, but from the shock of the military tracking him down. Crevace was a trusted mentor and leader whom he served with in Iraq. Russell volunteered to be part of Crevace's elite snatch and grab team for high-value former Iraqi leaders. A few months before, Crevace was the one who hand-selected Russell to take a team into Liberia to obtain valuable information on former President Charles Taylor in order to charge Taylor as a war criminal. Russell was plunged into a cat and mouse game with international terrorists who tried to take Liberia back to civil war. Russell led a team into Cameron to capture the former President Charles Taylor and turn him over to the international criminal courts at The Hague for prosecution of war crimes. Russell survived Liberia, but he was banged up from numerous firefights and needed several months to recover.

"I need you to deploy to the Congo within the next twelve hours." Crevace requested in a stern voice.

"Sir," Russell paused, "Can't talk right now." Russell said as he pulled his right arm and kicked his leg up onto the small ledge of the ice shelf. "Call you back." The abrupt nature of the call shocked Russell, and probably the Colonel who outranked him. Russell hurried to complete the rescue and call his old boss back.

In the more secure area of Kinshasa, the Intercontinental Hotel loomed large. Layers of security blanketed the compound. From the guard shacks to the security cameras to the fence, the compound was as secure as any place in the world. The NGO community arrived in the Congo shortly after UN forces secured the capital city. Foreigners flocked to the Congo. Some came for the high salaries in a combat zone. Some believed they could finally bring aid to Congolese without fear of reprisals or death. Unapproved drugs were sent to the Congo and illegally tested on kidnapped locals. Control of the massive nation, the size of Texas, was impossible. Mountainous borders compounded the challenge. Diamonds were freely smuggled across borders. The agreement developed in Kimberly, South Africa, referred to as the Kimberly Process, had been extremely difficult to enforce in the war-ravaged

Congo. The Kimberly Process was developed in response to the flow of illicit 'blood' diamonds from West Africa nations that endured brutal civil wars. Warring factions in Sierra Leone transferred 'blood' diamonds to Liberia for sale onto the world's market. Titans of the international diamond trade purchased thousands of rough diamonds to curtail a flood on the market. As the Congo crisis erupted, only forty-three nations signed onto the Kimberly Accord. None of the former Soviet states and most notably China had not signed - more than likely China would never agree to the terms.

At the rooftop bar inside the Intercontinental Hotel, the mood was grim. Dozens of foreign aid workers tried to assess the situation. Many wanted out of the Congo. In a rapid fashion, everything appeared to have spiraled out of control. The sound of gunfire became a common occurrence. The UN peace mandate that oversaw the transition of power from President Mobutu had been violated. Warring factions instigated violence to take control. After Mobutu was forced out of power, warlords postured for control and rebel factions kidnapped a next generation of child soldiers to wage war.

Foreigners huddled at the bar and devoured glass after glass of scotch as they discussed options. Among them were Belgians, French, Germans, Dutch, Portuguese, and Canadians. In the corner of the bar, an American named Dan Gertz appeared anxious even though he had the protection of several large bodyguards. Gertz was heavily involved in illegal diamond trade and recently moved into the more lucrative sale of weapons to warring factions.

"The ship will arrive in eighteen days." Gertz stated as he looked at Rajik Nabee who was a weapons smuggler with links to Hezbollah. Gertz continued. "We will need a diversion." Gertz knew he needed the Hezbollah gun runner, although every bone in his body told him not to trust Rajik. More importantly, Gertz kept his secret close that he was of Jewish descent.

Rajik Nabee came to Kinshasa from Monrovia, Liberia. He made his way to the Hezbollah training camp along the Congo River. Lebanese orphans known as Ashbals were sent to Africa and educated in warfare. In a matter of weeks, Rajik asserted more control over this ragtag outfit of orphan fighters. When Rajik arrived, he had brought a pile of rough diamonds and two hundred thousand dollars in cash to fund the terrorist training camp.

"My Ashbals will kill." Rajik stated in a cold voice. "We just need to give them more drugs." Gertz smiled wide as his plan had started.

Safely off the Mount Rainer, Russell assessed his conversation with Crevace and the tone of his voice. Russell knew something was wrong, terrible wrong. He hastily departed the barely furnished house. As he sat in Seattle-Tacoma International Airport, Russell reviewed the package of information he downloaded in the twenty-five minutes that it took him to pack. He pulled out emergency cash, nearly twenty thousand dollars from a hidden safe under his bed; whatever he forgot to bring he would buy. Russell immersed himself in the Congo affairs as he traveled from Seattle to Kinshasa via Washington Dulles, Brussels, and Accra.

For the next twenty-six hours, Russell tried to understand what he was walking into. He pulled out the map of the Congo and rolled it over several airport seats. He immersed himself in navigable roads, trains, rivers, and towns. The immense size of the Congo made him ponder what Stanley and Doctor Livingston must have experienced where no road existed. Russell understood from his time in Liberia how the deep jungles of Africa could affect man. He recalled Mr. Kurtz from Joseph Conrad's famed novel Heart of Darkness and how Kurtz lost his mind. He pondered if the same would happen to him.

Russell focused on the most recent Congo conflict. Laurent Kabila was assassinated on January 18, 2001, several days before the next US President assumed office. Prior to the Kabila assassination, the Mobutu regime had strangled economic development for thirty years. Mobutu's arrogance was everywhere, even in the new name of Zaire he chose for his nation. Near his ancestral home, deep in the jungle, Mobutu built a massive Presidential Palace while most of his constituents lived in squalor. The boiling point came when the economy crashed and massive inflation resulted. Within days, Mobutu lost control of the military.

Older reports caught Russell's attention. In 1960, the Belgian Congo was thrust onto the world stage as the U.S. and the USSR bargained for political control. Based upon the growing unrest in

Belgian Congo and the atmospherics of neighboring African colonies that sought independence, Belgium granted independence to the Congo, thereby ended seventy-five years of colonial rule. The Congo's new Prime Minister, Patrice Lumumba, rattled the Belgian King at the transfer ceremony when he blamed the colonial power for a hundred years of abuse. Sinister plans emerged as Belgian companies did not want to give up vast mineral mines in the Katanga Provence in southern Congo. A puppet Katanga government backed by Belgian investors was established, and it sought secession from the Lumumba government. Violence erupted. Tension in Katanga escalated. The crisis forced UN intervention and several thousand UN peacekeeping troops deployed. However, Belgium sent their military to protect the lucrative mines. In the streets, the Belgian forces fired indiscriminately on the protestors and killed hundreds. There was a tremendous international outcry, yet no one was brought to justice. The volume of information strangled Russell's mind. He closed his eyes and prepared himself for the shit storm he was about to enter.

In the Kinshasa darkness and several blocks from the Intercontinental Hotel, a boat with no lights powered forward. The thirty-foot vessel did not arrive at the commercial port that was controlled by UN troops. It landed on a small deserted beach. An athletic woman who wore all black jumped into the water. Immediately, she was soaked. She knew the boat driver would not get too close in case a rapid departure was needed. She pointed the Uzi sub-machinegun toward the shoreline. On her chest harness were several fragmentation grenades and four magazines. On her right hip rested her favorite weapon, the famed and extremely lethal Israeli Desert Eagle. The fifty caliber pistol was a cannon compared to other firearms. Any gun collector knew the weapon knew the recoil could break a man's hand. On her left hip dangled a nine-inch serrated combat knife. The sixty-pound pack on her back contained more ammunition, a collapsed sniper rifle, and most importantly an array of cocktail dresses. Inside her neckline, she wore a charm that possessed a small family photo when she was about eight years old. Her mother died weeks after the photo was taken. Her death was a result of a Hamas bomb blast in Tel Aviv. On the back of the necklace, there was an inscription embossed, *'For lack of guidance a nation falls, but many advisers make victory sure.'* The inscription was well known in Tel Aviv for both being from Proverbs 11:14 and the seal of the Institute for Intelligence and Special Intelligence, otherwise known as the Mossad.

Francesca Waszey wore the rank of Lieutenant Colonel in the Israeli Defense Force and was on permanent loan to the Mossad. She remained in Africa to hide from her overbearing father and fulfill her Mossad duties as an international terrorist hunter. If her father found out about her illicit affair while on assignment in Liberia, her father would be livid. She had an unsanctioned love affair with an American military officer, named Tom Russell. Francesca had a lot to fear as her father was the primary Mossad agent who developed American assets when he was assigned to the Israeli Consulate in Washington, DC. Her father turned several career government employees to provide secrets for Israel. She learned everything she could as a teenager growing up in Alexandria, Virginia. The family parties included many Americans who worked in the Pentagon. She was trained at an early age to witness how to recruit, train, and manipulate assets.

Francesca was worried that her father would obtain information on her most recent love affair with an American military officer. She wanted to protect Russell and kept his name out of her reports. She knew Tel Aviv would track him for the rest of his life. More importantly, she knew her father would execute her love interest. Her father would neither allow Francesca to fall in love nor be placed in a vulnerable position. Francesca knew she had violated one of the most important parts of being a female Mossad agent - she had a close intimate relationship. She did her mission well, yet she fell in love.

Yacef stood on the shoreline as Francesca pushed through the water. Yacef was the local Mossad agent assigned to the Congo. Israel was very concerned with what happened with the Congo's vast diamond mines. Yacef attempted to greet her and pointed towards the vehicle parked fifty feet away. She brushed past him. She had no expressions of warmth. Yacef heard that she was a killing machine. He turned his back to her without thinking as he opened the back gate of the vehicle. For a moment he wondered if she would kill him, but she put her gear inside without a word. Yacef knew that if she was sent to kill him, it would already have occurred. Yacef looked older than the fifty-four years in his profile. Francesca felt bad for what was going to happen to him when he got back to Tel Aviv. The cover story told to Yacef was that he had received a promotion to run operations in Great Britain. He believed Tel Aviv. He enjoyed the sizeable advance check as reward and purchased a new wardrobe, especially as London was tremendously more expensive. As Francesca dropped her gear, Yacef unloaded his four suitcases and struggled to carry them to the boat. Francesca kept her eye on the perimeter with her pistol drawn. She peered back and saw Yacef waddle through the water to the boat. He had to make four trips to his getaway ride out of the Congo.

Francesca sped the vehicle away from the beach and drove several side roads. She kept the vehicle's lights off as the UN initiated a curfew based upon the latest rebel attacks. Anyone on the streets at night would be arrested. She memorized the sketch map. In the darkness, the landmarks were identifiable. She sped down the darkened streets. The half blown out bridge was still open for traffic. A UN soldier waved for her to stop; however, she pressed the pedal to the floor. She accelerated the vehicle across the bridge and the vehicle became airborne as she struck debris. She memorized the directions. She turned right at the destroyed church that received artillery rounds during the civil war. Francesca remained focused. Kinshasa's landscape was heavily scarred. Vacant, blown out buildings dotted the skyline, but the buildings had residents. Thousands of squatters flocked to the city. Buildings appeared dark, yet if she stopped to look closer, she would see desperate faces. The only lights visible were above the river where all of the diplomats lived in lavish compounds.

Francesca pulled into the open garage and locked the large wooden door. Up the back staircase, she lugged her gear and weapons. She entered the apartment building with the key Yacef provided and was surprised to see two men who sat at the table. Her right hand reached for the Desert Eagle pistol.

"My name is Galpin and this is my brother Krause." The man had a machine gun across his lap and directed at her. Francesca was exposed, and she did the only natural thing - smiled widely.

"Where do I stay?" Francesca inquired. She eased her hand off the Desert Eagle pistol. She had no leverage.

"Here." Galpin pointed as he stood. The South African was large and muscular for an older man. Francesca read the dossier on the South African brothers. Galpin was sixty-three years old and his brother was fifty-seven. There was a third younger brother, but he was killed in the Apartheid uprisings. The brothers were accused of retaliating against the locals who shot their brother. They had killed eighteen locals and burned their homes. Twenty years ago they left South Africa as wanted men. They were very bitter on the changes in South Africa and unable to return to a post-Apartheid nation. "Is this apartment ok?" Galpin inquired. Francesca nodded as she needed these contacts.

After the brothers departed, Francesca stripped and took a shower. She held the towel close to her waist as not to reveal the eight-inch horrible scar on her left side. She felt a presence that she was being watched and did not want to give up any identifiable marks. Galpin had installed several cameras. In his car, he watched her get dressed. She looked slim, muscular and slender. He liked how she placed the small pistol overtop of the black negligee.

Francesca's mission was to clean up after a top secret mission. In 1973, well before the end of Apartheid, South Africa reached an agreement with Israel to share atomic weapons technology. A new type of atom bomb based upon use of Cobalt and Uranium was developed. Mossad agents had learned that South Africans wanted to use the weapon of mass destruction on its own colored population in the event of a major uprising. Mossad leaders believed the atomic weapon was smuggled out of South Africa and sold to former Congo President Mobutu. Francesca held an aged photo that showed the atomic weapon. She had little time to secure the weapon of mass destruction.

CHAPTER 2

Fred Schultz, the CIA's Chief of Station at the US Embassy in Kinshasa, puffed on a large Monte Crisco cigar. Schultz received the pleasurable gem in a diplomatic pouch from a longtime friend stationed in Havana. He was far away from the reach of Washington and frankly did not care if he got in trouble for smoking a Cuban cigar. Schultz was the senior CIA official in Africa's Great Lakes region and was responsible for all the agency's operations in the Congo, Zambia, Rwanda, Burundi, and Zimbabwe. Schultz had a good grasp on what happened in the Congo and the region, or at least he thought. Wars in Iraq and Afghanistan shifted a majority of intelligence assets out of Africa. Few in Langley even cared what occurred in the Congo. Schultz's wrote a scathing report on the potential disastrous outcome if high-grade Uranium 238 arrived on the world's black market. Schultz believed many foreign powers desired the uranium for nuclear enrichment and the Congo became the hot spot for black market uranium.

Schultz looked at the multitude of fires that burned across Kinshasa's skyline. He shook his head in disbelief. No one expected that the rebels had the capability to advance so fast. They were loosely organized, mostly undisciplined criminals. Everyone expected the UN to hold the city's perimeter. Nobody expected the rebels would break through the UN's international military force, yet within days, holes in the protective security blanket around the city became apparent. Twenty-two Pakistani, thirty-five Jordanian, and eight French soldiers were killed. Rebels from all over the shattered country traveled hundreds of miles to wage violence. Many organizations within the American government - CIA, FBI, NSA, State Department, US AID, and the Pentagon – were perplexed by the current crisis. Cooperation in Africa remained dysfunctional.

Schultz knew that there were many international players and no one would wait for America to sort out their strategy. Israel was concerned as the Congo possessed substantial diamond reserves. China wanted a foothold to garner more exploration of rare earth minerals. North Korean engineers were sent to help reopen an old uranium mine while Office 35 of the North Korean Special Intelligence section had managed to smuggle high grade uranium out of the Congo. Iran sought technology for its secret nuclear weapons program. Hundreds of South Africans lived in exile from their criminal actions during the Apartheid reform movement. Former KGB agents bribed Congo government officials to gain more control. Hezbollah operatives sold illegal weapons to rebel factions who operated throughout the Congo. Lebanese operated most of the hotels and restaurants. Most of all, several influential Belgians tried to keep a handle on their former colony. Schultz's head hurt for all of the factors that imploded in the Congo. He puffed hard on the Cuban cigar. It was his only pleasure. He was in a pile of shit and did not know which way to dig out. He needed help and fast.

In the Langley situation room, several men in their late fifties stood around the video monitor and watched the video feed Schultz piped in from the embassy server. From the top of the US Embassy, he held the camera steady. Far below, Schultz heard the Marines assigned to protect the embassy shout orders back and forth as they ran to reinforce the entrance. The Marines were in full riot gear and carried twelve gauge shotguns. Hundreds of protesters converged at the front gate and screamed for help. Many wondered where the United States was in their time of need. The smoke was thick and polluted the air.

"Can you see?" Schultz inquired.

"Yup, we got good video feed. The smoke is thick. How far out are they?" The senior officer in Langley asked.

"About a mile," Schultz replied. "The UN moved more troops into the city, but they only have APCs. There are no tanks here." APC stood for Armored Personnel Carriers, an eight thousand pound vehicle on six-wheel chassis with no windows. APCs could stop a small rocket but not the 7.62 millimeter armored piercing rounds that the rebels recently received from Hezbollah gun runners. The CIA desk officer on the other end understood the significant lack of resources to stop the rebels. "What did New York say?" Schultz referred to the UN headquarters in Manhattan.

"Nothing." The man far off in Langley stated. "Silence."

"They don't want to escalate the situation." Schultz retorted. He was disgusted at the lack of progress for the UN's training for the new Congo police force.

"Who's behind it?"

"Not sure right now." Schultz replied. "I have several guesses." Schultz paused for a moment and continued. "Whoever is bankrolling the rebels has a lot of free cash to give up."

"Whoever is behind it needs to be terminated."

"Understood." Schultz contemplated his current mission for a moment. There was no justice in the Congo, just repeated retaliations that never ended. "The rebels will tire out in another day. My biggest concern remains the uranium." The stiff shirts on the other end agreed.

Schultz completed the call after he received the usual advice from the pen pushing Langley desk officers to stay safe and not take any unacceptable risks. Schultz heard it before and was glad he did not have to serve as a desk officer. He had been a field operative for fifteen years and avoided assignments at Langley headquarters like the plague.

The Chief of Station sat behind his desk in the basement of the embassy. The secure room had routine scanning for listening devices. Schultz trusted few and knew several of the State Department career diplomats had loose lips. He was deeply concerned about the release of information.

Schultz looked at the stack of photos he had retrieved from the safe. The game had changed. Illegal uranium smuggling increased substantially and plagued world stability. If a rogue nation obtained the very potent Uranium 238, they would have the edge on developing a nuclear weapon.

Schultz was amazed at how rapid the level of interest increased at Langley. After terrorists drove their planes into the Pentagon and Manhattan's Twin Towers, the Congo had been off everyone's radar. Schultz believed most of the senior leadership at Langley wanted nothing to do with Africa. The CIA had bad experiences in Africa, especially in the 1960s. There were many missteps with several CIA supported assassinations. Schultz believed many in the CIA forgot about the past failures. As a young CIA operative, Schultz served in the Congo when it was called Zaire under then President Joseph Mobutu. Mobutu's thirty-year reign of terror ended abruptly when he was removed for power in May 1997. Four months later Mobutu would die in exile from prostate cancer, a fate many Congolese rejoiced.

Instability and civil war raged onward after Mobutu's Zaire government collapsed. Schultz knew the bloodied history of the Congo all too well. The Congo's heritage had been victimized by the Europeans. In the 1700s, there were over 35,000 voyages that transported slaves to America. For every single European in the American colonies, there were four Africans kidnapped and enslaved in the new land, with a majority originating from the Congo River region. Schultz knew America's support to Africa was lackluster at best and only brought front stage when some Hollywood star made a statement about a refugee camp. Schultz knew the real story that a week later the star would be back in their California mansion while Africans remained in deplorable conditions.

Schultz pondered the classified reports in front of him. Putting a UN face on operations in the Congo had been paramount for US National Security interests as America feared getting caught into another Mogadishu 'Black Hawk Down' scenario. However; the operational capability of UN troops had been a colossal failure as partner nations have differing agendas, not to mention the language barriers. By the second week, Nigeria sent a battalion of seasoned combat troops, veterans from the fighting in Sierra Leone. The Nigerian battalion with 800 heavily armed soldiers pushed into rebel strongholds. From building to building, they killed hundreds of rebels. Many of the rebels emerged into the sunlight with split heads and blood drips across their faces. The Nigerians unleashed a ruthless campaign. Most of the remaining rebels ran for their lives and took off their uniforms to blend in with the massive amount of refugees.

Meanwhile, the WNN (World News Network) reporter on top of the Intercontinental Hotel directed his crew to pan the camera across Kinshasa's burning skyline. The camera came back towards the reporter. The fifty-year-old man who went to Bosnia, Afghanistan, and Iraq had significant wartime experience. He arrived in Kinshasa two days ago and searched for the ground truth and began his broadcast.

"Congo stability is in crisis as more violence has erupted." He paused for dramatic effect and continued. "Fires rage across the once pristine Kinshasa skyline." The WNN reporter spoke. "UN troops have fought for six days against rebel forces that have infiltrated Kinshasa. Little progress has been made. The brutality of war echoed today across this forgotten land. This is Lester Beckman reporting live from the Congo." The WNN reporter quickly moved away from the edge of the roof. Gunfire was heard in the distance. The bright camera strobe light caught the attention of rebels on the ground, and he heard several rounds zing overhead. His combat experience taught him not to become a target.

After the live broadcast, the reporter and camera crew went downstairs to the hotel bar and ordered several strong drinks. The bar was packed. The smell from the bathroom repulsed many of the foreigners. The men succumbed to walking up on top of the roof and risked a stray round to take a piss. The few foreign women who were trapped in Kinshasa erected a small screen with old curtains. They relieved themselves in a bucket. Centralized plumbing in Kinshasa after the recent brutal civil war was non-existent. The waste disposal plant built by the Russians in the late 1960s decayed with age and the remaining scraps of metal were looted. War-torn Kinshasa relied upon a system of five thousand gallon septic tanks and a regular infiltration of pump trucks to empty the human sewage. The Intercontinental Hotel had four of these large drums linked together along the backside of the compound. For the first several days of the uprising, the abrupt stoppage of pumping out the sewage tanks plagued the foreign pampered guests. The hotel's lower rooms overflowed in human waste, and the guests had to be moved to higher floors. Pallets of bottled water lined the hotel lobby and provided some comfort to the foreigners. The pile slowly evaporated on the second day as the foreigners were glad to pay two dollars per bottle. As the flow of shower water completely halted on the morning of the third day, there was a mad rush by the foreigners to purchase cases of water at a time. Prices surged and in a few days, the hotel sold bottled water for twenty dollars each. Any amount of purified water was a luxury. Food was spoiled and the freshest food commanded the highest price. The restaurant menu was revised to show current prices from the crisis that inflated by three hundred percent. Most of the staff ceased to come to work and the only cooks were Lebanese who lived within the compound. The UN did not provide life support for the NGOs as they told them to contact their own government for support. Only a few countries had a diplomatic presence. The US Embassy was packed as thousands stood in line for military rations and bottled water. Many prayed for the resumption of departing flights out of the Congo. Latest UN reports stated enemy anti-aircraft guns would hit the arriving flights. A UN cargo plane was shot at the day before and nearly exploded from the multiple armor piercing rounds, courtesy of the massive weapons black market operated by Hezbollah.

Across town in a secure building inside Nakor Industries, Dan Gertz watched with pleasure as Kinshasa burned. Nakor's office building was surrounded by a fifteen-foot concrete wall with barbed wire. Guard towers overlooked everything and Gertz maintained his own small militarized security force. He was by far the wealthiest man in the Congo with an estimated wealth approaching two hundred million dollars. What was striking about Gertz was not his young age of thirty-seven, or his close connections to the new Congo government officials based upon large donations. What was striking about Dan Gertz was his ruthless tactics and how he employed his mercenary army of former Polish Special Forces. Gertz was paranoid about his own security and lived within his twenty story office building's top three floors. Congo diamonds amounted to twenty percent of the world's known resources and Gertz wanted control, at all costs. He dialed the number in his phone and talked to the leader of the National Patriotic Liberation Army (NPFL). Gertz told him that he was pleased with the fires and asked for more car bombings. The NPFL leader was pleased with the chaos and was glad to make more money. Gertz hung up the phone and wondered if the man was actually a Colonel or just playing the role of rebel commander. Gertz called his driver and within a few moments departed Nakor in a four vehicle column of his own personal security detail on his way to the Intercontinental Hotel. Gertz was proud of his little war that raged into the seventh day.

A few moments later, Gertz sat in the corner of the hotel bar and ordered a bottle of champagne and waited patiently for the new Congo Minister of Information. Gertz supported him with weekly bribes of twenty thousand dollars. Gertz became impatient and motioned to his head of security to track down the tardy minister. Nakor security services were headed by a brutal thug named Braum, who was a former Polish Special Forces soldier. Gertz did not know if that was his first or last name. Everyone knew him by his last name Braum. At six feet four inches and two hundred and sixty pounds, Braum was a massively sized man. The diameter of his biceps was the size of a man's leg. His eyes were a glassy coal color. Braum never showed a response or emotion. The most distinguishable feature was the ten inch ponytail that stretched from his pure black hair. Braum took pleasure in killing, regardless of skin color, age, or sex. He was ruthless and not allowed to ever return to his native Poland after murdering a senior military officer whom he disliked.

Under the current crisis, Gertz knew he could easily slip in weapons and smuggle out diamonds or even the higher prized uranium. And the best part was no one would know he was connected as the shell companies under Nakor Industries kept him out of public view. Dietger Laurent was pleased to have a chilled glass of champagne waiting as he sat down across from Gertz. Dietger Laurent, the most corrupt Belgian businessman in the Congo, reviewed the three documents in front of him. The first was a listing of all the smuggled weapons that arrived yesterday on the Hope of Africa container ship; the second was a list of names of potential buyers; and the third was a much smaller list of those UN and new Congo government officials he needed to bribe. As poverty remained rampant among a majority of Congolese, a group of ultra-rich emerged on the scene.

"Two more weeks." Dietger looked up from the papers.

"Is that all?" Gertz inquired as he looked around the room.

"Keep the pressure for two more weeks and the UN will fold."

"Then Kinshasa will be ours." Gertz held a toast.

"And all of the Congo." Dietger replied.

"We will have to kill the South Africans." Gertz paused to see the impact on Dietger's face. Dietger had been impressed with the South

African brothers, Galpin and Krause Vanetten. The South African brothers were the most reliable arms smugglers in the Congo. Word quickly spread in the international community that the UN was grossly incompetent at controlling security within the Congo. Weapons could be smuggled to warring factions and diamonds could be illegally exported. Gertz continued, "They're getting sloppy. They have history."

"Every white man has a history in Africa and you my friend will be no different when you depart this god forsaken land." Dietger stated coldly. He had survived a lifetime in the Congo. Dietger had committed many atrocities, and in his mind he thought it was justified. After all, the Congo was their former colony. There was generational hatred of the local populace. Under King Leopold's II guidance, Belgians butchered and murdered countless Africans, yet no one was ever brought to justice. When they lost power, a new emergence of Belgians raped their former colony of all possible mineral wealth.

Inside the United States embassy, the Ambassador convened a high level meeting. Charles Ringfield III, a significant political donor, believed an adventure in Africa would be thrilling and financially fruitful, especially as several extremely wealthy Manhattan diamond merchants wanted him to pursue the position. Besides, no other ambassadorial level candidates jumped at the opportunity to live in the Congo. A few sizeable contributions to several influential Senatorial campaigns solidified his Ambassadorship.

Ambassador Ringfield informed the embassy staff that security would be tightened and all nonessential personnel would commence the evacuation protocol. As Schultz departed the meeting, he shook his head as the situation on the ground was dire. Schultz came into the CIA right after he completed his Master's program at Johns Hopkins. He focused on International Affairs and had become very close to his advisor, an older professor who became like the father he never had. One night after a heavy drinking ritual with his mentor, he learned the truth about his mentor who retired from the CIA, a piece of knowledge that could get them both killed if known. Schultz joined the agency and completed operative training twenty-four years ago. Schultz's mentor was old breed CIA, original OSS from World War II. This exposure provided Schultz a graphic look into long forgotten CIA operations throughout Africa and invaluable lessons learned for those who made the ultimate sacrifice.

Within Kinshasa, Congolese huddled for survival. One of its residents, Tshambe Kuleli worked at the U.S. Embassy, yet he could not get there. Tshambe served as Schultz's driver. He watched out the hole in the wood where a glass window once stood. He heard female screams from the street. The vehicle's headlights illuminated a woman being attacked by several men who appeared to be rebels. Their laughter overrode her panicked screams as they assaulted her. Tshambe could not do anything. He placed the piece of plywood back in place over the broken window. He needed to keep his family safe, especially as his wife was killed. He was the only one left to care for his three children. Six months ago his wife went to check on her mother. She never returned. He had no news. Few Congolese owned cell phones. Only the foreigners could afford them. Finally, he received news. Tshambe's wife was murdered and dragged behind a vehicle with several other bodies. Her torso fell apart as her legs remained tied to the rebel's vehicle as it sped away. Tshambe could only bury part of her.

The night was cold and Tshambe pulled the blanket up on his youngest child. Tshambe's disfigured face was not noticeable as he lay on the bed. The machete that sliced across his head in the last civil war nearly killed him. Tshambe should have died. His wife dragged him for two days on a makeshift stretcher to her village. She navigated between government and rebel lines. She pulled with all of her might to get him to safety. The ten inch scar from Tshambe's right ear to his mouth reminded him every day how much his wife loved him. Tshambe thought the UN would protect the city from the rebels. He would never have returned to Kinshasa if he had known the UN forces would crumble.

CHAPTER 3

At Kinshasa's International Airport, Schultz observed the chaotic scene unfold as foreigners tried to depart the embattled city. The arrival lounge was deserted. Schultz had no problem finding the highly regarded Marine officer. A white man in his mid-thirties stood out in the crowd. Russell was exhausted from the shift in time zones and the extremely long travel time, but he knew that there would be no time to rest. Thirty-six hours after he departed Seattle, Schultz greeted Russell. Schultz pointed to an exit door guarded by a UN soldier from Spain. Schultz flashed his credentials to the UN soldier and Russell bypassed Congolese immigration. Russell was pleased as his checked bags contained half a dozen knives and specialized military gear. The UN weapons embargo across the Congo restricted even knives from entering the country.

"How was the flight?" Schultz asked.

"Long, too long. Seems like I just left Africa."

"Weren't you in Liberia last month?"

"About six weeks ago."

"I read your report and also what the UN had to say about you." Schultz paused and looked with a smirk. "They really did not care for you. You were called reckless and worse than a mercenary." Russell was put in a tough position in between a slow, inept UN Mission in Liberia and a fast moving tidal wave coming as deadly forces loyal to Charles Taylor tried to shake up stability.

"What are they going to do?" Russell asked. "Shave my head and send me back to Iraq?" He paused for Schultz's laugh, "The UN is incapable of the smallest military task."

"Understood." Schultz focused on his new arrival's comments. "Since you have already operated in Africa, I don't need to remind you how significantly different counter-insurgency operations are here compared to Iraq or Afghanistan. Lots of military guys miss that point and are behind the power curve coming in."

"No, I got it. I had a great mentor." Russell replied. "A British Colonel named Kitson."

"Frank Kitson?" Schultz inquired. Russell nodded agreement. Schultz heard about Kitson. Every operative in Africa with any sense had heard of Kitson. His exploits in Rhodesia were legendary. Kitson came from a lineage of British soldiers who served in Africa. Relatives could be traced to early British colonial missions, which dated back to when Great Britain controlled half the known world. His father was even more of a legend for his fight during the Mau Mau rebellion. In the 1960s, General Kitson made fame as the primary negotiator with Jomo Kenyatta and other Mau Mau leaders to curtail the violence on white settlers. However, Kenya erupted in violence and white settlers were massacred. General Kitson walked into the rebel compound and negotiated the rescue of hundreds of captured settlers. Twenty years later his son performed the same daring move. As a Second Lieutenant in Rhodesia, the younger Kitson walked three hundred meters out from his platoon's compound and waited to negotiate the surrender of 400 tribesmen. Both father and son were highly regarded in counter insurgency doctrine.

The smell of extreme body odor from men hard at work resonated throughout the baggage area. Tshambe grabbed Russell's bags and carried them to the Embassy vehicle. The armored sedan was used mainly for the arrival of VIPs. Once inside the vehicle, Schultz handed Russell a psychological background profile on Dietger Laurent, who became the most powerful Belgian in the Congo. Russell read about the dark secrets that surrounded the Laurent family. In early 1940, German SS moved into Brussels and they took control of the country. In the ensuing four years before the Allied invasion at Normandy, a special team of German SS oversaw the building of a heavy water plant for use in Hitler's first atomic bomb. Dietger Laurent's grandfather was among the Belgian scientists who helped the Nazis. Germany's ambitious project was based upon the use of heavy water to split uranium atoms. Allied aircraft repeatedly bombed and destroyed the facility. German SS realized the continued threat from Allied bombers and secretly moved Hitler's development of a catastrophic weapon to the Belgian Congo. The Laurent family moved to the Congo under direct control of the Nazi SS.

"The Germans were heavily invested in the Congo," Schultz said as he Russell handed an aerial photo dated 1943. "The search for uranium was pivotal for the first atomic bomb."

"And the Congo became ground zero."

"Everyone was after uranium."

"Luckily, we developed the bomb first," Russell said. He continued reading how the Roosevelt administration and the Office of Strategic Services (OSS) headed by Will Donovan raced to find the only known source of uranium in the world, which happened to be in Katanga. Before the Germans arrived in the Congo, an American company owned rights to the Shinkolobwe mine in Katanga Province. In the early 1900s, uranium was used as a cancer cure, or thought to be a cure until the scathing reports caused the market to fall out. Over one thousand metric tons of uranium ore had been mined out of Shinkolobwe and shipped to America. Soon the American government bought all of the uranium and secretly began the Manhattan Project. The race between America and Germany for a massive weapon of biblical proportions was on.

As the armored sedan approached the US Embassy, throngs of people crowded and blocked the street. Hundreds of locals waited in makeshift lines trying to get US assistance out of the Congo. At any moment, both Schultz and Russell thought the crowd could get unruly and violent. Marines and locally hired security guards pushed through the crowd towards the armored vehicle. Once Schultz flashed his credentials and Russell's military ID, they entered the interior embassy compound. Within the main chancellery building, Schultz brought Russell into the secure basement room reserved for the Chief of Station. For several hours, they poured over intelligence reports, aerial photos, satellite images of the deep Congo jungle, and taped phone conversations. The volume of raw intelligence was daunting and hard to piece the jigsaw puzzle together.

"Who's behind the uranium smuggling?" inquired Russell.

"A man named Gertz."

"Who's helping him?" continued Russell.

"I know of at least two South African brothers involved in smuggling." Schultz responded.

"We find them, we find the uranium. I go home." Russell paused shortly and injected, "Right?"

"Don't think it will be that easy." Schultz had learned a lot about the Congo in the past year.

"It never is." Russell lowered his voice and looked at the photos of Kinshasa on fire. "It never is." Russell continued reading the dossier. Gertz monopolized diamond exports from rebel-held territory. Gertz was not concerned who purchased the rough, untraceable diamonds. Inadvertently, Gertz dealt blood diamonds to Al Qaeda and other terrorist organizations. Several Congolese nuclear officials were arrested last year for their involvement in illicit uranium exports. The Commissioner General for Atomic Energy and the Head of the Center for Nuclear Studies sold low-enriched uranium fuel from the Regional Center for Nuclear Studies in Kinshasa. The search for uranium pitted America against the Russians. During the Cold War, the Soviets secretly fought for control of Congo minerals. The Soviets needed vital supplies of cobalt and tritium to fuel their missile race. After the fall of the Soviet Union, a diabolical organization comprised of former KGB and senior generals called themselves the Russian Military Brotherhood. As they lost control of their own country in free democratic elections, they went underground and formed a criminal syndicate known as Voctrad. Voctrad funneled money globally and utilized precious uncut, rough diamonds as easy means to launder vast fortunes. Voctrad managed to keep illuminating the flame of fear, similar to the former Soviet Union methods.

After he completed his research, Russell requested a meeting with the US Ambassador. The forty-five-minute session helped little to increase his situational awareness. The frail sixty-eight-year old man regretted coming to Africa. Russell was not impressed as he heard the Ambassador would not listen to Schultz. The inexperienced diplomat was overly concerned about being accommodating to the massive influx of NGOs from not only the United States, but also Canada, Japan, France, Germany, Russia, Italy, Norway, Sweden, and Finland. He allowed nearly four hundred non-Americans move into the embassy compound.

Russell wanted to get out of the embassy compound, yet to do so he needed to fill out several sets of forms, a new policy instituted by the Ambassador. The duplicate pages and relentless questions on the forms on why he had to leave the security of the embassy made him frustrated. Russell was not used to so many bureaucratic rules. He found Schultz in his office.

"Let's go for a walk." Schultz led him up to the top of the Embassy roof. "Take a look to the west." Russell held the high powered scope up to his right eye. "The rebels are held up in an old church." He pointed to the large plume of black smoke. "Hopefully, the UN can take the building."

"What about the violence in the streets?" Russell asked.

"Every idiot who wants to rob, rape, or pillage comes out of hiding. Many have old grudges that they can get settled." Schultz replied.

"Are more troops coming?"

"A Nigerian battalion arrived two days ago." Schultz said. He looked at Russell and sensed that he was impressed the Nigerian military arrived.

"How many men?"

"Eight hundred." Schultz looked up at Russell. "It's the same battalion that went into Liberia to take out Charles Taylor." The hollow expression that fell over Russell's face signified he knew the gravity of bringing in the Nigerians. The ruthless fighting exhibited by this Nigerian battalion became legendary. In the early days before Charles Taylor departed Liberia under the UN mandate, Nigeria parachuted an elite battalion to seize Robert's International Airport. A blood bath ensued with hundreds of dead on both sides. In the end, the Nigerians captured the airport and decimated Taylor's army.

"How long until they gain control?" Russell said. He knew that the horrible security condition would more than likely impact his mission.

"Five, maybe six days. Nigeria is the only close African Union member that has a standing force and can, or should I say will, respond." Schultz did not sound optimistic.

"What about the US, what about the Marines."

"Not this time, guess the two ongoing wars are enough. More importantly, many Americans lost faith in the Africa cause after the disaster in Somalia."

On the other side of Kinshasa, a terrorist named Kamal looked at the photo taken earlier in the day of the Israeli spy. He wanted to kill her now with a bullet, yet he knew an interrogation would be more beneficial. Kamal looked into the sniper scope toward the apartment's window. A body had moved past. There was only one occupant according to his South African contacts whom he paid handsomely for the information. They were happy to hand over information on the Mossad agent, and Kamal assessed that they wanted the Israeli dead as well. Kamal shifted his position and thought about taking the shot. He could justify the killing. However, he was informed to capture and interrogate.

As the son of a prominent Cairo physician, Kamal Abdullah was groomed to follow in his father's path. Everything had changed when his mother died, and his father married a French woman. To appease his wife's religious beliefs, Kamal's father became a non-practicing Muslim. His betrayal to Allah disgusted his only child. Throughout his college years, Kamal secretly met with members of the Muslim Brotherhood, one of Egypt's most notorious paramilitary groups. Three weeks before Kamal was supposed to graduate medical school, he murdered his father and his new wife. The Muslim Brotherhood provided him sanctuary and a path toward Al Qaeda. Kamal received his indoctrination training at a remote terrorist base in the desert on the border between Yemen and Saudi Arabia. His medical skills were needed and he was first sent to the Tora Bora region of Afghanistan. Senior terrorist leaders cherished his battlefield medical skills. During the Tora Bora campaign by the invading Americans, Kamal served as one of three physicians by commander Bin Laden's side at all times. After he moved to Pakistan, Kamal received his specialized interrogation training with the Inter-Services Intelligence (ISI). In Somalia he was the only terrorist who had this advanced interrogation training and everyone turned to him. After a dozen interrogations that usually resulted in death, Kamal became emotional cold. His brutal skills made him the perfect terror weapon. Rapidly he rose within Al Qaeda's ranks and was assigned to handle high priority missions. Kamal closely trailed the Israeli spy in South Africa where they intercepted and decoded several messages. Kamal was excited at the chance to kill an Israeli.

In the cool evening Kinshasa air, Francesca departed the limousine and walked into the restaurant. She wore a strapless dress and the change in temperature chilled her. She arrived for the meeting and wanted to be early to get the seat against the wall. She did not see the South African brothers all day and surmised they already heard that Yacef had taken a bullet to the back of the head when he returned to Tel Aviv. She mused that the Mossad let him die on native soil. She gazed out across the room at the international aid workers who made a career out of traveling from one hot spot to another. There were several tables filled with foreign businessmen who entertained government officials with heavy doses of alcohol. Food followed, yet the officials were interested in the free booze. A night of heavy drinking equated to a week's salary for them. The locals on the street could never afford the luxury of purified, clean alcohol. Most succumbed to drinking home grown moonshine that could potentially blind them. Francesca stared out across the room from the rear table and made sure her back was tight against the wall. Her contact had arrived late.

"This is why I am here." Francesca said as she slid the photo across the table upside down.

"What is this?" The Congolese Minister of Information asked as he made sure no one saw the photo and added. "Information likes this will cost substantial." As the face and voice for the new Congo government, he went to great lengths to hide secret bribes. Corruption was rampant among the newly formed government as many ministers openly held out their hands. The Minister of Information was one of the most corrupt.

"We can do this the easy way or I can make very difficult for you." She passed a cashier's check across the table from the Bank of Tel Aviv. There was no name written. The dollar amount listed was fifty thousand US dollars.

"It's not enough."

"What do you want?"

"I want out of the Congo."

"That is not possible."

The Minister of Information looked at the check again and paused for a while. "I will tell you what I know. There were rumors of a camp that had been operated by Germans. It was deep inside the country. It may not exist anymore."

"Is that where the weapon went?" Francesca asked. Her Mossad training forced her to watch his every move and facial expression. She knew that he told the truth.

"No, the bomb was taken to his jungle palace. Mobutu rode around on it at parties."

"What did he want to do with it?"

"Don't know. Perhaps he sold it. The Russians would not help him. They thought he was a madman." The minister paused for a moment and continued. "Mobutu knew it was a matter of time before the KGB or CIA would come after him."

"Mobutu's dead now." Francesca was direct. "Someone else must have called the shots."

"Don't know. Mobutu used the threat of selling uranium on the black market to remain in power."

"And the uranium from Katanga was not good enough." Francesca said as a matter of fact. She had done her research.

"No, it needed a lot of processing. It required tons just to make a little isotope and was expensive. But everything changed a few months ago when a new mine for Uranium 238 was discovered."

"Where?"

"Near Lubumbashi. Close to the border with Zambia." The Minister looked around. He was visibly nervous. She did not know if his fear was real or an act. Whatever it was, the newly appointed minister sweated profusely. He continued, "You must see. My life is over. I need to get out of Kinshasa."

"I can't help you." She looked at him and spoke in a directive tone. "I need you to show me where the mine is."

"It's dangerous. The radiation will most certainly kill you. There was a team of American archaeologists who stumbled upon the uranium." The Minister smiled as he offered. "They were looking for King Solomon's Mine."

"What happened to them?"

"Radiation poisoning." The Minister of Information looked around the room at his drunk peers and assessed his personal situation. "I want out of the Congo."

Kimberly Roberts looked the part of adventurer and thrill seeker as she stared into the mirror in the hospital bathroom. Her hair was long and unkempt. Outside of splashing water on her face and under her armpits, she had not cleaned her body for three days. The visits back and forth to the U.S. Embassy and the hospital were non-stop. She had not been back to her apartment since she received the urgent call to come to the hospital. Five of her team members from the Smithsonian Museum were deathly ill and the doctors feared Ebola or some other tropical disease. The first one died on the UN helicopter ride. The second and third archeologists died within moments of arriving at the hospital, which caused the emergency room to be locked down for fear of an epidemic. The fourth died the next night and the team leader, her boss, was still alive. He was traveling and found everyone sick when he returned. He called in the emergency evacuation. She leaned over his body. He could not speak. He motioned for a paper and pen. On the paper he scribbled several lines that crisscrossed. The tips of the lines were bent. She had no idea what it meant. The radiation poison had taken its toll. The man gulped hard and stopped breathing.

CHAPTER 4

Schultz came out of the daily meeting with the Ambassador Ringfield and held his head. He punched his right hand into the solid concrete wall. It hurt. He cursed himself after he lost his composure. The US Ambassador drove the entire embassy staff insane with constant prodding. By the time Schultz returned to the vault, Russell was in place reviewing recent Interpol documents on criminal gangs in the Congo.

"We got a big mountain to climb." Russell pointed to the stack of papers, "understanding what really is going on here."

"No one has a clear picture of the calamity here." Schultz dropped his papers on the desk. "I have been here for over a year and I still do not have a full picture. The situation changes here constantly. It is managed chaos."

"Who's calling the shots?" Russell inquired.

"Too many to choose: former KGB who have no home; Belgians who run most of the businesses; North Koreans after illegal uranium; diamond smugglers who move cheap blood diamonds; rebel factions who operate freely; and mercenaries from all parts of the world."

"Sounds like a shit storm." Russell replied.

"And now we have Hezbollah operating here."

"Hate those bastards." Russell shot back.

"We have few to rely upon." Schultz looked at Russell and smiled. "The British are sending someone to help us out."

"Who?"

"Your friend Kitson."

"Really?" Russell paused. "He was injured and had to be evacuated." Russell was very impressed with Frank Kitson's knowledge of African operations and knew he would be an extremely valuable key to the team.

"Guess he is ready to serve again." Schultz replied.

"He's someone you want when the shit hits the fan." Russell thought about the team. "Who else can we count on?"

"We have Major Zulu assigned to you for a month to support helicopter missions around the countryside," Schultz said. "We got you a good cover story. The Congo government requested the UN to provide aid shipments to remote villages. Helicopters are the best means to get around the bush. There are very few roads out there."

Major Jabes Zulu of the Zambian Air Force reported for duty. Over the next several hours, Russell got to know Jabes through detailed questioning. At first, Russell asked simple questions and expanded into more analytical reasoning. Jabes told him about the European staff officers on the UN staff and the Chinese junior officers who fetched drinks, but really spied on everyone. The UN headquarters was in the isolated zone near the US Embassy and British Consulate. Jabes explained his boss who was a Ghanaian Colonel who had the arrogance that his nation was far better than other African Union members. Jabes did not respect him as the Ghanaian Colonel talked down to him. The mix of cultures at the UN headquarters looked great on paper; however, there was an observed hierarchy of power even among the African nations. Jabes explained how participation in UN peacekeeping operations provided African countries significant money. Russell quickly concluded the UN operations were ineffective managing the Congo crisis. The underlying factors of security, proper governance, and disenfranchised former soldiers helped trigger the recent uprising. Jabes showed the local paper, which depicted a UN soldier who raped a young local girl. The photo sparked tremendous outrage and the soldier was kidnapped from the UN compound and beat to death by an unruly mob.

"Will that be a good enough cover story?" Russell inquired.

"No, we need to plus it up some more. You are from the National Smithsonian Museum providing support to the archeology expedition currently underway. They had a team searching for the historical context of King Solomon's Mine."

"Where are they?"

"Last word was Lubumbashi." Schultz said. Russell looked at him quizzically. "Katanga province by Zambia."

Nakor Industry headquarters bustled with activity. The offers for illegally mined uranium flooded into his office and Gertz was pleased.

North Korean officials made repeated visits to his office in the past weeks. Word quickly spread a new mine for Uranium 238 had been discovered. No new uranium mines had been discovered in the Congo for over twenty years. The existing uranium mines were closely monitored by the International Atomic Energy Commission. Small amounts of Uranium were smuggled out on the black market through arms smugglers, but a large amount could not be stolen without UN knowledge. The samples brought to Kinshasa were the highest grade pure content Uranium 238 ever discovered in the world. Gertz sensed a lot of money could be made; however, he knew that he was on shaky ground with Tel Aviv, especially if Iran purchased high grade Uranium 238.

Gertz reviewed the illicit proposals. Based upon what his mining engineers told him, they would have almost a ton of high grade Uranium 238 by the end of the week. His private security team guarded the shipment along the railroad for the 1,200 kilometer transport to Kinshasa. Gertz knew better not to keep the North Korean General waiting. He did not worry that he was a North Korean, what scared him was the general was from the infamous Office 35 in Pyongyang, known for obscure torture techniques. Gertz met with the general for about an hour. The meeting was longer than he wanted. The much needed translation took longer than he expected. Gertz called for his personal female staffer Moira and his driver. As Gertz walked out of his building for his meeting, he saw a beautiful woman walk towards him. Her megawatt smile in the early darkness caught his attention. The female Mossad agent walked briskly towards the man who held dual citizenship in United States and Israel. Francesca knew that he was well connected. From the transmitting device Yacef placed in Moira's handbag, Francesca knew where Gertz was going and when he departed.

"Good evening Dan," Francesca said in a sultry voice.

"Do I know you?" Gertz said. He knew most foreigners. It was his business to know everyone.

"I'm your new Tel Aviv contact." Gertz looked surprised, yet he knew the Mossad acted quickly. He would have to find out what happened to Yacef.

"Oh, well I am in a hurry," Gertz said nonchalantly.

"I can travel with you," Francesca said. She looked at the large bodyguard in the front who pointed a pistol at her head. The Mossad trained her to deal with all types of situations and she blew a kiss at the bodyguard with her puckered lips. Inside the car. The private security, Moira, looked at her with a jealous, contentious look and Francesca immediately knew Gertz used her for sexual favors as well.

"When did you get into Kinshasa?" Gertz quizzed her. He made a mental note to dig up as much information as he could from his Tel Aviv contacts.

"Not long ago."

"Where did you come from?" Gertz asked. He used his phone to secretly take her photo.

"Here, there. You know how it is. But let's talk about you," Francesca said. Gertz did not like her tone and gave her a stern look. "How is the illegal diamond business going?" Francesca was not about to take any crap from him.

"I don't know what you are talking about."

"Tel Aviv knows more than you think and you can count on a visitor if you do not help me."

"Still, I do not know what you are talking about. I am an American and your threats don't scare me." Gertz's voice was louder.

"You carry a dual citizenship," Francesca said. "You may want to think about that the next time you get on a plane and suddenly find yourself in Israel." Gertz had heard stories of Israeli citizens being taken captive abroad, drugged, and brought back to Tel Aviv to answer for their crimes.

"What do you need?" Gertz asked after he calmed down. His diamond trade relied heavily on the Tel Aviv market where a majority of the best diamond cutters existed.

"I want this back." Francesca showed the picture. "It could end up in Tel Aviv or your precious New York." Gertz did not know what he was looking at in the picture. The long cylinder tube about a foot in diameter was fifteen feet long and the ends were capped. There was nothing strange about the photo except the date 1971 in the upper right hand corner. What caught his attention was the verbal description written in Hebrew on the other side.

"What do I get in return?" Gertz asked as he returned the photo.

"Well, let me put it this way." Francesca looked at the other female in the car and smiled her megawatt teeth one more time and replied back to her boss in a regular tone, "You get to live." Francesca asked to be dropped off. She did not want the Iranian delegation to see her with Gertz or have her photo taken. She wondered if the Iranians knew Gertz maintained dual citizenship. But it probably did not matter as every international arms dealer knew Gertz was open for business regardless of nationality or conviction or political cause. What mattered to Gertz was money and lots of it.

In the secure room of the American embassy, Russell listened intently to the tape recordings made at the Intercontinental Hotel bar. The National Security Agency eavesdropping devices on commercial cell phones did not help. The best intelligence source had been the microphones placed at the tables. Russell had no idea what the Belgian was saying. For that matter, he had absolutely no idea of what the North Koreans were speaking. The interpreters that crowded around Russell and Schultz listened carefully. Russell waited patiently for the translations. There were over twenty different languages being spoken in the bar area. The Intercontinental Hotel manager was bribed to keep the music low to allow for better listening by the translators. Schultz had microphones hidden all across the room to pick up the discussions for later translations and printed out versions of the script. The American embassy did not have speakers from every country and had to send the voice tapes on a compressed file to Langley for written translation.

Schultz was pleased that senior officials at Langley would know what was being said and finally realized the Congo was about to erupt. Several times, Schultz sent backdoor classified cables outside of the State Department political channels. The CIA's history in the Congo had been volatile. Schultz believed many in Langley wanted to forget about Africa and definitely the Congo. Since 9/11, the new CIA war against jihad Islamic terrorists stripped resources from Africa. No one cared about the Congo, until Schultz submitted a report on the recently discovered high grade Uranium 238 mine. The CIA had lost the intelligence battle on the massive amounts of processed uranium supposedly smuggled out of Niger to fuel Saddam Hussein's nuclear program. The CIA would not get caught with their pants down again on Africa uranium smuggling. Schultz suddenly found a plethora of intelligence resources sent his direction. He had a team of special operation soldiers at the ready for intrusion into the Congo once he found the illicit uranium shipments. Schultz was given the green light to close down the Congo uranium smuggling. Schultz knew the State Department bureaucrats desired arrests and convictions in international courts; however Schultz knew many would flee and seek protection somewhere else. Schultz instinctively understood things were about to get dirty.

Back at his sanctuary, Gertz looked at the smoke filled the Kinshasa air. Gertz looked out over the burning skyline from his plush surroundings and wondered for a brief moment if he did the right thing. He resumed looking at the stack of rough diamonds on his desk. He held the large pink one up to the light. It was over one hundred and twenty carats and would fetch an unbelievable amount in Moscow. He knew that he could not bring it to Tel Aviv, New York, Brussels, or Zurich. He had to get it into the black market channels as there would be too much inquiry. He looked across the table at the Zimbabwe Cabinet Minister to President Mugabe. Gertz's henchman, Braum, smiled as he put away his gun. Braum had shot the Zimbabwe Cabinet Minister in the forehead. Gertz watched the blood trickled down the cold face. Once the Cabinet Minister landed in Kinshasa, Braum followed and watched. Gertz knew Mugabe had vast amounts of diamonds and under the Kimberly Process no one could legally do business with Zimbabwe. The Cabinet Minister offered to sell the large pink diamond to Voctrad; however Braum captured him before the drop off. Braum smashed his cell phone and dismantled a tracking device inside. Gertz held the large pink stone under the magnifying glass. He guessed that is must be near eighty carats. Gertz knew the precious stone would fetch three million cash on the black market.

Gertz became nauseous as he stared at the dead body. Braum took the hint, departed the room, and returned with a roll of plastic. He tossed the corpse out of the chair and onto the plastic. Braum did not care about police forensics as those processes did not exist in war-torn Congo. He cared more about Gertz's beautiful Persian rug underneath the dead man's chair. Braum hoisted the bundle over his shoulder and headed out of the executive suite. Moira looked up from her desk. It was late and she was tired. As Braum approached, she jerked her head down as if reading a document. Moira was scared to death. She could not escape. She knew far too much. She would be killed. Braum groaned as he trudged down the hallway. He walked toward the rear elevator and dumped the body in the street outside of the compound. The Zimbabwe Cabinet Minister's death would be chalked up to yet another string of violence that gripped Kinshasa.

On a dreary London morning, Colonel Frank Kitson, Jr. walked out of 10 Downing Street. He was headed back to Africa for another deployment. The retirement plan escaped him yet again. Several years ago, he submitted retirement papers; however, he was asked by the Prince of Wales to deploy to Afghanistan to help watch over his son. Colonel Kitson taught both Prince William and Harry at Sandhurst Royal Military Academy and knew them well. Kitson was widely known and regarded as a premier counter insurgency expert. In 1979, he was a young Second Lieutenant in Rhodesia and ordered to capture rebels. A young Kitson sensed that his sixteen man platoon was surrounded. In the morning he dressed in his finest military uniform, walked out of his small patrol base unarmed. He placed a table and chairs and waited. As the sun set, he was blinded and could not see the hundred heavily armed rebels until they were within fifty feet. He stood and offered the rebel leader a cup of her Majesty's finest tea. Over the next hour, he negotiated the surrender of over 400 rebels. No one would have known, except for London Times' photographer who traveled with the rebels. In two days, his face was on the front page of the London Times with the caption, 'British Officer Captures Rebels with Her Majesty's Finest Tea.' For his actions, he received the Queen's Medal. Colonel Kitson lifted his battered right leg into the waiting sedan. He gave the driver instructions to bring him to MI6 Headquarters. He leaned back in the leather seat and thought of his wife and how to best explain his new orders. Colonel Frank Kitson Jr. was headed back to Africa.

CHAPTER 5

The US Embassy was potently active with the massive influx of foreigners from numerous nationalities. Everyone tried to get out of the Congo. The latest violence targeted foreigners. Eight white French women were pulled from a UN van and murdered in the streets. Fear gripped the NGO community and hundreds of foreigners rumbled into the secure US Embassy compound, some with only the clothes on their backs. Deep within the chancellery building, Russell found the Chief of Station's secure office. A pile of papers rested on the table. Maps of the region were charted across the walls. Schultz had received more attention than he either wanted. The secure phone had rung relentlessly. Schultz greeted Russell by passing him a highly classified CIA document on criminal activity in the region. Many despicable groups descended upon the Congo. Hezbollah operatives were present along with former KGB, South Africans, Iranians, North Koreans, and many other exiles.

Russell read the report. The Congo had claimed the infamous status as Africa's First World War, yet few outside of the Dark Continent understood the context. Over a nine year period, nearly five million Africans died from war, malnutrition, and disease. In this period, eight separate countries invaded the Congo boundaries and waged war. Brutal rebel attacks forced many villagers along the far eastern Congo border to flee. The massive exodus of refugees went unnoticed in world affairs as well as the ruthless massacres in remote villages. Anyone with a gun ruled the day. Nearly a million women became victims of abuse. Thousands were kidnapped as bush wives and never seen again. Out of Rwanda, Burundi, Uganda, Sudan, and Central African Republic, government forces launched hundreds of cross-border attacks. The deep remoteness and lack of protection caused unimaginable despair.

What took the CIA by surprise was the introduction of mercenaries. Russell was intrigued by the most vile who were former Polish Special Forces, otherwise known as GROM. In Polish, the acronym stood for Grupa Reagowania Opperacyjno Manewrowego, in English it meant Operational Mobile Reaction Group. The GROM represented the most vile, ruthless, and dangerous group of Special Forces in the world. These thugs were a throwback to the former Soviet Union lethal grip. GROM soldiers were trained by the KGB alongside Russian special operation soldiers known as the infamous Spetsnaz in secret camps in the Ural Mountains. Slawomir Petelicki formed the GROM in the early 1990s. Petelicki was trained by KGB in reconnaissance, sabotage, and killing. As the Soviet Union dismantled, Poland co-operated with NATO for operations in Kosovo and with America for Iraq and Afghanistan. GROM were trained in explosives, special ops, scuba, airborne, and sniper. GROM operatives were trained primarily to eliminate targets versus capture. The GROM's weapon of choice was the Bushmaster M4A3 assault rifle with grenade launcher. Snipers employed the PSG-1 7.62 mm rifle. When the Iron Curtain disbanded and Poland received independence, one of the first acts of the new democratic government was to disband and abolish the GROM. Without functional job skills, they found them mercenary work around the world. From Angola, Somalia, Yemen, Sudan, Libya, Iraq, and Afghanistan, former GROM soldiers were put to work as mercenaries. In the Congo, they were hired by Gertz as public security. Russell looked at the photos and memorized the faces.

"I believe Gertz is paying for GROM services." Schultz broke in to disrupt Russell's stare into the documents. "There is a thug named Braum who works directly for Gertz."

"How many GROM are here?"

"Last count, twenty-two." Schultz handed him some photos of the aftermath from a fire fight. "Last month, two were killed by rebels near the Angola border. The rest retaliated by annihilating everyone in that rebel camp." Russell looked at the photos and from he read was not surprised. A well trained special operations team could rapidly and silently conduct a search and destroy mission. From his experiences in Liberia, he knew Africans did not fight well in the darkness. The night held almost mythical danger for Africans. Russell kept reading. He wanted to know who called the shots – in addition to Gertz. Many factions pulled at the fiber of Congo society and reaped rewards in the chaos. Russell needed to get the real on the ground intelligence.

Russell walked out of the secure building. There was a long line of NGOs who awaited entry into the embassy for protection. Russell heard a few complain about the long wait. He wondered what they would say if he offered to send them back into the deadly streets. Russell pushed past the crowd. He needed to get out of the embassy. More importantly, he wanted to get a hands-on assessment of the situation, and there was no better place than the local foreigner occupied watering hole. Russell found the Intercontinental Hotel with ease as it loomed above most of Kinshasa. On the top floor was the once world-renowned bar that was damaged by fighting. The hotel bar was packed with NGOs, diplomats, foreigners, and some of the Kinshasa ultra-rich. Russell strolled up to the bar. Several mammoth sized gorilla hands ripped off some dead chimps spread across the bar counter were used as ashtrays. Large, half-smoked cigars rolled in between the colossal fingers making a gorilla hand look as if it had eight digits. He had never seen such obscure extravaganzas. Russell was disgusted as these animals gave up their lives to be fixtures at a bar.

Russell gazed across the faces and became interested in the corner table. There were two Asian men who Russell surmised were Korean. They sat alongside several Russians. Russell knew former KGB generals moved into Africa and became involved with any and everything illegal. Smuggling drugs, humans, weapons, and diamonds were their specialty. Russell stepped to the bar and waved to the bartender. He folded a crisp hundred dollar bill in half and slid it across the bar. Russell asked him to point out Dietger Laurent. The bartender motioned his head to the rear of the room. A gigantic man with his hair pulled tightly into a ponytail stood next to him. The giant looked eastern European. He caught Russell's glimpse and stared back intently.

Russell failed to observe the entire room. The female Mossad agent slithered behind him. Francesca gently rubbed his shoulder with her left hand and pressed her lips into his ear. Russell's body jolted throughout. He moved his hand to strike, an automatic reflex but she already moved to block it.

"Well hello Tom," Francesca said as she smiled widely. She tried to think of something humorous as she knew he would not be pleased to see her after she dumped him and left Liberia. The only thing she could add was, "Nice war going on here."

Russell was shocked and pulled away, or at least tried. Her gentle massage of his shoulder turned into a harder grasp to the side of his neck. She had two fingers pressured at his chin line in a move he knew would shut off his oxygen supply if she wanted. Russell knew the voice, knew her perfume smell, and most definitely knew how she kissed.

"What are you doing here?" Russell asked abruptly.

"Did you miss me?"

"What the hell are you doing here?" He looked around. "Are you following me?"

"Tom," Francesca offered. "The world is a small place." She drank some of his beer. "Besides, you're not hard to spot." She touched his short hair and said. "You really need to invest in a disguise." Russell kept his hair relatively short and wore conservative clothes. Indeed, he surmised that he stood out in the NGO, save-the-world type crowd.

"What the hell are you doing here?" Russell repeated. She smiled back at him and drank more of his beer.

"Saving the world." Francesca replied nonchalantly.

Russell thought back to the last operation where they met in Liberia. They stared at each other intently for what was an awkward minute. Russell continued, "Why did you leave so fast? You did not even say farewell." He looked into to her crystal green eyes and inquired again, "What are you really doing here?"

"I told you." She drank more of his beer. "Saving the world."

"Hardly... You are one of the most lethal people I know. I understand your idea of saving the world is blowing everything up. I saw that first hand in Liberia."

"Tom, don't be so melodramatic." Francesca controlled the conversation. "You knew what you were getting into."

Russell did know, yet her abrupt departure out of Liberia still aggravated him. "I know if people care for one another that they just don't get up and leave." Russell thought for a moment. Something inside of him tore him apart. Two months ago, they were deeply in love or so he thought. Both had separate missions in Liberia that eventually folded together in a united American and Israeli common understanding – to hunt down and kill terrorists. For three months, Russell did not know her true identity. She portrayed herself as a volunteer with Doctors Without Borders as her cover story. To his surprise it worked well, especially since she was indeed a real doctor. Russell thought their relationship was something more. "Again I ask, why did you leave?"

"I needed to get out," Francesca replied. "There was a price on my head." She responded as she looked to the corner of the bar.

"I turned you in."

"I know." Francesca smile. "You did it because you loved me."

"Don't be so sure of yourself."

"I'm not but I do know you love me," Francesca paused, "and you still love me."

"Are you so sure?" Russell replied. In Liberia, night after night he slept next to her. After the mission, Russell thought of her every day. Francesca looked at him with what he thought were innocent eyes, so soft and green, yet there was something more deep and sinister inside.

Across the room, deadly steel eyes did not waiver from the former lovers. Braum watched intently. He had a pistol holstered on his waist that bulged under the large suit jacket. Francesca observed two more men as they entered the bar. Everyone was supposed to be frisked at the main checkpoint in the lobby. Russell found the guards half asleep. Two more eastern European men walked into the bar. Russell picked out the two new arrivals quickly. No one wore a long overcoat in Kinshasa, not even in the African winter months. It resembled a scene out of an Al Capone gangster movie. Francesca noticed the bulge out along the side of the second man's leg as he walked forward. She did not need for them to take action. She reached under her dress. Russell caught the movement and suspiciously watched her as she placed a hand up her skirt. For a brief second, he thought she was rudely adjusting her panty hose, but the look in her eyes told him something different. Russell reached for his ankle and pulled out the snub nose pistol attached to his ankle. Within several seconds, Francesca and Russell both pointed and fired at the two men. The gangster dressed men were taken off guard and struggled with the cumbersome jackets. As they unraveled the large machine guns from the jackets, they were taken by surprise. Blood burst across the overcoats as Francesca and Russell shot the men in their chests. However, the smaller caliber weapons did not stop them. The goons fired and bullets littered the air. Several bystanders were struck. Russell fired again at the man on the right and emptied the five remaining shots into his chest. Francesca was a better shot and placed a bullet in the middle of the first man's head. She had four shots left.

"Move...this way!" Russell shouted. "Go, go!" he screamed. Francesca followed him out of the bar and onto the balcony. Russell did not wait to see as he jumped over the railing. Francesca followed without questioning his actions. They landed forty feet below in the pristine bushes and Russell rolled out of the prickly needles. Russell yanked her out of the bush by her right arm and as her feet hit the pavement they were running. Her bare legs were scratched and soon bled. Several shots rang out behind them, which sent locals diving for cover. Russell did not have time to explain his predicament to a cab driver. The man emitted a shocked sound as Russell tossed him to the ground. Bullets ripped into the cab. The back window was blown out from the full automatic firepower. Francesca jumped into the driver's seat and started the cab. Russell pushed the cab driver with violent force to the embankment wall. He moved the man out of the direct line of fire. Russell ran towards the cab as Francesca accelerated down the street. He jumped on the back of the cab, crawled over the truck, and pulled his body through the blown out rear window.

"Just like old times." Francesca shouted from the driver's seat. Russell was not amused. She twisted the cab around the exit gate and past the serpentine wire and concrete, guarding the entrance from car bombs. Russell rolled around in the back seat as she shifted the vehicle back and forth in the fast moving traffic. He brushed off the glass and climbed into the front seat.

"Who the hell was that?" Russell asked. "Are you a target?"

"Not sure," Francesca said as she glanced into the rear view mirror. "Could be you?"

"Who knows I'm here?"

"Seriously?" She asked. Francesca turned and looked at him with a big grin across her face, "probably half the city now." She zigzagged the cab around the traffic and yanked the wheel hard to get back in the correct lane.

"Your driving is still horrible."

"But tonight, it got you out of trouble," She said and added, "once again, I saved your life." Russell counted three times that Francesca saved his life in Liberia and now he had to keep count in the Congo. He hated relying on anybody. Russell wanted to distance himself from her. He did not know what to think. Conflicting thoughts raced inside his head. Was she the one for him? Would he wake up to find her gone again? Would she drive him insane? Would she get him killed? Neither of them spoke for fifteen minutes as she zigzagged down blackened, deserted streets.

"Drop me off here," Russell said as he recognized the area. The location was close enough to embassy row. He had to get out of the car and had his foot on the pavement before she stopped it. Francesca said something offensive but he could not hear the remark as the engine erupted and the car sped down the street.

Russell walked down the block toward the American embassy. Some of the neighboring embassies were vacated. Finland, Italy, and Spain pulled out their diplomatic missions. He held his head down and was not focused. He thought of her. Outside of the alley, he did not see the figure move quickly. Russell felt the heavy thud across the back of his head. He dropped.

Russell woke up for what seemed like several hours later. The bright light ripped into his eye sockets. He could barely open his eyes in the high intensity illumination. Several figures were seated at a table drinking and speaking a slang version of English. He was tied to a chair in what he surmised was a basement from the furnace, stacks of boxes, and cinderblock walls. The place smelled. Russell saw the two men approach him.

"Now we have us a big tough American." Galpin lifted up Russell's face. Russell recognized the South African brothers from the photos Schultz showed him. By their accents, he definitely knew that they were from South Africa. By seeing their faces, Russell knew he was a dead man.

"You don't have a clue what tough means?" Russell responded back to Galpin. Krause held the shotgun against Russell's chest.

"You Americans think you are so mighty... Super Power?" Galpin laughed slightly. "You're nothing. Your country is nothing. I'm going to put a bullet in your head. What do you think tough guy?"

"I think you are biting off more than you can chew." Russell gave a wiseass response. Galpin placed the pistol barrel against the front of Russell's forehead and pressed hard. Russell closed his eyes tightly from the force of the pressure. After five seconds, he opened his eyes slightly to see the South African's grip on the pistol.

"Not just yet, you're going to suffer first." Russell did not know what hope or faith was, yet he wanted something to get him out of this, a prayer, or a divine intervention. The first punch shattered a front tooth. Russell gulped in pain. The second, third, and fourth fist shots sent pain throughout his head and neck. He spit out blood, a lot of blood. "You're going to tell us what you're doing here." Russell had been fully integrated before. When he prepared to join Special Forces, he experienced water boarding at the mock prisoner of war camp in the mountains of Colorado. During the mock interrogations, the participant could tap out and request a pause; there was no pause now.

"Who are you working for? CIA? FBI?"

"No one, I'm an archeologist." Russell said.

"Wrong. What are you after?"

"I'm not after anything." Russell said. He knew that pain would follow. Galpin did not like the answer and hit Russell across his right knee with a baseball bat. Russell screamed in pain. Galpin hit him again and again. Russell's body clinched. Russell remembered his interrogation training as never to threaten the interrogators with violence as they would be more inclined to permanently take care of the prisoner. He did remember humor works well. "Are you sure you didn't play baseball for the Yankees." His brother laughed while Galpin contemplated the situation.

"No, I played football." Galpin replied. "What you Americans call soccer." Galpin quickly crossed the ten feet to Russell's chair and kicked him out of it with a forcible strike. Russell fell out of his ropes and was finally able to hold his right knee. The South African lined up for a strike and knocked Russell unconscious with a hard kick to the head. They tossed Russell like a sack of potatoes into a locked room.

After she dropped off Russell, Francesca pulled the cab into a dark alley and thought about what had just occurred. Israeli intelligence was usually never wrong and Francesca read the damaging reports of information Yacef leaked to the South Africans. Since his execution, Francesca sensed she had been watched and followed. She drove fast down the darkened streets. She kept the cab's lights off and avoided the UN checkpoints. She knew it would be hard to explain the blown out back window and what she was doing in a stolen vehicle. In the deep darkness that eclipsed Kinshasa in the night, she pushed onward. Something told her deep inside that she had to get out of Kinshasa. Gertz had a lot of contacts and was a man not to trust.

Francesca changed vehicles at the new safe house. The older version Land Rover she purchased would have scared off many travelers but when she saw it and inspected the suspension underneath, she knew the vehicle was solid. The local dealer was surprised that she did not choose the newer vehicle which had air conditioning, yet was made of more plastic than steel. Francesca accelerated the Land Rover toward the UN check point and swerved to the right side near several of the Nigerian guards who jumped out of the way. In the rear view mirror she saw the commotion and response of the guards. Within moments, the Nigerians were in a UN vehicle with flashing red lights and in pursuit. Several minutes up the road, she pulled off near a stream. She climbed underneath the vehicle and pulled off the tracking transmitter. She surmised that the dealer placed trackers on vehicles to sell information on locations or to steal the vehicle back. She tied the transmitter to a log, placed it in the stream, and sent it traveling. She had no idea where the side road would take her. Anything would be better than the main road as they would be waiting for her. She got lost in the countryside. Higher and higher she climbed into the pristine jungle. There were no roads, just paths. She continued her journey.

In the eastern Congo along the border of Burundi, the plateaus were steep. Scattered across the terrain were massive mountain gorillas.

44

Their numbers had been ravaged substantially. Disease caused many infant gorilla deaths, but then war arrived and catastrophically altered Congo's gorillas forever. Rebels shot the large primates for meat. Doctor Eddy spotted a silver back male gorilla. He watched as the male pushed his way through the thick brush. At sixty-four years of age, Doctor Eddy was physically fit. Doctor Eddy was not a real surgeon or even a veterinarian, but he was the closest thing to help the gorillas. Twenty years ago, he was hired by a woman from National Geographic. He intently observed her as she patiently photographed the mountain gorillas.

As a boy, Doctor Eddy heard tribal stories that described gruesome detail of men who came in contact with the mammoth beasts. However, he was adventurous and enjoyed working with the female National Geographic photographer. The white woman came within feet of massive bull gorillas and showed servitude by staring downward. He watched as over time she gained their trust. Repeatedly, she came back to Africa and hired Eddy to support her. She paid for Eddy to become a veterinarian. Eddy felt close to her. More and more, he believed that he should protect her, but he could not. Five years ago, poachers came and shot her. In her will, she left money to start a gorilla protective foundation. Doctor Eddy maintained a camp for the infants to keep them off of the floor so they did not freeze to death. He hoped some of the orphans would be adopted by surrogate gorilla mothers.

The morning mist was thick and hung in the air. Doctor Eddy looked across the plateau for any movements by the male silver back gorilla. The chill in the high altitude air kept many of the Portuguese volunteers in their sleeping bags. Doctor Eddy was pleased to have help and even more pleased to have the donated supplies from the foreigners. He felt something was indeed wrong, a premonition. In the distance, the three female gorillas yelped as they were shot. The poachers fired indiscriminately into the tree line at the large apes. The baby gorillas sat next to the older gorillas that screamed in agony and died. The male bull gorilla charged at the poachers and caught several by surprise. The white hair silverback streaked across its back stood on edge as the primate vaulted into the open. With the swing of his massive arm, it ripped the face off one of the men. One of the soldiers tried to run, but the bull male

45

jumped on the poacher's back. It raised its massive arms and repeatedly bashed at the back of the man's skull. Blood shot out in the air. The Argentine collector aimed his high powered elephant gun at the middle of the bull male gorilla's chest and fired. Blood erupted as the large caliber projectile engulfed its chest. The bull male silverback gorilla died instantly. The Argentine inspected the baby primates and was impressed by the capture. He estimated that he could get two hundred thousand dollars for the five baby gorillas. The Argentine poacher motioned for his men to place the gorilla babies in makeshift wooden cages. Even in the chilled mountain air, the fat Argentine sweated profusely. He cursed the African humidity. He cursed the long uphill walk. As he caught his breath from the activity, he saw white people running up the trail. The Argentine did not waste time to hear their gripes and unloaded the last five rounds in his clip in their general direction.

The assault on the primate camp lasted just ten minutes. Doctor Eddy ran as fast as his legs would take him. Several of the Portuguese volunteers moved faster. Doctor Eddy breathed hard as his old legs trudged up the hill. He pushed towards the gorilla habitat. Doctor Eddy heard more shots and screams across the landscape. Foam dripped from his dry mouth as he pushed his body beyond its limits. He fell on his hands and knees as he saw the horror in front of him. Dead gorillas littered the landscape. Doctor Eddy yelled at loud as he could and fell to the ground.

CHAPTER 6

Within Kinshasa city limits, only a few buildings possessed power. Lights were powered from generators that hummed in massive, secure compounds. Only the elite could afford such an expense. Blind darkness overpowered many Congolese. Candles barely illuminated apartment buildings. The hydroelectric plant was decimated during the latest rebel intrusion. Three weeks ago, the fifty UN soldiers who guarded the key infrastructure were caught asleep and massacred. Within hours, looters stormed the hydroelectric plant and stole the equipment. Reinforcements arrived three days later and found irrevocable damage. The UN contracted a French company to rebuild the hydroelectric plant. The project plan stated it would take five months to mobilize resources and seven more months to complete. In the meantime, Congolese endured a lethal darkness as criminals roamed unabated in the night.

Inside the bright restaurant, Dietger Laurent drank whiskey, not the usual brand. Dietger drank one of the most expensive whiskeys in the world. He called a meeting of several prominent Belgian businessmen. Like many of the Belgians who lived in the Congo, he had controlling interests in many businesses. The Congo still harbored the ghost of King Leopold. Every facet of Congo life revolved around the foundation set by the Belgians. King Leopold was ruthless and his brutality was unparalleled. Barbaric practices fueled mistrust of the white European and institutional fear resounded in the minds of locals. In the later 1950s, the Congo found the attention of the Soviet Union and United States and a struggle for control of the mineral rich regions ensued. Both the Soviets and Americans needed tritium, cobalt, and uranium to fuel the space race. The Katanga Province, in southern Congo, had a preponderance of the nation's mineral wealth. Control of Katanga equated to control of the Congo and the Belgians were in the middle of it all.

After dinner, Dietger and several of his most trusted associates went into the back room of the restaurant. In the center of the room, the table contained a lead box. The inside contents held a high grade of processed uranium, levels never seen before.

CRISIS IN THE CONGO

"Where did you get this?" Dietger inquired.

"Once I tell you, I die." The local mining engineer replied. If he mentioned anything about the uranium shipment, his entire family would be killed. The Lebanese tried to smuggle the box out of Kinshasa on a passenger ferry, but was caught by a Congo Customs Official who immediately turned him over to Dietger. Dietger Laurent had many Congo officials on his secret payroll.

"Tell me."

"No, you will kill me." The local man did not know how much the box was worth. He found the box in a room upstairs from him. The room had been vacant for some time. He heard the occupants were archeologists and had died in an accident. He used the opportunity to steal whatever he could. He was pleased to see a box with uranium labeled on it. Everyone in Kinshasa knew uranium was worth a considerable amount of money on the black market. No one talked out loud about uranium. It was the Congo's dirty little secret.

"True, but it does depend on how you want to die." Dietger pulled out a metal bar about three feet long and an inch thick. With a large overhand strike, he broke the man's leg. After his dramatic performance, he looked at the other wealthy men and placed the metal bar on the table. Next, he lifted a syringe and squeezed the fluid out of the needle's head. The toxic chemical landed on the floor.

"Are you scared?"

"To death."

"Good. I am pleased you are scared. It would not be as fun if you were not scared of death." Dietger was well adept at using needles and truth seeking serum. Dietger smiled widely as he injected the needle into the man's vein.

The South African brothers, Galpin and Krause, were brutal. In their native South Africa, the Soweto Uprising was quelled rapidly with extreme violence. On June 16, 1976, black students rioted in the Soweto streets. The disgruntled black students fought against the Apartheid rules governing what language would be forced upon the indigenous population. Over 20,000 students participated in the riots and nearly 200 were killed. At the time, Galpin was a police officer assigned to the Soweto district. In the adrenaline of the moment, Galpin drew his handgun and fired in the crowd. Bodies fell. Newspaper reporters took numerous pictures of Galpin as he fired. Galpin took the time to reload his six cylinder pistol and fired again. He repeated the loading action eight times. After Galpin used all of the ammunition, he walked back to a police car and took a shotgun out of the trunk. He shot at anyone nearby. Those wounded on the ground looked upward and witnessed the wrath of a madman as he held the shotgun barrel inches from their heads. He blasted three more students to death. The photo made every international paper and injected a furor of dissent and solidarity to fight against Apartheid. Galpin was betrayed by the police commissioner who gave the approval for the massacre. Galpin would be arrested, yet he received advance word of his arrest warrant and fled South Africa. Years earlier, his brother Krause joined the South African Defense Force and flew helicopters. He fought alongside many of the South African blacks in Angola. The motto was no apartheid in the foxhole. Krause became disgusted as he felt leaders talked about fighting the communists, but realistically the rich companies wanted Angola's mineral rights. Krause became disgruntled more and more. When Galpin was forced to leave or go to jail for murder, Krause deserted from the South African army and followed his older brother.

Galpin handed Krause several photos of the female Mossad agent. "We need these posted over town, especially in the slums." He looked at the photo of the beautiful woman. "She will show her face."

"Too bad we have to kill her."

"Too bad." Galpin had primeval thoughts of what he wanted to do to Francesca. He drank straight from the whiskey bottle and handed it to his brother. "Let's go and finish off the American tough guy."

Russell could barely move. The ropes were deathly tight. His face hurt. His bound arms hurt. His head hurt. The flash of light from a penlight drifted from the corner of the basement. Tshambe scrambled across the room. "Mister Russell, you ok?" Tshambe slapped his face several times to wake him up.

"Get me out of here." Russell mumbled. He kept his tone low.

"Yes boss."

"Gun?" Russell asked. Tshambe looked at him as he started to cut the ropes and Russell asked again. "Do you have a gun?"

"No boss. Knife. I have knife."

"Where's Schultz"

"He's outside. Those white men left." Tshambe said as he lifted Russell out of the chair and served as a crutch as they walked across the basement. Tshambe carried him up the stairs and pushed out into the morning sunlight. The brightness blinded Russell.

"Damn, you look like hell." Schultz sounded concerned.

"Yeah." Russell responded with a slight laugh. "Bastards used me as a soccer ball."

"What did you tell them?"

"Not a damn thing." Russell spat dried blood onto the pavement. He used his finger to blast out his nostrils. Hardened blood clots bounced off the pavement. Within a moment, fresh blood flowed freely out of his nose. Russell wiped it away. He tore part of his shirt and tried to control the bleeding. "Gun? You got a gun for me?"

"You know the rules. UN embargo restricts," Schultz abruptly stopped before completing his sentence. The rage in Russell's eyes told him he knew the risks and what was at stake. "Here, take mine."

"How did you find me?"

"Tracking device in your shoe." Schultz paused for a moment. In his Chief of Station role, he had to state the obvious. "The South African brothers will not make the same mistake twice."

In the dilapidated Congo governmental building along the avenue shared by the foreign embassies, the well-dressed man from Amnesty International did not look like the typical totalitarian liberal trying to save the world. Gunther Blackledge who worked for Amnesty International sat across from Congo's newly appointed Minister of Information. Gunther was dressed in a grey suit with a black vest. His long hair was perfectly combed to the rear and greased in place. His manicured fingernails and hands were similar quality to those seen from fashion hand models. Gunther was highly educated and possessed an aristocratic persona. Gunther spoke superb English with a slight Zurich accent. "Not one Congo government official has been prosecuted for illegal mining," Gunther paused for effect, "not one government official has been prosecuted for rapes," and paused for effect, "not one government official had been charged with murder, let alone genocide."

"We don't know what happened in Kuvulu." The Congo Minister of Information continued, "Much bad information and initial reports are never true."

"My sources are reliable." Amnesty International had a far reaching network that bypassed many corrupt governments.

"Until we get investigators to the village we will not know." The Congo Minister smiled.

"I can tell you don't need investigators at the village." The man from Switzerland looked right into his eyes. "You need investigators here. Congo soldiers raped and butchered helpless civilians."

"Accusations," the Minister repeated himself, "accusations." He paused for effect and continued. "These discussions will not get us anywhere." The Minister of Information tried to quell the situation. Gunther heard corruption was rampant within the new Congolese government as newly appointed Ministers gobbled up control in the power vacuum. Fleets of executive cars and staff were employed, yet the government did not invest one cent into renovating their buildings. He continued, "We need all the help we can get. We are coming out of a long period of violence and our military is doing the best they can." The Minister of Information was perfect at displaying the myth of extreme poverty and needed the substantial foreign donor money.

"May I tell you, did you know there are over forty dead and almost three hundred women raped in four days?" Gunther prided himself in his politeness, but his patience ran out.

"Why do you care so much for forty dead souls?" The Minister leaned across the table and hammered his right hand into the plywood table. His voice was strong, convincing. "Millions have died here in Africa. No one came to investigate our World War... no one." The Minister was adept and rehearsed to alter public opinion, extremely adept.

"Your pain and grief are understandable."

"Don't tell me what I should feel like. You white Europeans have butchered us for over a hundred years." The African was on the offensive. Many people thought he was not smart from the manner of his speech; however, he was cunning, deceptive, and skillful at persuasion.

"I'm not here to discuss last century." Gunther would not sway in his conviction. "I am here to talk the present. A Congo army unit went into Kuvulu and committed atrocities beyond comprehension. The UN arrived two days after the army unit departed. Are you telling me Sir that the UN and the army are not conspiring?"

Silence ensued. The Minister did not say a word.

"Let me tell you what is going to happen. I am going to the village tomorrow and get my report first hand." Gunther looked for some sort of visual response and found none. As Gunther walked out of the room, he turned. "I will be making a full report to Amnesty International and it will be an official record."

The Minister of Information watched Gunther as he closed the door. He went into the hallway and motioned for one of his bodyguards to follow him. The Minister pulled out a large Cuban cigar from the gift box presented by the Iranian delegation. He rolled the moist treat in his fingers. It was noon and he was ready for a stiff drink. He poured a four finger shot of bourbon and looked out the window. From his fifth floor corner office, he scrutinized Gunther as he lunged into an awaiting white van. His man sped after on a motorcycle. The Minister drank the stiff drink and pondered if he would have to order yet another murder.

Francesca looked out of place along the side of the road. The Land Rover's axle was bent from her diversion past the UN check point. Even after a night of running and sleeping in the vehicle, she still looked incredibly sexy in the same black cocktail dress and caught the attention of many passersby as she contemplated her next move. Against all of her instincts, Francesca wanted to find Russell. She turned the battered Land Rover around and headed back towards Kinshasa. She could not go back to her safe house. Luckily, she hid her weapons in an abandoned building across from the apartment compound. Francesca hoped squatters did not find the secret spot. She knew that she could not arrive at any of three hotels still open that catered to foreign guests. She would stand out if she tried to hide within the local populace. She headed towards the American embassy. She abandoned the vehicle several blocks away. She walked through one of the toughest sections in the city. Local men watched. A few thought about jumping her, but saw the stern, fearless look in her eyes and backed off. At the US Embassy front gate, her fake Canadian passport quickly gained her access. She already memorized the layout of the embassy and guessed correctly where Russell would be staying as a visiting official.

"What freight train hit you?" Francesca asked as she into his small apartment. She walked over to him and placed her hand on his chest, not just to give comfort but to take the pistol in his hand.

"How did you get in here?" Russell asked.

"You Americans really do not know proper security protocol." Francesca replied as she showed her illegal Canadian passport.

"What are you doing here?"

"I need a secure place to stay." She rubbed her hand across his chest, "Let's just say I'm without a home right now."

"Your South African friends did a real number on my face." Russell moved his head back and forth to show the deep marks.

"They're not my friends." Francesca replied. "I would like to kill them both, but can't right now."

"Why not?" he asked.

"Complicated." She looked around the room to make sure no one was there. She memorized the locations of doors and windows. She looked upward and wondered if the room was bugged. Russell knew better than to ask. He did not know where his emotions were headed. Memories of Liberia jumped into his mind. They shared many intimate moments and Russell felt something strong for Francesca. Abruptly she left. The only thing that remained was a hand written note; *'Don't try to find me, it cannot be. We cannot be.'* Francesca stood from the bedside and walked to the cabinet. She pulled out a wine and popped the cork. She poured several large glasses. "You've got a lot of room here. Mind a roommate?"

"After Liberia, where did you go?"

"Joburg." Francesca replied. Russell looked confused and she corrected herself. "Johannesburg." She saw the look in his eyes and knew it was the best time to tell him. "My father sent me there. He was involved with a mission in the early 70s and it needed to be cleaned up."

"Does he know about me?" Russell was worried about her father and what the Mossad would do to him.

"If he did," she paused and looked into his eyes, "you would already be dead." Russell knew she was telling the truth. He was smart enough to know when he was in over his head and now was the time. He had South Africans after him, Hezbollah operatives, and now a pissed off senior Mossad official who happened to be her father. Violence and the chaotic situation in Liberia brought them close. The sheer adrenaline rush of near death experiences and numerous firefights enhanced their libido. When Russell discovered Francesca standing over a dead Hezbollah operative she had interrogated, he knew she was someone not to screw with.

Most of his love life dealt with short relationships as many prospective girlfriends called him an adrenaline junkie. One girl came close. At Columbia, he met Kristin. She was in law school and Russell started the MBA program. For a year, their relationship thrived. Russell believed they had a chance. Kristin became patriotic as many Manhattan residents had after 9/11 and loved her Marine. Russell wanted to drop out of the MBA program and go to Afghanistan. Kristin was frightened for him and Russell succumbed in order to appease her fears. He remained at Columbia. Kristin's father found out about them and more importantly how Russell was from second generation Scottish immigrants who changed their last name upon entering America. Mr. Vanderheuse hired a private investigator to conduct a background check on Russell before he met him. When Russell finally met Kristin's father, his first comment was, "Tom, you know I can trace my family roots back to the Mayflower." Russell was suspect. Under a hot summer sun at the luxurious Piping Rock Country Club in Oyster Bay along the famed Gold Coast of Long Island, Mr. Vanderheuse put everything in perspective. Russell remembered, "Tom, have you ever experienced a significant loss in the market?"

Russell replied, "Mr. Vanderheuse your idea of a significant loss compared to mine is on a different level."

"Tom, when I was scuba diving off Bali, I was down a million dollars by the time I came back to the surface."

In a stone-cold face, Russell replied, "Yeah, but those are just paper losses." Later, Russell did his own research and discovered Vanderheuse ancestors on Long Island provided information to the British on George Washington's movements. After he came back from Iraq, Russell walked along 34th Street in Manhattan. A crane dropped a container and made a tremendous concussion sound similar to an IED. Russell reacted. He tossed Kristin like a rag doll on pavement. She was horrified and cursed him, the war, and the Marines. He walked away from Kristin and never turned back.

Down the street from the embassy, Kamal watched the crowd of foreigners move in and out of the secure compound. The Al Qaeda operative memorized every possible physical attribute of the female Mossad agent. Kamal thought about shooting her, perhaps he will. Kamal despised Israelis just as much as Christians. He killed his mother who was Christian. He enjoyed the lethal interrogation he performed two months ago on a kidnapped German female tourist in Somalia. Kamal believed the caliphate, Bin Laden's vision for the Islamic control of the world in a thousand years would arrive in his lifetime and he would do everything possible to expedite it. Kamal watched the American embassy for the CIA operative he was ordered to kill.

The embassy cafeteria was crowded for the evening meal. More foreigners had had flooded into the American embassy for protection. Schultz found the two former love birds sitting at a corner table. As Schultz approached, he sensed hostility between the two of them.

"Who's your friend?"

"I could tell you she works for Doctors Without Borders or some NGO, but that wouldn't be the truth." Russell looked at her, "Do you want to tell him or should I?"

She reached her hand and shook Schultz, "Name is Francesca." She paused for a moment and added. "I'm from Israel."

"Mossad?" Schultz asked. Francesca looked to see if anyone else heard him and when no one caught the remark, she nodded. "So you're the one. Every intelligence operative in Africa has been talking about you." Schultz looked at Russell and back to her. "I heard you're extremely lethal." Francesca smiled and Schultz continued. "Also heard there is a standing kill order on you with a three million dollar price tag."

"Rumors, just rumors." She laughed slightly in a diabolical tone and became serious. "It's five million."

"What are you doing here?"

"I replaced Yacef."

"Yes, I know him well." Schultz replied as he was got off guard. "I did not know he was leaving. How is he?"

"Dead...Bullet to the back of the head." Russell and Schultz looked between each other. "He had a welcome home party in Tel Aviv." The two Americans did not need to state the obvious. The Mossad were ruthless and deadly to everyone against Israel. The Mossad was extremely poisonous to anyone who betrayed them, regardless of rank, privileged name, or wealth. Survival of the Israeli state came at all costs.

"What are you really doing here?" Schultz leaned closer.

"Looking for something."

"Is that why you left Liberia so quickly?" Russell searched for answers as to her abrupt departure. He thought that there was something between them and all of a sudden she was gone.

"After Liberia, I went right to Johannesburg." She leaned into the table. The others followed. In a hushed tone, she continued, "In the early 70s, Israel had an agreement with South Africa to transfer atomic weapons technology. The Apartheid government was concerned that they would be overrun, just like what happened in Rhodesia. A deal was brokered for a low-level atomic weapon called a cobalt bomb."

"I read reports on that, but all of the analysts believed a cobalt bomb was fictional." Schultz replied. "They believed the reaction would not work and a cobalt bomb does not exist."

"It does exist." Francesca paused. "Only one remains."

"And it's here." Russell stated as a matter of fact. "That's why you're here?" Russell was pointed in his questioning.

"If that gets to New York or Tel Aviv, it would kill millions." Francesca stated as a matter of fact.

"What's the explosive rating?" Schultz inquired.

"More powerful than Nagasaki, but the killer would be the radiological fallout that would be a hundred times more powerful."

"Shit," Schultz said as he looked at Russell. They had enough on their hands tracking down illegal uranium shipments to Iran, North Korea, and any terrorists that wanted uranium to fuel secret nuclear programs. Now, they had intelligence on an actual weapon of mass destruction that could potentially end up on the world's black market. "How many agents are with you?"

"Just me." She looked at Russell. "The South African brothers know why I'm here. Gertz knows why I'm here. And soon enough whoever has the weapon will be scrambling to get it out of here."

"Why now?"

"This has been the first viable intelligence that showed the bomb had been moved from South Africa."

"How long do we have?" Russell knew what was at stake.

"Don't know. Could be days, could be weeks. Bottom line, it will be moved…and soon."

"I need to call Langley about this." Schultz quickly analyzed the information. "Maybe, we can get a Special Forces team out here. We are definitely going to need more help." He would have to inform the Ambassador, but not yet. If he let it play out for a few days, he could accomplish a heck of a lot compared to the bureaucracy. There was not enough time for intelligence fusion and verification. He had a level of uncertainty on all of the players in the Congo. Schultz rapidly realized he needed Francesca more than she needed them. Schultz looked at Russell, "There are several retired CIA operatives in Lubumbashi that I want you to link up with."

"Copy that." Russell paused and added. "Anything to get out of the city." Russell looked at the tables packed with frightened NGOs trying to abandon Kinshasa in its hour of need. The foreigners devoured the free food courtesy of the United States and enjoyed the protection only the world's remaining superpower provided.

"But first," Schultz added, "We have been asked by the Ambassador and Congolese Prime Minister to track down what happened at the Kuvulu massacre."

CHAPTER 7

At the luxurious Intercontinental Hotel, Gunther Blackledge thought about the report he would send to Amnesty International. He drank his first shot of whiskey in one mouthful. Gunther needed that drink. He thought back to the gruesome scene in the photos dropped off in a sealed envelope at his hotel room. There were no marks on the envelope as to who delivered them. A short note within asked for Amnesty International to find the truth around the Kuvulu massacre. The horrific scenes from the photos resonated within him, frozen, dead faces tore into his gut. Back in peaceful Switzerland, Gunther worked in an office building and rarely traveled. In his first eight years with Amnesty International, he helped raise awareness on child labor violations in Asia. Six months ago, he asked for a transfer to the investigative division and received only one week of classroom training. He had seen war scene photos thousands of miles from where the atrocities occurred. Gunther had never been to the African bush. His only time in Africa was on safari at an exclusive five star Kenyan resort, a far cry from the Congo. Gunther hated violence and wondered if he made the right choice becoming an investigator. The bartender poured another shot and Gunther gulped it. He sat alone at the end of the bar. The mood in the bar changed, becoming increasing lively as news spread. Earlier in the day, UN forces had prevailed in a major fight for control of the port. Within moments of hearing the news, UN diplomats, elite Congolese, and the NGO community barricaded in the hotel erupted in celebration. Gunther found the joyous raucous strange as Congolese troops butchered hundreds of citizens in Kuvulu. He hated them for it.

Two women watched Gunther - the first was a hired Russian prostitute and the other was a female Mossad agent. The Russian, a twenty-year old runaway, was good at her job of manipulation. Her tight, black dress highlighted a figure she used to seduce men. She leaned close to Gunther as she ordered a drink. Her perfume caught his senses and her ravishing beauty more than caught his attention. Every few seconds she bumped and touched Gunther caressing his body. Gunther was aroused and within twenty minutes she had Gunther in the palm of her hand. Over the course of their discussion, Gunther divulged his plans for reporting what happened in Kuvulu. The more he drank the more he talked. The microphone in her purse broadcasted his plans to Braum who signaled to the Russian operative by running his right hand across his throat in a slicing manner. She smiled and nodded to the bartender who dropped a small capsule in Gunther's drink when he was not looking. It did not take long for the hallucinogenic drug to take effect. And it was no trouble for the good looking woman to convince Gunther to retire to his room. Gunther's became dazed from the drug in his drink.

Across the room, Francesca watched. Gunther stumbled down the hallway. The Russian agent helped hold him up. As they passed another corridor and moved out of the sight of the hotel security guards, she tossed Gunther to the floor. As she reached for the straight blade in her boot, she looked into the eyes of the man she was about to kill. The Russian was excited by the task and did not hear the fast movement behind her. Francesca kicked her in the middle of the back. The force sent the Russian across the corridor and onto the floor. The two violent women looked at one another. Gunther remained oblivious. The Russian jumped up and leapt at the Israeli. Several strikes back and forth were made and the inexperienced young Russian prostitute was no match for the trained Mossad killer. Francesca bounced her head against the wall several times and broke her nose. She heard it pop. The Russian operative collapsed to the floor. Francesca pulled the Swiss drunk out by his arm. Gunther tried to stand. Francesca walked him back towards the elevator near the bar. Several jubilant foreigners passed and laughed at the drunk. Outside of the hotel, Jabes held the car door open. Francesca pushed Gunther into the back of the car and they sped down the street. Gunther pushed his way up onto the car seat. Russell sat in the front seat and watched for any trailing vehicles. No one followed.

"Who are you?" Gunther mumbled incoherently.

"Just keeping the peace around here." Russell said. He tried to assess how his new captive would respond. The man's eyes were closed and his mouth hung open.

"Where do we take him?" Jabes asked after a few minutes into their brazen escape.

"Kuvulu" Russell looked at Gunther who appeared to be passed out. He turned to Jabes and asked, "Can you get a helicopter?"

"Why are you helping me?" mumbled Gunther. His eyes were sealed tight.

"Call it mutual interest." Russell and Francesca looked between one another and they both smirked. After Gunther rose from his intoxicated stupor, Russell explained to Gunther that his life was in danger. It did not take long for Gunther to realize that the Minister did not want anyone to investigate what happened at Kuvulu.

Russell assembled the team for the Kuvulu reconnaissance mission. As they waited at the helicopter pad, Francesca inspected her equipment. She carried a pack loaded with weapons and ammunition. Tshambe looked hesitantly at the helicopter as he had never flown before. The lift off and rapid shift in flight caused Tshambe to vomit, no one laughed. Outside of Kinshasa, Jabes banked the UN helicopter to the left and then right as they took incoming fire from the remote hillside. Jabes heard many locals fired on the UN helicopters indiscriminately in hopes of downing the aircraft, not for a political statement but for the salvage value of the equipment on board and the steel frame. Jabes saw several tracer rounds shoot in front of the windshield and in a split second rounds dinged against the helicopter's frame. Even with the headsets, Jabes heard the shots bang against the metal. Everyone heard the sound. Jabes looked at the instruments, saw every gauge was green, and smiled back. Jabes moved the helicopter low across the landscape. He knew that the higher he flew, the more rocket shots he would take. He read a recent UN intelligence report that stated the African black market now had possession of surface to air missiles from Chechnya.

For the next hour of flight time, there was nothing to see but the fantastic beauty of the African rolling hills and open territory. Animals roamed below. Over the headset, Jabes remarked to Russell how he had not seen any sign of the massive herds that used to cross from neighboring Zambia. There were too many poachers and too many locals without food. The Congo River Valley Authority, comprised of six nations, set rules in the region to protect the roaming herds of elephants, giraffes, zebra, and antelope in hopes of drawing tourists, yet stability in the region limited tourism to a few select parks. Most tourists stayed away from the Congo turmoil and journeyed to Kenya.

Jabes heard something in the headset. He turned up the volume. The sound was inaudible. Jabes pulled back on the stick to gain altitude. The rotor squealed as the helicopter lifted upwards. He risked exposure from a missile shot, but he needed to hear the transmission.

"UN flight 8825." The garbled transmission jumped in the air.

"Roger, UN flight 8825," Jabes replied.

"Emergency evacuation has been called at Virunga." The UN traffic controller noted. "How do you copy?"

Jabes turned to Russell. "They want us to divert east for an emergency pick up. Is that ok?"

Russell did not question the emergency. He understood his mission with utmost importance, yet something inside of him made him care too damn much. "Go ahead."

"Control, this is UN flight 8825. Confirm evacuation... changing course." Jabes adjusted his direction and increased speed.

Virunga National Park was listed as a World Heritage site in 1979. The diverse ecosystem stretched from river beds to the mountain slopes. With nearly a million acres, the massive pristine jungle served as the only solitude in the world for the mountain gorilla with less than eight hundred remaining in existence. The adult male silverbacks roamed the high altitude landscape. The massive males reached over six feet and weighed nearly five hundred pounds. The thick misty clouds masked most of the mountain gorillas' movements across the slopes. Doctor Eddy and his team of foreign volunteers lived close by to study the creatures, but became protectors of the massive animals as gorilla poachers inundated the Congo.

The down wash from the UN helicopter kicked up all of the brush and a significant amount of dust. As the wheels touched firmly down, Jabes looked at the instruments one last time before he powered down the aircraft. He had too many bad experiences with these old UN helicopters and did not want to get stranded in the remote jungle.

"Where's the trouble?" Russell asked as he jumped several feet off the rear open platform onto the ground. Several children ran to see the helicopter land. They pointed up the hill. After a mile hike, Russell saw twenty locals standing outside a bush hut. Many of them were visibly upset and crying. Inside the bush hut, Russell found three white men and one white woman being worked on. All of their faces were visibly shocked by the brutality.

"What happened?"

"Soldiers came for the gorillas." One of the volunteer Portuguese men pointed towards the mountain pass and in the general direction of Burundi. "Many shot." Russell sensed that the foreigners were shocked at the brutality. Gunther tried to help one of the Portuguese women who had multiple gunshots to the torso. Blood gurgled from her mouth. Within seconds, his light blue Amnesty International shirt was covered in blood. She grasped his hand with both of hers and temporarily lifted her body to fight the pain. She squeezed hard in the last moments of her life. Death eased over her and her lifeless body gently drifted back to the ground. Another volunteer had been shot in the leg. A tight tourniquet held back the bleeding. Blood covered everyone, even those not wounded as they tried to administer first aid. "We have a helicopter to take you to a hospital." Russell spoke to the injured Portuguese volunteers. They understood him, but spoke amongst themselves in their native Portuguese. The ones who were not injured helped load all of their belongings into bags. Russell, Francesca, Gunther, and Tshambe helped carry the injured to the helicopter. Locals helped carry all of their gear. The Portuguese team's journey to discover primate instincts between orphan baby gorillas and mature gorillas came to an abrupt end. Before they got to the helicopter, Russell already made his decision. He found Jabes in the cockpit as he completed preflight checks.

"Jabes, take them to Kinshasa and come right back." Russell grabbed his pack as he left the cockpit. He turned to Francesca. "I have to do this." Russell inserted a magazine into his sub-machine gun. The noise of the helicopter blades starting sent loud concussion sounds in the cabin. She could barely hear him, but knew what he was up to. She grabbed her gear and followed. The helicopter lifted off and banked over top of the grass huts. The pressure from the down wash vibrated the thatched roofs. Loose rubble sprayed Russell and Francesca.

The calmness of Virunga National Forest was unsettling. Prior to the massive influx of refugees from the Rwanda genocide, Virunga was the last bastion of peace and normalcy within the Congo. Nearly two million refugees fled the brutal Hutu bloody rampage. Over a decade ago, they arrived in Virunga and never left. Virunga's isolation and massive 800,000 acres proved a viable sanctuary from cross-border attacks. Small towns sprung up within the hillsides. Massive uncontrolled poaching and deforestation ensued. UN reports estimated over 9,000 hippopotamus were gutted in the lowlands. Fortunately, the gorillas who lived high in the mountains survived, until foreigners arrived and paid premium dollars for kidnapped infant gorillas.

Doctor Eddy carried the water up the side of the mountain for four hundred yards. Water sloshed over the rim of the two pails in either arm. He trudged his way up the steep slope. He was surprised to see a white man standing on the front porch of the laboratory.

"Let me help you." Russell moved to grab one of the water pails.

"Where did you come from?" Doctor Eddy asked. He heard the helicopter land and surmised he was there to rescue the Portuguese. "Who are you?"

"Nobody, just here to help."

"You don't have a name?"

"I do, but it is best that you do not know."

"Are you an NGO?"

"No far from it. I'm the guy that they call in when there is trouble."

"We have lots of trouble here." Doctor Eddy pointed down towards the lowland and said, "Many refugees slaughtered there." He paused for a moment and added. "They ran out of bullets and used clubs." The World Heritage Committee released a scathing report on the UN High Commission for Refugees (UNHCR) inability to control the massive influx of Rwandans. Huge amounts of charcoal, made for burning thousands of mature trees, were transported out of Virunga, often with the knowledge of UNHCR. From their vantage point, Russell could see large holes in the pristine forest where refugees conducted widespread burning. Doctor Eddy motioned for Russell and Francesca to follow him. They walked down the path to several brick frames that looked like partial buildings. Russell smelled death. Within a few feet, he saw the corpses of several large gorillas.

"These were the females. They nurtured the young orphan baby gorillas." Doctor Eddy pointed. Russell looked at the handless mammoth gorilla bodies. "They took their hands so they can sell them." Doctor Eddy cried hard.

"What about the orphan gorillas?" Russell asked.

"Taken." Doctor Eddy started to sob again. "They will sell them on the black market to collectors. No rightful zoo would buy the babies but there are many individual exotic animal collectors who will."

"Where did they go?"

"Burundi to sell them." Doctor Eddy was visibly upset. He fell to the ground and sobbed.

"Are there any rangers here?" Russell asked.

"No, all dead. Rangers were killed last year by exiled Tutsi rebels from Rwanda." He wiped a tear from an eye. "All killed." Doctor Eddy looked down to the ground.

"Are UN soldiers here?"

"Other side of the mountain, along Uganda border. They don't go near Rwanda border – too deadly." The Rwandan genocide was over ten years ago and Russell knew the cease fire had been violated hundreds of times. Cross border violence raged. "Those who did this," Doctor Eddy pointed to the lifeless primates, "they are not men, they are beasts."

Russell stepped close and put his hand on Doctor Eddy's shoulder and said, "I promise that I will return." Doctor Eddy looked into Russell's eyes and could sense he was going after the poachers. Russell loaded a magazine of ammunition in his weapon. The rebels had a five hour head start.

Francesca watched Russell as he inspected his gear. She never knew what real love was. As a Mossad trained killer, there was no room to let anyone get close and personal. If Tel Aviv wanted her married, it would have been a cover story. Her father was the contradiction as he joined the Mossad late in life and had to sign a waiver that if he was captured and divulged his real family, Tel Aviv would not protect them. No one protected her mother when the bomb blast killed her right after her eighth birthday. For a quick second, she placed her left hand against the necklace charm around her neck. She felt it under her black, thick canvas safari shirt. She turned back to Russell and said loud enough for Doctor Eddy to hear, "No survivors."

Schultz received word of Virunga attack within hours of it happening. The UN sent a flash message that two foreigners did not return with the emergency helicopter. It did not take Schultz long to put two and two together to know Russell was up to something. Tshambe called Schultz from the hospital. Gunther went back to the Intercontinental Hotel and called Amnesty International for a bodyguard team to protect him. Gunther needed to complete his review of the massacre. Gunther picked up a local paper and saw the photo of the Minister of Information. He read the article, *'Reports of rapes and killings by Congo troops at Kuvulu are unfounded,' stated the Minister to the reporter who questioned him, 'These things are brought up by those not wishing Congo peace. These things are discussed by those who do not know the truth and fabricate what they want everyone to believe.'* Gunther laid the paper down and knew he would have no support from the Congo government. Since the UN failed to act appropriately to protect the Kuvulu, Gunther knew he would have no support.

On the high altitude Virunga plateau, Russell and Francesca trudged through the bush. Francesca pushed faster past him and the race was on. Both looked back to one another more than out for the rebels. The intensity between them was thick. Five hours passed without a break as they trekked hard and faster. Russell was in top condition, yet he had difficulty keeping up with Francesca as she pushed faster. Several times, he slipped from the speed of the pace. He watched her thick legs pound against the earth. Both sweated profusely. Out of nowhere she stopped, turned, and turned back to Russell. With all of her might, she tossed him to the ground. Russell fell hard. He was near exhaustion. A butterfly could have knocked him over at this point.

"What do you want from me?" Francesca stared down at him. He looked up at her in disbelief.

"Nothing... not a damn thing." He replied in a deliberate tone. Russell sensed she wanted something more from him, yet he wanted answers. "Why did you leave Liberia?"

"My cover was blown."

"You wanted out." Russell was not letting her off easy.

"If I wanted out, I would have put a bullet in your head." Francesca clicked open the flap that held her Desert Eagle in its holster. She looked at him with piercing eyes. She had a secret that she could not tell him at this moment, a secret that would change her life forever.

"I don't know what to say."

"So I guess we are on the same sides for now?" The female Mossad agent knew how to turn someone, but she had difficulty with the man she loved.

"For now." Russell said as he pulled himself off the earth.

Up the side of the mountain, Russell and Francesca continued. There were only faint traces of light as the sun began to set. In another forty minutes, they would be in pitch blackness and paralyzed by the night without the aid of any starlight scopes. Francesca found a rock shelf. They ate some food and rested. The moment was awkward as both waited for the other to speak.

"I do love you," Russell said, "in some way I guess."

"Don't say it unless you mean it." Francesca replied. "You're not going to be able to live with me in Tel Aviv. My father would kill you and not quickly. He would make you suffer. He's old school Mossad."

"That's nice." Russell laughed and said, "Guess I don't need to ask him for your hand in marriage."

"Were you thinking that?"

"Sorry, just talking."

"Did you ever come close?" Francesca inquired.

"Yes, but her father had some severe issues."

"Why are you so inclined to be with women with insane fathers?" Francesca stopped and looked at Russell. She added. "Are you mad?"

"Some may think that." Russell thought about it for a moment and added. "I guess that I have always had a problem with authority.'"

"But you're in the military."

"Maybe it is more of a death wish." Russell said pointedly.

"My father can help with that." Francesca replied as she pushed past him.

Alongside the Congo River, Rajik was pleased with his Hezbollah terrorist training compound. He had a small army of young Lebanese orphans. Hundreds of these orphans were sent to remote camps all across Africa as staging and training bases for future martyrs. Hezbollah leaders were keen to sack orphanages and comb the hospitals after the fighting. Under the guise to help the orphans, they sent the Ashbals away to learn a new craft, an education based on the destruction of Israel. Child soldiers have not been anything new to Africa. At the height of the Congo war, the UN estimated more than 30,000 children were fighting with various factions. Rajik believed there was a viable threat of HIV and AIDS being used as a biological weapon by advisories. He heard similar rumors of Yasser Arafat being infected by HIV that led to his death. Rajik kept the Lebanese community in check with intimidation and death threats. Three months ago he barely escaped Liberia as a female Mossad agent fired at his boat after she blew up his SUV, with a rocket. Rajik managed to smuggle a large box of rough diamonds. The blood diamonds were from Sierra Leone and buried since their civil war ended in 1999. He created significant wealth for himself by stealing a pile of blood diamonds from an Al Qaeda assassin who was on his way to blow up the US Embassy, Monrovia. That was until Russell and his Israeli girlfriend interceded and foiled the plot.

Back in Kinshasa, the Nakor Industry building was empty except for the executive suite. Moira sat patiently by her office desk praying that she could get out in a reasonable time. She hated driving home in the dark. Moira knew of three women in Nakor who were brutally attacked. She was scared for her life. Moira did not look at Braum as he passed. The massive man entered Gertz office and slopped into the chair. Gertz mimicked to himself that Braum looked like an adult sitting in a kindergarten chair, but the chair was normal size. Gertz passed the envelope of cash across the table to Braum and then passed a photo of the American. Braum smiled as he departed. He was pleased to have permission to kill. Braum looked at the picture of the female archeologist. Laid across his conference table, Gertz studied the map intently. One of his paid informants at the hospital gave him daily updates on the dying archaeologists. Final death was sudden brought on by severe radiation poisoning. He understood perhaps they found the same Uranium 238 mine that he currently exploited, yet the radiation counts were off the chart. Perhaps that could be from exposure to the atomic bomb the female Mossad agent sought. Gertz was smart enough not to deal with the nuclear weapons black market. His network would surely become a target for attack. What Gertz was more interested in was something the dying archaeologist murmured in his somewhat conscious state. Braum put a pillow over the man's head and suffocated him, but before he murdered the near catatonic patient, he recorded. Gertz relayed the tape player again and again. The only word he could pull from the wrangled voice was "Solomon."

CHAPTER 8

Colonel Frank Kitson Jr. walked out into the blistering African sun, a sharp contrast from the dreary London weather. He had arrived in Kinshasa on the last flight, the previous evening. Sometime after midnight, he met Schultz outside the airport terminal. The deadness of the night surprised him. No one moved as the UN curfew remained in effect. Kitson got settled at the embassy in the early morning hours. After only a few minutes of sleep, he was on the move. He walked away from the security blanket that surrounded embassy row and into the Kinshasa streets. Kitson held his wallet tight as he pushed through the crowd of beggars. His satellite phone buzzed, yet he knew better not to bring it out in the open as he would be a target. He did not know who watched him - gun runners, blood diamond exporters, uranium smugglers or what groups – Hezbollah, Al Qaeda, or KGB? Kitson survived half a dozen attempts on his life. He served in Rhodesia, Sierra Leone, Kenya, Northern Ireland, Afghanistan, and most recently Liberia. Based upon his experiences during a vast twenty-seven year military career, Kitson became a master at surveillance and counter intelligence operations. Moreover, he spent two years assigned to MI6, but that position was summarily absent from his military record.

After assigned to MI6, Kitson deployed to Northern Ireland and became entangled in the struggle for peace against some of the world's most hardcore terrorist groups. While deployed to Belfast, he controlled a specialized team of local spies that fed raw intelligence on Sin Fein movements. Within weeks, he found his name on the IRA's target list and realized he was being tracked. After midnight on Christmas day 1988, he caught his tracker, interrogated him, and prevented a major terrorist bomb attack in Dublin over the holidays. Kitson learned the identity how proper counter-intelligence was conducted. Kitson was on another high profile mission.

Along the Kinshasa streets, Kitson stepped up his pace. He pushed through the crowd of beggars and potential criminals who saw him as a soft target. The tourist safari hat and large sunglasses concealed his face. The tan shooting jacket contained large caliber rounds for big game hunting. Over his shoulder, he carried what looked like an expensive camera. His cover was a British citizen on safari. He sensed a tracker, someone who traced his movements. Kitson stepped up his pace. He was exhausted from the flight, yet he knew the situation called for an extra burst of adrenaline. As he turned into the alley, he plugged a small remote camera with a gel adhesive against the wall. The makeshift shops bustled with activity. With utmost sped, he moved through the crowd. Kitson looked down at the handheld screen and watched several white men stop and look around. One pointed down the street while the other two headed down the jam packed alley. Kitson dropped the hat on a vegetable stand and placed a brown long hair wig on his head. A local boy quickly grabbed the hat and ran off. Other boys chased. Kitson pulled off his shooting jacket and rolled it up. He was not about to surrender his favorite shooting jacket. Kitson discovered a coffee house, a basic room with two beaten plastic chairs that could barely hold a man's weight. One was occupied by a local young professional dressed lady, a foreign NGO worker, who enjoyed a morning coffee. Kitson grabbed the other chair and leaned close to the young lady for a brief question on where best to eat. The trackers moved past and did not even give him a second look. Kitson headed the other way. He had ten minutes to meet his contact.

Kitson was familiar with the two economies in post war-torn Africa. High prices paid by UN, NGOs, and foreign businessmen helped inflate the cost of basic goods. Cargo ships rarely entered the port, out of fear of being taken over or vandalized. The Lebanese used their own ferry boats to purchase goods from of Johannesburg. The only thing that kept the bridge of supplies together were the Lebanese. Kitson headed towards the main street that divided Kinshasa from the slums to the mansion compounds. The pungent odor of human waste resonated and choked him. Kinshasa's sewage waste plant stopped working six months ago after the only man who could operate the equipment was killed in mob violence. The plant worked for a week before the equipment seized. A contractor was brought in to assess the antiquated plant equipment at a cost of $5600 a day. The lack of sewage treatment highlighted everything that was wrong in Kinshasa.

Kitson found the Christian Fellowship School. It was empty – looted – destroyed - left to rot. The painted words on the side of the building still remained, *Impacting Lives, Equipping Saints, Changing a Generation.* Kitson wondered what happened to the dreams of youth who once roamed these halls. Dietger Laurent sat in a brand new lounge chair. He sipped a local coffee.

"You must be Kitson." Dietger stood and offered his hand. Kitson sat in the adjacent lounge chair. "Coffee?" Dietger pointed to his butler to serve Kitson. "We have some of the best coffee in Africa. Forget what the Ethiopians say - Congo coffee is the worlds' best." As the butler departed. Kitson observed a compact machinegun strapped across his back. Kitson knew even with the UN weapons embargo that wealthy men had their own security and openly carried weapons.

"London says you may be of help." Kitson did not want to refer to MI6, but Dietger knew who he referred to.

"Belgium and Great Britain have long been allies in Africa." Kitson picked up Dietger's reference to the former British Empire. "It is hard to let our colonial holdings go...kind of like letting a child go off to school. You hope the child matures, obeys the rules, and flourishes. But we know that is not the case in Africa. Do we?" Kitson remained silent. He did not want to get into an argument about how brutal the Belgians were in the Congo. The British had their own obscure and turbulent history in Africa, yet the crown never brutalized a population like the Belgians. In fact, Kitson believed no European power was as brutal as the Belgians. "Now look at this school. Some Christian organization from your old colony America came here and abruptly departed once the first rounds started." Dietger waived his arm in the arm and added. "It's a shame. Education is so important. Look at this mess."

"I agree." Kitson replied. "Without education we cannot break the bonds holding back the Africans." Kitson could already tell Dietger was a racist, but he needed the information. "As I said, London believes you can offer information."

"Illegal diamonds are the root of evil in Africa." Dietger continued to digress as he pointed to an article in the paper on captured diamond smugglers. "So much has been lost searching for rare diamonds. So many lives impacted. And now there are more diamonds that will flowed the market."

"Katanga?" Kitson inquired. "I thought the diamond mines had good security against theft." Kitson referred to Katanga province that held the world's largest known supply of diamonds. International conglomerates held majority interest in the Katanga diamond mines and it was in their interest to limit the flow of illegal diamonds. Diamond syndicates were registered in countries that signed the Kimberly Accord and adopted the Kimberly Process to track rough cut, untraceable diamonds onto the world market.

"No," Dietger said and added. "Mugabe."

"Zimbabwe? They are banned from dealing openly on the world's diamond market." Kitson thought for a moment and quickly came to the conclusion. "Smuggling into the Congo and mixing with the Katanga rough diamonds would bypass detection."

"Smugglers can easily bring across the most desirable diamonds and nobody knows how big Zimbabwe's reserves are." Dietger drank his coffee and motioned for his butler to serve more.

"About twenty billion dollars' worth." Kitson responded as a matter of fact. Silence came across the room as each formulated in their heads the magnitude of twenty billion dollars. Kitson fully understood and let the ramifications sink in for a moment. He thought of his own experiences. Kitson served in Rhodesia, which became Zimbabwe. He kept current over the years on the ruthless affairs of the most brutal dictator in the world. Mugabe opened a dozen diamond mines in the past ten years and used prison labor to dig for diamonds. Mines repeatedly collapsed and buried the prisoners. Guards remained at the entrance. If the prisoners wanted to eat or drink they had to come back to the surface. Before they could get anything, the prisoners were stripped searched for diamonds. Those who tried to hide diamonds in body parts were shot.

Kitson knew Mugabe took over all of the banks in Zimbabwe once he gained power. He constructed a massive vault inside of the capital city Harare's largest bank. No one knew exactly how many blood diamonds Mugabe pulled from earth. MI6 had best guessed about five hundred million. Kitson realized that Mugabe must have been extremely fortunate to discover a large diamond deposit, possibly a deep kimberlite tube. From his time in West Africa, he knew kimberlite tubes were formed by rapidly cooling volcanic geysers that stretched several miles deep into earth's crust. Kimberlite tubes were rare and hard to find, yet they yielded some of the largest diamonds ever discovered. He was intrigued about Zimbabwe diamond mines. Kitson continued, "Mugabe could flood the world's diamond market and cause complete collapse."

"Someone may try to leverage this chaos."

"Who?" Kitson asked.

"An American named Gertz." Dietger passed him a photo.

Along the slope within Virunga National Park, Russell and Francesca pressed forward. The poachers had a head start; however, Russell had hoped carrying the kidnapped baby gorillas would slow them down. There was only one mountain pass that led to the Burundi border. Through the sparse foliage, Russell could see Lake Tanganyika, which separated Tanzania from the Congo. Burundi was one of the nine African nations directly linked to the Congo. Lake Tanganyika served as a buffer to keep cross-border violence from raging in Tanzania. A rapidly flowing stream obstructed their pursuit. Russell waded through the fast moving water. Within a moment his entire body was soaked. As she crossed, Francesca accidently dropped the survival bag with food into the water. The fast moving water tumbled the bag over the small waterfall and into the big pool below.

"Wait...the bag." Francesca shouted. Russell pushed the remaining ten feet to the shoreline. He saw where the bag went over the waterfall. He peered down forty feet to the lagoon.

"Can you bring down the gear?"

"I can manage."

"And my clothes." Russell added as he stripped down to his underwear. Francesca gave his body a hard look. He was toned and chiseled from his regular climbs in the Seattle mountain range. Russell walked across the rocks in his bare feet and jumped. After a four second free fall, he smashed through the cold water. His skin sizzled from the sudden exposure to extreme cold. He punched back to the surface and breathed hard. Visibility was good for him to find the bag. He swam ashore and found Francesca already on the side with the pack and his clothes. He was freezing and knew that he needed to get warm. As he approached her, she could see him shivering. He hugged her tightly to get warm. She did not mind and squeezed hard as she could.

"We need to move or I will go into hypothermia." The cool mountain air coupled with the cold water pinched his skin. They picked up the pace.

"There." Francesca pointed. "Five hundred meters." She handed Russell a set of binoculars. Russell could see a small orange glow from a fire. They were in luck. The poachers were undisciplined and needed an open fire to keep warm. The Burundi border was less than a mile away. Russell surmised the poachers must be waiting for a morning pickup to bring them into the capital city Bujumbura where the black market for animal sales thrived. Russell motioned toward a rock face and Francesca followed. They huddled close as night started to fall. Russell enjoyed the tight grip as he shivered uncontrollably. Within moments, Russell felt the warmth.

Francesca pulled the high powered night vision scope from the bag and attached it to the sniper rifle. Russell put on a set of night vision goggles. As darkness surrounded the mountains, the two were off on a search and destroy mission. They did not have headset microphones to communicate, yet the professional soldiers knew how to move. Francesca initiated the star light scope and held the sniper rifle tight as she walked. Russell held the sub-machine gun at waist level. There were no guards awake. Francesca remained on the outside boundary of the camp and sighted the scope on the sleeping bodies.

Russell lifted off the night vision goggles and stepped silently into the camp. The coals from the previous fire glowed. As he directed his weapon in the air, he heard a man snore and did not lose the opportunity. Russell fired into the Argentine's tent and heard a moan as the man fell off his cot. Several of the poachers ran and Francesca fired at them. She delivered five direct hits in a span of eight seconds on the moving targets. Russell blasted another clip into the tent. Russell peered into the tent and observed a dead white man. He quickly pulled the man's identification and found the Argentinean passport. He checked the face to the picture and folded it into his pocket. Francesca held the perimeter as Russell grabbed cages. Within two minutes from their assault, they exited the camp. The baby gorillas screamed at the noise and sudden awakening. For an hour, Russell and Francesca climbed up the mountain and away from the raid. They did not slowdown in case rebels were in the area. As morning approached, Russell and Francesca were exhausted, yet they pushed onward.

Sixteen hours had passed since Russell and Francesca departed Doctor Eddy. Near the camp, Jabes landed the helicopter in the field and had waited six hours past his scheduled departure time. UN authorities in Kinshasa were getting more and more concerned that the helicopter would be left out there unguarded in the night. Jabes knew the UN cared more about their precious equipment than service members, yet he would not leave Russell. When they staggered out of the jungle, Jabes was pleased to see them.

"The baby gorillas." Doctor Eddy screamed. "You saved them." Again he shouted, "You saved them!" Doctor Eddy fell to the ground as he ran. He picked up his body with the help of his cane and hurried to his chimps. "Thank you my friend, thank you." Except for Doctor Eddy and two young boys, the camp was deserted.

"Are you ok here?" Russell knew the man would not leave his life's passion, but was concerned for him. In a few days, someone in Burundi would be wondering where the poachers were and soon would be asking questions.

"We will be fine." Doctor Eddy rubbed his grandsons' heads as they fed plantains, African style bananas, to the baby gorillas.

"I'll make sure the proper authorities know what happened here." Russell said. He ran towards the helicopter as Jabes started the engines. Russell would have to explain to the Regional Security Officer at the US Embassy why he was involved in a civil issue and why he did not arrest the poachers. Russell wondered how much paperwork awaited him.

Kamal made sure no one saw him pull the Lebanese boy about twelve years old into his newly formed Al Qaeda interrogation lab. Kamal tied his victim to a chair. At several points, he struck his victim's skin with a scalpel and his victim bled. The young boy had duct taped over his mouth. His eyes bulged as Kamal thrust a dull screwdriver into his chest. The boy shook violently. The ropes held the victim firmly to the chair. As Kamal retrieved the screwdriver, blood shot out from the wound. Kamal was impressed that he hit a lung on his first attempt. As the boy breathed, blood squirted.

"Where can I find the bomb?" Kamal asked his victim. The interrogation had just begun and Kamal enjoyed the fight the Lebanese boy already put up. His death would be a pleasure.

CHAPTER 9

Rajik kept the cobalt atomic bomb in a large wooden box. The Hezbollah terrorist read the description from the thirty year old pamphlet. The bomb was actually a hydrogen atomic bomb with a blanket sheath of cobalt metal. Supposedly, the cobalt metal blanket would maximize damage from radioactive fallout as escaping fusion neutrons were captured. Rajik looked at the pages from an older 1950s U.S. government book on the effects of nuclear weapons. It clarified the neutrons activated from the cobalt were deadly fission products. Thermo-nuclear weapons released more neutrons and acted as what is known in present day as dirty bombs. Gamma radiation would be intense, nearly 15,000 times more in the first hour and would dramatically decrease to 35 times potent within a week. The initial blast of radiation would generate lethal doses within a ten mile radius. Rajik realized the bomb would generate more fallout than explosive force. More importantly, the sheer panic the weapon of mass destruction would cause was good enough for him.

Rajik changed the cipher door lock every hour. He became obsessed. Back and forth he walked all day and most of the night. He sat on what could be the most historic terrorist attack in all of humanity. He would personally be responsible for the direct killing of nearly a million individuals within a week. He was so impressed with the potential catastrophic outcome that it started to drive him mad. Did he remember the right altitude for the bomb to initiate on the plane? Did he have the right longitude and latitude? Should he utilize a ten digit GPS grid coordinate and would that be more precise? He burned the maps and later the same night dug his hands into the ashes to see if he was correct in his time and space calculations. Paranoia started to drive him. He yelled at them to get back to their posts. He was impatient with everything.

"When will the bomb be ready?" Rajik asked.

"Soon," replied Galpin, "you must have patience."

"It could blow up at any time." Rajik raised his voice louder, "and we could miss out on the greatest terrorist attack in history."

"It is my revenge that will be the greatest." Galpin tried to compete with his fellow conspirator. Galpin thought for a moment of putting a bullet in the back of Rajik's head when he turned, but realized that he needed him more than anything.

"It won't come soon enough. I want this bomb out of here now." Rajik looked at his radiological tracking meters, which were good for three hours. "Someone is watching us. I can feel it."

"Who?" Galpin asked, "The blue helmets?" Everyone referred to the UN forces as blue helmets for the UN sponsored countries that joined the mission. There were over fifty different countries that sent troops to the UN mission in the Congo, yet they all wore the same blue helmet. Galpin continued, "They are inept. Do not worry about them."

"No, someone else. One of my Ashbals disappeared and was tortured to death." Rajik knew who ever did would be coming for him. "The person who did this was brutal." Rajik did not know the Al Qaeda interrogation physician named Kamal had arrived. A few months ago, Rajik stole diamonds from an Al Qaeda operative in Liberia before he vanished in daring escape by speedboat. Rajik watched out for Al Qaeda operatives seeking vengeance.

"You need to increase your guards and take more precautions. If word leaked about our mission, we will all be dead."

"That is why we need to move up the timetable." Rajik was more nervous. "I want the bomb out of here now." The meter maintained a green light to signify it was safe.

"The detonator must be completed correctly." Galpin was direct. "Everything hinges up the triggering device. It must activate the bomb at the correct altitude."

"When can I have the rest of my money?" Rajik asked.

"Once we move the bomb to the final location, then you will be paid." Galpin reassured Rajik that the three million dollars previously agreed upon would be deposited into his Swiss bank account. Rajik never had such wealth before. His blood diamonds were sold at rock bottom prices as everyone had diamonds for sale in the Congo. The only business that turned a healthy profit was weapon smuggling. His Ashbal camp cost him a lot of money to keep his young orphans trained and equipped. The Ashbals believed that they would go back to Lebanon to wage war against Israel and seek revenge. However, Rajik had bigger plans to sacrifice them in his elaborate plan to escape out of Africa once and for all as a wealthy man. Rajik had changed out the detectors more than the locks. The threat of radiation engrossed him.

In the secure embassy compound, Kitson watched Russell as he greeted Schultz. The two of them talked briefly until Russell noticed his old mentor sitting on the balcony. Russell respected Kitson based upon their service together in Liberia a few months back. Kitson was assigned to watch the illegal flow of blood diamonds out of Sierra Leone into neighboring Liberia.

Throughout the Sierra Leone civil war that raged in the late 1990s, Liberia exported over a billion dollars of rough diamonds onto the world's market. Governments could not stem the flow of loose, untraceable rough diamonds and diamond cartels became more powerful. Kitson established a base camp of operations at the old Firestone Rubber Plantation outside of Monrovia, Liberia. The British Colonel mentored Russell on the impacts of revolutionary thought and counter insurgency doctrine in Africa. Kitson served on the Dark Continent for most of his thirty year career.

Kitson was more than ready to retire, until he got the call from the Prince of Wales to serve in Afghanistan alongside the Second Lieutenant Wales otherwise known as Prince Harry. His tour of duty was abruptly curtailed as media fanatics got word of Prince Harry's service in the warzone. Kitson had a few months left on his military orders and took the Liberia assignment. In the midst of the Liberia deployment, the remote MI6 secret compound was attacked. He had pre-arranged explosive charges ready to blow the communication building. As the intruders attacked, Kitson blasted them and subsequently the bungalow roof collapsed on top of him. He was pulled from the rubble and transported to the UN hospital in Monrovia. Russell heard of the attack and rushed to the UN base, only to find his mentor was sent to London.

"Just like old times." Russell lamented and handed the British Colonel a very strong gin and tonic. "Good to see you Colonel."

"Hopefully this time, I don't get evacuated."

"Sorry that I wasn't there for you." Russell replied in a soft tone. Russell was not there when Kitson was injured and felt tremendous guilt. The two old friends talked about the Liberia mission for several hours. Kitson heard of the dramatic events around the arrest of Charles Taylor for war crimes. Russell filled in a lot of the blank spaces on how he took a team into Nigeria to arrest Taylor who was in exile. However, Taylor got word of the upcoming raid and had already fled north to Cameroon. Russell explained how he was able to get a helicopter, fly to another country under the radar, arrest Taylor, and bring him back to Liberia to face justice. Russell explained the last days of his deployment to Liberia and the intense fire fights he had with Hezbollah operatives. The worse part was Hezbollah gunrunner Rajik had escaped.

"What are the atmospherics here?" Kitson inquired as he wanted to focus back to the moment.

"Bad," Schultz jumped in after listening intently. "The newly appointed Ministers are even more corrupt than Mobutu's regime of terror. The UN has been completely ineffective protecting the locals. Congo soldiers have committed rapes and are suspected of a huge massacre in Kuvulu. There is so much corruption here. Nothing gets done without a bribe."

"Are any NGOs helping the Congolese?"

"Most have left." Schultz replied. "Those who remained are frightened for their lives. Few ever leave Kinshasa for the countryside. Education is at an all-time low. Everything is smuggled out: uranium, diamonds, gold, even humans. Iran and North Korea are looking to fuel nuclear weapons programs and some terrorists are looking to make a dirty bomb."

"Anything else happen since I left Africa?"

"Your boy Russell has a new girlfriend." Schultz remarked.

"Really?" inquired Kitson as he looked at his protégé.

"I wouldn't say that." Russell jumped in.

"Israeli Mossad agent and smoking hot." Schultz ruffled Russell's feathers and could see him fume. Schultz liked to press people's buttons to see how they reacted to questioning and more importantly he needed to know Russell would not place any romantic feelings above accomplishing the mission.

"Didn't you meet her in Liberia?" Kitson asked. He already knew the answer that Francesca had worked undercover for Doctors Without Borders."

"Her cover was blown," Russell said. "And she had to leave."

"From what I know about her." Kitson stated pointedly. "She's deadly … very deadly."

"Yeah, Tom sleeps with one eye open." Schultz laughed. Russell was not amused.

"Do we know Israel's interests in the Congo?" Kitson asked.

"Diamonds." Schultz looked at the new member of his intelligence team. Schultz knew Kitson had strong ties within Africa and many contacts. "There is man named Gertz has dual citizenship with Israel and America. Gertz has somehow found a way to smuggle diamonds out of the Congo and into the New York diamond district. He's from Brooklyn and well connected with New York Rabbis and politicians. He believes that he is above the law."

"But I thought the Katanga diamond mines follow the Kimberly Process." Russell commented. He learned a considerable amount about how to track and stop illegal blood diamonds in West Africa and more importantly the human toll that rough, untraceable diamonds had on locals. He led a team into Sierra Leone on strong intelligence of a blood diamond camp. Deep within the borders, his team liberated forty citizens held hostage by rebels to scour the riverbed for diamonds. The Kimberly Process was supposed to end the sale of illicit diamonds on the international market, yet only a fraction of nations signed the accord and some major diamond importing countries such as China, Russia, and Syria refused to sign it.

"There are still many untraceable rough diamonds on the world's black market. What about diamonds from Zimbabwe?" Kitson asked.

"Have not heard anything." Schultz received regular updates from Langley on the companies exporting diamonds from the Katanga mines that had been operated by international conglomerates for several decades.

"MI6 is concerned about what is going on in Zimbabwe." Kitson pointed out. "Zimbabwe has untold diamond reserves. Over the past decade, Mugabe has used prisoners to farm diamonds. The Central Bank of Zimbabwe contains a massive underground safe full of rough diamonds."

"What does Mugabe plan to do with the diamonds?"

"Mugabe needs to stay in power. The atrocities he committed on his own people have all but eliminated foreign donor aid. The World Bank will not lend him money. If he succeeds in funneling rough diamonds out of Zimbabwe, he could feasibly bribe his way to stay in power. Rough cut diamonds would have to be moved through a middleman."

"Who?" Russell asked.

"More than likely this man Gertz." Kitson said.

"In fairness of sharing information with our partners, we are after uranium smugglers." Schultz replied. His CIA superiors already cleared him to share all available intelligence information with MI6's lead man in the Congo. Schultz did not need a memo that informed him, he would have done it anyways. MI6 operatives have saved him from a bad day on more than one occasion.

"We should be able to help one another." Kitson understood the need for cooperation.

Dietger Laurent's retreat along the Congo River was spectacular. His mansion was the most massive resort that lined the river. The most powerful and wealthy families in Kinshasa maintained riverfront mansions to relax from the brutal heat. More importantly, the river mansions served as a launch point for a means to escape when violence erupted. All of the mansions were occupied as the ultra-wealthy waited for the violence to subside. They became prisoners of their own wealth.

Along poolside, beautiful local females relaxed on the lounge chairs. Each were tested weekly for the HIV virus. Dietger worried about getting involved with infected girls. Two of his house wives became dirty with herpes and were summarily executed in front of the entire house staff. Their bodies dumped into the river for the crocodiles. Sexually transmitted diseases were rampant as the UN lost control. Ladies lounged alongside the pool, which was nearly a half-acre in size. The mammoth amounts of water were pumped by three 200 horse power pumps. Objects were majestically placed and water cascaded steadily out of concrete mouths. Mythical Greek gods and goddesses were represented in solid concrete fashion. The office was on the third floor of the cement building. An open porch surrounded the office. Dietger walked outside with a drink in his hand to admire several of the beauties. He was pleased at the high level meeting he called and had his most beautiful women on hand to entertain. His guests sat on the veranda and drank whiskey.

"Is the shipment ready?" Galpin asked.

"Soon," Rajik responded. "But we have a problem that needs to be taken care of."

"The American?"

"Yes," Galpin looked at the photo and handed it to Rajik, "and there is also an Israeli here too." He placed photos on the table.

"I know this Mossad parasite. I should have killed her in Monrovia when I had the chance."

"We heard a female Mossad agent took out one of our cells in Johannesburg. It could be the same one."

"More than likely it is. She's deadly. I will not make the same mistake?" Rajik ripped her photo into pieces, tossed the scraps on the floor, and spat on it in disgust.

"We will kill the Israeli and the Americans. We can take them all out in one move." Galpin lifted his drink in a cheer.

"And bring the world to its knees." Dietger replied. He stumbled as he finished his fifth drink and picked up a weapon. He fired a machinegun across the water. Locals rushed for cover. Dietger smoked his large cigar and laughed as the innocent locals dove for cover.

At Kinshasa International Airport, the private jet marked NAKOR painted on the side traversed the runway ahead of all of the UN aircraft. Gertz had paid contacts all across the Congo. Compared to the local Congolese citizen, Gertz lived as royalty. He had more power than the Congo's President. Gertz bribed the Minister of Information and aggressively targeted the newly appointed Minister of Defense. He was confident he would have the new minister on payroll by the end of the month. If not, he would have him killed. Gertz played for keeps.

As the aircraft pushed through the low level clouds, Gertz looked out across the skyline to witness the vastness of the Congo. In back of the plane, Braum and three of his goons sat idle - no words spoken - just waited for orders. Mercenaries were paid well and Gertz kept the best on his payroll. Gertz motioned for Braum and handed him a stack of aerial photos that were magnified into five by six foot photo sheets.

"Have these photos matched to the UN bases." Gertz directed Braum. Initially, Braum looked confused and his lack of understanding irritated Gertz. "Here, mark the UN bases on top of the photos to see if we will have company." Gertz made a few marks and pushed it towards Braum who grunted. Gertz knew not to push him too far mentally. He knew Braum was a killer and extremely gifted at that craft. Gertz kept several close up images of a large mountain. He knew the site. Several Belgians invested a lot of money for drilling core samples for a potential uranium mine. The area was also where several archaeologists had come back with mortal illness. The five middle aged men showed signs of radiation poisoning and subsequently died.

As Gertz's private jet landed at Lubumbashi airport, several more GROM thugs waited. Within minutes, the diamond merchant was airborne again. The Russian made Hind helicopter had seen better days. The old metal beast hovered over the tree tops, and Gertz wondered if the body of the helicopter would clear the tree line. The Hind helicopter screeched and the engine's shrill noise pierced the sky like the sounds of fingernails dragged across a chalkboard. The former Russian military pilot chain smoked cigarettes as he smacked the gauges with his free hand. The landscape was thick. Nothing moved down below. No people, no animals, nothing lived near the mountain. It appeared as a dead zone. Gertz directed the pilot to circle the isolated mountain several times. There was no spot to land and Gertz motioned for the pilot to get lower. On a high ledge, Gertz found what he was looking for but still could not land the helicopter. The helicopter hovered for a moment close to one of the most important historical finds in modern history.

Chapter 10

Schultz reread the thin intelligence report on Nakor Industries. There was not much information on the company, yet instinctively he knew that the company was crooked. Schultz watched the entrance of Nakor Industries. He remained on the exterior of the compound and several hundred feet from the main gate. He borrowed a vehicle from the embassy maintenance shop as to not attract any attention. Schultz snapped several photos as limousines arrived and discharged passengers. He noted the times. After an hour, he counted fifteen vehicles and over forty men who entered the large twenty-five story office building. Nakor Industries existed only on paper; size, mission statement, and funding were all unknown. The company's financial structure shifted between several offshore corporate accounts and weaved back and forth into subsidiary holdings. Schultz passed a request through Langley to track the money flow. Also, Schultz had requested assistance from Interpol, MI6, and the UN. Requests were made six months ago and the latest status reports identified no concrete explanation how Nakor made any money. A shroud surrounded Nakor. By late afternoon, Schultz had the photos scanned into Langley's mainframe computer. Within hours, he had criminal background checks on the men who had entered Nakor Industries. A majority emerged as hard core criminals from the Interpol database. Some of the older men had no profiles, and he circled their faces. Schultz needed more information.

Outside of the Nakor executive office suite, Moira kept her desk very neat. She was not allowed to keep anything personal. Gertz demanded that she shred every piece of paper and then burn the confetti strips. Moira looked inside the cracked door. The large group of men sat around the conference room table. Moira had never seen them before. Their bodyguards remained pressed against the wall, waiting for some threat to squash. Maps were spread across the table. She brought in coffee, but was yelled at by Gertz to get out. A bodyguard came and retrieved the coffee. Moira was aroused by the intrigue. The sight of her boss as he directed the men in discussions made her want him even more. Moira loved her boss and she believed that he remained sexually loyal to her and did not sleep around. She heard numerous stories about men who contracted communicable diseases from local women, worse HIV. She prided herself on how much she kept her boss satisfied so he would not look for some dirty locals. Moira hoped her boss would someday love her back, she just needed more time.

In the restaurant several blocks from embassy row, Russell entered and immediately sensed tension. He knew the CIA and KGB fought and disagreed over many issues, mostly Cold War relics. As he entered, the Russian men stared at Russell with pierced eyes, maybe it was because they were Russian or maybe it was because they lost the Cold War. Whatever it was Russell instinctively felt these men wanted to put a bullet in the back of his head. Russell looked at Igor Tretiak as he drank his red wine. The former KGB general held the wine glass up to the light to admire the wine's legs, which crisscrossed the glass. Russell gladly accepted a glass of extremely rare and highly valuable 1961 Rothschild. Five men sat around the table and drank the wine. They belonged to the Russian Military Brotherhood, commonly referred to as Voctrad and each one watched Russell closely. Russell wondered if they would be killed tonight. Two of Tretiak's armed guards, former Russian specially trained killers called Spetsnaz, were seated in the corner.

For over an hour, Russell sat across from the men who spoke native Russian freely in front of him and smirked back and forth. None of them asked Russell a question or generated small talk with him. The mood quickly changed as the others arrived. Francesca wore a form fitted black cocktail dress, short to the knees and a revealing neckline. The Russian's mouths dropped open. "Sorry we're late," Francesca said. Schultz never divulged who would attend the meeting. Russell was not accustomed to playing this cat and mouse game.

"No problem," Tretiak sniped. "We were just enjoying some fine wine with our new friend." Russell looked at the local members of Voctrad. Tretiak waved at the panoramic view of the Kinshasa skyline. "Do you like the view?" Schultz admired the skyline and noticed they had a high powered telescope in the side window that was transfixed around the port area. Schultz made a mental note.

"You live like a king." Schultz replied.

"Not at all, just a humble man from Leningrad trying to make a few bucks."

"Speaking of that, let's get down to business." Schultz jumped in. "You all know who I am. And you probably know who I brought with me. Russell here is my right hand man in the Congo, understood?" Schultz paused for a moment. "Good." Schultz continued. "Intelligence reports highlight President Mugabe is sitting on twenty billion dollars in rough diamonds." Heads turned between the Voctrad members. "Yes, I said twenty billion dollars. As you know he is restricted by the Kimberly Process to dump them on the open market as more than likely they are blood diamonds. However, he is trying to smuggle them through Zambia and into the Congo. I cannot overemphasize to each of you that the international community will come down hard on anyone who helps him. The American government will be more than interested in this affair."

"What does the Israeli diamond syndicate say?" Tretiak watched Francesca intently. The other Voctrad members could not escape from her low cut neckline and robust cleavage, yet Tretiak looked right into her eyes. Everyone knew the Russians funneled diamonds outside of the Kimberly Process and competed directly against Tel Aviv jewelers. Billions of dollars in annual diamond sales were questioned, yet the source of the rough diamonds could not be traced. The stakes were high and everyone at the table knew it.

"The diamond cartel will not let illegal diamonds flood the market." Francesca said. "The Israeli government will do whatever it takes to keep a lid on Mugabe."

"Does that include taking him out?" Tretiak asked. Francesca did not respond to Tretiak's question and sipped her wine. Everyone at the table knew the answer. The Mossad had been known to carry out many successful assassinations.

"Let's just say the US and Israel see eye to eye on this," Schultz said. "If anyone has business holdings in Zimbabwe, it may not be good for their health."

Back at the embassy, Kitson walked out of Schultz's apartment and onto the balcony. The building was over two hundred feet from the U.S. Embassy's perimeter wall and the balcony was high enough to see over top of the wall and into Kinshasa. The main roads around the American embassy were tightly controlled. Local vendors pushed all sorts of goods in wheel barrels. Women balanced large baskets atop their heads. Children played. If one did not know, war raged a few blocks away. For those isolated from the carnage, they might easily conclude this was an African utopia. Kitson passed Russell a gin and tonic.

"Thank you, sir."

"No sir here. Remember I am a private British citizen on safari."

"Right." Russell laughed.

"What's your cover?" Kitson inquired.

"Doesn't matter much." Russell retorted. "As usual everyone wants to kill me."

"Having a bad day?"

"Sorry, just pissed at what I saw in the bush."

"At Virunga?" Kitson said. He had a big sip of gin and tonic. "I heard...any survivors?"

"Not many."

"Finish that one." Kitson said as he got up and went back in to the room to make another round of gin and tonics. Russell only had a few sips while Kitson emptied his glass. "What do you say we get drunk tonight?"

"I have no plans," Russell replied.

"And I don't have to go anywhere." The two old friends drank heavily for three hours and shared stories of the turmoil and tribulations they experienced in war zones.

As Francesca walked in, Russell noticed the sharp contrast to what she wore earlier in the evening. Loose sweatpants and one of Russell's oversized exercise shirts hung on her body. "So what do we have here?" she asked.

"Good evening. Please come here and sit." Kitson said. He stumbled as he stood. "Would you care for a drink my dear?" Kitson was immediately taken by Francesca's beauty, as many men were.

"No thanks." Francesca smiled. "On the job, no drinking."

"Oh, don't be such a tight ass." Russell shouted. "Have a drink." Kitson gave him a stern look for being offensive to the lady. Russell realized his mistake but did not care. Francesca made him angry, especially with the revealing outfit to make the Russians drool. It was all in the job, but Russell was getting sick of the job she was in.

"No!" Francesca repeated firmly. Russell stood and stumbled. He was beyond intoxicated. He walked across the room and fell on the bed fully clothed. Within seconds, he was passed out. After a few minutes, he awoke and vomited on the floor. Francesca used that as a sign to get out. She found Kitson sitting outside.

"What do you think of Rajik Nabee?" Kitson asked.

"Scumbag," she responded. Kitson moved the empty chair towards her. Francesca crossed her legs and looked at him intently. "Rajik is deadly."

"What about the Ashbals?"

"Deadly as well. Do you know about the Lucifer Effect?" Francesca knew a great deal about the main threat to her nation's existence.

"No?" Kitson replied inquisitively.

"Lucifer effect dates back to the Crusades and the religious manipulation of dark, evil signs. Basically, it is the mass control of a group to do bad things. Bad things happened to good people as they get swept up into trouble. Mental control of subservient individuals, become the master of the mind. Many Lebanese are generally good citizens but are caught up in the fervor for independence. The Ashbals are prime example of manipulations."

"Sounds like their orphanage program needs some refinement," Kitson pondered.

"Terrorists killed my mother and if I could kill every one of them I would." Francesca lost her mother when she was eight years old and never forgot the pain.

In the morning, Russell did not wait to face Francesca for any potential scolding for getting drunk. More importantly, he wanted to stay far away from her. It was not the time to lose his mind on some romantic escapade that would end up worse than Liberia. Russell had to meet the surviving archeologist. Russell picked up her address from the Ambassador's office. Kimberly's apartment was on the other side of Kinshasa. The apartment was on the fourth floor of a ten story building. The windows were covered with wood on the inside to prevent exploding glass from flying inward. The apartment complex served as the primary location for the once large population of NGOs who came to the Congo with ambitious ideas. The building was mostly empty. Squatters moved in as no guards remained. As a favor to the Ambassador, Russell volunteered to help move Kimberly onto the embassy compound. The Ambassador promised to get her on the next flight out with some non-essential embassy staff. As Russell entered her apartment, he saw how clean she made the place. He laughed inside as he knew squatters would trash the apartment within minutes of their departure.

"Do you have everything that you need?"

"Most of the expedition team's equipment was already sent back to Washington." She looked dazed and confused. Kimberly looked in drawers.

"What can I carry?" Russell asked. Kimberly pointed to the three large suitcases, and Russell wondered how much stuff she actually brought with her. Russell changed his poise as he heard several car doors slam hard. Outside of the UN forces, no one had vehicles.

"We need to get out of here." Russell said as he slid along the wall to spy out the window. Russell watched a man as he pointed a gun at local kids. The GROM thugs had lined up four teenage boys and forced them to the ground with hands beyond their heads. Russell wanted to take out the GROM, but he knew that he did not have the fire power and more importantly he knew that he should not compromise his concealed position. His pistol had silencer attachment. Against all of his operational instincts, he lined up the weapon on the fuel container on the back of corner of the vehicle and hoped for the best. The first round punctured the steel. The GROM thugs dove for cover and instinctively knew someone used a silencer against them.

Local rebels did not have that type of weapon and the GROMs knew they were the primary mercenaries in the Congo. Russell watched as the former Polish Special Forces soldiers dispersed. The fuel rapidly dripped but did not ignite. The mercenaries scanned the horizon with scopes and talked within their headsets. Russell looked for a possible rapid escape route and nothing stood out. He knew the GROM would move fast. If he stayed on top of the building, the GROM would have to clear each floor and would be on top of the building within fifteen minutes. Russell knew he would be isolated and trapped on top of the building. Russell looked at the power line attached to building and made his decision. The second shot he fired bounced off the concrete in front of the barrel and ignited the fuel. Russell gave away his position as he rolled to his side and ran across the roof. Automatic fire erupted. Bullets splattered across the adjacent apartment building ten feet above him and shattered windows. Russell fired his third shot at the power line and blasted apart the antiquated clay bulbs that held the wires. Sparks sprayed across the ground from the end of the line. He motioned for Kimberly to hang onto his back and follow him. Russell grabbed the power line and they ran towards the edge. They jumped into the empty air and both held on for life. Russell swung twenty feet towards the telephone pole where the wire came from and in a split second knew he did not have enough line to make the ground. He dropped the remaining fifteen feet to the road. They rolled several times. He had no time to contemplate his injuries. Kimberly was shaken up. Russell focused his attention on her. He needed to get her to safety. She limped as he pulled her up. He dragged her around the corner of the building. Up above, they heard shouts in Polish.

Across the street, Russell saw several men watch from the cover of a burned-out truck. Russell spotted a motorcycle and ran across the street. Machinegun fire erupted down on the street and dirt flew as rounds missed. Russell dove over top of the empty engine compartment onto the other side of the rusted out vehicle. Bullets ripped into the side. Local men were scared and hugged the ground. Russell motioned for keys and one of the men was more than happy to give up the motorcycle as not to get shot. Russell crawled towards the wall and pulled the motorcycle to the ground. Gas filtered out of the tank and spilled over him. He did not care. He kick started the motorcycle off of the ground. He revved the engine. Once he felt comfortable that the motorbike would indeed operate, he ripped open the throttle and accelerated down the sidewalk. The momentum lifted his body and the bike off the pavement. The concrete storefront walls were riddled with bullets as he sped around the corner. He shifted the bike in and out of alleys for several blocks and came up behind where he left Kimberly. From down the street one of the GROMs fired in their direction. On the motorcycle, Kimberly held his waist tight. Russell sped down the street. In several seconds, other GROM thugs stole several motorcycles and the chase was on. Along dirt trails, Russell sped farther away from the city. He knew the GROM would have more vehicles. He needed to get to the countryside and hide. Quickly, Russell noticed that they were very adept at riding the motorcycles. Kimberly held on for dear life as Russell bounced the motorbike over rugged terrain. He zigzagged the bike around downed trees and hanging tree limbs. Russell sped down towards the large stream that paralleled the highway. Kimberly held tight and Russell opened to full throttle and pointed the front wheel towards a gradual incline. He jumped the bike twenty feet towards the opposite side of the stream and landed in the middle of the stream. Russell came up short; however the jump took the GROM by surprise. As the stream's current pulled them under, Russell heard shouts in Polish. The bike bounced off several rocks, but Russell kept one hand on it. His other hand grabbed a hold of Kimberly's shirt. As water pounded his face, he saw the GROM stand on the side of the riverbank firing at them.

It took ten minutes for Russell to pull the motorcycle out of the water as the current yanked it toward a watery grave. Kimberly trembled more from the fear than the brisk coolness. Russell could not go back for the embassy vehicle. He cleaned out the spark plugs to get the bike started. He kick started the bike for twenty minutes before it started. Russell pointed the motorcycle down the rough path and continued to travel away from Kinshasa.

CHAPTER 11

Tshambe was unable to make his way home for the fifth consecutive day. The Congolese man was destitute. All of the streets in his neighborhood were closed with concrete barriers. Kinshasa was strangled with crime and danger. Locals prayed for peace, yet tranquility never came. Sewers became clogged with vial refuse. Piles of garbage, diseased rats, and sporadic dead bodies littered the streets. Tshambe sensed there was no future for his family. His children had not attended any type of school for a month. His oldest daughter, a mere nine years old, had been a target for sexual predators. Tshambe feared for his family's future. Schultz allowed Tshambe to sleep in the basement, against embassy rules. Schultz would have been counseled if the Ambassador found out, yet he did not care. Schultz knew that there were no other CIA operatives had lined up to come to the Congo in order to replace him. Tshambe looked out the window and saw smoke rise from burning tires in the streets. More fires burned in several buildings directly behind the embassy from Molotov cocktails. Kitson watched Tshambe as he stared into the abyss. The British Colonel had served many years in Africa and shared his grief with Tshambe.

"Are the Americans going to get you out of here?" Kitson asked. He handed Tshambe a beer.

"No, the Congo is my home. I will never leave Africa." Tshambe looked at the British officer and contemplated his country's fate. "Everyone leaves when things get bad."

"Lethal parasites have taken over your country." Kitson responded. "The UN will have difficulty bringing peace to the Congo. There is too much corruption. Your country will be destitute for years"

"But this is the Congo, we have lots of wealth."

"The Congo possesses more wealth than anywhere else."

"But why is my country so poor?"

"Most would rather steal your wealth than pay for it. Your former colonial ruler has not helped." Kitson knew intimately the history of the European powers control in Africa. Britain had numerous colonial holdings. Kitson believed British soldiers and magistrates brought governance and education to Africa, unlike many European nations, especially Belgium. "King Leopold took one arm for every one hundred to keep them in line," Kitson said as he made a mark across one of his arms with a knife.

"The Belgians were brutal. Too many have died at their hands." Tshambe sighed deeply. He was desperate. "I must get to my family."

"You will be killed if you go out there." Kitson said and added. "Either the rebels or the UN will more than likely shoot you."

"How can I get to my family?"

"Patience." Kitson sensed the man's turmoil and could do nothing. Tshambe would not see his children for yet another day.

Deep in the Congo bush, Russell and Kimberly were lost. After they plunged into the stream, water had filled the motorbike's fuel tank and helped seize the engine. Without a means of transportation, Russell looked at the map and made the decision to cut through a three mile stretch to reach the next town. They weaved in and out of the impenetrable tall grass. Movement was severely hampered. At times, Kimberly laid her head on Russell's back and nearly fell asleep during the slow movements. Russell pushed onward. The heavy dose of humidity coupled with their physical movement soak their clothes with sweat. After a mile, they found themselves in an open forest. The thick jungle canvas restricted any view more than thirty feet. Animal sounds echoed and penetrated the tranquil air. Chimps, large and small, drowned out each other's sounds. Birds of all colors flew past and zigzagged into the tree line. Russell believed he found a wonderful place to rest, yet he needed to push onward and make distance from the GROM thugs. Russell knew it would not take the thugs long to find a way to cross the fast moving stream and continue the search. The dense jungle pulled and held moisture as night started to fall. Russell was worried about hypothermia and started a small fire under a log to keep the glow minimal. He used several dozen branches to make a small ceiling and wrapped a tarp over the branches. A light rain started and ferociously picked up pace. Kimberly crawled under the makeshift structure. Russell placed a GPS locater on the structure, synchronized his tracker, and walked into the bush. He needed to check the light signature from the fire. He squatted and listened in different locations – no sounds emitted. The chimps and birds hid from the torrential rainstorm.

Russell was gone for less than thirty minutes and was surprised to hear shivering sounds emit from the structure. He crawled inside and shined a light into Kimberly's face. Her lips were blue and she shook uncontrollably. Her cheeks were bright red and pupils dilated. She became incoherent and mumbled something. His basic survival instincts kicked in. Russell undid and removed her clothes. She shivered more and tried to speak, yet nothing came out. Her mind raced and she was scared. Russell removed his wet clothes and stripped down to his underwear. He clung to her body. Her skin was cold and clammy. Russell squeezed her tight and embraced the coldness of her body. She was going into hypothermia. Russell spoke to her to keep her from going to sleep. After some time, she was finally able to speak softly. After an hour, Russell helped her get dressed with the dried clothes and he did the same. He stoked the fire more. He was damn cold but knew it was nothing compared to the snow in Seattle's mountains.

The morning light brought abundant sounds from the animals in the area. Birds sang in the morning warmth and Russell heard several animals move. He needed to get moving yet he knew she did not want to wake her. He nudged her more to get her out of the deep sleep.

"What?" Kimberly looked surprised.

"Time to hit the deck."

"I'm not in the military."

"I know... just trying to get you moving."

"You must have been a Boy Scout."

"Sorry, we need to move and quick." For several minutes, Russell packed up the camp and scattered the wood to hide any resemblance of a camp. He buried the ashes under the log.

"Thank you for saving me."

"No worries. You almost went into hypothermia last night."

"I cannot believe how quickly I started to shiver."

"Hypothermia can come quickly." His experience as one of the top search and rescue guides on Seattle Mountain Rescue showed.

Russell experienced the effects of hypothermia half a dozen times and knew the ramifications.

Within an hour of struggling through the jungle canopy, they arrived at the town on the map. The town was practically deserted, except for two dozen UN troops from Albania. Rebels had come through and threatened the local tribal chief. They had killed several men. Their bodies were hung by the legs from the large tree in the middle of a dozen bush huts. The UN troops cut them down, but Russell could still see where the ropes remained. In contrast to the carnage, Russell found a quaint and comfortable hotel to clean up. The small hotel was two levels, surprisingly something large for the African bush country. The hot showers cleaned off three days of nasty grime. Kimberly purchased some used clothes from a local women selling out of a wheelbarrow. She looked at her wrapped dress, which nearly touched the ground. She tore the material in half and made an instant mini-skirt. Russell and Kimberly settled into the hotel comfortably and they did not think anyone would recognize them. Except ten minutes after enjoying a hot meal, Russell's worse nightmare arrived. Francesca walked into the hotel, dirty, tired, and hungry. The hotel manager informed her that they were out of rooms, but she should stay and have something to eat on the house. She was pissed when she saw Russell and a female in the dining room. What Russell did not know was Francesca placed a GPS tracker in his shoe.

"What are you doing here?"

"I should ask the same." Francesca replied. She looked at the woman next to Russell and asked. "Who's your friend?"

"Hello, I'm Kimberly."

"She's the archeologist Schultz talked about." Russell added.

"You both look too cozy. I don't want to interrupt." Francesca shot a deadly stare at Russell.

"Not at all." Kimberly spoke and smiled back at her.

"I smell really bad." Francesca said. Russell did not say a word. Kimberly looked at him with suspicion. Francesca continued, "I need to get back on the road and find a place to stay."

"Why?" Kimberly inquired.

"Out of rooms." She looked at Russell with a glaring look hoping he would invite her to stay with him. Kimberly watched Russell closely. She also watched Francesca. At first she felt physically intimidated but then remembered she was an attractive female with a certain sensual appeal.

"I have two beds in my room." Kimberly offered. "You can bunk with me." Kimberly was genuinely sincere. Inside the room, Kimberly showed her the small bathroom with no shower or tub, just a toilet.

"Can I ask you a personal question?" Kimberly asked.

"Depends."

"Were you two lovers?" Kimberly was inquisitive and Francesca was not used to this line of questioning.

"You could say that. I saved his life several times in Liberia." Francesca started to take off her clothes. As she did, she tossed several knives on the bed. She kept her Desert Eagle pistol on her right hip.

"When was that?"

"Three months ago." Francesca said as she stripped off her clothes. Kimberly noticed the eight inch scar on the left side of her stomach. The scar looked grotesque.

"That recent." Kimberly said. She wanted to know if she had a chance at love, "but now you are not together?"

"No, we are not together." She looked at her with suspicion. Francesca did not like being asked questions. "My work got in the way."

"Why was that?" Kimberly asked. Francesca sensed the line of questioning leaned more towards jealousy. She could sense the younger more naïve girl thought Russell must be her crusader and knight in shining armor.

"Work complications," Francesca said as a matter of fact. She could not inform Russell's new love interest that she was a trained Mossad assassin.

"And you're a doctor?" Kimberly asked with a smile on her face. It was one of those Southern charm smiles that sized up her competition.

"I work with Doctors Without Borders," Francesca lied perfectly. "We met in Liberia."

"But you're not together now?"

"Correct," Francesca said. She wanted to be with Russell; however she was torn with her loyalty to Israel. If she could turn Russell to spy for Israel, perhaps her father would approve of their romance.

"He saved my life," Kimberly said. She chocked up for a moment and continued. "I was never so scared in my life." Francesca gave her a strong hug as she cried on her shoulder. Francesca kept quiet and laughed internally as she dealt with death on a daily basis.

Miles away at the Congo's main industrial seaport, Rajik opened several forty foot ocean containers. The Hezbollah operative was cautious. Crates of weapons and ammunition were packed inside. Rajik did not bother to conceal the crates with any type of produce or supplies. The local custom officials had been paid off. The UN troops rarely stopped by this end of the mega commercial port. All of the Congo was supported from this one port that was spread over three miles. Eight large berthing spots for supertankers lined the port. The commercial cranes heaved the large containers off the latest ship. Commerce continued within Kinshasa's port, but at a fifth of what it was before the latest civil war. Rajik motioned for the Ashbals to pull out and open a wooden crate. New AK-47s from Hungary glistened in the moonlight. Rajik used his own money to purchase the weapons from a Voctrad arms dealer. He paid three million Euros for six thousand AK-47s, two hundred RPG rocket launchers, and eighty heavy caliber machineguns. The shipment arrived right under the eyes of the UN weapon's embargo. Rajik found the Congo's current chaos lucrative.

Rajik found a buyer. He checked the Interpol's most wanted list for crimes against humanity and matched it to Africa. On top of the list was Joseph Kony who was charged in 2005 by the International Criminal Court with crimes against humanity, war crimes, murder, rape, and enlisting children as combatants. Kony commanded The Lord's Resistance Army (LRA) and would pay three times the value in rough diamonds. Last month, Rajik met Kony along the Congo and Rwanda border. The meeting went well and Rajik was pleased to see Kony's camp full of children soldiers without weapons. They walked around with clubs and sticks to beat people. Rajik saw an opportunity.

"I need more weapons." Joseph Kony said as he smoked a large cigar. "When can I get my weapons?"

"Soon, very soon." Rajik studied the UN guard post in his binoculars. He could blow up the security station and gain access to the port, but he would find 800 Nigerian soldiers descending upon him with unspeakable brutality within an hour. Rajik knew not to piss off the Nigerians. His Ashbals were no match to the Nigerian soldiers. What the Ashbals failed to possess in tactical and technical proficiency, they made up in enthusiasm. Rajik knew that was not enough to take on a superior African force. His orphan fighters could easily fight the Indian and Bangladesh UN soldiers with good results. In several raids, these young ragtag soldiers destroyed several Congolese trucks. After several shots, the Congolese soldiers had a habit of desertion under fire. Regardless of how big the Congo army grew, Rajik felt secure. He knew senior officers were easily bribed. The UN's plan for improving the Congo army had failed. Everyone in the Congo knew the army's fate.

"You don't want to double cross me." Kony puffed out a large cloud in Rajik's direction.

"Your weapons are safe."

"How will you get them out of the port?" One of the world's most notorious war criminals asked. "There are too many UN troops."

"Right now, there may be a lot of troops, but just wait until the next bomb goes off in downtown Kinshasa. The UN has no taste for casualties, especially foreigners."

"Your little war is working out well for you." Kony smiled wide. Rajik knew Kony paid high prices for many more guns. Rajik heard rumors the LRA had kidnapped and drugged hundreds of children to become soldiers, yet he did not care as it was business.

"With war there are many opportunities."

"Indeed. Many fortunes have been made in Africa." Kony replied. "I have been at war with Uganda and Rwandan forces for many years. Everyone wants to kill me. They think that I am a bad man. So what if I use children soldiers. No one else is giving them jobs." Rajik knew Kony was more than just a jobs program for children. He stole and drugged his child soldiers. Kony had no compassion.

"Your weapons will be out of the port tonight." Rajik kept a duffle bag filled with fifty thousand dollars to bribe the Congolese port officials, but he would still need to get the UN soldiers out. The back of the truck was filled with eight propane gas cylinders. He would send his Ashbal on a suicide attack that would cause considerable destruction. Rajik needed a diversion and would gladly sacrifice any of the Ashbal, orphans no one wanted.

"Good...good." Kony said as he motioned for his driver to come pick him up. "I have an offensive next month that I want to be ready for." As Kony walked to the open door in the rear of the limousine, he turned back to Rajik. "I hope we can do more business in the future."

Kamal watched from the hidden vantage point. The Al Qaeda terrorist would report back that Joseph Kony had been seen in Kinshasa. Kony's head would be a prize for Al Qaeda. Many inside of the new terrorist group wanted to remove the old rebel leader. Kamal believed the African wars needed to change. Bin Laden's caliphate would rule the world in fear. Kamal was ready to steal Kony's child soldiers that he kidnapped in many raids across the vast Congo region. The child soldier was the perfect recruit for Al Qaeda.

CHAPTER 12

In the executive study at his massive riverside estate, Dietger Laurent looked through the pile of historical family papers stacked on his desk. Many documents were scrawled in his father's handwriting. His father was a prominent member of the Belgian community for many years up until he was killed by rebels. Dietger knew the history of the Belgians in the Congo all too well, but he searched for important information on a remote mountain deep in the bush. Dietger scoured the references to the search for King Solomon's mine. He knew Hitler was obsessed with discovering old world treasures and anything that would give legitimacy to his brutal Third Reich.

Dietger sat back in his leather chair and looked at the picture of his father. The photo was undated, yet Dietger knew he was about eight years old. His father told him the family story over and over again. Dietger recalled his father's words. In May 1940, a large number of Belgian government officials fled as the Germans blitzkrieg advanced and isolated the small nation. The Maginot Line of fortified positions forced Germany to take a divergent avenue of approach. The relic of the First World War opened an easier flank for Hitler to invade France through Belgium. The Belgian army was ineffective against the fast moving, rapid German Panzer tank advance. Communications allowed the Germans the ability to quickly react and adjust tactics. King Leopold surrendered the Belgian army and received significant criticism from former government officials who safely traveled to Bordeaux, France and then to London. The Belgian government maintained control over colonial possessions and Hitler expressed desires to negotiate the permanent transfer of the Congo in lieu of lost colonial holdings from World War I. With the fight in North Africa and with Russia, the Germans did not possess adequate resources to seize control of the Congo.

A month after the Belgian victory, Nazi SS officers came to the Congo on a German U-boat to inspect the uranium mines in Katanga. Authorities in the Congo with the approval of the Belgian government-in-exile in London declared war on November 26, 1940, which was more political as the Congo had no army. The OSS sent a team to the Congo in early June 1942, which was nearly four years before the first atomic bomb landed on Hiroshima. Bill Donovan led the OSS, which was the precursor to the CIA and reported directly to President Roosevelt. The Americans needed to know if the Germans started an atomic weapons project that started with heavy water with a hydrogen isotope deuterium. The Reich Minister for Armament and Ammunition advised Hitler to take a more active role in stopping the Americans from developing an atomic bomb by controlling the Congo uranium mine. A special team of German scientists moved to Katanga, yet no one heard from them again.

Dietger walked to the dock and picked up an AK-47, aimed it across the river, and unloaded a full magazine. Bullets skipped across the Congo River. Several local fishermen bailed out of their boats. Others kept their heads down. Four of the hulled out wooden canoes started to sink. Blood spilled over into the water from those who were struck.

"That's how you get rid of the locals." Dietger pointed out.

"I could send a raiding party to their village." Rajik suggested. He put down his whiskey; pulled out his pistol; and unloaded several rounds in the direction of the locals. He knew the boats were too far away for the smaller caliber round, yet he truly enjoyed the added effect of scaring the fishermen.

"This is fun." Dietger smiled at his new friend. Dietger sat down and consumed a beer. He motioned for his local help to fetch him a new one. Dietger handed Rajik a large envelope filled with pictures. The aerial photos had crisscross marks across large highways with latitude and longitude grid marks.

"Here's the target location." Dietger said as he pointed to the photos next to the map.

"What plane will be used?" inquired the Hezbollah operative.

"UN cargo plane. There is a regular cargo plane used in delivering supplies to Lubumbashi and we will take it. We will load the weapon in that."

"What airstrip do you plan on using?"

"We have to stay out of Kinshasa." Dietger replied. "There's an airstrip in Goma." Goma was two hours away by road or twenty minutes by helicopter. There was a clearing by Rajik's compound capable of landing a helicopter but he did not have anything large enough to lift the crated weapon into any helicopter. Using an external sling load was out of the question as it could damage the bomb and more than likely generate a lot of interest as it moved through the air.

"When do I get paid?" Rajik asked.

"Soon."

"I'm taking all of the risks. I need something more." Rajik needed to hedge his bets that the mission would be discovered.

"Here are some diamonds to keep you interested." Dietger said as Rajik opened up a sealed plastic bag and emptied a dozen rough untraceable diamonds on the table. The largest was the size of a man's thumb. Rajik had seen many blood diamonds from the Sierra Leone conflict. However, he never saw any this size with beautiful pink tones. These were not the typical blood diamonds. These were magnificent, rare pink diamonds.

Back in Kinshasa the following day after her exploits in the African bush, Francesca sat next to Schultz in the back seat of the embassy as Tshambe drove the five blocks toward the Intercontinental Hotel. The roads were eerily deserted. Tshambe drove the vehicle across the empty streets, something was not right. All of a sudden, three motorcycles appeared. The motorcycles jumped the curb out from the alley and accelerated rapidly. Tshambe saw the headlights fast approach.

"Danger comes," Tshambe pointed his hand back towards the left rear of the vehicle.

"How many?" Schultz looked backwards in the window. Francesca methodically opened the compressed stock of the sniper rifle and attached the starlight scope.

"Three, maybe four," Tshambe said.

"How many men?" Schultz asked as he pulled out his pistol and checked the magazine.

"Several riders." Tshambe shouted. "Don't know boss."

"Take the bridge ahead. It'll get us to the embassy faster."

"I can take care of them," Francesca said as she went into motion opening the case that contained her sniper rifle. Within twelve seconds, she assembled the four pieces of the sniper rifle together. Francesca spotted the first motorcycle in her scope. She inserted an eight round clip. She preferred the older bolt action sniper rifles. She maneuvered the bolt action just as fast as a semi-automatic trigger. Francesca chambered the first round and shot the closest rider in the head. The remaining motorcycle riders returned fire. A rapid succession of bullets blasted out the rear window. Glass rained throughout the vehicle's interior.

"Hold on boss." Tshambe swerved the vehicle back and forth. More bullets flew past.

"Straighten out." Francesca yelled, "and slow down!"

"Are you crazy?" Schultz lifted his body off the floorboard. He wished that he carried a weapon. The UN weapons embargo was very specific and did not even allow embassy personnel to pack heat outside of their embassy compounds, to include CIA agents. Schultz surmised that the Mossad really did not give a damn about UN memos. He was glad Francesca had a weapon, yet wondered if she was borderline insane. Tshambe complied and slowed down. In a violent succession of four shots fired within just a few seconds, Francesca eliminated the remaining motorbike riders. Schultz looked at her in disbelief that anyone could make that shot: two speeding motorcycles at a distance of eighty yards, four targets, and in several seconds.

"Now, can we get some dinner?" Francesca disassembled her rifle and packed it back into her briefcase. "I'm starving."

As the embassy vehicle approached the main street, a UN check point was erected. Fighting had escalated again in the past few hours and more UN check points ringed the city. With their embassy credentials, they quickly passed. Locals were held up and a long line formed. The bar scene at the Intercontinental Hotel was vibrant. As she walked into the hotel bar, eyes opened wide and mouths dropped open. Francesca wore the black dress tight against her body and short to reveal skin. The three inch high heels accented her legs. Several inches under her dress and strapped to her thigh, a snub nose pistol waited.

"There's your contact." Schultz did not point. Agents never pointed. "Far right corner wearing a black suit." Francesca walked forward. "You're on your own." In another way of saying it, Schultz meant the United States had no official business supporting Israel's objectives in the Congo. She looked back over her shoulder and smiled with those brilliant white teeth.

"Pleased to meet you." The elder gentlemen reached his hand upwards. He did not stand. He appeared frail with age, yet Francesca suspected why he chose to remain seated. She saw the barrel end of a large caliber pistol that rested on his lap pointed at her. She reached under her dress. The move aroused the elder man. She pulled out the small caliber revolver, placed it on the table, and sat down. The elder man laughed and pulled back his weapon.

"You were in Mobutu's government?" Francesca inquired.

"First, I get paid." The man requested. Francesca handed him a small envelope that contained a locker number and combination at Kinshasa airport. The man was extremely nervous. "I was." He paused and looked around. "In the early days, Colonel Mobutu was a fine leader. Some say he was vital in the transition of the Congo after Patrice Lumumba was murdered by the Belgians. Some say he was a good friend of Lumumba. But I know otherwise."

"Go on."

"Mobutu wanted power, not just of the Congo, but of all Africa. He was crazed, a madman. He would not deal with white South Africans, but he had hired men who would. I have a good idea what Mobutu did with the weapon."

"How?"

"Mobutu built a massive compound deep in the Congo near his ancestral birthplace of Lisala. It is a massive palace, bigger than the presidential palace." Francesca had seen the ornate presidential palace resting along the ridge overseeing Kinshasa. The sprawling hundred acre complex was indeed colossal. Anything larger would be obscenely large.

"Is the bomb there?"

"Maybe...perhaps. I don't know anymore. It has been so long. Mobutu did not trust many. When he was deposed and sent to Morocco to die from cancer, we all felt betrayed. His family lived like royalty and took billions of dollars with them, never to be seen again. I did not get anything when the new transitional government was installed. I worked for Mobutu for years. Where is my share? Where is my exodus? We believed in Mobutu's rule. Why am I treated like a criminal now?"

"Who else knows about the bomb?"

"Many people, Mobutu would have wild parties with the bomb as a centerpiece. Mobutu was very proud of negotiating the sale of the bomb before the South Africa white government folded. He always laughed at how he got a great deal off the white Apartheid before everything they owned collapsed. I told him he was crazy and should hide the bomb, but he did not care. In those days, who was going to question Mobutu? He would have you killed in a minute. Your entire family would be dead by nightfall."

"If he was so brutal, why did you stay for so long?"

"When you make your bed with the devil, you have no place to go. I will die in Zaire." Francesca noticed he referred to his homeland as Zaire instead of the Congo. She sensed he believed in the Mobutu totalitarian, almost police state rule. Many foreign governments called Mobutu a dictator. Many diplomats courted favor with Mobutu over the years, especially during the famous 'Rumble in the Jungle' Mohammed Ali versus Joe Frazier fight. Yet as time passed, so did the relations. In the final months of Mobutu's thirty year rule, many democratically, free governments labeled his rule as one of the most barbaric in Africa's history. Francesca thought for a moment and responded back that she would have to check with Tel Aviv. She knew it would be extremely hard to smuggle a former high ranking member of the former Mobutu government out of Africa.

From the balcony of the apartment building inside the US Embassy walls, Kitson admired the dusk skyline as nightfall approached. Having served nearly half of his thirty year British military career on the Dark Continent, Africa was in Kitson's blood. As Russell approached, Kitson held out a chilled gin and tonic for his friend.

"What I learned living in Africa is that when someone claims to be an expert on African affairs, you need to run, because they have no real understanding." Kitson expelled.

"Bad day?"

"Dealing with bureaucrats."

"I remember you telling me in Liberia that once you lived in Africa, it is hard to get it out of your mind." Russell now knew the significance of serving in Africa, especially after he left and came back. Three months ago he conducted a covert military operation in Liberia to gain valuable intelligence on the former brutal dictator Charles Taylor. What surprised Russell was how quickly the operation escalated out of control. Hezbollah operatives had a stranglehold on illegal diamond smuggling out of Sierra Leone through Liberia. Kitson and Russell teamed up in mutual interest to hunt former warlord Joseph Koroma. By circumstance, Koroma was in Monrovia smuggling cocaine with Rajik, the leading Hezbollah operative in a partnership with Colombian rebels to fly large shipments of cocaine into West Africa as a hub for follow-on transport to the United States. Russell and his team captured four thousand pounds of cocaine valued in excess of one hundred million dollars. Koroma, the Argentine pilots, and two Colombians were detained, yet Rajik escaped. Koroma was brought back to Kitson's compound for future questioning by MI6. As the British needed to show progress in charging war criminals in neighboring Sierra Leone, Koroma was being transported to Sierra Leone to face war crimes for his role in several Freetown massacres during the late 1990s civil war. Russell was absent when Hezbollah operatives came looking for Koroma and the four thousand pounds of cocaine at Kitson's compound. In a daring raid on his remote camp, Kitson blew the communications building that also leveled the ceiling of his bungalow on top of him. Russell was indeed glad Kitson did not die that night. Russell made a lasting bond with Kitson and knew him to be a true warrior.

"Nothing is what it appears to be in Africa." Kitson spouted out over a swig of gin and tonic.

"There are too many criminals here operating freely." Russell pointed towards the smoke from recent fires near the outskirts of Kinshasa.

"Many of them are there." Kitson pointed in the opposite direction where the Democratic of the Congo government buildings resided. "The corruption among this government disgusts me. Many of the Ministers believe that they are above their own laws. The UN has been unable to weed out the bad elements." Kitson paused for a moment to reflect. "If they did arrest Congolese officials for corruption, there would be no one left in positions of authority. The UN just turns a blind eye to what really goes on here."

"There are more and more UN troops arriving every day." Russell added. "Last estimate, I heard UN troop strength would exceed twenty thousand. And with the thirty thousand Congo soldiers, you would think the rebels would be running, but they are gaining traction."

Kitson put on his philosophical hat and said, "There's an old African proverb that says 'the meat that has fat will prove it by the heat of fire.'" Kitson caught Russell's quizzical glimpse. "Africans are used to turmoil and know when the shit hits the fan, their former colonial masters will leave them to die. The new Congo army will not fight and why should they risk their lives. They know the UN will pull out and run when the situation gets bad. The UN always leaves in a crisis."

The British Colonel understood counter-insurgency. More importantly, Colonel Frank Kitson understood the significance of negotiations. As a young Lieutenant in 1979, Kitson was assigned to bring in a rebel group in Northern Rhodesia. He was sent deep into the bush to set up a small camp. Kitson felt like he was being watched. The following morning, the young officer dressed in his finest military uniform. Lieutenant Kitson walked out three hundred meters, set up a table with two chairs, sat down, and waited. For hours he waited in the brutal heat. As the African sunset blinded him, Lieutenant Kitson could not see the rebel force of four hundred strong approach him. Young Kitson stood and greeted the rebel commander. The two sat and Kitson poured some of England's finest tea. Fortunately for Kitson, the rebels wanted to surrender. What Kitson did not see as the rebel commander handed over his pistol was the London Times photographer who had taken the picture. Two days later, the front page read, *Young British Officer Captures Rebels with Her Majesty's Finest Tea.* For his bold move, the Queen decorated him with England's highest decorations.

Kitson remained humble from his recognition and perhaps that helped fuel his strong relationship with Prince Charles who wanted Kitson to protect his youngest son Harry in Afghanistan. Kitson was well regarded among by many of Britain's leaders.

Russell looked at the Congolese government buildings and observed no lights within the buildings. The government could not even obtain the petrol required to run the generators. Russell looked at his mentor and inquired. "Who do you think is funding the rebels?"

"Don't know. MI6 reported Joseph Kony of the LRA fame had been seen in Kinshasa buying weapons. He could be connected." Russell knew LRA stood for Lord's Resistance Army and Joseph Kony was one of the most ruthless warlords.

"If Kony is indeed supplying the rebels with weapons, the situation could escalate out of control." Russell said.

"MI6 satellite images of Kony's camps estimate that he has over eight thousand rebels fighting for him, mostly drugged up children soldiers. They are heavily armed and living freely in the northeast corner of the Congo near Rwanda."

"From what I understand, the UN has not done a damn thing to control that area. They are more worried about keeping their precise executive compounds secure in Kinshasa."

"They don't have a damn clue do they?"

"Nope." Kitson replied.

Russell and Kitson continued to watch as the luminescent haze from the fires made a somewhat hypnotic sunset. Gunfire could be heard in the distance. Kinshasa residents reeled from the latest surge in the counter attack against the Nigerian eight hundred man battalion.

"I don't believe the Congo will ever have peace." Kitson downed the remaining of his drink and walked inside.

Russell looked across the Kinshasa skyline at the fires. He knew there was a lot at stake. He remained on the balcony for some time and contemplated the British Colonel's comments. Peace was something hard fought and even harder earned. He wondered how much more pain and anguish the Congolese could endure. The fires raged and there was dead silence as no fire trucks would emerge in the darkness.

CHAPTER 13

Francesca pressed the tape recorder button several times to hear the conversation. The female Mossad agent focused on the tone and inflection of the elder man's voice. Her meeting with the former high ranking member of the Mobutu government yielded solid intelligence. She believed the missing atomic weapon had been transferred out of South Africa. Only three people in the Israeli government knew about the current situation and two were Mossad – Francesca and her father. The other was the Israeli Prime Minister. Francesca had not talked to her father in three months and instinctively felt that he had been trying to contact her. Her father was the agent who worked with South Africa on a secret atomic weapons program. In secret negotiations with Israel, the South Africans purchased the atomic technology. Several Israeli scientists were sent to a remote nuclear research facility about two hours northeast of Johannesburg. After the Apartheid regime collapsed, the research facility was abandoned and all Israeli scientists returned with all of the detonation triggers and design plans. Everything was accounted for except for an experimental cobalt atomic bomb that her father personally escorted on a ship to South Africa for three weeks. Information surrounding the sale of atomic weapon technology from Israel to South Africa had been leaked. She needed to get answers.

The career Mossad agent never showed emotion. However, her feelings for Russell started to tear her insides out. They had a wild romance and the adrenaline junky craved violence. She had saved Russell's life. In the final chase to stop an Al Qaeda plot to blow up the US Embassy in Monrovia, Francesca and Russell fought off a dozen terrorists. As Russell jumped on a fast moving, hijacked 5,000 gallon UN fuel truck, he riddled the cab of the truck with machinegun fire and took control of the vehicle bomb. What he did not know was the remote explosive trigger failed to detonate. A helicopter operated by one of Al Qaeda terrorists circled above and he screamed obscenities as the wet electronics failed to ignite the bomb. Russell drove the fuel truck down a long pier inside Monrovia's harbor. As he jumped, the remote trigger finally worked and exploded the fuel truck - two miles from its intended target. Unhurt, Russell jumped on a motorcycle and was chased through Monrovia's winding streets. The terrorist fired a large caliber machine gun from the helicopter. The fast helicopter had Russell pinned down. As the Al Qaeda terrorist leveled the machinegun onto Russell's position, Francesca fired a shoulder launched missile that ripped apart the helicopter. Russell would have been dead if Francesca's aim was not on target.

Francesca walked through the gate of Nakor Industries and felt like she had just walked right into a trap. Out of the corner of her eye, she noticed the security cameras mounted on posts and the side of the building. The camera rotated and scanned towards her direction. The steady beams of surveillance lingered on her movement as she entered the main building. The Nakor building was nothing to speak of on the outside. Gertz did not want to expose Nakor as a rich company while many of the locals lived in poverty and filth, but the inside was splendor. As she looked around, Francesca was amazed at the twenty foot tall artist rendering of an African safari scene. The object was made out of tin with gold plating and hung lavishly from the ceiling. She surmised the object must have been extremely valuable. As the security guards approached Francesca, she saw the metal detector wands in their hands. After several swipes of the wands and the constant ringing, she reached her hand underneath her dress and surrendered her pistol. Now, she felt completely naked. The elevators were in the far corner. The four local security guards stayed close until Francesca stood outside of Gertz's office. Moira looked up from her desk and recognized the Israeli agent. Moira did not smile. The Israeli was far more beautiful. Ever since Francesca jumped into Gertz's limousine, Moira felt jealous.

"You wanted to know what happened to your bomb." Gertz stared out of the windows as she entered. He neither greeted her nor offered her a seat. Francesca stood. He remained in his chair and focused on the smoke from fires burning across the streets within Kinshasa's landscape. The screams and shouts from mortal combat were too far away to hear, yet Gertz felt proud of his little war.

"I know it is in the Congo." Francesca sensed a large body move behind her and out of the restroom. Braum towered over her by over a foot as he passed close. He did not speak, but made a muffled groan so as to scare her. Francesca remained still to the human eye, but her thick leg muscles slowly shifted weight to prepare for a vertical kick if she needed to. She knew her punches would be useless against Braum and opted for a karate kick if needed.

"The Congo is in complete chaos." Gertz said. "Look at this terrible fighting. When can we finally have peace so we can help rebuild this nation? There is too much suffering here. And now we have a bomb to deal with."

"Who has it?" Francesca asked.

"You have to understand that I'm just a businessman. Nakor is an international company and we have many dealings with all types of businesses. We have many operations here." He paused for a moment. "Even with the fighting," Gertz paused for dramatic effect, "many of my employees have put their lives on the line all the time. That is why we had to hire our own private security." Gertz motioned to Braum. The giant moved closer out of the shadows. Gertz continued, "We feel so helpless with the lack of UN security here. You must understand that we mean no harm." Francesca wondered about the bullets Braum fired at her. She was too well trained to let feelings get in the way of her intelligence collection. Gertz mumbled on further, "These times will pass. Our business relationships will keep us strong. Nakor has a very solid partnership with many of Tel Aviv's diamond merchants." Francesca remained silent as Gertz rambled on for another ten minutes on how he was an innocent man trying to make money and provide a future of hope for the Congolese. After his rant, he pulled a photo from his desk and slid it across the desk. "If the bomb is not at Mobutu's jungle palace, then this man may have it. Of course you did not hear it from me." Gertz looked for any effect on the Mossad agent's face. When he did not see any, he continued. "His name is Rajik Nabee. He is Hezbollah and deadly. He came to Kinshasa three months ago with a considerable amount of rough diamonds. He paid premium prices for black market guns from an arms dealer in Hungary."

"Are you positive?" Francesca said. She recognized the face of Rajik Nabee, the Hezbollah operative who tried to kill her in Liberia three months ago.

"Hezbollah has been heavily involved in Congo smuggling." Gertz continued. "Rajik makes lots of money in the gun running business. There is a Hezbollah camp along the Congo River that is guarded by Ashbals." Francesca knew intimately of the Lebanese orphans taken out of schools and trained from an early age to become future Hezbollah killers.

"You mentioned Mobutu's palace." Francesca had to confirm the story about Mobutu that she heard from one of the old regime's officials who she paid. "Why do you think it may be there?"

"There is an underground bunker behind the swimming pool. He was paranoid and kept all of his precious items there. From Ferraris to jewels to gold bullion to his private atomic bomb, he kept those things close." Gertz said. He turned and looked out his window. As Francesca stood to leave, Gertz wondered if she would shoot him in the back.

Meanwhile, Tshambe drove Russell and Kimberly towards the more secure area of Kinshasa that held many of the government buildings and foreign embassies. The archeology team's office was in a half burned down office building. Black smoke stained the walls before the flames could be extinguished. Only the bottom floor was impacted from the riots and thieves. The rest of the office building was fully functioning. The archeologists wanted to keep an office outside of the American Embassy compound so they could have more locals come in with potential information on King Solomon's mine. Word had spread among the Congolese that the archeologists paid good money. Much of the information was useless, yet there were several consistent tales about one large, remote mountain deep in the Congo interior.

Russell knew something was wrong before he opened the door. He quickly checked the perimeter of the door frame for explosive wires. The door was clear. Fresh looking scratch marks around the lock signaled someone had recently entered. Russell slowly opened the unlocked door and felt a wire on the inside. The hook on top of the door held the wire taut. He motioned for Kimberly to step back. She did not understand and he motioned faster with his hand to back up.

"Stop." Russell shouted. "Don't move."

"What...why?" She peered over his shoulder and tried to get closer. Russell stopped her by thrusting her body to the floor with his free hand. He used his other hand to secure the wire from any further movement. Russell lifted the wire off the top of the hook and slowly opened the door while keeping the wire taut. After he squeezed through the opening, he spied the connection wire that led to the bomb. It was a simple explosive device with a pull toggle connected to four pounds of military grade explosive; more than enough to blow the room apart and anyone entering. In fact, it was more than enough explosive to tear apart the entire third floor. Russell wrapped the wire around the knife on his right hip to free up both hands. He delicately removed the triggering device. Russell checked the kill switch on the backside and was surprised to see a mercury leveled motion detector trigger. The mercury bulb was in the center of the two inch capsule. On either end of the mercury capsule were electronic diodes that linked to wires on either side. Any movement of the bomb to the left or right by ever a slight quarter inch would have blown him up. Russell wanted to kick himself for not checking for multiple triggers before touching the bomb. From his explosive training, Russell knew to analyze the entire situation and think beyond what he saw. For nearly two minutes he stood still and examined the room for the direction of the blast. On the floor, he saw several pieces of paper. There was a slight rise in the middle of one. He walked along the wall and squatted next to the papers that were directly in the walking path entering the room. He lifted the sheet and saw the adjustable metal one centimeter spikes. There were three of them rising from the wood floor. He pulled out his knife and removed the floorboard. Inside, he found a step triggered grenade. On the side was a screw to secure the adjustable metal trigger spikes. He defused the bomb by gently tightening the screws. Whoever placed the bomb was indeed a true professional who disguised the bomb as a simple wire trigger with the primary detonator as the mercury capsule.

The archeology team had maps posted all over the room, or they had. The maps were torn from the walls. Scraps of paper littered the floor. Tables were flipped over and the single couch ripped open. The guts of the couch were flung across the room. Russell thought the soft white foam interior resembled snow and the room had a blizzard.

"Oh my god," Kimberly said. "What were they looking for?"

"Whatever it was they did not find it." Russell said nonchalantly.

She looked at him with a disapproving look. "Terrible, absolutely terrible." She cried while picking through the snow stuffing to see what was underneath. Kimberly sat on the floor and wept hard.

"We need to move." Russell paused. He caught a glimpse of a large man moving on top of the adjoining roof, "and now!" He grabbed her arm. "Go! Go!" The window glass burst inside the room from the multiple shots fired at the building. As Russell pulled her across the room towards the door, the rounds followed them and indented into the wall. She shrieked and fell on the floor. Russell dragged Kimberly by the arm, yet he had to get her out of danger. Russell yanked her arm down the staircase. There was no time for negotiation, no time for conversation, no time for dispute. He got them out of the danger zone. Outside the back ally, he put her back on her feet. By the expression on her face, she was in deep shock. Tshambe saw them move fast and instinctively bolted the vehicle to rescue them. Russell yanked Kimberly inside and within seconds, Tshambe sped the car out towards the country. Russell thumbed through the text message from Francesca and gave Tshambe directions towards the Congo interior and Mobutu's remote palace.

The next afternoon in the Congo bush, Francesca waited patiently as she sat on the hood of her Land Rover. She skillfully cleaned her sniper rifle. The sexy dress was tossed aside and replaced with her comfortable black Israeli Special Forces outfit. She wore the rank of Lieutenant Colonel on the insignia. As Russell approached, the site of Francesca sitting on the vehicle with a high powered sniper rifle stirred emotion within him. They had a torrid love affair in Liberia. They got off to a rocky, somewhat combative start in the Congo, but the sight of her brought back good memories. They had worked closely together in Liberia and thwarted a major Al Qaeda terrorist attack. And now, they were after a loose atomic weapon. The stakes were high and he needed her on his side.

"What took you so long?" Francesca asked.

"Not easy to find this." Russell remarked as he looked at the immense mansion. "Even this big, it was difficult to see with all of the jungle growing around."

"Did you find anything?"

"No. I did not think it was here." She showed him a map. "I did not trust my source so I followed him. He had a small compound along the Congo river here." She pointed to the map. "That is not far from the Hezbollah compound. My gut tells me we are on a wild goose chase here and my informant sold it to Rajik."

"That bastards name keeps coming up."

"We need to take him out." Francesca said pointedly. "I should have killed him back in Liberia." She recalled the speedboat as it hurled out of Monrovia's port as she tried to fire a missile at it. Her shot was wide as the speedboat bounced around in the ocean. Rajik had escaped.

"But first we need to find out who is behind everything." Russell said. He tried to calm her.

"I need to get back to Kinshasa and find out more about Getz." She said. "Something is not right about Nakor Industries." As Francesca drove into the jungle, she did not see the man on the motorcycle follow her. He hid himself well in the thick bush. Kamal accelerated the motorcycle towards the Mossad agent. The Al Qaeda physician smiled as he thought about the pleasure he would have killing an Israeli.

At the dilapidated structure that was the former Mobutu's palace, Russell walked on the outside of pool area to make sure Francesca told him the truth. She played many games with his head while she was undercover in Liberia. He did not know her true identity until well after they became intimate. Russell looked up at the immense marble columns that outlined the entrance to the mansion. The colossal pieces of rock weighed several thousand pounds and were one of the few items not ransacked or stolen. Russell walked inside the dilapidated building and could not see more than twenty feet. The massive entrance foray was darkened by lack of light. Previously, eight foot high designed pane glass windows lined the octagon foray. Now, the windows were covered with solid brick. Russell pointed the rifle in the air. The moonbeam attached on the side of his weapon shined only a few feet.

The first movement did not catch Russell's attention in the monitor. However, the viral shriek froze him. They were under attack and Russell knew that he had only a few moments to act. He recognized the threat and wanted to open fire. He looked through the night scope one more time and could make out the devilish face with an enormous nose pierced with a bone. The head was covered in some type of long grass style wig. The eyes were wide and violent. Russell pulled a concussion grenade from his vest and was ready to toss it.

"Wait," directed Tshambe. "They may not be evil."

"They're armed." Russell kept his eye trained on the target, which carried a large spear.

"This is not your country."

"You're right." Russell lifted his finger off the trigger. "Should we go and ask them what they want." Russell motioned to Tshambe. Into the darkness, Tshambe walked. Russell kept his weapon trained down the darkened corridor. Up ahead, Russell heard some whistling and several other strange signaling sounds he never heard before. Ten minutes later, Tshambe returned to the room with the local village chief.

"He asked for our help."

"Why?"

"His village was massacred when some of the men went hunting. He thought we might have been the ones who attacked his village."

"I have to get back to Kinshasa." Francesca picked up her gear. Russell wanted to say something, but could not find the words. Francesca did not look back and spun the tires in the dirt as she accelerated. Russell, Kimberly, and Tshambe followed the village chief.

The village looked like a war zone. The few living inhabitants were bandaged with blood soaked clothing. Some of the children had arms amputated. Their little arms were sliced off with machetes. Some of the older women were assaulted. Boys were stolen for forced labor. The bodies of the men were strewn across the ground. Remains of the huts smoldered. The smell of burnt flesh lingered in the air. An old man dragged a body out of the destroyed grass hut. As he pulled the corpse, an arm ripped out of socket and became dislodged. The tendons and ligaments that once previously held the arm in place had disintegrated from the intense fire. The old man stopped and abruptly looked at the ripped off arm. After a short reflection, he folded the dislodged arm into the remnants of clothes on the corpse's chest. He walked around and pulled the body by the legs. Tshambe helped lift the corpse off the dirt. They walked one hundred feet to the village cemetery, or what the Congolese called a cemetery. There were no head stones. No flamboyant marble slabs etched with names, birth dates, and deceased dates, just small wooden crosses.

Russell's mind flashed back to the bloodshed he witnessed in Iskandariyah, Iraq. The post traumatic images raced through his mind. In Iskandariyah, a bomb blast exploded in the street and destructively rattled two hundred and forty Shiites who peacefully assembled at the police station. Innocent civilians were blasted into oblivion by a powerful car bomb. Mangled body parts rained over the Iraq streets as over two hundred died on 10 February, 2004. Russell tried to help the dying but could not save them. Burnt bodies littered the Iraqi street. The explosive fireball consumed everything. Scenes from the massive car bomb that decimated the Iskandariyah police station floated throughout his mind. Russell was point lead on negotiating for the transfer of several high ranking former members of Saddam Hussein's government captured near Iskandariyah, thirty-two miles south of Bagdad. As his armored military vehicle rounded the corner, an explosive force ripped across the front. As Russell surveyed the carnage, he accidentally stepped on what was left of a human body and slipped on the ground. Red blood stained his military uniform. He would not be able to get the blood out and had to burn his clothes. As he approached the Iskandariyah police station, startled figures emerged - shocked by the catastrophic explosion. Blood flowed from their smoke polluted faces. Russell thought they resembled zombies.

Russell looked back at the carnage of the village. He could not get the dead bodies out of his mind. His past was catching up to him. His hands vibrated violently. He could not control the tremors. A vengeful rage came to his mind.

On the other side of Kinshasa, Francesca slowed her jeep as she noticed the motorcycle tail. Something did not resonant well with the rider. Very few men in the Congo wore helmets. More importantly, very few motorcycles were operated at a safe consistent sped. She observed dozen bikes speed past her on the side of the road. Motorcycles moved in and out of traffic moments before a resulting head on collision. Aggressive driving was accepted. If a driver was not aggressive in the Congo, they were taken advantage of and risked death. Francesca turned the jeep into on-coming traffic and pulled back at the last moment. Horns from large trucks squealed and smoke ensued from the rapid depression of brakes. She tried again and kept the jeep steady as she faced a large truck less than a hundred feet away. The head on collision would be only a few seconds away. The truck driver lost his nerve and swerved to his left and moved past Francesca on the side of the road.

The Al Qaeda terrorist watched as the Israeli moved in and out of traffic. Kamal thought she was wild. He sped up the motorcycle. He only had a few weeks training on the motorcycle and felt impressed that he kept chase. As the Israeli moved back into traffic, Kamal thought how much a pleasure it would be to interrogate and torture a Mossad agent. His mind raced with thoughts of her torso ripped open with his scalpel. He would cut her feet off and toss them into a bucket. He thought about all of the evil things he would do to her private parts. Kamal was distracted by his thoughts. His eyes squinted as he saw a large truck move in front of him. Kamal reacted and turned the motorcycle off the road. He could not slow the motorcycle down fast enough and entered the high grass. As the motorcycle's front wheel struck a hole, Kamal flew twenty feet in the air. The Al Qaeda human missile landed safely in the tall grass; however, he broke his arm and had a severe concussion.

CHAPTER 14

The village massacre had shocked Russell. Dead bodies were strewn across the ground in random fashion. Some of the dead were close together. Russell thought how they must have been family members - closeness in life sealed in their deaths. Locals walked about the littered bodies in shock. Cries erupted as they found relatives, everyone knew somebody in the death pile. The Africa dirt was stained with blood.

"You cannot do anything for these people." Tshambe stood in front of Russell. "This is Africa. Evil happens here all the time." Tshambe sounded like an educated university scholar.

"This violence has to end." Russell was disgusted and showed his contempt for the violence.

"It will end in due time." Tshambe replied. "When the good Lord shines over and illuminates man's evil darkness."

"How can you act so civil with this horror?"

"This is my home and I have seen far worse brutality."

"We must find those responsible." Russell demanded.

"Doesn't matter...There will be others. Violence is a common thread in African society. You cannot change that. Even dictators such as Mobutu killed more than the plagues. But your western governments touted him as a great leader of the Congo because he kept the peace with neighboring nations. In truth, Mobutu tried to take over and destabilize the region. He even had a hand in supporting the Rwanda genocide, but where are the charges for war crimes? Mobutu got to leave the Congo and die in exile. He should have been hung from the center of Kinshasa."

Russell had to get away from the village to calm down. He wondered down a path farther away from the horrific scene. Russell wondered about Joseph Conrad's mysterious, dreadful character Mr. Kurtz and what evils of the dark jungle possessed and drove him to madness. He opened the novel Heart of Darkness to the section containing the discussion between Kurtz and the young naïve Willard. *Kurtz said, "I expected someone like you. What did you expect? Are you an assassin? Willard replied, "I'm a soldier." With Kurtz giving his landmark reply, "You're neither. You're an errand boy, sent by grocery clerks, to collect a bill."*

Russell knew Rajik was evil. Could a man be so committed to the destruction of Israel that he would risk detonating an atomic bomb over top of Tel Aviv and have the ash cloud strangle Beirut? Indeed Rajik was evil, but was he indeed the mastermind behind this doomsday plot? None of the paid informants had seen Rajik in or round Kinshasa for weeks. Rumor swirled about the Ashbal compound along the river.

Russell thought of what Schultz told him about the problems with the aid organizations. Giving children shoes was one of the worse NGO decisions as it made children's feet soft after there were not around to hand out larger sizes over time. The lack of cultural understanding was one of the bigger misgivings by uninformed NGOs that flooded into Africa. Good hearted individuals saw the infomercials on poor African children and pledged donations without knowing clearly where the money went. Some NGOs received ample stipends and incentives to work in the most dangerous parts of Africa - the more dangerous - the more money spent. As overcrowding and disease killed millions, some NGOs enjoyed the plush lifestyle in secured compounds. Everything in Africa was segregated by wealth. Those who could pay received the best medical care. There was a vicious cycle of poverty. Many people lived on the street, barely existing. The NGO community remained at several secure compounds within Kinshasa out of fear for their lives. Few dared to venture to the outer countryside where disease and poverty were even more prevalent. Russell contemplated his next move. He needed to keep his mind fixed on the mission. There were too many distractions - corruption, poverty, disease. A massive amount of Congolese had died.

By the next afternoon, Francesca found herself back in Kinshasa city limits. She abandoned the Land Rover and purchased a motorbike from a local on the street. There were no mirrors on the motorbike. The gas tank was strapped together with grey duct tape. The entire bike juggled and jolted from each bump in the road. She felt huge gyrations in the bike's handlebars. It was the best she could find. She sped down the street and pushed the envelope as the motorbike nearly broke apart. From a side street, Francesca surveyed the safe house the previous

Mossad agent had rented. The small complex had a large outside wall with barb wire strung across the top. She did not think anyone ever lived there. Francesca knew it from a satellite photo. She slowed down as she approached on the street level. Within seconds, she sensed the place was under surveillance.

The men looked out of place as they drove behind Francesca and were not concerned about concealing their weapons. Two held weapons out their open windows. The GROM thugs had targeted Francesca. In a split moment, machinegun fire cascaded across the dull grey cement brick façade of the building and ejected large pieces of concrete. Locals dove for cover. Francesca sped the motorcycle in and out of traffic. The handlebars were close to falling off. The little engine screamed, yet she accelerated faster. After she passed the large bus, she turned her head to observe any pursuers. She lost them. Up ahead there was an overpass over the four lane highway. She could see three men standing on it. One pointed in her direction. She slammed on the brakes and twisted the bike into oncoming traffic. She shifted the bike left and right quickly to avoid cars flying at her at over fifty miles per hour. Two hundred yards in front, she saw a black SUV approach. Men hung out the windows with guns pointed in her direction. Again, she slammed on the brakes and twisted the bike with the flow of traffic. Francesca moved up behind the large bus which concealed her from the men on the overpass. She accelerated the bike full throttle and passed the bus underneath the overpass. She kept her head lowered for wind shear and did not look back. Bullets riddled past her as the men overshot her. Rounds exploded into numerous vehicles around her. Surprised drivers panicked and slammed on brakes. Several cars to her right collided. She kept the throttle open all the way. More rounds flew past her. A church van caught a heavy volley and flipped. As she passed, she connected eyes with a mother who tried to protect her baby. For a brief moment, there was a connection that was abated by the utter chaos. Collisions occurred and forced cars off the road. Tires gripped the pavement as the rubber burned. The GROM thugs maneuvered around several disabled vehicles until they could not pass any further. One thug jumped on the vehicle's roof and fired at will. Francesca outdistanced the shots and sped out of Kinshasa – destination unknown.

The Minister of Information looked across his thatched together plywood desk. Gertz pulled out a large envelope and slid it across. Gertz could tell the envelope's thickness intrigued the Minister. Gertz looked the Congo Minister in the eye and professed, "This should be enough."

"You foreigners think that you can bribe us."

"Call it an investment." Gertz replied.

"I'm a simple man trying to make a life for his family. I chose to stay in the Congo when many left after Mobutu died. I remained to help my nation get back on track."

"I need your endorsement on these shipping documents."

"Why should I sign this?" The corrupt Minister inquired. Before he looked up from the document, he could sense Gertz was upset.

"Because you know what is at stake." Gertz stated coldly.

"Yes, yes. I do know what you have signed me up for." The Minister was visibly upset. "You and me, we are tied together." He pointed his right index finger back and forth several times. Gertz was accustomed to the Minister's theatrics and was not surprised when the Minister stated. "Voctrad knows what you are doing."

"I am not worried about them."

"You better be concerned." The Minister said as he smiled. "If you are taking their clients, you will not wake up."

"Don't worry about them or the American CIA." Gertz said as he stood. Both knew the UN forces were corrupted and easily bribed. Gertz had already paid large installments to several high ranking UN diplomats.

"When do you need the document back?" The Minister inquired. He had to endure the Congo bureaucratic red tape and bribe the Minister of Transportation.

"In three days. It must be signed before we move forward with the next shipment."

"How many more will there be?" Minister now appeared nervous. There would be more questions.

"With the North Koreans as new customers, we will double our shipments."

"But how many more?"

"Until the mountain is empty." Gertz walked out of the office. He held his nose as he walked past the office staff and he almost nauseated from their body smell. Soap was a luxury item in the Congo.

Russell could not stay at the massacred village as the post traumatic thoughts of Iraq lingered in his mind. He left Tshambe to help the village chief bury the dead. Russell had to get to Lubumbashi to meet his contacts. Kimberly was excess baggage, but he could not leave her there, especially as she was the only white woman within several hundred miles. Kimberly looked at Russell as he geared up with his equipment. Neither had showered for several days. The African winter was far from cold and the heat of the day penetrated their pours. They both smelled. Kimberly tried to clean herself the best she could with water from the stream. Russell filled all of the containers they had with the fresh stream water. He did not know how long they would have to go or if they would see fresh water again. He brought a hydration system that decontaminated water. The small attachment was light weight and hi-tech from the Seattle Mountain Rescue team. She was amazed at all of the gear he carried; she was especially interested in the automatic weapons.

"Can you show me how to shoot?"

"Why?"

"I feel safe with you around, but what if you are not close and they come for me again?"

"Weapons are very dangerous and worse in the hands of those who do not know how to use them."

"Well you can teach me?" Kimberly asked. He knew she never fired a weapon before. He did not have to ask. From the background he learned about her, she lived a sheltered life in academia. From undergraduate college at Brown, she moved to Washington, DC and studied at George Washington University for her Doctorate degrees. She did not hold the pistol correctly and Russell stepped closer to hold her arm. Her first shot was wide right and the sound of the shot made her more nervous as she kept squeezing more shots and more noise came out from the pistol. She screamed. Russell grabbed the weapon, now he hoped she would not ask for a weapon again.

"Teach me properly," she paused. "I need to know." By the expression on her face, Russell knew she was dead serious.

"Alright," he responded. Russell wrapped his right arm tightly around her waist; even with the bulky clothes he could tell she was thin. Her hair smelled but he moved close. He pulled her closer to him. "Hold the weapon forward, lock your elbows, and fire." The burst of eruption scared her again, but he sensed it and he held her tightly. He gave her more instructions and used his left arm to help support her arms. He let her fire the entire clip and showed her how to replace it. Her shots were all over the place yet Russell remained patient. He carefully showed her how to properly handle and take care of the weapon.

Russell and Kimberly walked forty minutes to the next village, which intersected with the railroad. A long train equally divided between passenger cars and flat cars that possessed bundles of large trees for lumber. The executive car was at the front of the train. Russell and Kimberly were the only white people within fifty miles as they walked passed hundreds of interested eyes. Fifteen passenger cars were over-packed and some chose to sit on top of the train. The conductor informed Russell that the journey to Lubumbashi would take two days, yet he looked at the long line and the old beaten engine and surmised the trip would take three days. A well-dressed man in a perfect white dinner jacket greeted them at the door of the executive car. Inside there was an open dining area, three small cabins, and a full bathroom. The bathroom was elongated compared to the sleeping cars to make room for a gold embroidered large marble tub. Fine china and pure white linens covered the three sets of tables. In the corner of the car, a small bar was stocked with fine liquor and bottles of expensive South African wine. Kimberly did not take long to drop her bag and strip down to her underwear in the bathroom. The hot water gushed out of the faucet, which made her extremely happy. She soaked in the tub for over an hour as the train started to roll down the line. Russell walked around the car and saw old pictures of President Mobutu. Russell looked at her as she emerged from the bathroom and wore a satin blue robe tightly around her thin waist.

"We got the only room on the train," Russell said. Kimberly shuffled past him into the bathroom. The coachman went into the bathroom, picked up her dirty clothes, and handed them to a young woman who waited at the door. Russell grabbed a shirt and slacks out of the closet.

"These are for unexpected guests," the coachman informed him. Russell pondered how many times the old man witnessed foreigners emerge out of the bush along the train route and needed luxury surroundings, probably a lot more than he would think. The one hundred percent cotton and white dress laid out on Kimberly's bed looked horrendous to her, yet she needed something to wear.

"You look wonderful." Russell said as he walked back into the bedroom.

"Thank you, just something I threw together," she laughed. The old man came back into car and poured glasses of fine South African wine. They enjoyed several glasses while waiting for dinner. After thirty minutes, the old man arrived with roasted chicken covered with steamed vegetables. Large bowls of rice and fruit were placed in the center of the table.

"I feel guilty." She looked up at him and the pile of food in front of them.

"I know." Russell said. "It doesn't seem right that we are here and hundreds of locals are packed behind us."

"But let's enjoy it best we can." She raised the wine for a toast

"What are we toasting?"

"Here's to my private body guard."

"Anytime." Russell replied pointedly.

Kimberly looked at Russell as he devoured the food with a complete lack of grace. She was not offended. She was aroused. "You are a very interesting man."

"Four out of five former girlfriends polled would call me an adrenaline junkie. Most do not hang around long enough." Russell was playing with fire as he knew a sex crazed, extremely jealous, and lethally trained female Mossad agent would be watching his every move.

Kamal awoke in a hospital bed. He looked around the room and saw only Africans. As an Egyptian, he had a dark complexion, yet he easily stood out next to any locals. Kamal motioned for a nurse. He looked at the blood soaked rag around his broken arm. The bone had protruded out of the skin and was wrapped with a dirty towel. He could still see dirt around the wound. Kamal tried to sit up, but his head hurt. He remembered the fall as he landed and blacked out. He concluded that he must have received a concussion. He asked the nurse for a clean bandage and she laughed. The other Africans in the room had wounds from the recent rebel attack. A few had amputated legs. There was a stack of four legs in the corner of the room that awaited burial. Kamal knew if he did not get proper antibiotics that he would die from infection. By the look of the conditions in this hospital, he knew that he had to get to Kinshasa to purchase drugs on the black market. He would need to set his arm. He cursed the Israeli and wanted her even more now.

The Al Qaeda terrorist barely survived his accident and worried that he would lose his left arm due to infection. Kamal knew that he would be an easy target if he went to a hospital in Kinshasa. UN security men would ask questions. Kamal's photo had been posted on a terror watch list. The CIA knew he was in Afghanistan and Pakistan with Bin Laden. Kamal had done the best he could to set his arm. He pushed the bone back into place and yelled. However, no one came. He placed a diluted concrete mixture over top of a white sheet he had wrapped around his arm. The makeshift cast held. Kamal used a burner cell phone to talk with his contacts in Uganda. He would need a safe house to move to and recuperate after this mission. But first, he had to capture and torture a female Mossad agent.

Near the center square within the southern Congo city of Lubumbashi, the crowd was large. Locals were packed like sardines in the city center. National elections were less than a month away and the campaigns became heated. Kimba Lumumba had a slight lead in the Presidential polls. He came to Lubumbashi to solidify his support base. If he succeeded in amassing support in the Katanga Province, one of the largest populated areas, he could achieve victory. Kimba believed corruption reigned throughout the new Congo government.

"The Congo must be taken back." Kimba Lumumba shouted as he stood on the top of the truck and shouted in the blow horn. The crowd was two thousand strong and listened intently. "The white man has destroyed everything. My grandfather fought the white man." The crowd cheered. Kimba referred to Patrice Lumumba, who was the first elected Prime Minister after the Belgian King gave up control. "Foreigners are stealing our wealth. It's ours. It's our right." Kimba became more irate, "It's our heritage." He paused for effect, "It's our destiny." The crowd cheered and chanted "Lumumba...Lumumba" - words that have not been cheered in over four decades.

The political rally was his tenth in the last week and he surged in the polls. Kimba had less than a month until the presidential election and put all of his hopes on winning Katanga Province. The crowd was in frenzy. Kimba waived his arms in the air. Hands reached forward to grasp the hand of the man who would change the Congo.

Across the street about three hundred yards away, the former Polish Special Force sniper sighted the rifle. The crude rifle had to be African and left at the scene. He tried several times to fix the sighting mechanism and did his best to aim in the middle of Kimba's chest. The sound from the rifle shot was loud. Dozens dropped immediately from fear. Others pointed and shouted in the direction of the shot. The accuracy of the weapon was jilted by the age of the weapon and the round penetrated Kimba eight inches off target. Kimba fell off of the truck into the arms of his bodyguards. The arm that once carried the warrior's sword above his head was bloodied. Kimba closed his eyes. The pain was excruciating. A bright light erupted in his eyes. Kimba thought that he was dead.

CHAPTER 15

The train lumbered towards Lubumbashi and through the thick African bush. From the executive car, Russell looked out at the countryside. He saw large swaths of land. The Congo had many ecosystems: thick jungles, pristine forests, high altitude mountains, and most notably the immense Congo River. A mighty river flowed throughout the country with origins deep inside the Dark Continent. Animals were scarce as many were killed for food. The most horrific war in Africa that forced so many refugees triggered mass animal killings in the countryside. With no animals to see and lack of security forces, tourism dropped to nonexistent.

The last hours of the train ride were brutal for Russell as Kimberly sat right next to him. She wrapped her arms around his with octopus-like grip. He tried to read background information on African counter insurgency operations, but gave up. She grabbed onto him after their passionate night. Russell knew better and was forced to suffer as she cuddled close. At last, she closed her eyes and Russell concentrated on the books Kitson gave him. Russell read the counter insurgency campaign during the Boer War in South Africa. He tried to understand more about the South Africans and what made them tick. Russell was amazed racism was still alive and well in South Africa. As well as, he was shocked to read the UN report on economic slavery in Africa at the hands of former colonial powers. The governments may have changed but business holdings lasted. Nakor was at the top of the list for violating human rights. Strikes and labor protests were dealt with harsh and brutal tactics. Labor organizers and reformers had disappeared. Something was missing, a clue to the past that would bring it all together. Russell did not know what it was, but knew it was there.

Schultz provided Russell a good description of his contact. The elderly lady would be dressed similar to a majority of the NGOs running around the Congo - tan slacks and shirt, big hat, lots of sunscreen. The man would hold a cane in his right hand. Russell had no idea what to expect from the retired CIA agents. In his past, he met retired senior military officers and nine times out of ten they all tried to relive the magic of bossing people around and telling anyone who would listen how important they were. He did not know what a retired CIA operative would be like. Schultz gave him the run down on Harry and Elsie Martin, if indeed that was their real name. Russell was a quick study to comprehend no one appeared to be what they professed in the intelligence community. In this case, Schultz provided Russell with a legitimate background that had him spellbound.

In the early 1950s, Harry Martin was stationed in West Berlin at the American Embassy. His cover job was a janitor. He actually cleaned floors as part of his cover and at night went on secret missions into communist controlled East Germany. On one mission into East Berlin in 1953, he met Elsie. Her father was a notable professor in Leningrad who tried to defect with his only living relative - his twenty year old daughter Elsie. Upon meeting Elsie, Harry was impressed with her English and knowledge of America. She had longed to live out from under the veil of communist control. As a musician, she traveled the world with the Bolshoi Theater. She and her father tried to defect before, but feared the KGB who tracked their movements. Harry took Elsie to have new documentation papers made. Minutes later the KGB came to arrest her family. Her father was shot dead as he attempted to escape out the back window. As they returned, Harry saw the neighborhood packed with KGB agents on the hunt for Elsie. Every house was searched. Harry knew that he had to get her out of there. He turned the truck around and headed towards Czechoslovakia. For over a month, they worked their way through the Iron Curtain and evaded KGB agents. At every turn, KGB killers were on their heels. Harry knew if he tried to cross back into the West from East Berlin, she would be captured. Deeper into Soviet territory they traveled. They had to pass as a married couple. Elsie liked being called his wife for their charade. On the steamship freighter out of the Kiev along the Dnieper River, Harry finally kissed Elsie. Eventually, they made their way to Istanbul and to freedom. Harry was assigned back to Langley and asked Elsie to join him. The agency looked into Elsie's background and eventually hired her. They could not go back to Europe as the KGB had a price on Elsie's head so they were sent to Africa where they spent three decades bouncing from country to country. Most of their time was spent in the

Congo. Harry and Elsie knew the country's violent history better than any outsiders.

Elsie looked around and something was not right. She observed the threat well before Harry. Elsie was always better at assessing danger. In a split second, she knew the three men were not right - their clothes, what they drove, how they walked. Instinctively, she knew the men were mercenaries and it did not take a rocket scientist to understand the potential threat as the mercenaries watched the restaurant where they were going to meet an American Marine officer and an archeologist.

Russell looked down the street and did not see anything out of the ordinary. His mind raced with thoughts about the mission. He had a hard time focusing and he missed the obvious signs that he was being followed.

"What's wrong?" Kimberly asked as they crossed the street. She was genuinely concerned about the man she started to fall for.

"This assignment has gone to hell quick." Russell stated in a bold and direct manner. "You should not be here."

"But your cover?" Kimberly questioned him intently. "You may be exposed. What if they do not think you are a legitimate archeologist?"

"Can't be too hard." He knew that he offended her.

"It's a lot more than just digging up bones."

"Understood." Russell never knew how to properly apologize his entire life. He did the next best thing and changed the subject. "Once we find this retired couple, you need to get away from me." He paused. "Far away."

"Why?" Kimberly asked. "Is something dangerous going to happen?" Kimberly leaned across the table to hold his hand. Russell sensed that she had no clue what was about to transpire.

"Chaos. Utter chaos has arrived here in the Congo and we are walking smack dab into a shit storm." Russell looked around the restaurant.

Across the street, Braum watched closely as the two white people had entered the café. The large GROM thug easily spotted the only foreigners visible on the entire street. Inside the café, Russell picked a corner table in the packed room. He ordered a sandwich. Kimberly did not dare eat anything. His food just arrived when Russell witnessed the door open and a flying object strike against the far wall. The canister burst open and spewed gas into the air. Locals gasped and choked on the CS gas. As chaos erupted, tables were tossed and overturned. Several people vomited. Russell looked at the clogged exit as patrons fought to exit. He tried to smash the restaurant window with a chair; however, the glass held firm.

"Are you ok?" Russell looked into Kimberly's eyes and she was shocked beyond belief. She coughed and choked. She waved her right hand in the air and tried to cover her mouth with her jacket using the other hand. She vomited. Russell had to act as the CS gas burned into his eyes. He felt a hard twist in his stomach and almost vomited. Every instinct in his body told him to get out of that location and save himself, yet he could not leave her. He crumpled over in pain and fell to his knees. As he coughed heavily, he lifted his pistol and opened fire on the glass window. He emptied the entire clip of thirteen rounds. Glass particles bombarded the patrons. His gunfire added to the chaos and high pitch screams engulfed the scene as patrons ran for their lives. Russell coughed hard again and vomited. He looked down and could barely see the mess he emptied on the floor. He slipped in the greasy digestive mess. He gained his footing, grabbed Kimberly, and hurled her body through the large empty hole where the large plate glass window once stood firm. They rolled on the pavement and gasped.

Complete and utter chaos rang out in the street as everyone ran for cover. The locals did not know where the shots came from. Russell heard the sound of tires screeched to a halt. Several foreigners jumped out of the open sliding door. Russell could not resist the captors as they zip locked his hands with plastic restraint straps. His eyes flooded with tears. He could not make any faces and within three seconds someone circled his head with duct tape that covered his eyes and ears. He continued to cough violently and spat viral stomach juices in the air. His spat connected with one of the GROM Polish Special Forces who reciprocated the pleasure as he punched Russell in the gut. From the time the CS canister pin was pulled to the time they had Russell and the female archeologist in the van was no more than four minutes.

Braum was pleased with Gertz's decision to kill Russell, but first Gertz wanted information. Braum laughed to himself as the American was easier to calculate than he thought. There was no possible way he would be able to get out of the cafe's single door as the locals tried to escape the harsh CS gas. Braum concluded the only option the American had was to blow out the window. He calculated correctly. Russell was easy to judge. The van sped out of town. Braum mused to himself that he still had yet to hear any UN police sirens. The former Polish Special Forces team remained silent. They had remote headsets wired yet still used hand signals in the vehicle.

Russell believed whoever took them were professionals. Russell rolled towards Kimberly to hold her hand. Her body shook violently. The vehicle stopped several times in quick succession. Russell realized that they must have arrived at a safe house. Within a minute, the captors pulled them from the van and tossed them into a room. Russell felt a needle in his arm and instinctively knew he was drugged as he passed out. A while later, someone had pulled tape from his eyes. Russell opened his eyes slowly. Across from him was the missing Amnesty International investigator. Gunther appeared badly beaten and bruised. His face had dried blood as he was taken over four days ago. The abuse stopped after Gunther divulged everything he knew about the American archeologists.

"What happened to you?" Russell asked as he tried to move. There were metal leg irons around his ankles and handcuffs on his wrists.

"Taken at Kuvulu." Gunther responded softly. He was beaten.

"Why did they take you?"

"I have been asking too many questions." Gunther said. He did not know what happened. This world was a far cry from his plush lifestyle. "Who do you think is behind this?"

"These thugs are former Polish Special Forces. They all work for a diamond merchant named Gertz. Does that sound familiar?"

"No, no it does not. The only man I have dealt with has been the Minister of Information." Gunther paused for moment. "Perhaps he does not want me finding out what really happened at Kuvulu."

"The Minister does not have the clout to pull the trigger."

"After we came back from Virunga, I hired a local driver from the hotel. They must have followed me out of Kinshasa. They shot my driver in the back of the head. I have been here for days. No food, no water. They beat me every few hours. I do not know anything. I told them that I thought you were archeologists. They do not believe me. They are mad. They beat me more."

"You were watched before you ever came to the Congo."

"Who are you?" Gunther sat up. "They beat me because I met you and traveled with you. Who are you working with?"

"You do not want to know."

"What?" Gunther asked. "I am going to die here because of you."

"The only piece that I can tell you is somehow this is all tied to what happened in Kuvulu."

"Why are you investigating what happened in Kuvulu?"

"I am not," Russell said, "but someone must have thought that you gave me information on Kuvulu."

"What are you after?"

"I can't tell you," Russell said.

"What can you tell me?"

"A lot of people want us dead." Russell wished he had not told him that information as he heard Gunther cry aloud.

At Nakor Industry headquarters, Gertz slapped his executive assistant Moira so hard she fell out of the chair. When she was on the ground, he kicked her in her face. He suspected Moira spied on him but he did not know who for and he did not care. Word of his brutality would spread, and he hoped his own people would fear him more.

"You see what you get for lying to me," Gertz shouted, "who did you tell about the uranium?" Life did not matter much in the Congo and Gertz knew he could have people disappear easily.

"No one, no one." She whimpered.

"I can't move it, if you told the Americans." Gertz wrapped a towel around his right hand. With his left hand he picked Moira up by her shirt and punched her in the face with the other hand. Gertz continued his interrogation. "Who did you tell?"

She wanted the pain to stop. She wanted it to end. At this point, she would agree to anything. "The Americans made me tell them. They threatened to send me away from you. I love you. Please stop...please."

Moira cried hard. Her lungs heaved up and down with deep gargled breaths. Gertz poured water into the blood soaked towel and cleaned up the face of the woman who had been his executive assistant for four years. In his strange way, he respected Moira as she was very efficient. He had sex with Moira many times, yet he would never let her spend the night at his house. Gertz made her a commodity. No one at Nakor dared to ask her on a date as they knew Gertz used her. Gertz walked out onto the patio. The fires across Kinshasa had ceased and peace talks were again being made. Gertz did not like that.

"The container is staged at the port." Gertz said. "I cannot have my security staff seen with it as it will come back to me. We need someone else."

"How about the Hezbollah gun runners?" The Minister of Information asked.

"Agreed." Gertz handed over the manila envelope with two hundred thousand cash.

"What about her?" The Minister looked at the blood on the side of her face. She was crumpled on the floor.

"Take her with you." Gertz replied. "Give her to the rebels and tell them she's a bonus."

Gertz picked up the phone that dialed to the main security desk. "I need a driver." Gertz looked down at Moira as she tried to lift her badly beaten body. "Also, have you seen my executive assistant Moira?" Braum knew Gertz did not want Moira back. Braum looked at her and thought that she might make a good bush wife for the rebels. Braum laughed inside as he thought about all of the carnage the rebels would do to this white woman. A bullet to the head would be too peaceful for her. Braum chose the more brutal means of disposal and called the rebel leader Gertz had on payroll. Moira became the love interest for several rebels until she took her own life after she jumped off the two hundred foot Boyoma Falls.

Chapter 16

Kimba Lumumba walked out of the hospital to cheers from his native Congolese. The crowd was substantially larger than any he had encountered before. Twenty UN policemen pushed against the throngs of locals who hoped to touch Kimba. As he was thrust into a van, his shirt was partially ripped from his body - a memento for one of his supporters. At a slow sped, the motorcade made its way past thousands who lined the streets to show support for not only Kimba but the Lumumba family name. Kimba reflected on his family history. He had valuable family information that would cost him his life if the South Africans found out what he knew. A secret was buried, long forgotten. Four decades ago, Kimba's grandfather was catapulted on the world stage. In the late 1950s, Joseph Mobutu was by all means ignorant, until he found Patrice Lumumba. As one of his first acts taking over the Congo government, Prime Minister Lumumba promoted Mobutu to Colonel and gave him control of the fledgling military. After Lumumba was arrested and murdered, Mobutu served under a transitional government for five years until he had enough power to stage his own military coup. Mobutu took over the Congo in 1965 and renamed the nation Zaire soon after. For decades, Mobutu inflicted fear and terror throughout Zaire and the Congo River region. However, his reign came to an abrupt end in 2007. Mobutu was delirious from the cancer medication and had advance signs of Alzheimer's. Kimba was invited to Mobutu's jungle mansion and he stole a box of papers. Kimba thought the documents would educate him more on his grandfather's murder. What Kimba found was a treasure trove. Kimba found evidence Mobutu sought a secret atomic weapons program.

Excruciating pain encompassed the left side of Russell's face. The interrogator was right handed and smacked him extremely hard. The blunt force joggled several teeth out of position and Russell spat a tooth filling onto the concrete floor. He did not hear any voices for about an hour. His arms remained bound behind his back. Every time he rolled, the bonds cut into his wrists. He looked around. There was no other exit from the closed room. Gunther moaned on the other side of the room. He was tied with a small gauge wire, which Russell could have easily escaped from. Gunther did not attempt to escape as fear gripped him.

Outside of the warehouse, Elsie watched as the she strolled past with the assistance of a cane. She did not need the cane. It added to her cover as a nice old foreign lady out on a stroll. She walked back and forth along the outside perimeter fence and found a concealed spot to enter. The GROM thugs loaded into the van and drove past her. She waived her hat to swat some fake flies away, which was the signal for Harry to bring the jeep around backside of the warehouse.

"Russell, I presume?" Harry said as he pushed open the door.

Russell knew immediately that his rescuers were the retired CIA operatives Schultz talked so highly of. "You got weapons?" Russell was banged up hard, yet ready for a fight.

"Here," Elsie whispered as she handed Russell a nine millimeter pistol. "We need to move quickly my dear." Elsie said as she cut Russell's metal chain bondage with bolt cutters. Russell tried to stand and fell. Kimberly helped pull him off the floor. Harry and Elsie tried to help Gunther from the floor but they could not lift him. Once Russell was standing, Kimberly helped them lift the Swiss man. Gunther had more of a hard time moving. He had been locked up and repeatedly beaten for days. His body was shutting down from the lack of water and food. The interrogators deemed him an expendable catch: someone to abuse, and discard once dead. They climbed into the back of the jeep and Elsie put blankets over them.

Elsie drove the large suburban vehicle to their compound on the outskirts of Lubumbashi. They arrived slightly before nightfall. To the new arrivals, Elsie seemed the perfect host and painstakingly cleaned up the battered men. Kimberly took extra care to nurse Russell who did not mind a massage on his beaten back. After some rest, Russell found Harry sitting by the fireplace.

"How long have you been here?" Russell inquired.

"This place or the Congo?"

"Both."

"We've been in this place for about six years. Back and forth, we have been in the Congo for nearly thirty years." Harry said. For the next hour, he explained the cat and mouse game played with the former Soviets in Congo affairs. Harry first came to the Congo in the early 1960s as an agricultural engineer for the State Department. Later he came back to the Congo when he joined the agency in 1965.

"I understand the Nazis immigrated to the Congo."

"A few German scientists did. Don't know if they were hard core Nazis or not. But what I do know is some Belgian government officials helped the Germans come to the Congo."

"Why?"

"Germany had a top secret mission to build a hydrogen bomb. Once the Allies started to bomb the hard water plants in Belgium, the Nazis needed to smuggle loyal socialist scientists out. The Germans had control of Belgium and there were enough Belgians in government positions willing to help their occupiers."

"Are they here still?"

"Don't know if any of them are still alive. When I was here in the mid-60s, we received word the Russians kidnapped a German scientist in Katanga. He was working in the uranium mines for the Belgian company."

"Did Mobutu know about the Nazi scientists?" Russell asked.

"At an embassy cocktail party, I asked Mobutu and like usual he denied any knowledge." Harry paused. "But you have to remember Colonel Joe Mobutu was someone who could not be trusted."

"I heard Mobutu killed as many Congolese as Hitler killed in concentration camps."

"He was on par." Harry stated in a cold tone.

"Why didn't we take him out?"

"You have to remember the Cold War." Harry said as he folded his hands together like a Buddhist monk. "Our involvement was guided by controlling the growing communist Soviet red peril that flowed all over Africa. The Congo became the battleground in the early 1960s."

"The Red Peril?" Russell referred to the Soviets.

"It seems like a far off story, but it was real. Hardcore KGB agents came in force. The Congo was put into a tug and war match between the US and the Soviet Union." Harry contemplated for a moment. After nearly a minute of silent reflection, he continued. "What I will tell you has been declassified now." Russell nodded. Russell possessed a Top Secret government security clearance, but even he knew instinctively that the highest state secrets were solely on a need to know basis. "Khrushchev found that all roads in Africa do indeed lead to the Congo. He wanted to exploit the vast amount of rare earth minerals needed for Soviet missiles." Russell knew the story well. He read the detailed reports. In the early 1960s, European colonial powers such as Belgium, Portugal, France, and even Great Britain lost control. Pan Africanism, the belief in post-colonial sovereignty, took shape. Locals sought freedom from centuries of colonial rule. Patrice Lumumba became the first Prime Minister of the Congo. Khrushchev believed African revolutionaries such as Lumumba could be trained in the Lenin doctrine and the Congo was the perfect place to test. President Eisenhower feared the Congo and all of its mineral wealth was headed for communism. The Director of the CIA under Eisenhower was Allan Dulles and he took direct measures to get rid of Lumumba. Lumumba was ousted from power with the help of his old friend Colonel Mobutu and arrested. Three days before JFK was inaugurated, Lumumba was murdered by three Belgian officers.

"What happened when Lumumba disappeared?" Russell asked.

"From what I was told by my predecessor, the Katanga province exploded in violence. There were major protests," Harry said. "No one worked in the mines. Riots were everywhere."

"What did America do?"

"Nothing. No one did anything. The riots continued. The real spark for intervention came when ten white women were raped and killed in the streets of Elizabethville." Russell knew that Lubumbashi replaced the arcane Queen's name as the largest city in Katanga Province. "Belgian paratroopers landed two days later and started shooting."

"Who were they after?"

"Didn't matter. They shot anyone in the streets. They killed over two thousand locals."

"Were they charged with war crimes?"

"No." Harry replied and added. "The Belgian troops even shot up schools and killed children."

"And then came Mobutu?"

"At the time, no one knew Mobutu would turn evil. He had us all fooled."

"You knew him?"

"Too well. I have visited the jungle retreat. Mobutu sure knew how to party. We would be up all night. The parties got crazy sometimes. I remember Mobutu started shooting a shotgun into the pool when he was drunk. Everyone ran for cover. The unfortunate swimmers were not so lucky. That was the last time I went to one of his parties."

"How many people do you think he murdered?"

"Hard to tell." Harry thought about it for a moment. "Probably quarter of a million."

The vehicle headlights caught Harry's attention and he looked out the window. The arrival of Francesca, Kitson, and Tshambe broke up the conversation. They flew with Jabes in a UN helicopter from Kinshasa. Jabes remained behind to finish maintenance on the helicopter and would catch a ride later. The sight of Russell's bruised face caught Kitson and Francesca by surprise. Russell brought them current on his kidnapping. Kimberly sat close to Russell and rubbed his bruised arm. Francesca looked at her competition for Russell's love and wanted to put a bullet in her head. She thought of the Desert Eagle pistol and how quickly she could blow the archaeologists head apart. She thought about the explosive power a fifty caliber bullet would cause.

Russell's debrief was interrupted by the dinner chime. Elsie was pleased to have Russell, Kimberly, Francesca, and Kitson for dinner. Everyone was impressed by the food prepared before them. The retired CIA agents had not forgotten their touch hosting a dinner party. Across the table were local flowers. Russell made idle conversation with his hosts trying to avoid eye contact with Francesca on the other side of the table and Kimberly who sat next to him. He definitely needed to watch Francesca's emotions. Russell learned from their past romantic interlude that their entire relationship was based on lies.

"You went out of your way to make this," Kitson said as he waved his arms across the table. The British soldier passed around several gin and tonics he poured. Francesca refused one.

"Not at all," replied Elsie, the cute little grandmother. Her doting husband sat at the end of the table. Harry provided a toast to the group.

"Can you tell me about Mobutu?" Kitson turned to Harry.

"I came to the Congo on an African study program when I first joined the agency. Mobutu was not even a soldier when I first met him and when I came back two years later, he was a Colonel and in charge of the army."

"When I served in Northern Rhodesia, we thought he might send the Congo army to fight alongside the rebels. In the end, Ian Smith signed a peace treaty and Mugabe came to power." Kitson said. He referred to Robert Mugabe who was elected after the international pressure on Ian Smith to transition power to a majority black rule. A majority of white Rhodesians disagreed with the decision and a civil war flamed for five years. In 1980, Mugabe finally took control as the elected president and that was the last fair election in the renamed country of Zimbabwe. Many of the white Rhodesians fled to South Africa and other parts of the Africa.

"I don't know who was worse Mobutu or Mugabe." Harry said. "But I can tell you, they both filled graves of those who disagreed with them."

"And Mugabe is still filling graves." Kitson kept pace with what happened within Zimbabwe from his old contacts. The stories of government abuse on locals were horrific and unbelievable to many, but not Kitson. He knew Mugabe was a criminally insane butcher.

"Did Mobutu have a hand in the assassination?" Russell wanted to know more and could sense he was bringing up bad memories as Harry squirmed in his chair.

"At the time, we didn't think he had a hand in Lumumba's assassination. We now know Mobutu and three Belgian officers were present when one of the Belgian officers shot Lumumba. They decapitated him and spread his body to several secret graves to prevent his death from became a martyr."

"Did the agency know it was going to happen?" Russell asked.

"Washington wanted Lumumba dead. Eisenhower and Dulles thought he went rogue as he got military support from the Kremlin."

Russell recalled his background declassified CIA cables from then Director of the CIA Alan Dulles to Chief of Station Larry Devlin."

"When did anyone know Lumumba was dead?"

"Devlin told me that he did not hear anything for weeks. There was speculation from many foreigners that the CIA was involved, but Devlin refused to carry out a poison plot on Lumumba and walked a fine line with Langley. I remember Devlin confided in me that he would be kicked out of the agency, if Dulles had his way."

"I read a report at the embassy that Devlin did not get along with Director Dulles." Russell added. "Was that true?"

"Very few of the old OSS operatives got along with Dulles." Harry offered. "He was more of a Washington bureaucrat than an operative."

After dinner, the guests moved onto the back deck for drinks. Kitson already poured three fingers of brandy for himself and Russell. The vibrant sounds of African nightfall radiated throughout the compound. Monkeys screamed aloud in mating calls. Insects of all types could be heard. Russell wondered about their security posture in this remote compound. Harry allowed several local families to reside on the sprawling twenty acre site that possessed a complete perimeter fence.

Harry looked at the Mossad agent and asked, "What's Israel's interest in Africa?"

"Israel has many enemies." Francesca raised her voice. "Terrorists that want to kill us hide in Africa. We will go after them wherever they are." Francesca looked at everyone at the table.

"But why are you here?" Harry asked. "Why now?"

"We traded weapon technology with South Africa and we seem to have sold them an atomic bomb in the 1970s."

"Is that the one Mobutu purchased?"

"Indeed it is the same."

"That bastard used to parade around at his wild parities riding it. He would be dressed up in a cowboy outfit shooting blank cap guns. At first, I thought it was not real. I thought no one if their right mind would parade around and sit on a real atomic bomb."

"From everything I have heard or read Mobutu was a madman." Kitson stated. "My own country did not do enough to take him out."

Inside the kitchen, Kimberly helped Elise clean up the dirty dishes. "You have a wonderful home." Kimberly said.

"Thank you dear."

"I really love your family photos. Your grandkids are so cute."

"Indeed they are. We are very fortunate to have such a lovely family." None of the guests knew the truth that the family pictures were a cover story.

In the middle of the night, a dog barked and was quickly silenced, but Russell heard its last whimper as the bullet from a silencer pistol pierced its side. "Kimberly," Russell said softly. "Kimberly, wake up." Russell slid the blind open and saw a figure move in the night. A few seconds later and to the right about fifty feet, something else moved. Russell did not need anything else to know that they were under attack. He placed his hand over Kimberly's mouth and told her to keep quiet. Russell heard a creek on a floor board in the hallway. He almost opened fire. His mind raced. How could they be in the house that fast? He jarred the door open slightly and saw Francesca dressed in strapless negligee carrying her super powered Desert Eagle fifty caliber pistol. In her small hands, it looked like a howitzer cannon. Russell connected eyes with her quickly as she lifted the pistol towards his head. She removed her finger from the trigger and lowered her pistol. She nodded to go straight and Russell followed. Russell pointed to Kimberly and motioned for her to remain still.

"They're professionals." An older man's voice spoke. Russell looked towards the dining room and saw Harry with night vision goggles attached to his head. He had a shotgun in one arm and an Uzi sub-machinegun in the other.

Chapter 17

Within a moment, automatic weapons fire erupted and shredded the building. Russell stayed close to the floor. The scene was chaotic. Window glass exploded over Russell's head as he crawled towards Harry. The automatic fire ripped into the wood exterior. When Harry first moved into the house, he reinforced the interior walls with ballistic sheets to stop small caliber rounds, something fired from infamous and abundantly available AK47. Harry kept his head low and prayed that they did not have anything more powerful. However, his prayers went unanswered as a RPG rocket ripped into the kitchen wall. The explosive force blew a football size hole into the wall.

"They're going after the gas tanks." Harry shouted. The deafening sound of the explosion punctured his ear drums and made him shout louder as he could not hear himself speak. Russell knew that if they hit any of the propane gas tanks, the entire place would blow.

"Open fire!" Russell yelled as he took the safety off of the legendary fifty caliber Thompson machinegun. Russell had eyed the legendary piece that hung on the library wall and relished the idea of unloading a magazine on full automatic. Russell moved into the open where a window once was and blasted across the area in a zigzag motion. Whoever was out there now knew that those in the house had some serious firepower behind them. Another RPG rocket erupted near the kitchen wall. Russell spotted the shooter behind a tree as he fired and ripped twenty rounds into him. He saw the man's body bounce as the impact nearly lifted him off the ground.

Shrapnel from the RPG rocket rained into the house and several fragments penetrated Harry's leg. He tried to roll over but could not. Notwithstanding he had a bad hip. Small pieces of molten hot metal impacted his legs. One of the pieces shattered his thigh bone. Harry was fortunate. Another half inch higher would have punctured his femoral artery and ended his life. His pants were soaked and he thought for a moment that he actually pissed his pants, something he was prone to do in older age when he could not hustle fast enough to the bathroom. Harry gasped and raised his hand. "Elsie," he repeated himself, "Elsie."

Elise did not hear Harry's screams over the gun fire. However, she observed something was wrong. In a quick motion, she pivoted on the floor in front of the blown out bank of windows and slithered across the carpet. She felt the wetness in the carpet and realized she touched a blood spot. She rolled Harry over and saw the wound. Harry gasped for air. Pain shot through his entire body. Elsie applied pressure with her right hand and all of her weight on the wound. With her loose hand she undid her belt and slid it over the highest part of his thigh, above the near fatal wound. She attempted to tighten the belt; however, blood skyrocketed and splattered her face. She instinctively knew he would bleed out if she did not secure a tourniquet. She pulled the belt as tight with all the strength her sixty-three year old arms mustered.

Russell jumped out of the open window with the fifty caliber machinegun and three fully loaded magazines. He saw two darkened figures move towards the rear of the house. Russell concluded that the intruders were going after the two natural gas canisters located behind the kitchen. There were no citywide natural gas connections in the entire area and the only means to cook and heat water was by natural gas. The two canisters of highly pressurized gas rested on a cement pad. Russell knew the explosion would kill everybody in the house. As Russell jumped over a small fence, he rolled onto the ground. The attacker holding the RPG rocket launcher turned around as he heard the thud. Russell blasted him with a volley of shells. The man wore all black to include a mask that concealed his face. The fifty caliber rounds ripped the intruder's mid-section open. Russell tossed the RPG rocket launcher into the pool. The splash signaled his general location. A flurry of shots penetrated the bushes where he just left. A figure moved along his right side, and Russell was about to open fire until he recognized the half-naked man.

"Just me, chap." Kitson said, "I got two by the barn."

"There's one more over there by the pool." Russell replied.

"You get him and I will sweep back around by the barn. We shouldn't stay in the open long."

"Watch out for fire from the house." Russell said.

Sporadic fire came and went from the house. Tshambe picked up an AK47 and shot randomly. Russell thought how much of a horrible shot he was and made a mental note to teach him firing discipline. Elsie was taking care of Harry. The only other shooter Russell did not hear from was Francesca. Russell did not see Francesca from the roof top position she crawled up onto. Her black negligee fluttered in the breeze as he observed the attackers from behind the brick chimney. The starlight scope on her sniper rifle illuminated the shadows. Bright muzzle flashes bounced across the nighttime sky. She centered the cross hairs on the target which peered out from the barn. She saw the half-naked Kitson move toward him and witnessed the man raise his weapon. The dull thud of the silenced round ejecting from the sniper rifle raised Kitson's senses. He dropped to the ground and heard the man moan as Francesca shot him in the chest. Kitson crawled forward and on top of the attacker. He whispered into the man's ear and tried to get a name out of him, but the man's blood gurgled to the top of his mouth as he died. Francesca shifted her starlight scope to the pool area.

As Russell walked softly on the patio bricks, he watched out for the large snails, which came out at night. The slowly crawling night creatures had gargantuan shells, some the size of baseballs. If he stepped on one his position would be compromised, but it also gave him an opportunity as he listened. The first crack could have been the wind blowing in the bushes. The second and third cracks gave him a potential position ten feet away. He pulled his nine inch serrated blade knife from its sheath and slowly placed the machinegun on the patio bricks. With cougar like reflexes, he hurled his body at the man and closed the distance within several seconds. The attacker had only enough time to turn around. In his right hand was a grenade. The force of the thrust from Russell's knife into his chest made him drop the grenade on the ground. Russell dove into the pool as it exploded. The shock of the blast hurled the man's corpse into the pool. Russell fought to get away from the smoldering body and out of the water. The grenade explosion and splash caused the remaining attacker to hone in on Russell's position. As he exited the water, Russell did not see the man come within ten feet of him. Francesca knew she had one shot and placed the cross hairs in the middle of the man's head. Russell heard a dull thud as a high powered sniper round blew off half the man's face. Russell turned to see the attacker fall and knew Francesca had saved his life once again.

Inside the house, Tshambe tried to keep Kimberly still, but she struggled with him to get away. He repeated several times. "Stay still" Still she wanted to run. She had no survival training and Kimberly became more hysterical with the sound of gunfire. She screamed and violently twisted her arms. Tshambe caught an elbow to the nose that forced him to loosen his grasp. As she stood to run, a ricochet bullet clipped the top of her shoulder and sent her to the floor in pain. Tshambe crawled to her and pinned her down again. He covered her mouth. She bit hard into his hand, yet he kept it in place.

"You need to get me out of here." Kimberly paused and screamed. "Now!" Tshambe put his hand back over her mouth to keep her quiet. She struggled more. "I need a doctor," Kimberly yelled.

"Let me see your wound." Russell crawled along the hallway floor. He shined a pen light onto her shoulder. The ricocheted bullet fragment struck her clavicle bone. Since it did not have the full force power of a straight bullet, it did not exit and was lodged inside the meaty portion of her shoulder. "Hang on." Russell said. "I can get it out, but we need to wait until this is over." Russell crawled toward the rear of the house.

"Don't leave me...You bastard...Don't you dare leave me." Everyone in the house heard her screams and fit of rage.

"What's wrong with Miss Prissy?" asked Francesca.

"She took a ricochet in the shoulder." Russell replied.

"That's it?" Francesca asked. "I thought she might have had her leg blown off." Francesca added. "What a wimp."

"Not everyone's a trained killer like you."

"True." Francesca paused. "Wait one." She lined up the sights and fired. "Got you, you bastard." The final intruder dropped dead. "Good guys seven; bad guys zero," she piped.

Tshambe patched up the ricochet that stung Kimberly's shoulder. She was an unwilling participant, and he pinned her down. Tshambe poured the twenty-five year old Scotch whiskey over top of the wound and wrapped it tightly. He allowed Kimberly to have the bottle and she gulped the remaining contents in several deep swigs. Tshambe found Russell crouched behind the overturned desk near the door that was blown open and into pieces.

Tshambe pointed in the direction of the barn. "There's one dead guy there." He pointed towards the pool. "There is another one there." He paused. "He's all burned up and wet too. He had this knife sticking out of his chest."

"Yeah, it's mine." Russell took back the knife and placed it in the hip holster. "Where did you put her?"

"The girl?" Tshambe asked. Russell nodded and Tshambe pointed upstairs. "She up there. She not happy with me so I come downstairs." Russell looked at him with sympathy. "I had to take the bullet out of her. She wanted a hospital but I tell her again and again that she is in the bush and there are none."

"Can you take her to the hospital?" Russell inquired.

"And tell them what?" Tshambe asked pointedly. "Do you think I can walk up to the local hospital and drop off a white woman and say she was shot? The police would lock me up, and more than likely beat me into a confession that I shot her. Justice does not happen in the Congo like it does in your America."

"Good point." Russell never thought of the consequences in case they ran into heavy resistance. He faced a death trap, a suicide mission to track down illegal diamonds, a secret uranium mine, and a loose nuke. "I can take her to the UN check point at the airport and see if there are any medical personnel there."

Russell went upstairs to check on Kimberly. As he stepped into the bathroom, he saw blood all over the tub. She rested on her bottom with her back against the wall. Her right arm was in a sling. Tshambe cleaned up the blood the best he could. Her ripped blue nightgown shirt was soaked deep red from the blood.

"How much have you had?" Russell looked at the liquor bottle. He paused for a moment and added, "You'll be alright."

"There you are." She blabbered as Russell attempted to get her on her feet. "Where have you been? I needed you and you were nowhere to be found." She made a big circular motion. She looked at Tshambe and whispered loudly as if telling a secret. "You know we had sex and now he does not want anything to do with me." She saw Francesca walk down the hallway. "It's because of that bitch," Kimberly said. "You should love me. I'm pretty, aren't I?"

"Yes, Kimberly you are very pretty."

"Don't patronize me," Kimberly said as she paused for a second as they placed her on bed. "You bastard, you don't love me." She had a sudden sense of rationalism. "You took advantage of me. That's right; you took advantage of a poor naïve girl."

"Kimberly, you are not a naïve girl." Russell sensed she was intoxicated, which he believed was the best course of action at that time.

"Sure that's easy for you to say." Kimberly replied in a sarcastic tone. "Mister Indiana Jones swinging in on his rope to save the day." Russell thought to himself how the heck he got himself into this situation. He liked her and most certainly was not in love with her. He knew better than to get romantically involved on a mission. He was a fool and now had to pay the price. Russell wished it were simpler. He wished it were easier.

Russell looked into Kimberly's eyes and said, "I'm truly sorry." She cried, sobbed, and incoherently said something. Russell told her everything was going to be alright. She passed out within seconds.

Harry grimaced but did not scream. He had endured pain many times in his life, shot twice by the Viet Cong, interrogated by the KGB, and roughed up by the East Berlin secret police. Harry found himself shot up in a shitty little town in southern Congo whereby he should have been relaxing in retirement on some beach in a Florida retirement community. However, Harry vowed to right a wrong he committed in the Congo some thirty years prior. Harry grasped Elsie's hand.

"We need to get you to the UN hospital." Russell said as he looked at the wound.

"No, I don't trust those bastards." Harry clenched his teeth tight. Russell knew whiskey was not going to help curtail his pain level. He continued, "There is a local witch doctor that can actually take care of gunshots. I know him. He's reliable."

"What are we waiting for?" Russell helped Tshambe carry Harry outside in a makeshift stretcher. Jabes walked behind them with the passed out and mildly wounded Kimberly.

Meanwhile back in Kinshasa at the Intercontinental Hotel bar, Galpin passed the note to the Iranian undercover agent. The man looked at the note, thought about the translation to Arabic. Seconds later he burned the note. Others in the hotel bar did not think anything of the man's action as the fire ignited the paper. Secrets were common in Kinshasa. Many agreements were made in this shadowy bar.

"Make sure it will work." Galpin said.

"The electronics are probably corroded." The Iranian professed.

"But it will work?"

"It should." The Iranian was an expert in atomic weapon technology, trained in France.

"How?"

"The fission reaction is based on...," He stopped as the waiter passed by to check on their drinks. Dietger waved him off. Galpin motioned to Krause who pushed the local barkeep away from the corner table. "The fission reaction is based on the same principles regardless of weapon type. Once the protons are brought into the isotope, the reaction will initiate and become uncontrollable."

"Will it explode in the air?" Galpin was concerned about his exit strategy. He was not about to go on a suicide mission. He wanted to make sure he would be able to get out of the aircraft.

"The trigger switch will be crucial and that is why I need to look at it; the sooner, the better."

In the open Kinshasa streets, Schultz pushed through the crowd of beggars. Pain and anguish were cemented in the faces of many Congolese. Uncertainty after Mobutu's 2007 death led many to reach back farther in their history. The Lumumba name gave them hope. In the early 1960s, Patrice Lumumba emerged as the force against colonial rule as a voice of defiance. In his inauguration speech and in front of the Belgian King, Patrice Lumumba eloquently lectured the Belgians that the Congo was not open for business. Patrice Lumumba became a liability to the immense fortunes being made in Katanga Province, southern Congo. Katanga was the most fertile ground in the world for rare earth elements. Belgian, American, and French companies had a lot at stake. What was more perplexing to all parties was the viral hatred between the Americans and the Soviets. Michal Khrushchev needed favorable trade negotiations in the Congo for cobalt and tritium, rare minerals needed for soviet missile development. Patrice became expendable. By his own right, he made himself a liability. Repeatedly, the new Prime Minister told the Belgians that all of the brutality associated with their colonial rule would not be allowed. The new Congo government would take possession of Belgian owned mining companies in the mineral rich Katanga Province. Patrice Lumumba signed his death sentence. As the senior CIA officer in the Congo, Schultz knew the history all too well.

The Al Qaeda terrorist watched the American CIA officer assigned to the embassy as he walked in the Kinshasa streets. Kamal had explicit orders from senior Al Qaeda leaders that he should not kill any Americans in the Congo. Any assassination or terrorist attack would draw unwanted attention. Kamal disembarked on his hunt for the old atomic bomb. He was going to use every means possible to find the weapon of mass destruction. Kamal wanted the atomic bomb. His master Bin Laden lived isolated in Pakistan and the world believed the Al Qaeda professed caliphate was a joke. Kamal planned to smuggle the weapon out of the Congo on a riverboat. He devised a plan to outsmart any who would look for him. Kamal's plan involved going deeper into the Congo towards Uganda vice using the open ocean to transport the atomic bomb to Somalia. Two years ago, Kamal established a base camp along the Uganda and Sudanese border. The area was no man's land, a heavily mountain area with few villages. Kamal would get the weapon to his secret camp. From there he would drive the bomb through the Sudan desert to the Red Sea. Kamal had a ship at his ready to transport the bomb off the coast of Israel. He would use the infidel's own weapon against themselves. Kamal would ensure the caliphate succeeded and Israel would be destroyed.

Kamal walked faster into the crowd of beggars. His broken arm hurt tremendously, yet he refused to inject drugs into his body. He needed to remain alert. Any mistake would cost the mission. Inside his right sleeve, he held a syringe with a knock out drug concoction he developed. The drug would make the victim vomit at first and then go into a seizure. As the victim fell to the ground, Kamal would offer assistance as a physician and claim that he would transport the patient to the hospital. Of course, the patient would never make it to the hospital. Kamal had used his concoction four times and each time he got better and better with the drug combinations. He perfected his debilitating drug. Form injection to convulsions, Kamal calculated ten minutes. He had the perfect weapon.

Schultz sensed something was not right about the man who walked ten feet behind him. The man did not look right. He had a strong Middle Eastern look about him, something of a rarity in the Congo. All foreigners stood out in the throngs of Congolese, regardless if they are neighboring countries. The Congolese had a dark thickness to their skin color, perpetuated by the mix of the Congo River people during the slave trade. Schultz easily spotted his tail and hastened the pace. The man moved awkwardly. His left arm seemed to be in some type of makeshift cast. Schultz made a mental note of all his features. A line of motorcycle riders stood on the street and smoked cigarettes. They were rich by Congolese standards as they made illegal fares from their bikes. The new government had no means to tax them. Schultz waved at a man and jumped on the back of his bike. The man geared the engine and catapulted Schultz on the ride of his life as they zigzagged in and out of traffic. Schultz turned and saw the man who followed him turn away. Perhaps, he was not up for the experience of a lifetime on the back of a motorcycle in the chaotic Kinshasa streets.

CHAPTER 18

At the Hezbollah compound, Dietger Laurent watched the Iranian scientist as he worked on the atomic bomb. The large Belgian man with fattened fingers from his glutton lifestyle knew that he was not equipped to handle such a delicate process. Dietger looked from a distance. The atomic warhead was encapsulated by large pieces of cobalt. The bomb was heavy and not easy to move. Dietger was amazed at this treasured find. He now possessed a hydrogen bomb with a jacket of cobalt metal. The cobalt blanket would capture the escaping fusion neutrons to breed a radioactive isotope that maximizes the fallout hazard from the weapon rather than generating additional explosive force from the fission process. Dietger knew the environmental damage from radioactive fallout would be deadly.

Deep in the Congo bush, Gertz watched from the protection of the armored vehicle. The windows were blackened. No one saw him. Nakor Industries owned Anvil Mining Company, which produced cobalt and tritium in low quantities. Gertz purchased the once thriving mine four years ago and contemplated closing the site; however, he developed a sinister plan. Anvil mine was located outside of the village of Kilwa with a population of nearly two thousand. Kilwa was eighty miles north of Lubumbashi and in the deep forbidden jungle. The mine had an economic stranglehold on the locals. Gertz was not pleased with the recent labor uprisings and wanted to send a message. Kabila Lumumba made several speeches in Kilwa that promoted a pacifist, Gandhi-type pacific resistance. Some of the locals had enough with the deplorable working conditions and low wages as Anvil accumulated massive profits over the decades. Enough was enough and a small band took over the Kilwa police station. The rioters set their sights on Anvil mining headquarters and looted everything. Within hours government troops were flown out by Nakor Industry helicopters. Congolese troops opened fire and killed the looters who remained.

Afterwards, the workers from the Kilwa mine were taken in the middle of the night and blindfolded. None of them knew the location of

154

the new mine and Gertz wanted to keep it that way. The dense Congo jungles prevented them from knowing where they were. Some recognized the large mountain. An old man told the others that the mountain possessed evil spirits. Men who visited the top of the mountain died from sickness. What they did not know about was the radiation seeping from the destroyed German isotope reactor. The massive doses of radiation from the high grade Uranium 238 ignited the dosimeters. The sharp red color on the dosimeter and smear patch forced Gertz to take a hard and deep breathe. Gertz had discovered a potent radiated area that would yield vast sums of wealth.

"How many did we get?" Gertz asked Braum.

"Twenty-two last night." Braum looked at his notepad. He could easily kill, yet he had difficulty remembering the smallest numbers. "That brings the total to one hundred and eighty."

"That's still not enough to run the mine." Gertz looked at the local miners. Many were old men and young women who lost their husbands. "Have them round up the teenage boys tonight. No girls. I don't want this operation turning into brothel."

"You want survivors?"

"A few," Gertz paused and watched an old man be restrained as he shouted to let them free. The local African security guards hired by Nakor beat him with a bat. "Make sure to dump his body in the jungle."

In the office trailer, Gertz reviewed the production reports from the Congo's three legitimate uranium mines. He knew that he could not obtain approval to open a new uranium mine. Initial estimates from potential black market sales showed he would make over eight million dollars selling one container of the rare, high grade Uranium 238. Gertz gambled on his strategy moving away from smuggling diamonds with the discovery of the new uranium mine. Gertz believed that there would always be plenty of rough, untraceable diamonds from West Africa. Any large, bird sized egg rough cut diamonds caught the immediate attention. Gertz was in direct talks with international diamond merchants and kept a close watch on illegal diamond sales. Illicit diamond sales accounted for ten percent of the world's market, yet that equated to several hundred million dollars annually. Gertz paid pennies for black market diamonds that sold for much more, thereby generating substantial wealth. Gertz was not satisfied. He wanted more.

Outside of Lubumbashi, the rest of Katanga Province was primitive. Russell was amazed at how quick life changed for those who lived minutes from the small city. No central power grid existed. Only a few generators dotted the landscape. No phones, no satellite, no radios, no lights; nothing worked. There was no magic power station. There was no advanced solar technology to power up the phones or infrastructure to distribute power. Nothing worked and there was no hope on the horizon to get power. Electricity had a luxury.

In the jungle, locals lived on the same rustic lifestyle as their ancestors. Some modern amenities such as generators and cars arrived into the isolated Congo bush, but for the most part those luxury items belonged to the tribal elders as gifts or bribes from the government. There were no rich locals who resided in the bush. If they had some wealth, someone else wanted it. The only thing that mattered was tribal justice. In the bush, people disappeared. Locals would say the jungle took them, meaning a vigilantly mob took matters into their own hands. The brutal truth of tribal justice was hard to comprehend. Russell had his own thoughts on the horrific nature and kept his opinions to himself.

Tshambe drove the large suburban, a four wheel drive behemoth. Russell grabbed several cans of black spray paint and put large UN signs on the door. In the bush, Russell knew the locals would have more positive impression of the UN's support than in Kinshasa. Few UN personnel ventured deep in the Congo bush. Kimberly and Francesca sat in the back seat next to each other, yet they did not utter a word between them. Jabes was in the far rear of the vehicle that was packed in with gear. The roads were bumpy and his head hit the roof of the vehicle so many times that he put his flight helmet on. For over three hours, the team pushed deeper into the interior. Roads and bridges were washed away. Fortunately, the vehicle had what was called a snorkel on the front hood that extended three feet above the hood. The snorkel was attached to the engine block to allow the vehicle to be driven into deep water without stalling. Prior to departing, Russell inspected the snorkel especially as he knew from his time in West Africa that the vehicle could easily get stuck in a rapidly formed river without a vehicle snorkel. In the African bush, not having a means to escape equated to death. On top of the vehicle, Tshambe latched down eight fifty-five gallon fuel cans. Russell inspected his tight knots as well.

As darkness fell in the wild jungle, Tshambe turned on the headlights and four large spot lights attached to the top of the suburban. Someone crossed the road and stunned Russell. He motioned to Tshambe to slow down. Another figure passed and another. An old man carried a woman who was covered in blood. Tshambe stopped the vehicle. The figures ran away from the search lights. Russell motioned for Tshambe to continue at a slow pace. The road sign pointing to Kilwa has seen better days. The piece of wood barely hung onto a metal post as it pointed down a dirt road. Across the street, the bright white sign pointing up a different road for Anvil Mining Corporation was a sharp contrast. The statement underneath the company logo stated, '*Bringing a bright future to the Congo*'.

"Stop," Russell shouted. In the rear of the vehicle, he heard Francesca slam a magazine of ammunition into her weapon. Next he heard her chamber a round in her Desert Eagle pistol. Before Russell could get his fingers around the magazines attached to his chest harness, Francesca was already out the door. Men and women ran past, screamed, and threw their hands in the air. In the darkness, she could see red blood across their clothes and on their black faces. Tshambe and Russell emerged from the vehicle. Kimberly screamed as an old man pressed his face against her window to see inside. Russell turned and pointed his machinegun at the man and he ran off. "Tshambe," Russell directed, "find out what happened here."

After ten minutes, Tshambe returned. The look in his eyes told Russell that something evil happened. Tshambe had managed to find the village elder. He had been shot several times and had lost a lot of blood. The man died soon after. Tshambe appeared frightened and said. "They say government troops came and took many of the boys. They put them in Anvil mining trucks and drove them away." Tshambe pointed down the rough dirt road and continued. "All the men disappeared and now children have been taken." Russell looked at the pain on their faces. Several women saw that is was safe and carried a battered figure. Her lips had been sliced off. Her face was a mask of gauze and tape. Tshambe pointed to her and said, "If anyone talks, the soldiers said that they would come back and slice off everyone's lips."

The brutality of the Kilwa village attack shocked Russell. His senses were awash in an aggravated memory. Iskandariyah erupted over two years ago. His mind thought back to that morning. It was bright and sunny for an early February day. The chillness of the air was lifted by the illuminated desert sun. His armored military vehicle was two hundred meters from ground zero impact at the Iraqi police station. The distance did not shield his vehicle from the explosive force of the car bomb that ripped apart the city center and killed nearly two hundred. Body parts rested at all types of angles. The fresh tangible scent of blood resonated in the midst. Russell staggered about for over an hour in front of the police station not knowing what to do. Partly, he was in shock and had a perforated ear drum from the explosive impact. Kilwa sent him back to his violent memories. Russell punched himself in his right side to get control of his mind.

"We need to get them out of here." Russell said as he looked at the team. "If they know about this massacre, those responsible will be back to make sure there are no witnesses." Tshambe nodded his head in agreement. Russell continued. "We have to take care of them, no one else will." Francesca nodded. Kimberly was in tears and offered several of the children water. Francesca pulled out her medical bag and changed the dressing on the woman's face. Kimberly gasped in horror at the sight of a woman's lipless face. The butchers took her lips and tongue so she would never speak again. Her grotesque features stirred a lot of feelings among the massacre survivors. Russell helped move those near away to let Francesca perform as a doctor. Russell wondered at how effective she was as a doctor and wondered how someone so deadly could be a doctor. Tshambe helped load as many as possible of the injured and survivors into an old school bus. As the morning sun rose, they started their journey. Russell motioned for him to drive and waved for Jabes to follow with the suburban. An hour up the road, Russell spotted a large white cross on the side of the road.

The Portuguese Angels of God cared for locals in the jungle. The hospital ward was clean and children's voices could be heard from the orphanage several hundred feet away. The compound was open, the gates were never closed. The white angels hurried into and out of the hospital ward carrying dead bodies. Their little frames were solid and proud. Russell watched as they walked three hundred yards with the latest corpse to the massive brick incinerator. The stench was overbearing and he pulled back away and gasped for clean air. Smoke billowed from the brickworks. Russell saw the cemetery but realized the epidemic must have been brutally dangerous as the white women skipped digging individual graves. Russell watched several of the nuns closely and followed the elderly nun into the hospital ward. Mosquito nets draped over the beds and concealed the patients. He placed a surgical mask over his mouth. He did not know what the disease was and could not speak the nun's Portuguese. Boils were exposed all over the skin. The Angels of God rushed between the beds with bed pans and sponges to clean the sap drip from the boils. Tshambe stood still at the entrance gate. He would not move forward. Fear even gripped every Tshambe. He heard stories of the disease camps. Places were death gripped like an octopus.

"Death came here." Tshambe said.

"We can't help them." Russell spoke in a dismal tone.

"What do we do with the villagers? We can't leave them here." Tshambe was visibly upset. Russell knew he could not bring them back. The bus carried eight children, six women, three old men and two elder women. The village bus was extremely old and slow.

"We need to move...and fast." Russell blurted. Tshambe jumped behind the steering wheel and turned the bus around. Plumes of black smoke exhausted the tail pipe as the old diesel engine engaged. The bus jettisoned down the one lane dirt road. Overhanging branches ripped into the side of the rusted bus skin. Francesca rested the Uzi sub-machinegun on her lap. Russell laid on the floor in the rear of the bus and pointed the sniper rifle out of the large hole he made. Within two miles, the bus turned onto the major jungle highway, which happened to be just two lanes of somewhat paved asphalt.

The bus stood out, not just because of its loud engine and massive size. The bus stood out because it was the only non-smuggler, non-NGO, non-UN vehicle on the road. Russell knew they would have company and was not surprised when he saw the brake lights on a truck as it passed. The pickup truck driven by GROM thugs sped past them and slammed on the brakes. The vehicle spun around and sped towards them. Russell positioned the scope on the hood. The truck was over two hundred yards away and accelerated fast. Russell fired four bullets into the grill. The hood ripped open. Smoke and black oil plastered the windshield. The truck swerved and rolled over several times across the pavement. Russell knew they had better get off the road, but there was nothing else. Russell's instincts alerted him that more than likely there would be a roadblock up ahead with heavy machineguns that would destroy the bus and everyone inside. Russell knew they had no chance to return fire. A large caliber machinegun could strike them from over two thousand meters before they had any chance to return fire.

"Tshambe, we need to get off the road." Russell said as he pointed towards a path on the right hand side of the road. Tshambe pushed the bus up the path. It was the farthest thing from a road. Deeper and deeper, Tshambe pushed the bus until it stopped on top a large downed tree. The front tires lifted in the air and spun out of control. Tshambe turned the engine off. Russell helped the villagers out of the bus and carried two children as he trained his sniper rifle off his hip towards the front. Francesca followed as she fired her Uzi. Tshambe raced ahead as he saw several thatched huts two hundred yards ahead. Several men came out of the huts with large spears. Russell knew these men were not the typical Congolese he met in the big city. These were real bush men. He slowly approached as Tshambe tried to talk with them and explain why they arrived. Russell could tell Tshambe had difficulty with the dialect. Russell stopped and let the children down. He kept the sniper rifle lowered, yet was ready to blast the bush man if he swung the blade. Two more minutes passed as the remainder of the party arrived. Several of the adults spoke with the bush man and he understood them.

More villagers came out of the other eight bush huts. The small village was probably one of the more remote places in the Congo and Russell thought a perfect place to hide. Russell and Tshambe went back towards the bus. Russell looked at the large downed log, concluded it was put there by the villagers to keep them isolated and protected. The bus was not going anywhere. Tshambe started cutting large branches and leaves to cover the rear of the bus. Russell climbed on top of the bus and placed branches over the metal structure. To the left forty feet away, he heard a large movement. Russell slung the sniper rifle off his back and spotted the enormous hog. With one shot he blasted a baseball size hole in the head. The hog was over four hundred pounds. Tshambe went back to the village to get all of the men. Muscles bulged as they dragged the hog up the path. Several of the men made a tripod made out of logs and pulled the hog in the air. Women meticulously carved out the intestines and caught the bloody pulp in buckets. In the bush, nothing went to waste. The men built a fire inside the large rock pit. In the embers, they rested large pieces of meat on metal grates wrapped in banana leaves. Darkness blanketed the village. Red hot coals from the fire gave warmth. Everyone sat around the fire pit and enjoyed the meat.

Russell found a semi-secluded area. He needed to talk with Schultz and provide him an update. For the first ten minutes, Russell updated him on Mobutu's remote mansion and the remaining villagers who they saved. Schultz turned the conversation back to the latest actions that occurred within Kinshasa.

"We have phone taps on the Minister of Information." Schultz advised. "He sold out to Gertz to smuggle a large amount of uranium."

"Doesn't make sense," Russell quickly replied, "Gertz had been selling diamonds to Tel Aviv. There was a report that linked Gertz with conflict diamonds out of Zimbabwe. Do you really think Gertz is stupid enough to deal in uranium?" Both men knew anyone who dealt uranium on the black market would be branded an international terrorist.

"Gertz is greedy. I would not put anything past him." Schultz said. "There are a lot of uranium buyers here. Between the North Koreans, Chinese, and Iranians, anyone of them could be the buyer."

"Gertz needs to be at the top of our list to take out." Russell said, and he added. "He's the primary financier for these GROM thugs running all over the Congo."

"Concur." Schultz replied. "Also, we need to take out the fat Belgian." Schultz gave Dietger Laurent the code name fat Belgian.

"Don't forget about Rajik. We know he had sold smuggled weapons to the rebels."

"But we still do not know who had financed the insurgency." Schultz shot back at him. He knew that Russell wanted to kill Rajik and his personal vendetta had clouded his judgment at times. Russell became obsessed with taking Rajik out. Russell viewed Hezbollah as a direct threat to the large population of honest Lebanese who operated many of the restaurants in Kinshasa. Rajik threatened the local Lebanese with his drugged up Ashbal orphans. Schultz continued, "If we trace the money trail, we can take out the financier and end the insurgency."

"At the same time, we need to find this bomb." Russell proposed. "Do we know who has the weapon and what they planned to do with it?"

"Langley does not know the target and speculate New York, Tel Aviv, or London."

"Is it Al Qaeda?"

"At this time, it does not look like an Al Qaeda plot;" Schultz added, "however, that could change once we get more information."

"The South African brothers are on top of my list for conspirators." Russell said. Schultz knew that Russell was still very steamed after the two brothers worked him over good. "Those white supremacists are up to no good."

"We got a lot of bad guys here. I requested a spec ops team to help us out." Schultz sent the classified message to Langley and onto the Pentagon behind the Ambassador's back. Schultz viewed the statesman as an impediment to progress when things turned bad. "We should get a SEAL team."

"Is it confirmed?"

"Not yet. However, we have a loose atomic bomb floating around the Congo. We have a long list of potential conspirators. We have a full-fledged insurgency. And we have an extremely incapable UN force. Do the math." Schultz blasted Russell on the phone. He paused for a moment. Both ends of the phone were quiet. Schultz added, "Sorry."

"No worries," Russell responded.

"There are few in America who deem events in Africa a threat."

"We are in a pile of shit. Everywhere we try to dig out, we find more shit." Russell responded. They finished the call. Russell promised to get back to Kinshasa by the end of the week; however, another mission would delay him further.

Russell's head hurt and the last thing he wanted was a confrontation with his former lover. Francesca waited for Russell to finish his call. She watched and waited. As Russell came close to the fire, she pounced like a hungry lioness.

"Do you love her more than me?" Francesca stared at Russell.

"What makes you think that I am in love with either of you?" He half joked yet that did not stop her from swinging at him and connecting with his jaw. Russell landed on the ground.

"Bastard!" Francesca shouted as she held her hand, which was in excruciating pain.

"What was that for?"

"You have no idea what I am putting on the line to be with you. I am an Israeli Mossad agent, trained to kill, trained to manipulate, trained to torture, and definitely trained not to fall in love. You have poisoned me."

"I wouldn't call it that."

"I would." Francesca said point blank.

"You are insane. You were the one who jumped me in a casino's bathroom in Monrovia. You were the one the drugged me to put me out while you escaped out of Liberia." Russell paused for a moment. He tried to calm his temper, but he was unsuccessful. "And what was that note you left. Did you not tell me to stay away and not come find you."

"I did tell you that and here you are, right in the middle of my operation."

"No, you are in the middle of my operation." Russell said.

"So what do we do about her?" Francesca said. She pointed towards her competition.

"Don't even think it." Russell knew what she was capable of and had a quick dreadful thought as to what a sex crazed, love maddened, trained killer would do to a simple archaeologist.

Chapter 19

The Lubumbashi streets bustled with merchants and fresh groceries – a far cry from the capital city of Kinshasa where fear gripped everyone. Many foreigners migrated towards Lubumbashi as the violence raged in Kinshasa. Lubumbashi was originally called Stanleyville, after the great explorer. However, after the murder of the first Congo Prime Minister Patrice Lumumba, the city's name was changed. The mystery around the murder of Patrice Lumumba remained cloudy until a 2006 report by the International Court identified several Belgian Army officers by name as the ones who pulled the trigger, yet the main ring leader remained unknown. What became more complex was the fact that Lumumba's grave was never discovered. Rumors had parts of his skeleton sent to the corners of the African continent as a reminder to all not to question colonial rule.

A distant relative of the first Prime Minister, Kimba Lumumba watched his team of supporters push through the crowds. Hands touched his head and some tried to tear off pieces of cloth. His near death experience and namesake made him a viable Presidential candidate. Kimba pushed his way into the café as throngs waited outside. Harry sat at a corner table waiting for him.

"Thank you for meeting me." Harry stood up with the assistance of a cane. From the attack on his home, he suffered several shrapnel wounds from the RPG rocket. The doctor released him, yet Harry still had significant soreness. Kitson watched from the corner of the room. The standard issue MI6 weapon, Walther PPK pistol, rested on his lap underneath a newspaper. Kitson was extremely worried about more GROM assassins. The total body count from the other night's assault at Harry and Elsie's compound were six dead GROM thugs.

"What does the CIA have that would interest me?" Kimba Lumumba inquired as he sat down across from Harry. Kimba refused to shake the retired CIA agent's hand that was outstretched in a friendship gesture. Harry understood and retrieved it. Harry observed the two large security men as they sat down at the next table. Harry sensed Kimba was fearful as he wore a bullet proof vest.

"I'm retired." Harry said.

"Once CIA, always CIA." Kimba offered.

"Not anymore." Harry paused, looked at the guards, and back to Kimba. "I am hoping for peace."

"Peace is a hard thing to come by in Africa, especially the Congo." Kimba replied and inquired. "What makes you think a foreigner can have any influence in Africa?"

"Because I bring peace, not war."

"You foreigners talk of peace. Look at what all of the colonial holders did to Africa. Look at what the Belgians did to the Congo. Short sleeve, long sleeve." Harry knew the horror stories that were true in Joseph Conrad's famed novel Heart of Darkness. "Everyone comes to the Congo trying to fix the past. Some Congolese want to forget the past." He paused for a moment and leaned across the table. "I do not wish to forget the past. You butchers killed my grandfather."

"Belgian officers killed your grandfather, not America." Harry leaned closer. "Patrice Lumumba did not want support from America and made his bed with the Soviets and Castro."

"America would never help him. You think he wanted the Soviets to have the Congo." Kimba sipped on the coffee that finally arrived. "No, my grandfather Patrice was a patriot, a nationalist. He was the farthest from being a communist." Kimba teared up. "History has shown."

"It was a different time." Harry said. "No one trusted the Soviets and the world was almost plunged into another world war."

"In Africa, we are always at war." Kimba shot back. "I wondered what would have happened if papa Patrice had not been so vocal and open about his ambitious thoughts for the Congo. What if he had just played the Belgian's game and not insulted the Belgian king on our independence day." Harry knew the story well. The rich Belgian King sat and listened to Patrice Lumumba's sharp tongue as he lambasted colonial authority and brutality. Harry was present at the 1960 inauguration event and believed Patrice signed his death warrant.

"Do you really think the Belgians ever wanted to give up power?" Harry said as he leaned close. "The face of the Congo may have left Belgian control, but they surely did not give up economic control."

"Is that why my grandfather was murdered?" Kimba sensed that the retired CIA officer had information that could be valuable.

"Partly," Harry opened more about his time in the Congo. He knew everything he was about to say was against the oath he took at the CIA thirty-five years ago. "There were other factors. Not just the Soviets and Che Guevara, but also the South Africans. Thoughts of Africans freedom and dismantling Apartheid sent shockwaves through white South Africans. For the problem in breakaway Katanga, your grandfather went to the UN; he trusted the international establishment to resolve the conflict peacefully. No one wanted to help him, not America, not France and most certainly not the Belgians. Lumumba turned to the Soviets who were glad to send military advisors and equipment."

"The UN is not a peace organization," Kimba seemed restless as if he was going to speak at the pulpit, "have you seen so much UN come to Africa to wage war, only in Africa could this happen. I used to dream the UN would be a peaceful organization but that is not possible. The UN is the will of Europe and now China to impose its will on third world countries. Americans and Belgians believed Lumumba had allegiance to the Soviets and had him murdered. Our African brothers were once again puppets."

"I'm truly sorry." Harry paused for an extended moment. He reached his hand across the table and placed it onto top of Kimba's arm. "I am truly sorry for all your family's suffering." Harry passed him a folded map. "We need your help." Kimba unfolded the map with several points marked on it. The three circles were several miles apart in an area west of the city. "Here is what we need." In the surveillance photo Harry passed was Dietger Laurent along with several Iranians next to an oblong shaped object. "We need your help to find this location."

Back at the remote village, Francesca awoke and needed a shower. The closest opportunity was the stream. She kept her Desert Eagle pistol strapped to her right thigh. She twisted and turned her way though some brush. Something inside her told her that she was being watched. Out of the corner of her eye she noticed a brown animal move fast. Francesca did not wait to pull her pistol and took off running. She could not run any faster. The lioness chased her in full stride. Francesca turned to see the large cat in pursuit. Something in her told her not to shoot, perhaps a common sisterhood, or the fact both of them were killers. She ran back towards the village. Heart pounded out of her chest. Veins bulged from the exertion. She reached max speed and still the lioness came closer. She turned her head every fifth and tenth step to see the pursuer. In stride, she pulled her pistol and fired into the air to scare the large cat. Russell and the others came out of the huts to see the action. Francesca sprinted right past them. Russell blasted ten rounds into the dirt in front of the lioness that made the animal stop. Russell saved her and the score was even in the Congo.

Russell, Francesca, Kimberly, and Jabes watched silently as Tshambe participated with the other Kilwa survivors in a tribal ceremony to honor the dead villagers. All of them were in dead fear to return home and sought sanctuary with the kind tribe they stumbled across. Russell and the rest of the team bid farewell to them and packed up the suburban for the final leg of their journey. With four hours of driving along a riverbed where there were no roads, Russell examined the GPS coordinates and ordered Tshambe to stop the vehicle. Outside of the suburban, each looked upward at the mammoth mountain that etched to the sky above them. At nearly seven thousand feet, the mountain was larger than the surrounding hills in the range. The mountain was one of the largest in the southern Congo and stood out. Tshambe remained with the vehicle and pulled small bushes to conceal it. Russell did not know if there were any threats, but he did not want to take a chance. There were no airstrips for fifty miles in every direction. The only means to get out was either by vehicle or walking.

The climb up the side of the mountain was an easy feat for Russell as an experienced world class climber. However, the others huffed and took longer. Russell stood on top of the ledge, nearly eight thousand feet above sea level and the jungle floor. He anchored a grappling hook into a rock formation to secure a new rope line. He tossed the rope over the side and it uncoiled three hundred feet down to the rest of the team. For the last few hundred feet, the rock wall was a shear, slippery face and Russell made the decision to go it on his own. From his new vantage point, he could see at least fifty miles in either direction. Nothing below the jungle canopy could be seen. The painted green landscape looked daunting. Jabes was the final climber arriving thirty minutes afterwards.

The cave entrance was not hard to find from the GPS coordinates Kimberly provided. Her boss made several sketches of the mountainous terrain, but it was the exact coordinates that helped them. Not much other information was left about the cave, just the coordinates. Russell pulled his gear up on a tow line to the ledge. He looked around and noticed the four life sized gorilla statuses covered in vines. Natural decay from three hundred years chipped away at the solid rock gorillas. Russell hacked away at the vines with his machete and made a two foot opening, large enough to crawl into. A stone walkway emerged on the other side. Eight foot square plates connected together making a pronounced entrance. Ahead, he saw the remnants of a recent camp site torn apart. Tents were shredded to pieces and strewn about the area. Debris was littered everywhere and resembled the aftermath of a massive tornado. Russell picked up a scrap of paper and noticed the Smithsonian seal. Out of the corner of his eye, he observed a rapid movement in the trees forty feet away. Russell pointed his weapon and was ready to fire. A large gorilla snarled and passed deeper into the trees. Russell held his fire. Kimberly ran to the middle of the camp and fell to her knees crying. Her sounds masked the gorilla's movement. The rest of the team pointed weapons into the bushes as she cried for several minutes.

After several turns through a maze of stone walls made from gigantic rocks, Russell led the team into the final opening. He felt that he was being watched. Another gorilla ran past thirty feet in front of the formation. He kept his weapon at the ready and walked carefully over the ancient walkway. An eight foot poisonous black mamba snake slithered over a fallen wall. From his time in West Africa, Russell knew the black mamba was very territorial and raised his right hand to signal the team to remain still. The snake slithered on. After the deadly creature moved twenty feet from them, he signaled to the team to move forward. He turned as he heard a silencer pop. Francesca blew the head off of the snake. Russell gave her a disapproving look and Francesca shrugged.

Russell found a man-sized cut out hacked into a wall of vines. The cave face was small and it opened up into a significant sized space that Russell believed to be manmade. Russell pointed the light deeper into an opening that appeared to be a mine shaft. The tunnel into the mine shaft was shored up with large timbers. At the end was a solid metal door, at least eight inches thick. Russell could see patches of lead were soldered over top of the metal. As he scraped away the dust, Russell saw the fresh hand prints in the dirt. He observed one of the most horrific symbols every devised by man – the swastika. Kimberly now knew what the symbol on the sketch of paper that her dying boss provided.

It took every bit of muscle he had to move the hinge that sealed the door in place. The marks and scrapes against the metal looked recent. He surmised that it must have been the Smithsonian archeologist team's work to get into the mine. He pushed the door slightly open and injected a straight rod which he connected together. After a dozen pushes, he extended the rod ten feet into the darkness. As Russell flipped the switch on the detector, the needle went berserk and signaled a heavy, fatal dose of radiation present. The nuclear biological suits were light. New technology enhanced the materiel's content and durability. The suits had built in radiation meters and communications. Jabes was borrowed them from an International Atomic Energy Commission (IAEC) team visiting the Congo to check on illegal uranium shipments. The IAEC team regularly wore the suits as the IAEC team inspected suspicious containers in Kinshasa's port.

"Can you hear me?" Russell asked the others. Everyone nodded. "Once we go through the door there is no going back. If you do not feel comfortable, say so now and you can stay back."

"No, I'm ok. It just takes getting used to, kind of reminds me of scuba diving." Kimberly said.

"It's close to a deep ocean suit." Francesca replied sarcastically.

Inside the mine shaft, old mechanical gears were rusted. The large isotope reactor resembled something he saw on a farm to pasteurize milk, except everything was rusted. Farther down the passage they traveled, deeper into the mine shaft. Ahead the passageway stopped, unusually ended. He shined the light on the cave bottom and noticed relatively new mortar. He hit his flashlight against points along the wall. After five strikes, he heard a dull thud. Russell pushed against what appeared to be a seam within the rocks and pushed inward. A small opening emerged. Russell shined the light within and informed the team. "I think it's a kimberlite tube." He was careful not to rip open his suit. He gently pushed his head within and saw what amazed him. The diamonds were gigantic, the size of a man's hand. He pulled several small stones from within and sealed them in a lead box. The story Harry told Russell about former Nazi scientists in the bush must be true. In 1943, a small group of German scientists came to the Congo and set up several labs within the interior as not to be detected by the Americans. The heavy water plants in Belgium had already been destroyed. The German scientists had difficulty developing a uranium based bomb. Large generators were brought in to power the colossal amounts of water required to cool the isotope reactor. A big explosion released large amounts of radiation. Many of the Germans died from radiation exposure, a few survived and eventually made it back to Kinshasa. On their death beds, they talked of great diamonds, the size of a man's hand, the beautiful colors. Russell thought of the historical reference to King Solomon's mine that intrigued many adventure seekers over the years. Russell concluded that the potential find of vast mineral wealth must have enticed the National Smithsonian and Royal British Museums to support the exploration.

Outside the mine shaft, Kimberly sat on the edge of the rock that overlooked everything eight thousand feet below. Inside the jungle, the river waggled back and forth consuming more pristine jungle with each massive rain. Parts of the river were visible. A small camp was built next to one that caught Russell's attention. Kimberly pointed to the camp at the base of the mountain, which had a lot of activity with a new convoy of trucks.

"Will they find this place?" Kimberly asked.

"Not sure who they are." Russell replied.

"Will they find us?" Kimberly was more direct. There was fear in her voice.

"We should be fine. They're a thousand meters below. We just need to watch out for any fires or lights."

"It would have been nice for those trucks to be used for aid instead of smuggling whatever they are up to."

"Moving food and medicine does not pay well."

Russell called Schultz on his satellite radio and received an intelligence update that Gertz had discovered a new uranium mine somewhere near Russell's position. Russell advised of the camp he observed below and they both concluded that must be the location. Russell provided the reading updates on the uranium exposure and the diamonds from the Kimberlite tube that reached deep into the Earth's crust. They talked at length and determined the best thing to do was destroy everything – the entire mountain if possible.

The sun rested in the sky and revealed the most beautiful sparkles of last light across the Congo's wilderness. The scene and view were beyond breathtaking, yet Russell could not take in the sight as he planned a strike. Russell climbed over the top of the mountain above the new uranium mine and set two objects in place. The first was a long range motion detector with thermal monitoring in case the GROM sent out a search patrol. The other device was placed twenty feet away inside of a rock crevice. It was a digital tracking unidirectional laser that linked into two others Russell emplaced for a high level triangulation of the strike site. The signals could be tracked up to twenty thousand feet for accurate bombs. The lasers had enough power for thirty-two hours.

The strike mission was already approved by the CIA before Russel and his ragtag team had climbed the mountain. The orders were approved by the White House and passed off to the Pentagon. The best bomb type to bomber combination required a B1 Stealth Bomber out of a secret airbase in Qatar that would take almost seventeen hours one way. The bomber's take off time hinged on Russell's confirmation of his team's evacuation plan and timeline. Schultz confirmed that the bomber would circle overhead about thirty thousand feet until the final bombing run that was set for late the next day. The plan would allow for his team to gather more information from the mine shaft on the Nazi plans and get out of the danger zone safely.

171

Russell found the rest of the team huddled inside the cave. The temperature dropped even more in the hour since he had left. Russell sat down and closed his eyes for a moment. Jabes took the first watch and turned it over to Francesca. She held her sniper rifle closely. The five inch silencer attachment extended the barrel, yet she was easily able to handle the additional weight with no interruption to her deadly accuracy. She heard the first sound and thought it was the wind knocking a rock down the cliff. The heavy huff of air from a beast signaled to her that they had company. The first mountain guerilla stood at the edge of the cave opening. She trained the night vision scope on its chest. She did not want to fire and was about to pull the trigger when Russell popped a red flare. The bright light blinded her and she dropped the weapon. She rolled on the ground and clutched her shooting eye. Russell tossed the burning flare at the chimpanzee and ran towards the primitive ape. He pulled a knife out of the holster just in case. The large chimp departed and the group of about ten primates stood still. Russell debated whether to extinguish the flame or toss the flare at them. He did not have the chance to decide as Tshambe ran past him at the group screaming like a madman in a tongue that no one recognized. The animals quickly dispersed. Russell extinguished the flare; turned to the group; and said, "We need to go now."

"What about climbing down at night?" Jabes asked. "You said that it would be dangerous."

"It is but we don't have a choice now. If the GROM goons saw that flare, the mission is doomed." Russell explained.

"But it was safe inside the cave." Kimberly was warm and cozy and did not want to leave.

"You don't realize how far lights can shine in the night jungle.' Russell replied and added. "We cannot risk it."

"Can't you get someone in here to fight them?" Kimberly asked. "We need to protect one of the most important discoveries in eighty years." Kimberly said as she looked at the rest of the team.

"Sorry," Russell said as he tried to be empathetic, a trait he was not very good with. Russell started packing up his gear and checked his harness.

"There's something you are not telling us." Kimberly demanded. "My life is at risk. I need to know what is happening here."

"It's more than you." Russell replied. "It's more than all of us."

"What?" Kimberly raised her voice. "What is so damn important that we need to risk our lives climbing down a mountain at night?" Russell stood up and looked at Kimberly and the others. He knew what the plan would be for a long time, even before he left Kinshasa. The CIA was not going to allow weapons grade uranium on the black market. The decision to bomb a sovereign nation was singed off in an executive order from the White House.

"An air strike is inbound." Russell said coldly.

"You're going to destroy this place?" Kimberly shouted.

"Yes." Russell replied calmly. "I know if we do not leave right now a bomb will land here and destroy everything within a mile radius."

"You don't understand a damn thing." Kimberly shouted.

"We need to get away from here." Russell demanded. "There is an Air Force B1 bomber being scrambled out of Oman. It departed two hours ago and will be here in eight hours."

"What happens if this is King Solomon's mine?"

"It doesn't matter." Russell replied.

"The sculptures, the writings?"

"Can't risk it."

"We can get an entire team here now that we know what made them all sick. We have the map. We know the location. This could be one of the biggest discoveries in history. We can be on the verge of understanding what happened here, erased from history." Kimberly paused deliberately and slowly stated. "We can find out what happened." Kimberly believed firmly in preserving the ancient history, yet she knew Russell was not asking to preserve the archeology site.

"I'm afraid to tell you." Russell paused as he pointed toward the mountain. "Your government called in an air strike. There is nothing you can do. If you stay near here, you will die."

"Then I will die," Kimberly felt betrayed.

"Not on my watch." Russell said as he grabbed the archeologist who started to scream and fight him. Russell tied her hands behind her back as Kimberly kicked him and tied a cloth across her mouth to silence her protests. The others looked on and did not offer to help.

Each team member stepped into the harnesses and Russell tied off the rope between them. Russell went to the rear as the most experienced climber and put Tshambe in front. Francesca followed. Jabes was next in line and then a bound up Kimberly. Russell shortened the distance between them because of the lack of night vision goggles. He held the only set on his head but did not initiate the device just yet. Using the goggles would kill his depth perception. Slowly, they progressed down the mountain. At the slow rate, they lowered Kimberly down the mountain. She wiggled against the ropes, yet Russell would risk a loud protest that could alert the GROM thugs. Ascending down the mountain, they were easy prey. Half way down the mountain, Russell asked Kimberly if she would be silent and she nodded concurrence. Russell cut off her binds and released her. In the darkness, Russell did not see her hand coming, yet he felt the hard slap against his face. The sound echoed across the mountainside. Russell instinctively knew that Kimberly would have no more romantic feelings for him. And Russell was alright with that.

CHAPTER 20

Russell was quiet as they drove away from the mountain - the entire vehicle was quiet. Everyone was exhausted. Russell felt good about his decision to speed up the timetable. Schultz passed on the change of plans to move up the strike. The massive Air Force bomber refueled mid-air and approached the Congo from the Atlantic Ocean. The U.S. did not have time for clearance and went with the strike plan from the water.

Russell pulled out some of the files Schultz gave him and began to read. The report began with the statement that the sustaining influence of the Belgians remained the dominant mechanism for economic growth in the Congo. Lebanese, South Africans, Chinese, Russians, Iranians, and North Koreans funneled into the Congo as visitors compared to the Belgian historical significance. The former colonial power had tremendous difficulty giving up their colony and many in Brussels deemed the new Congo government inept to handle the resource fortunes hidden beneath the earth's crust. Belgian mining engineers traveled throughout the widespread and dense jungle in search of potential rare earth sites. When word arrived in Brussels that a potentially highly lucrative uranium mine emerged, dozens of mining experts flooded into Kinshasa. Satellite images pegged the mountain as an unknown.

A 1948 survey of the mountain was pulled from the files and dusted off. The survey revealed nothing significant other than a stream, which was dredged in 1953 for potential gold deposits. The only mineral in higher than normal doses was tritium. At that time, the correlation between tritium and uranium in rare earth deposits was not known. The report was filed in a remote storage room and never digitized. Over time the information was lost. The satellite image did not show anything out of the ordinary. The deep channel dug by the Nazis was overgrown. The massive metal doors deep in the mountain were undetected by any overhead imagery. Russell read about the historical impact of German influence in Congo. Alfred Krupp was convicted at Nuremberg Military Tribunal as a war criminal for his firm's use of slave labor. In 1999, a new company emerged as ThyssenKrupp and became one of the world's

175

largest steel producers. He shook his head in disbelief as he knew businessmen from the Congo's former colonial master and those from Germany, France, Portugal, Russia, America, Britain, and now the Chinese had their claws in Africa's mineral wealth.

Russell asked Tshambe to stop the vehicle after about an hour of driving. Due to the rough terrain, they had only made five miles distance in the time. A heavy rain had washed out part of the road. Tshambe could not drive along the riverbank and had to find an alternate route that navigated through some very thick bush. The suburban's wheels spun wildly as the eight cylinder engine powered over tall bush grass and small trees. Tshambe did not slow down once he had momentum. He maneuvered along paths that perhaps one time were roads. The spot he stopped at was an open field.

Standing on top of the suburban, Russell thought he heard a jet. He called the Air Force combat operations center on the Iridium satellite phone. He had to remember the ten digit code key to activate the crypto fill in the phone. Once he was in a secure mode, he confirmed the coordinates for the airstrike. Russell sat on the tire bolted to the roof of the vehicle and waited.

"How much longer?" Jabes inquired.

"Should be about twenty minutes out." Russell offered.

"What about the camp?"

"With the laser designators we emplaced our Air Force brothers will put the MOAB on target." Russell said. MOAB stood for Mother of All Bombs and was over seventeen thousand pounds of explosive weight. Russell continued, "The morning strike is best as no one would be at the mine yet. The kidnapped workers from Kilwa should be safe. Hopefully, they can escape once we cave in the mine."

"Probably not." Jabes shot back. "If there is uranium, they will have captives every rock out by hand to get the mine back open."

"At least we can delay them until the UN sends out a team."

"I wouldn't count on the UN." Jabes said, "Too many hands getting payouts." Both knew bribes were running wild in Kinshasa. "We have to take out the guards ourselves."

"Perhaps," Russell paused for a moment to think. "But not our mission right now."

"Then when?"

"Not now." Russell said as he sensed Jabes concern. "We have a more pressing concern. There's a loose nuclear weapon floating around the Congo that we have to track down and destroy."

The B1 Air Force stealth bomber slid into final approach pattern. Russell could not see anything in the darkness and asked Francesca to check with her starlight scope. The bomber was moving too fast and at too high of an altitude for her to pick it up. Russell kept an ear to the Iridium satellite phone as he heard the air controller and pilot talk. He watched the skyline and said, "Bomb release." Jabes and Francesca stared across the sky from top of the vehicle. Kimberly sat inside with Tshambe and she did not say a word. She pouted and cursed Russell to his grave. The explosion ripped into the mountain. A brilliant white light ignited the darkness and shattered the tranquility. On top of the vehicle, they felt the concussion wave from the explosive force. A wave of rocks cascaded down the mountainside. Several of the GROM thugs inside of the portable air conditioned trailer next to the mine were buried alive. In the darkness, Russell was not able to inspect the damage and requested satellite imagery at first light.

At Nakor Industry headquarters, Gertz looked at the shipment manifest. The smuggled uranium was destined for the Iranian port of Bandar Abbas. With several ubiquitous phone calls from an unassuming connection that originated out of the Seychelles, Gertz's put his plan into motion. Gertz knew he played with fire as Dietger Laurent controlled the uranium black market. Gertz was also concerned about the South African brothers Galpin and Krause who had been known to deal in smuggled weapons. Gertz heard that the South Africans worked with the Hezbollah operative named Rajik. The one thing Gertz had on his side was the fact he paid off former KGB operatives with several handfuls of rough untraceable diamonds to get intelligence reports. Gertz knew he had a target on his back. Within twenty minutes, he was outside of Kinshasa's commercial port complex waiting in his limousine.

"Were you followed?"

"No." The Minister of Information looked out the tinted ballistic proof window glass. "I can't be sure. I made a lot of turns."

"Drive." Gertz directed Braum who slapped one of his thugs on the back of the head and spoke in Polish. The driver rapidly accelerated the mammoth armored vehicle.

"The shipment will be four containers."

"I don't feel comfortable with this." The Minister gave the same line that Gertz was used to in the Congo.

"How much more?" Gertz asked

"You don't understand." The Minister looked at Braum. He was intimidated as Braum rested his right hand on a pistol. The Minister heard reports of GROM's murderous ways and did not want to be next. "The UN has sent many more troops to the port. The latest attack near the oil terminal scared them."

"Don't worry about the UN troops." Gertz looked at Braum and nodded. "We'll take care of them." The Minister heard rumors that someone financed the rebels, but he did not know who the culprit was until now.

"When will the containers be in the port?" The Minister asked.

"Should be four to five days." Gertz said as he paid close attention to the Minister's body language. Gertz planned the distance from his new mining operation to the port and added another day as it was Africa where nothing went as planned.

"Okay," The Minister said. "Place the containers on the far end away from the oil terminal."

"We will need local security passes."

"That was not part of the agreement. Those are hard to get approval for...the bureaucracy." The Minister snapped his head towards Braum as he heard him load a bullet into the pistol's chamber. "It will take more money...the bribes...I will need much more."

"Fine." Gertz handed the Minister of Information a thick envelope that contained eighty five thousand U.S. dollars.

A nervous Dietger Laurent fumbled his phone and dropped it on the floor. The fat Belgian had not slept for several nights as the final coordination of his masterful plan came into shape. He was exhausted and fueled up on caffeine. Dietger dialed the number he had for an Iranian sleeper. Only first names were known and Dietger had not known if the names provided were real. Across town in a small building that had more rubble than walls, the Iranian sleeper cell came together. Each had come from other parts of Africa to meet in the Congo. Arash was a nuclear physicist and understood what quality of uranium was needed. Arash was his real name. He refused to use the alias name Tehran pressed upon him to go undercover. Arash stood for hero in Persian folklore and he was extremely proud of his Persian heritage and indeed believed Iran would someday rule the entire Middle East.

"When can you have the trigger device completed?"

"Should be another day." Arash was frustrated by the magnitude of the mathematical calculations and sweated profusely.

"Why so long?" inquired an impatient Dietger. "I am paying you a lot of money."

"It is not my fault. It is the atmospheric conditions here. They are much different than the Arabian Gulf. I must have the calculations correct, or..." Arash stopped.

"I understand." Dietger said and added. "We need to be safe." Dietger attempted to keep the timetable for the plan he imagined five months ago when he first heard of the cobalt atomic bomb. Dietger was exhausted and could not think straight anymore. Anxiety gripped him and tore at his sleep. He was a walking time bomb.

Kamal contacted his superiors in Somalia. He requested more men for the mission. His injury had impacted his ability to blend into the surroundings. A leg cast was easily recognizable. The new recruits would do the work and Kamal would remain to conduct the much needed interrogations. Kamal drove the Kinshasa streets throughout the day and watched all of the foreigners. He hoped to find the Israeli. Kamal had a body in the back of the van that started to smell. Kamal opened the electronic window. The victim had worked near the U.S. Embassy as a security guard and provided several interesting points before he breathed his last mouthful of air. The security guard made an interesting observation about a select few who departed the American Embassy, especially as there were long lines everyday filled with foreigners who tried to gain access. By the time Kamal had broken the man's third finger, he had a detailed description of the Israeli female,

American CIA agents, and the British MI6 agent. The security guard did not know much more, but regardless Kamal wanted the man to feel pain. More importantly, Kamal wanted to prove that even injured he remained a superb interrogator.

The UN security vehicle that followed Kamal had a flashing red light attached on top. A siren echoed and Kamal looked behind him. What Kamal did not know was Schultz published a photo and description of a Middle Eastern man about forty years of age and medium build. Even in the SUV, Kamal stood out. The UN vehicle moved closer behind Kamal and the driver blasted the siren again. Kamal pulled over. The UN vehicle had four men inside. The two from the rear got out and walked up both sides of Kamal's vehicle. With his only good arm, Kamal lifted up a TEC-9 pistol that had been converted to fully automatic. Kamal sprayed rounds at the UN soldiers. Rapidly, Kamal accelerated the van and drove towards the port terminal complex. Kamal would not outrun the UN radios and found himself hunted. He heard a UN helicopter emerge overhead as he entered the port complex. He drove through the gate manned by several Ghanaian soldiers who tried to wave him down. None of them fired at his vehicle.

Kamal drove towards the pier where the getaway boat was moored. Kamal watched the UN helicopter as it passed overhead. In a moment, he weaved in between stacks of containers and slammed on the brakes. Kamal grabbed his interrogation bag filled with all of his specialty tools. He pressed a board between the seat and the gas pedal. The engine squealed loudly. Kamal jammed the gear into drive and watched the van as it launched forward down the pier. The UN helicopter circled back overhead, and the pilot watched the vehicle fly into the Congo River. Kamal contacted his superior in Somalia and informed him that he had been compromised. Kamal climbed into the getaway boat and accelerated it up the Congo River where he would find refuge at a secret terrorist camp near the Ugandan border. Kamal vowed that he get his vengeance and memorized the photo of the American CIA operative named Russell.

The North Korean general arrived in Kinshasa on the morning flight and went directly to the Intercontinental Hotel. He knew the airport executive lounge well as this trip was their third in the past month and tenth in the past two years. With all of the foreign nationals who had arrived in the Congo, especially from Asia, his arrival went mostly unnoticed. His trusted sergeant stood by his side. The sergeant was massive, specially selected and trained as a personal bodyguard. Gertz sat in the hotel lobby alone and saw the two North Koreans as they checked in. Gertz had never met the North Korean General Yal and asked Dietger Laurent for an introduction. Dietger was not surprised as he knew Gertz pedaled illegal diamonds; however no one knew Gertz had moved into illegal uranium shipments. Dietger had establish cover stories for the two North Koreans as Asian businessmen looking for minerals needed in the next generation of smart phones. Gertz knew North Korea wanted uranium and he attempted to contact the remote uranium mountain, yet no one answered.

With the Presidential election only a few weeks away, Kimba Lumumba worried about his chances more than his own life. Kimba refused to hide, as some of his closest advisors recommended. Kimba wanted to change the Congo, just as his grandfather died for trying. Kimba waited patiently for the American CIA officer who Schultz wanted him to make contact with. Russell entered the café and raised his arms as two very large Africans frisked him. Russell heard from Schultz that assassination paranoia had gripped Kimba's security staff. Russell concluded that they had a lot to be concerned about.

"Do you have enough security?" Russell asked.

"I am not afraid." Kimba said.

"Why don't you consider taking our Ambassadors promise?"

"For more protection? Your white guards will stand out."

"The extra guards would be African American military men who are trained in diplomatic protection."

"Does not matter what color they are. My people will know them as foreigners. I will live and die in the Congo. Hopefully I will live long, but it is God's will. Not my advisories." Kimba looked at Russell and continued. "Your country has never protected us from the Belgians brutality. Now we have the Russians, Chinese, Iranians, and Hezbollah in my country. There are too many foreigners in the Congo. They need to go away."

"If you're elected, will you kick them out?"

"My first order of business will be to nationalize the diamond mines. Belgians have rapped our diamonds far too long." Kimba said. Russell gave him a hard stare.

"I would offer that your advisories are very powerful." Russell said. He sensed that Kimba wanted his helped.

"And very rich off the backs of my brothers and sisters." Kimba interrupted.

"They'll do everything possible to kill you."

"Death is something that I have come to grips with. I have made my peace with God." Kimba looked at Russell. He already heard rumors of the exploits this American had fighting against the GROM and Hezbollah. Kimba sensed something about Russell. "Have you made peace with your God?" Russell did not worry about his own future.

"Schultz wanted me to talk with you. From what I have seen in the Congo, life is not worth much." Russell leaned in close. "You have the opportunity to make a difference, more than you may ever imagine. The foreigners will never leave the Congo. There is far too much money on the table and they will not walk away. Even if you build a competent army to oust them, the foreigners will either bribe your own generals to reject your orders or they will bring in mercenaries to annihilate them. You have the unfortunate dilemma of living in a country that possesses more mineral wealth than anywhere else in the world. Mark my words, more foreigners will come."

"Everything comes at a cost." Kimba repeated, "At a cost." Kimba looked down at the floor. Russell's comments helped Kimba put his life and the future of his Congo into a clear perspective. "I will take your offer for security. I need to be elected President for my people...for the future of the Congo."

CHAPTER 21

Russell walked into Harry and Elsie's home and could not believe his eyes. Since the five days he departed, the house was repaired with new windows installed, china replaced, and the rooms were freshly painted. The bodies were discarded in the jungle for the animals to feast upon. Harry had some long time contacts in the local community. When word of the attack spread, locals arrived to help. Harry sat in the study drinking an afternoon gin and tonic. Russell walked in and went right to the bar.

"How was the mission?" Harry inquired.

"Good," Russell replied. "We were able to knock out two birds with one missile shot."

"Was it King Solomon's mine?"

"Hard to tell. There were many drawings in the cave. Kimberly was pissed we blew it up and could not wait to get away from us."

"Where is she?" Harry offered, "Perhaps, I can talk some sense into her."

"She wanted out and took a flight yesterday."

"For the best."

"Guess so." Russell replied and added. "I keep screwing up my love interests."

"Part of the job." The career CIA operative offered and he added. "But Francesca still cares for you." Harry said and Russell nodded, yet he remained silent as he poured a stiff drink. Harry continued, "I think she loves you."

"Perhaps, but her father wants me dead." Russell wanted to change the subject and reflected back to what he observed at the mountain. "What was interesting at the site was how the German scientists built an elaborate bunker complex. They had everything there, labs, operating room, library, decontamination showers."

"I heard rumors over the years of German scientists who came out of the jungle maddened and delusional from exposure to heavy doses of radiation. At first, they never realized the effects of U-238 and radiation isotopes on the body."

"They had a pretty good set up there." Russell said. "I wonder what happened. It looks like it was abandoned."

"Back in my first assignment in the Congo, I interviewed a German scientist. The man claimed a plague came through and wiped the camp out. Without Hitler anymore trying to develop an atomic weapon, most of the scientists dispersed and went back to their lives. A few returned to Germany and subsequently kidnapped by the KGB to work on the Soviet missile program."

"What about the uranium mine?" Russell asked. "Do you thing Gertz will try to get it running again?"

"More than likely. Gertz has always been out for himself. His Polish mercenaries are extremely deadly." Harry pointed to the outdoor patio area where Russell fought hand to hand and killed several GROM thugs. "But they did not expect us to have so much fire power. They'll be back."

"What are your evacuation plans?"

"I'm too damn old and set in my ways to be running away from a fight. I lived a great life and loved my wife. We're fine here."

"What about moving to Kinshasa and the embassy compound?" Russell inquired and he added. "There's plenty of room."

"We're fine." Harry stated sternly. He turned his eyes towards the window and gazed outside. Russell wondered what demons haunted him and why he wanted to remain.

In the kitchen, Elsie and Francesca were cleaning weapons and loading ammunition into a dozen magazines. They both looked upward with blank expressions. Open ammunition boxes lined the counter. Hand grenades were neatly aligned on a serving platter. Over a dozen throwing knives were stuck into a wooden cutting board. Russell did not have to think too hard on what they were up to. Russell did not want to ask them and needed to get out of the house to think. He sat by the pool for an hour. Finally, Russell concluded that he would not let them go alone.

In an upscale area of Lubumbashi, Russell spotted several white men who walked out of an apartment building. Elsie got a tip on the location from a local informant. The men drove a blackened SUV. Elsie followed. Within a minute the vehicle turned around in a sharp directed move. One of the GROM thugs launched his arm out the window and started firing. Rounds impacted the windshield. Elsie ducked her head and turned left down an alleyway. She sped the vehicle down the narrow road. Russell grabbed the hand grip hung from the vehicle's ceiling. Elsie twisted her neck around to look at the vehicle that chased them. Russell wondered if she sprained her neck with the extreme jerk, but she did not complain. Elsie viewed the approaching bridge and calculated the distance to the center of the bridge and the pursuing vehicle's speed.

"Watch him; we'll pull him in closer." Russell did not know what she was thinking. He held the Uzi submachine gun tightly. There was no shot. Bullets ripped through the back side panel of their vehicle close to the gas tank. Elsie slowed more. Bullets riddled across several beat up vehicles that they passed. Elsie slammed on the brakes and twisted the vehicle into a half turn. Russell emptied his weapon into the front windshield of the assault vehicle. Fifteen rounds were exhausted in the eight seconds it took to complete the maneuver. Several of the rounds hit the driver and front passenger. Two goons in the back received slight facial wounds from the shattered glass. They rolled out of the vehicle before it stopped. They both took cover on either side of the road and opened fire before they stopped.

Elsie floored the vehicle and aimed it towards the man on the right. She lowered her head against the steering wheel. Russell saw Elsie slouch and knew she aimed the vehicle right for the goon. They ducked as well. Glass shattered on top of them as the goon emptied his weapon. As he turned to jump out of the way, the right front bumper caught him in the mid-section and sent him aloft fifteen feet in the air. He landed on the pavement. Elsie looked up and turned the vehicle in a spin. She saw the man crawl forward. Without any remorse or forgiveness she accelerated the vehicle as fast as she could in the short distance and ran right over top of the goon. The other goon witnessed the assault and took off running. Elsie turned towards him. He zigzagged while he ran and fired a pistol haphazardly over his shoulder. He ran towards a store and had only twenty feet to safety. This time Elsie kept her head up and was attentive. She sped fast. Russell turned towards Francesca. Both did not say a word and by the look in both of their eyes they knew that they better hold on tight. In the five feet before the store's door, the GROM thug fired his last shot. The vehicle plowed directly into him sending him through the store's glass door. Elsie never touched the brakes and the vehicle sailed into the store at full speed. Several shoppers and the cashiers in the front dodged for cover as the entire front section of the store collapsed from the forceful impact. As the vehicle came to rest in the third aisle, it lifted upwards on top of debris. Russell looked over at Elsie. She still had a death grip on the steering wheel. Her tiny veins bulged as she held the steering wheel. She breathed fast, puffs of air wheezed out of her lungs. Russell leaned over, pushed the gear into neutral, and turned off the ignition key. The motor hum and the spinning tires caught on the broken shelves ended.

"We need to move... and fast." Russell said as he grabbed Elsie. Francesca helped pull Elsie out of the vehicle. Russell motioned towards a taxi cab. Francesca burst out from the broken glass. She pressed her Desert Eagle cannon into the driver's chest. He unwillingly obliged. Russell opened the back seat and placed Elsie in the back. She did not speak and Russell wondered if she was catatonic. Francesca wasted no time and sped off as Russell climbed into the passenger seat. He tossed her a dirty look as he tried to close the door in the rapidly accelerating car. On the road back, she slowed down as she saw a half dozen UN police vehicles drive towards the scene. Lights flashed and sirens blasted into the air.

"Looks like I'm not shopping there anymore." Elsie lightened the mood with her joke. Russell smiled at her. He never knew his own grandmother as she passed away when he was a child. He wondered what type of grandmother Elsie would make. Perhaps he would adopt her as his own grandmother.

After returning back to Elsie's house, Francesca grabbed all of her things and bolted without saying a word. She needed to get away. She needed to think. She moved into a small hotel. Once again, she let her emotions cloud her judgment. Francesca pulled out her satellite phone and called Tel Aviv. She had not talked to her father in the four months since she left Liberia. She was scared to explain how she fell in love with an American and compromised her cover story. Her father was abrupt on the other end of the line and she knew by the tone of his voice that it was far from over. She knew Russell would be killed. Francesca finished the call. Locals who sat around her in the open air café on the main Lubumbashi promenade had no clue what she said in Hebrew. She finished her coffee and turned on the range finder. Francesca located Russell within ten minutes based upon the transmitter she snuck into his boot. She knew that he would look inside his pockets. Her last tracking device went silent. Francesca needed to find him and remembered that to catch a wolf, sometimes you had to tie a lamb to a tree. The Iranian agent needed to be brought out in the open. Francesca heard Gertz had a place within Lubumbashi and had a jet fly kosher food in from Kinshasa every week at a cost of twenty thousand. She could not understand why. The shops looked abundant. The locals were pleased with the merchandise and crops.

At Lubumbashi airport, Russell met the UN military transport aircraft that arrived from Kinshasa. After several large Nigerian soldiers departed, Russell saw Schultz scamper down the back ramp.

"We have actionable intel on the uranium." Schultz handed Russell a picture of Gertz and the North Korean General Yal.

"I knew that bastard Gertz was up to no good." Russell shouted.

"The North Koreans need the Uranium 238 and are willing to pay top dollar. The report from our guy doing surveillance said the MOAB caused a major avalanche that covered the mine entrance and killed a few GROM thugs." Schultz said as he handed Russell updated satellite imagery.

"That's a good thing. The less GROM around here, the better."

"In one of the photos, you can see figures move away from the camp." Schultz speculated, "More than likely the kidnapped villagers ran off when the guards were distracted."

"Don't worry. Gertz will find some new bodies to get his mine operational. The critical point of failure is the North Korean general. We need to take him out of the equation." Russell looked at the photos closely. He was glad the kidnapped villagers got away, but knew it was not over. Russell continued, "Do you really think the UN will stop Gertz from opening the mine again?"

"Probably not, but we need to divert our limited resources to tracking down the loose nuke."

"Anymore updates on locations?" Russell asked. "We could start hitting places hard." Russell was anxious.

"No, not yet." Schultz thought for a moment. "If we start a random search that could spook them and send them into deep hiding."

"It could get us closer to finding it." Russell thought about the situation. He was still a novice CIA operative.

"I doubt it. There are so much misinformation and hidden agendas here." Schultz provided more insight to working in Africa. He had over fifteen years of experience as a CIA operative and a majority of that time was in Africa. Schultz added. "They could try to move the bomb or bury it for a future operation. The bad thing about the atomic weapons program is that most of the components remain critically active and it's the trigger mechanisms that erode with age."

"The weapons grade uranium could make a dirty bomb." Russell thought for a moment. "That may be a likely scenario?"

"Probably not." Schultz stated coldly. "Whoever is behind this is waiting for a major terrorist attack."

"Regardless, we can't let those North Korean bastards get a hold of a functioning atomic bomb."

"Agreed." Schultz looked at the photos again. "The North Koreans have been after nukes for decades and will pay top dollar." Schultz shuffled into the stack of photos taken at Kinshasa immigration control. "Here, look at this one." He handed Russell a grainy photo. "I found out that there is an Iranian engineer who arrived several days ago and word on the street is he was brought into country to develop a new trigger device."

"Who's supporting him?" Russell thought about it. "He can't just be here just alone."

"No, he has company. We have long determined that an Iranian sleeper cell operated in the Congo to buy uranium on the black market."

"Do we have an address?" Russell asked further, "A location?"

"No, they are deep underground." Schultz looked at Russell directly and said, "There are others behind this. Somehow I feel that there is a dangerous plot brewing." Schultz handed him photos.

"Do we take out the North Korean?" Russell asked.

"Not we... You." Schultz took the picture and burned it. "Kitson and I are going after Gertz. You take out the good General and meet us at Nakor."

"I take it you are not interested in any line of questioning?"

"Nope," Schultz said as he looked at Russell with a hard inquisitive glance and wondered for a moment if Russell would carry out the assignment. "Are you?" The North Korean general was approved by Langley to be terminated.

"Not really." Russell said in agreement to the mission.

Francesca waited in the café and sat against the far wall. She held several napkins on her lap that concealed her mammoth Desert Eagle pistol. She patiently waited. Her contact was long overdue, but she knew the roads were not good. The old man traveled far to meet Francesca. He drove all the way from Kinshasa to Lubumbashi with everything he owned and several of his family members. When Francesca saw him sitting at a table with six others, she could tell by the look on his face that he was desperate to get out of the Congo.

"Here's a picture that was taken two weeks ago." The old man handed Francesca the photo. She looked at the bomb with a magnifying glass and noticed the special markings that would not mean anything to an outsider. The twelve digit mix of numbers and strange markings were known only to four people in the world. Three of the individuals were high ranking members of the Tel Aviv government and the fourth was Francesca. She knew it was the atomic bomb she was after.

"Who are these men?" She knew the answer.

"The two in front are South African brothers. The man touching the bomb is Hezbollah. I do not know his name, but I have seen him in Kinshasa and heard from the Lebanese that he is indeed Hezbollah." Francesca knew Rajik Nabee when she saw the photo. She missed her chance to kill him three months ago in Liberia. Francesca had worked with Russell and Kitson to take out a terrorist cell that ran around Monrovia and was supported by the now deposed Charles Taylor. Francesca wrapped her hand around the photo and crumpled it up.

CHAPTER 22

Conditions in Lubumbashi had worsened. Russell observed the shock looked expressions on the faces of several locals as he drove. Most locals were surprised to see a white man drive alone and equally shocked to see him get out of his car. Russell walked several blocks as he checked the addresses. The numbers were faded and hard to see. In this area of Lubumbashi, the streets were desolate. The area was prone to horrific crimes, not even squatters lived in the old buildings. Criminal thugs controlled the area. Russell saw a few men who watched him. He pulled his pistol out of its holster and made it visible. Across the street, Russell saw the building number that Schultz believed was the rendezvous point.

The hotel manager was on Harry's payroll and kept close eye on the North Koreans. He had notified Harry when the foreigners were on the move. Schultz informed Russell moments earlier that confirmed the North Koreans were holding a meeting with the suspected Iranian agent. Additionally, Schultz got an update Kinshasa that the North Korean general took a large box from the only international bank prior to flying to Lubumbashi. Time was ticking and Russell needed to find the missing atomic weapon. Schultz gave him the green light to take action and do whatever it took to find the missing weapon of mass destruction. Russell climbed the back staircase at a fast rate. He swung the pistol around each corner as he moved higher and higher. Russell moved slow and more deliberate as he approached the top floor apartment.

In the small apartment, the North Korean general became impatient and sent his trusted Sergeant to find out where his late guest was. General Yal looked surprised as Russell emerged from the back of the apartment. Russell kept his weapon raised and was ready to fire. Russell scanned the room and focused back toward General Yal who was utterly surprised to see the American. Russell lifted his pistol towards the North Korean's head. He moved close.

"Where is it?" Russell asked as he knew that General Yal understood English. An intelligence report stated Yal studied extensively in Switzerland and was fluent in five languages to include English.

"I'm not armed." General Yal replied and added with a slight smile. "I do not have money."

"You know who I am and what I am after." Russell paused and asked. "Where's the bomb?" Several years ago, Russell conducted several rehearsal exercises in South Korea at Yongsong based upon North Korean invasion plans and appropriate, rapid response by the United States and other allies. The only thing he formulated from the training was the fact that many North Korean leaders were widely unpredictable. Most significantly, he recalled - never; absolutely never allow them to make the first move. Russell knew the man would not tell the truth.

"I don't know anything about a bomb. We are here for diamonds." His Korean accent was thick, but he could put out an understandable short phrase or expression. The report from Schultz stated the North Korean officer knew more English than he let people believe. He was educated in Switzerland like many elite North Koreans aligned to the communist government.

"I have no patience for your lies." Russell stated calmly as he continued to aim the pistol at the general's head. "Tell me where the bomb is or I will put a bullet in your head." Russell needed to get to the point before the South Africans or GROM showed up. There were too many unknowns and too many mercenaries running freely, undaunted around the countryside. Russell also knew the general's large enlisted aide would be missing him soon and would show up.

"You'll never find it." Yal said. In the next split second, the North Korean sergeant emerged from the stairs and was surprised by what he saw. "Easy" The general spoke to Russell. He also said something in Korean. The soldier stood still and assessed the situation. The sub-machine gun was looped around his back. Russell observed as he slid his hand slowly around towards the weapon.

"Well here's to diplomatic peace." Russell said as he raised his pistol and fired two shots into the North Korean General. The first landed in his chest and the second blew out the back of his skull with brain matter blasted against the concrete wall. Russell did not wait for negotiations. He sprinted towards the closest exit in the front stairway as bullets rattled the wall near his location. Pieces of brick rocketed past him as the North Korean missed. Russell sprinted up a set of stairs toward the roof. He did not wait to see why the North Korean did not pursue him.

The North Korean sergeant would not leave the side of his dying general until he breathed his last breathe. The North Korean gripped his leader tightly and sang their national anthem lightly into his ears. He lowered his dead body onto the floor, screamed out loud at the top of his lungs in a carnivorous grunt, and grabbed the sub-machine gun. Rage encompassed his face as he ran up the stairs after the American.

Russell had very few choices as he looked down from atop the battered building. Across the rooftop, there was broken glass, bodily waste, and garbage. He jumped over several piles of trash and found his way to the old radio antennae, which in its day provided live music throughout the city. He ripped the sleeves off his shirt and wrapped them around his hands. He climbed down the side of the building. He knew that he would not have enough cable. Even with the rag in his hand, the frayed cable ripped and bloodied his hands. He felt excruciating pain and focused away from the blood, which streamed out of his palms. Russell knew what was at stake and his mind rapidly compared a little pain and blood compared with a dozen bullet holes from a high powered weapon. Several feet below him, the cable ended. The remnants of the fire escape were another thirty feet below. The North Korean helped Russell make up his mind to let go as he unloaded the sub-machine gun onto the side of the building. Bullets ricocheted and blew apart the brick. Russell fell and the rusted metal frame bent under the weight and force of impact. Rusted shards blew into the air as the North Korean fired onto the fire escape. Russell limped and pulled his body into a window. He found the staircase. Within a few seconds, Russell hobbled down the street.

Russell arrived back at the CIA safe house by nightfall. He still hobbled and was too beaten up to travel back to Kinshasa. Elsie waived her hand as Russell entered. Harry was fast asleep in his favorite recliner. The events of the day exhausted him. Elsie was still going strong. Russell was surprised at how much energy she had as if she were a boxer in the tenth round of a twelve round title fight and getting her second wind. Elsie pulled a bullet fragment out of his right calf and bandaged the wound. Russell had numerous cuts from concrete fragments that became projectiles. As Elsie finished with the last bandage, Russell looked surprised when he saw Francesca.

"Are you alright?" Francesca asked as she looked at the several bandages wrapped around her former lover.

"Do I look fine?" Russell shot back.

"You didn't ask for my help so you get what you deserve." Francesca said in a cold tone. She paused for a moment as she opened the bottle of twenty year old scotch that rested on the dining table.

"Not your mission." Russell responded.

"So it's classified?" Francesca inquired. "Within your CIA halls. You don't think I can find out what you did?"

"You need to stay within your lane." Russell directed.

"Don't tell me what to do." Francesca flung the bottle over Russell's head. The bottle smashed against the wall. Francesca turned to Elsie and said, "Sorry...he brings it out in me."

"I understand my dear." Elsie said, "Harry was the same way." She paused for a moment. "We were always on a mission."

The phone rang and Elsie answered. She conversed in a native Russian language that Russell did not understand. Elsie's expression changed as abruptly as a vehicle collision. "We need to move."

She kissed her husband of thirty-eight years on the forehead farewell and picked up her sub-machine gun. She handed Russell a RPG rocket launcher. Russell knew better than to ask, especially since Elsie was a career CIA operative and lived a fruitful life in some of the most dangerous parts of the world.

Elsie jumped into the driver's seat and did not even allow Russell the opportunity to take control of the vehicle. Without a word, she accelerated the vehicle at a fast rate. She headed toward the warehouse district of the city. After twenty minutes into the drive, Russell observed a moment to ask her. "You love him a great deal?"

"Harry?" Elsie asked. "Yes, he's my soul mate."

"I know we cannot think about it now," Russell said, "but I want you to know that we do whatever it takes to bring down those responsible for the attack on your home."

"You really have no idea what extreme violence is, do you?"

Russell thought at it for a moment. He quickly flashed back to Iskandariyah to the police station bomb blast he barely missed. "I am smart enough to say no."

"Bravo Tom...Bravo." Elsie paused and looked at him, not with the endearing grandmother eyes he witnessed twelve days before. Russell saw squinted pupils and a long range stare, something out of a western gunfighter's eye stance before quick draw. "I have done things that will make me answer to the devil."

"Such as?"

"In the name of American diplomacy, I have killed many - direct or indirect associated - many have died." She paused for effect and continued. "A majority were evil. The kind of scum you rarely see this day and age. Back then, the world was filled with many more despots." She stopped the discussion abruptly and mumbled something that sounded like a prayer. "I will have to atone for my sins. I knew what I was getting into when I joined the agency."

"Why didn't you leave?" Russell inquired. "For your children?"

"That's a cover story." Elsie looked at Russell. "We never had children. We were too busy saving the world."

Elsie received another call and abruptly shifted the vehicle again down another road, or what Russell presumed was a road. Branches bounced off the hood of the vehicle as she sped along. Russell looked over to see if she would edge off of the pedal, but she did not concede. More branches hung over the road blocked visibility and continuously bounced off the hood. Elsie slammed the horn several times. The horn blasts echoed and warned everyone near the road to get out of the way. Russell held on for life and he witnessed a possessed Elsie catapult the vehicle through the brush. Finally, they hit a hard paved road and the tires skidded onto the pavement.

"Ten more minutes," Elise said as she looked across at Russell, "better lock and load. We will be coming in fast... no surprises this time." Russell reacted rapidly and shifted his body around to position his weapons. Francesca slammed a magazine into a machinegun and her Desert Eagle.

The South African brothers smoked cigarettes and chatted about the homeland they missed. Neither could return, yet they still reminisced. Both turned as they heard a fast approaching vehicle. The South African brothers ducked for cover as Elsie slammed on the brakes and the jeep skidded to a complete stop. Russell dove out of the front door and somersaulted several times. He heard rounds fly over top of him. Elsie fired her weapon as a distraction. Galpin anticipated an attack at the airfield and waved a red clothe in the air. Out of the jungle, Russell saw over thirty Ashbals run at full speed toward them. Elsie ripped them apart as she fully triggered the sub-machine gun for automatic fire. Her arm muscles bulged as she kept the weapon level. The force of the full auto fire lifted the weapon upward. Elsie emptied the weapon. Several Ashbals observed an opportunity to attack Elsie after the weapon silenced. Within fifteen more seconds, Elsie ripped them apart with another fully loaded magazine. Bullets blazed across the area. Russell loaded a RPG rocket and blasted the vehicle the South African brothers hid behind; however, they were already gone.

The entire firefight lasted no more than a few moments but the experience exhausted Elsie. Russell drove back to the CIA safe house as Elsie rested the entire way back. Her eyes were barely awake, yet she responded with clarity.

"Why did you do it for so many years?" Russell asked.

"For him." Elsie responded. "I love him and could not be away."

"You love him a great deal." Russell paused. "I can tell."

"You would never know by seeing him in his older state but in his day, Harry was intense, a seasoned warrior. He came into East Germany to get me out."

The Minister of Information locked his door, but it took Kitson one solid kick to break the door. Kitson tossed the garbage can that rested by the door at the Minister as he picked up a pistol from his desk. The flying garbage surprised the Minister and caused him a momentary lapse. Not accustomed to handling a weapon, he fumbled with the safety. Kitson launched across the room and slammed the Minister against the desk. The loosely put together plywood crumbled under the weight and the Minister crashed to the floor. Kitson placed a knee into his back. Grunts and groans resonated underneath as he grabbed hold of the right wrist and dislodged the pistol from the Minister's grasp.

"You can't do this to me."

"Oh yes I can." Kitson shouted. "We pay the bills here."

"You have no jurisdiction here. This is sovereign territory and the government of the Democratic Republic of the Congo." He shouted, "You have no right!"

"You're a common criminal and will be dealt with as such. The only thing that can help you is to tell me about the illegal uranium?"

"I don't know what you are talking about."

"Liar." Kitson inserted his other knee into the Minister's back. The man groaned. Kitson pushed both knees into the lower back and had his left hand pushed against the Minister's head. He pushed harder against the head and drove it into the plywood particles dispersed from the crash. "Stop... stop. You are hurting me."

"That's the plan." Kitson said with stern tone. "Now tell me what I need to know." He lifted his fist. "Where's the uranium?"

"There's no uranium, just diamonds." The Minister grunted harder. His voice quickly changed to a more friendly tone as he said, "I can cut you in on the diamonds. There is plenty. You can retire rich."

"Are you bribing me?" Kitson slammed his other knee in the Minister's back. The effect sent more pain in his body and conjured up a deathly shrill.

"Stop...please stop."

"Where's the uranium?"

"Kinshasa Port. A large metal container painted in dark blue in the holding area."

"Now that was not so hard." Kitson motioned for several UN security officers who remained outside the door. Kitson played the recorded conversation from the tape player. The Minister of Information held his head low as he was escorted out of the government building by UN security officers in handcuffs. Kitson followed and smiled at the other Congolese government workers. He nodded his head up and down. Kitson looked into the eyes of many men who were all of a sudden scared that they would be exposed for corruption. Kitson enjoyed the sunshine on his face as he exited the building and surmised it was going to be a great day after all.

CHAPTER 23

Rajik walked back and forth; faster than usual. His recent ramblings became more obscure. He grew more impatient. The Iranian scientist removed the designed triggering device from a shock resistant container. He tested the circuit panel with a specialized, non-magnetic voltage meter. Rajik watched the nuclear physics professor place the trigger into the atomic weapon. Rajik did not know if it would detonate at any moment. With the utmost precision, the scientist utilized several precision screwdrivers to secure the trigger, which rested on the top front panel of the bomb. The barometric cylinder was the size of a large cigar and was linked by three pieces of titanium, each one quarter inch wide. The mercury was encapsulated in the vial and slowly moved. Rajik sweated profusely. He could not stand still, yet did not want to distract the scientist and quietly bolted out the door. Several of the Ashbals were playing soccer and enjoyed themselves. Rajik walked over and slapped one. He informed them to keep quiet while the bomb is completed.

Since Russell needed rest and wanted out of Lubumbashi, he took a ride back to Kinshasa on the regular UN transport airplane. He was exhausted. Over the past two weeks, he had been shot at more times than the thirteen months in Iraq and eight months in Afghanistan. He had to get out of Lubumbashi as there was one very disgruntled, heavily trained North Korean sergeant on his trail. Russell thought about going on the offensive to find the North Korean. Any non-black foreigner was easy to spot and track. However, Schultz inquired with the local police on the whereabouts of any Asians in Lubumbashi and heard nothing. No body was found. Schultz even asked several local informants to look around the area and they found nothing. The two North Koreans had disappeared. Russell found his room in U.S. Embassy compound and dropped his gear. Everything in his bag smelled. Russell's entire body smelled, but he had no time to take a shower. Time was moving too fast and there was still a loose atomic weapon in the Congo.

"You look like hell." Kitson said as he observed how much weight Russell lost in the week since he last saw him. Kitson handed him a cold beer. It was slightly after two in the afternoon and too early for gin and tonics. Russell drank a hefty gulp and belched. The British officer was repulsed by the sound and gave a disapproving glance.

"I hate to say it, but it feels good to be back in Kinshasa."

"Not for long."

"What do you mean?" Russell asked.

"I need you to fly with me to Zambia. MI6 received reports on a high level meeting happening tomorrow. Plane leaves in twenty minutes." Kitson paused. "Make sure you pack some of your best clothes as we will be heading to a top resort." Kitson picked up his garment bag with his tailored suits inside and turned to Russell as he stepped into the passageway, "And try to remember to bring your manners." Russell smirked and laughed slightly at the suggestion.

The plane departed Kinshasa on time and an unwilling Russell joined Kitson and Jabes on the journey. Jabes watched the pilots as they landed the ten seat passenger jet, which was on loan to the UN mission from France. Jabes had not been home to see his family in nearly eight months. His home was two hours north of Livingston. Even though he was so close, he would have to wait longer as the mission at hand was far more important. The luxurious resort was within earshot of Victoria Falls. The sound was deafening. The immense volume of water catapulted over the high cliffs. The balcony restaurant had a direct line of sight of the massive falls. Kitson ordered a strong drink and Russell followed suit. Kitson knew that they would stand out if they did not order alcohol. Kitson looked into his camera and snapped several shots of the men. He immediately recognized Joseph Mugabe, President of Zimbabwe, a man who terrorized his own nation.

Deep in the Congo bush on the outskirts of the Hezbollah compound, Francesca sat for over eight hours in the same spot. She neither moved nor flinched. Bushes concealed her as she lay prone on the bug infested ground. She watched Rajik's compound through the high powered spotting scope. The skilled Mossad agent regularly used the scope for long distance sniper competition to hit targets, upwards of eight hundred yards away. From the distance, she saw the Iranian scientist as he departed. Slowly with deliberate motions, she slithered back out of her position. Once out of view, Francesca sprinted to her vehicle. At first, she stumbled and nearly fell. Her legs became practically immobilized from lying still for so long. Blood rapidly churned in her legs and her muscles responded vigorously. She jumped into her jeep and sped down the isolated road. She kept her distance. Her natural instinct was to kill the Iranian, yet her intelligence training forced her to observe. There were only a few vehicles on the road and she had little trouble trailing the Iranian. The photo that she uploaded had returned from Tel Aviv with a background description of the Iranian and known accomplices. Rajik was top on the list as well as the Belgian named Dietger Laurent. She was surprised to Dan Gertz on the list and made a mental note to interrogate him further the next time she finds him. Francesca watched the Iranian closely. She sensed that he had not been trained in clandestine operations and she used that to her advantage. As he entered a building, she set up the perfect kill shot.

Meanwhile in Zambia's capital city of Livingston, several Chinese businessmen wore crisp Armani suits. They were not dressed as tourists. In the African bush next to Victoria Falls, the three Chinese stood out like a sore thumb. Kitson kept the camera trained on them. Underneath the newspaper, the ten inch telescopic lens was well concealed. Kitson attached the remote view panel to the camera and pressed several buttons on the hand held gadget. The lens maneuvered back and forth and zoomed in close. Several fast frame shots erupted.

"London should have facial scan in a few moments."

"Really?" Russell looked at the hand held gadget no bigger than the palm of Kitson's hand. In the upper right hand corner of the device an antennae signal flashed. Russell quickly ascertained that the device had a satellite uplink chip. Within five minutes, the device beeped. Kitson opened the file. Each face had a matched photo passport framed photo. MI6 had a direct line with INTERPOL and Taiwan Secret Police.

"The dossiers list them as international art dealers." Kitson looked at the report as it arrived. "They're out of Hong Kong."

"Are they legit?"

"Hard to say. Not much on them. The older one in glasses is Joug Wun. He came to attention of INTERPOL five years ago after a Monet forgery sale in Zurich. Made millions stealing paintings and selling them on the black market. Employs a small army for security."

"Why would they be talking to Mugabe?"

"It must be diamonds. Mugabe has not been known as an art collector. Wun must be shipping diamonds into Hong Kong for resale. It should be easy for him to move untraceable diamonds into China, especially after we gave Hong Kong back to the Chinese." Russell recalled the shift of Hong Kong and the concern British and the free world had as the communist giant expanded control over the small island. "If Wun can sell loose diamonds, it could be worth billions."

"Didn't China sign onto the Kimberly Process?"

"Officially yes, however smuggled diamonds can be a huge windfall." Kitson continued. "The Chinese appetite for diamonds has exploded. I imagine there are uber-rich Chinese who would pay the highest price for rare diamonds. Zimbabwe had some of the best diamond mines in Africa before Mugabe took power and was banned from trading on the world market. Who knows how many giant diamonds he has been sitting on?" Russell remembered the reports of mythical giant diamonds from King Solomon's mines and the Star of Africa that was over five hundred carats.

"What would Mugabe do with the money?"

"Probably buy more weapons to keep down any rival factions. I would be more concerned about Wun getting a hold of billions of dollars in untraceable diamonds. Something does not fit right."

"How would they get them out? Zimbabwe does not border the Congo directly."

"I witnessed several late night flights arrive." Kitson replied. "The UN controls the air traffic but the Congo Ministers yield unbelievable power. Many bribes have been paid. Everyone at the airport is on the take."

"Gertz is definitely involved." Russell said. "Langley traced financial transaction from banks in Seychelles. Bribes go there and funneled to accounts in Brussels and Zurich. Gertz must have account numbers and ledgers. If we get that info, we could take down the entire network."

"Do you really want to sign up for that?" Kitson looked sternly at the American. "International laws are hard to enforce in many parts of Africa. You may have to take them out." Russell knew what that meant and the implications. These men may never see a trail or jury. But if he let them live, the lives of thousands and perhaps many more could be endangered.

"Before we dismantled their network, we would have to know for certain what their intentions are."

"Would that make you sleep better at night? Mugabe murdered over two hundred thousand of his own countrymen and the international community did nothing. No charges were ever filed in international court. Few witnesses survived. No one would dare come forward. Mugabe's henchmen are ruthless and would kill you and your family in a heartbeat if they knew or even suspected you were collecting intelligence on their leader." Kitson leaned close. "To deal with men of this nature, you must use overwhelming and swift violence - the kind of swift violence that may go beyond a normal man's rational thought. Are you prepared to do that?" Russell did not have a chance to respond as he witnessed Kitson expression alter sharply. Russell turned to see several of Mugabe's entourage take an interest in their table. One of Mugabe's security details talked into the microphone in his sleeve and motioned to several others to move.

Kitson bolted from the table and Russell followed. Kitson kept his hat covered low across his face. Russell quickly caught up to him in their adjoined bungalows overlooking Victoria Falls.

"Did they recognize you?" Russell asked.

"I doubt it." Kitson said softly as he covered his face more with the oversized safari hat. Russell recalled how Kitson had his photo on the front page of all London's papers when he received the Queen's medal. "It's been too long." Kitson continued, "I don't think we have been compromised. Having Jabes here is a good cover."

"Glad to be of assistance." Jabes smiled. "Can I inform the UN of the meeting?"

"No, not yet. We do not want to spook Mugabe. If he has planned a large diamond shipment, maybe we can expose him and keep a significant amount of rough diamonds from entering the world market."

"Would it collapse diamond prices?"

"Possibly." He paused to think for a moment. "I went into a briefing deep inside the London diamond exchange and saw tables upon tables of diamonds being sorted." Kitson shifted to his scholarly tone. "The problems we have at hand are terrorists funneling the diamonds as a means of currency. Rough, untraceable diamonds are every smuggler's dream."

"How much diamonds do you think Mugabe can dump?"

"I would estimate at least a billion pounds worth." Kitson replied. Russell looked confused on the conversion. Kitson continued, "That would be about six billion in your dollars."

"Damn." Russel was surprised. "What would that do to the global diamond market?"

"Do you want me to conjecture?" Kitson handed Russell a MI6 document. Russell read the detailed report that identified diamonds from the Marange mines in Zimbabwe as conflict stones. Criminals and stolen people have been brought to the Marange mines to work under horrific safety conditions. Thousands have perished in tunnel collapses and many more murdered in open sight. Several members of international human watch groups who reported on the Marange mines have disappeared; bodies never found. Mugabe has worked out a deal with Chinese diamond importers. Sales of diamonds increased over three hundred percent from 2003 to 2005. Rough diamonds have become the only form of currency for fighting in many African countries, especially the Congo. Russell did what he was told and burned the report. Jabes did not need to read the report to understand what has occurred in his backyard. Most Africans knew the deadly tale of diamonds – the curse of Africa.

Back near the Iranian's safe house, Francesca slithered like a snake over top of broken glass and crumbled brick. Her sniper skills were pristine and she did utter a painful sound as she moved closer. Francesca set up her firing position across the road and turned on the laser range targeting scope. The Iranian scientist watched the red dot move along his chest. At first he thought it was a joke, someone pointed a light at him. He moved his hand onto the light and saw it cascade over the back of his hand. He laughed for a quick moment and suddenly realized the red dot was a laser sight. Not being agile or athletic, he clumsily moved across the room. He dodged the chairs and table. He reached to grab his drawings. The explosion in his chest skyrocketed blood all over the table. Blood covered his precious documents. As she entered, Francesca held the sniper rifle high to her shoulder and kept pointed into the house. She pulled the body off the table, grabbed the blood smeared documents, and plunged them into a bag. The crack of the glass to her right caused her to duck. She looked under the table and saw the grenade roll across the floor. She pulled the table onto her and the explosion riveted the room and blasted out the windows. Francesca stayed behind the table. Her legs and arms had dozens of splinters. Her blast resistant sunglasses saved her eyes while her chest armor saved her life. She slid the Desert Eagle 50 caliber pistol out of the right hip holster. She had less than three seconds to decide what action to take. Instincts kicked in to attack. She pushed off the floor and jumped through the remnants of the window just as another grenade bounced into the room. She kept low on the ground as the grenade fragments lofted above her. She rolled several times and aimed the pistol forward. The remaining members of the Iranian sleeper cell lifted their heads after the grenade explosion dissipated. Francesca blasted the skull of the first and recalibrated her shot after the immense recoil. The others dropped behind the truck. She kept rolling and blasted along the ground level at their feet. She emptied the remaining eleven rounds and more of the rounds caught parts of legs and eventually the body torsos as they fell to the ground as their legs were blown out. She crawled forward. Blood dripped steadily from her arms and pooled into the palms of her hands.

At Nakor Industries, Gertz was surprised to see Dietger Laurent enter his executive suite. The fat Belgian never came to the Nakor building. His presence startled Gertz. Dietger sat down in the chair. His large body hung over the sides.

"Your secretary seems to be absent." Dietger said as he looked around. "I called and they told me she had not been seen. I would have made an appointment, but there was no one to make it with." Gertz made a mental note to find a replacement. Gertz wondered for a brief moment how Moira enjoyed her new life as a rebel bush wife.

"What do you want?"

"Out of the Congo, just like every foreigner here. But we all must wait our turn. I lived here for most of my adult life. I have seen many things change here, some good, but mostly bad." Dietger had the respect of the Belgian community and a few foreigners. Gertz on the other hand did not respect him. Gertz made millions as he out smarted the Belgians in the illegal diamond trade. "There was no much concern about the Zimbabwe official found dead in the streets."

"Poor fellow." Gertz sounded empathetic. "I heard about him. Robbed and shot in the head by some prostitute." Braum had staged the entire crime scene. "I heard the police shot the prostitute as she tried to escape."

"Everyone would benefit from good relations with Mugabe." Dietger paused and continued. "We have a plan."

CHAPTER 24

At the massive luxurious resort in Livingstone, Russell looked out the window and saw several of Mugabe's security detail walk around the bungalows. The hotel security arrived and the group started to knock on room doors.

"We need a diversion." Kitson said.

"I have an idea." Russell said. "It should create a distraction, but more than likely we will have to punch our way out." Russell looked in his bag and started pulling apart the desk computer in the corner of the room. "Are you ok with a homemade bomb?" Russell smiled.

"Just don't blow us up." Kitson said in a stern voice. Kitson took two small towels from the bathroom and wrapped it around his knuckles. Kitson asked Jabes to wrap the towels with a roll of duct tape. Once finished, Kitson punched his makeshift boxing gloves together. Kitson watched Russell as he quickly stripped the computer circuit card.

"Short notice," Russell said, "this is what we got." Russell was pleased with his quickly configured bomb comprised of hand gel sanitizer and pieces of magnesium from the computer circuit cards inside an old soda bottle. "When I pull this wire, the magnesium will drop into the hand sanitizer." Kitson looked at the makeshift bomb and scratched his head. Russell burst out. "It will give us about four seconds. Make sure you keep your eyes closed after I hurl it." The three of them packed into the bathroom and waited. The knock came at the door and the joggle of keys into the lock. Russell peaked through the opening and tossed the makeshift bomb at the first security guy as he entered the room. Russell already pulled the wire, which dropped the magnesium into the sanitizer gel. As the bottle flew in the air, the security guard stopped dead in his track as the blinding white light from the magnesium blast temporarily crippled his vision. Russell punched the security guard in the stomach. The man coupled over. The next two were less blinded, yet still affected. Kitson and Jabes quickly beat them to the ground. They pulled the men inside and shut the door.

"Are we ready for check out?" Russell pointed towards the bags. "We can either carry them or leave them. What do you think?"

"Take them." Kitson quickly replied. "It will look suspicious if tourists arrive at the airport without bags. More importantly, we do not have time to sanitize everything in the luggage." Kitson looked around the room. "However, we do need to wipe the room down." Jabes looked at the cleanliness of the room and gave him a surprised look. "Fingerprints...nothing to identify. Wipe everything. Don't leave anything untouched."

"Are Mugabe's goons that capable?"

"Don't underestimate Mugabe. He's extremely cunning and most deadly." Russell remembered back to the story he had heard about a young Lieutenant Kitson serving in Rhodesia in 1979. After Kitson succeeded in receiving the surrender of over three hundred armed rebels with the offer of a hot cup of her Majesty's best tea, he was reassigned to Ian Smith's office, who was the outgoing Rhodesian Prime Minister. Kitson's father was a high ranking British general and well connected. After the young Kitson's face appeared on the front page of the London Times, Ian Smith knew he had to get the young officer away from any harm, especially after he received word from the Defense Minister that Kitson would be awarded the Queen's Medal. Within the confines of Ian Smith's office, he confided in Kitson many times about Mugabe and how vile a man he really was. As leaders from across the world praised Mugabe taking power from the white ruling elite and transitioning Rhodesia to Zimbabwe, Ian Smith showed Kitson hundreds of photos of men, women, and children who were murdered by Mugabe and his henchmen. Kitson rarely told the story and Russell knew that he had earned the British Colonel's trust when he confided in him. Jabes had not earned enough of his trust yet, but went along with Russell's nod in agreement.

Kitson wondered if Mugabe would have an assassination team waiting for them in Kinshasa. He did not want to risk being exposed and potentially jeopardize the Congo mission to find the missing atomic warhead. Once the UN plane was airborne, Kitson directed the pilots to alter course to Lubumbashi. Immediately upon landing, Kitson went to the store and loaded up on a crate of gin and several boxes of tonic. He even splurged on the fresh limes from the local grower. As they arrived at the retired CIA agent's compound, they noticed tighter security. Russell thought to himself how Elsie won that fight with Harry.

"Lads how are you doing?" Harry raised a toast from behind his desk in the study. Kitson and Russell did not see was the sawed off shotgun pointed under the desk. It was leveled at knee height and would have caused a deadly injury. Harry disengaged the trigger and put the weapon on safe. He removed his hand from the lethal weapon and used his cane to hobble over to shake the hands of his unannounced guests. "Elsie should be back in a few minutes. Francesca showed up this morning and they have been nonstop chatting all day long. With all this recent drama, Elsie thinks we are back in the eastern bloc countering the KGB." Harry paused for a moment as he realized that he rambled on for a moment. He needed someone to talk to and was happy to see Kitson and Russell. Harry continued, "I love Elsie very much. She is one tough cookie and someone you want in your foxhole."

"Amen." Kitson raised the first gin and tonic in toast.

"What about you and Francesca?" Harry asked as he handed Russell a fresh drink.

"Let's just say the drama is pretty extreme. When she shows up, somebody usually dies." They all laughed at the joke and toasted a few more times. Russell had more than his share and passed out hard.

"Morning sleepy head." Kitson said. Russell did not like the cheery British Colonel in the morning. Russell was amazed at how much alcohol his partner consumed.

"I feel horrible."

"You look horrible. Hope you are ready for today's activities." Russell almost forgot that they had to fly up country for aerial surveillance of potential locations where the missing atomic weapon could be located. "You should get something to eat." Russell looked at the plate of sausage and biscuits and nearly vomited from the thought. He pushed the toxic fluid back down into the pit of his stomach. Russell pushed his body upward and out of the chair. He partially collapsed and grabbed the table for balance.

"Hang on there." Kitson helped him stand. "You yanks can't hold your booze." Russell did not need a lecture now or an argument. He nodded agreement. Russell drank with Colonel Kitson in Liberia. In the solitude and protection of the remote camp they occupied, Kitson fed Russell afternoon gin and tonics, followed by wine at dinner, and completed with a malt scotch night cap. Every day for over a month the ritual was repeated. Sunday's were no exception. Religious observances and practices rarely existed in the African bush.

"Lift off in one hour." Jabes shouted from the front of the apartment. Russell could not form a coherent thought or sentence. He mumbled something and headed to the shower. He pulled the curtain for support and turned on the shower. With all of his clothes on from the night before, he immersed himself in a hot shower. Slowly he got undressed. Vomit stains randomly blanketed his pants. He held the clothes up into the shower head and soaked everything. After half an hour, he emerged naked.

Jabes started the helicopter's engines when he saw the van turn onto the flight line. Fuel would become a major concern. They were travelling into a very remote region with very few villages, no roads, and definitely no airport for a refueling point. The map chartered the mountains at several thousand feet with two mountains rising upwards of six thousand feet. The only other place on the Africa Continent with a higher peak was Kilimanjaro. Fuel consumption would significantly increase traversing the mountain range. Jabes checked the instrument gauges. All systems were operational. The eight fifty-gallon fuel drums consumed up most of the space in the cargo bay. Jabes checked his fuel calculations again. He maneuvered the helicopter at tree top height. He was still very concerned about getting a RPG rocket up his backside. Russell looked out across the small villages and the small children running and waving.

The bright white helicopter with big UN letters on the side had not been seen in the remote parts of the Congo since the renewed fighting. More and more UN troops moved towards Kinshasa every day to keep the current government in power. The exterior parts of the Congo lacked either any form of law or prosecution. Worse Russell thought was the fact that ghosts of King Leopold lingered. Like an info commercial with babies with swollen bellies hoping folks will send a few cents he saw unclothed children waving as hard as they could to get his attention. Russell was shocked by the abuse endured by the Congolese. Short sleeve, long sleeve highlighted the age old threat to keep in line or else. Abuse, intimidation, stealing wealth, no infrastructure built for the populace, Brussels became infected with deposed officials. Russell recalled the little girl outside the Kinshasa market who asked him, "*Will my arm grow back?*" Russell wondered what barbarian cut off the girls' arm. Russell was appalled at the violence that still plagued everyday life of the Congolese. The brutal tactics used by the Belgians were still used. Russell knew the horrific stories depicted by Joseph Conrad in <u>The Heart of Darkness</u> were factual. Forced slavery and intimidation remained prevalent. Russell thought back to the change from colonial rule. The Congo had a chance after the change from Belgian rule, yet with any new country, there were men content with greed and violence. Patrice Lumumba became an early casualty from the mindless perception that the Soviets gained a foothold in Africa. The Lumumba government was removed as Mobutu gained control. Patrice Lumumba's belief in self-reliance and removal of all foreigners died with him. Mobutu was paid well by the Belgians to keep the diamond mines independent. Mobutu was paid well by the Americans for uranium. Mobutu was paid well by the Soviets for rare elements that were used to make ballistic missiles. Russell understood that many African government officials became corrupt. Many Africans fought for freedom and few succeeded. In South Africa, Nelson Mandela was finally released on 11 February 1990 after twenty-seven years in prison.

Dietger handed several aerial photos to the South African brothers. Krause reached out and grabbed them. Galpin looked on as he did not know much about aviation and flying. There were several large circular rings around the city. Galpin recognized some of the historic landmarks of his native country and his former home in Johannesburg.

"The detonation must occur no higher than ten thousand feet altitude for maximum contamination." Dietger said.

"What about fallout?" Galpin inquired.

"Not with this weapon. The trigger has been manufactured for an aerial burst. There will not be any radioactive dust that would occur from a ground level detonation."

"Why don't just direct the plane into the ground before we parachute out?" inquired Krause.

"No, the weapon would not perform to maximum extent possible. The cobalt sheath wrapped around it will greatly enhance the radiological contamination."

"Airspace control and vector zones over the populated areas will restrict any flight plan." Krause looked at the map. "I have been home in years. I would imagine that the air tracking systems have been updated periodically. We could be sitting ducks up there."

"Not if the plane has UN marks and high priority travel documents for dignitaries."

"How?" Galpin knew the mission had to succeed.

"There is a UN cargo plane that will transport supplies to Goma in two days. As part of their propaganda, the UN has several dignitaries flying around the Congo handing out food. We will take the airplane."

"That should work." Krause replied.

"And we will all benefit greatly."

"We don't care about the money." Galpin plugged into the conversation. "Those bastards need to pay the price for toppling Apartheid."

"Your vengeance will be recorded in history." Dietger turned his attention back to Krause. "Are you certain you can navigate the plane properly?"

"This aircraft is not hard to understand." Krause looked at the map and wind speed calculations for bomb release and added. "We will need exact speed calculations."

"Don't worry about that. Arash is working the numbers now and should have something later today."

Gertz knew the location of the Hezbollah camp. He floated his boat slowly along the riverbank. Braum and three other GROM thugs held automatic weapons below the side of the boat. A young Lebanese orphan ran towards the bank as the boat drifted closer to the dock. He shouted loud as the Gertz slowed the boat's engine. Gertz guessed the boy must have been eight years old, yet he was old enough to hold an AK47. Braum kept his hands behind his back and screwed the silencer into the pistol.

The boy shouted louder and pointed the AK47 at Gertz. Braum did not give the boy the opportunity and shot him in the head. The boy's finger was on the trigger and he fired into the air as he fell dead. A dozen Ashbals ran out of the house.

"What do you want?" Rajik said as he walked up to the stand-off between his inexperienced Ashbals and the heavily trained, mercenary type GROM thugs.

"Call it mutual interest." Gertz said as he smiled. He leaned from the boat and handed Rajik a security surveillance photo of the female Mossad agent. "I have heard that you would like her dead."

"I should have killed her in Liberia three months ago, but my leaders would not allow me." Rajik looked at Francesca's photo, which she wore a black evening dress. Rajik crumpled up the photo and tossed it into the water.

"What about now?" Gertz tossed a bag of cash onto the dock.

"It will cost." Rajik said. He opened the bag and smiled at the eighty thousand dollars in US currency.

"Sorry about your boy." Gertz said as he powered up the boat's engine. Rajik looked at the dead boy's body.

"Not a worry. I have many more." Rajik said. He shouted something in his native tongue. Several Ashbals picked up the boy and tossed him into the river. Several crocodiles on the riverbank jumped into the river. Within moments, the boy's body was ripped apart.

Chapter 25

In Kinshasa, Francesca saw the Ashbals before the young boys departed the back of the dump truck. The inexperienced Lebanese orphans were easy to pick out in the crowd of Africans. The boys carried metal pipes and approached the table where Francesca had enjoyed her morning coffee. The street was active with local shoppers. Francesca gently sipped her hot drink. She looked at the roof tops for a potential sniper and did not see any. She looked at the open windows in the nearby buildings and saw a few local women who shouted down to their children. The only threat that encountered her was the five Ashbals who ranged in the age of ten to fourteen. The boys came up towards her on both sides. In unison, they banged the pipes on the pavement and shouted something that she could not understand.

Francesca continued to gently sip her hot coffee and waited for the exact moment to react. The oldest looking Ashbal came forward and raised the metal pipe above his head. Before he slammed the pipe on the table, Francesca tossed the hot liquid into his eyes. She flipped the table over and tossed a chair at the boy on her left. She did several roundhouse karate kicks and knocked the three boys in front of her off their feet. The only boy who stood yelled and ran towards her. She picked up one of the metal pipes and smashed him in the head. The force of the strike knocked him unconscious. The older Ashbal who had the hot liquid in the face pulled out a switchblade knife. He swung his arms wildly and moved towards her. Francesca grabbed the knife and twisted the boy's arm. With a rapid move, she flipped the boy. As he landed, she plunged the knife into his chest. She pulled the knife out and stabbed the Ashbal several more times. She withdrew the knife and causally walked over to the three Ashbals who moaned on the ground. She lifted each boy's head and cut their throats. Blood poured across the sidewalk. She kept the murder weapon so the UN would not get her fingerprints. After she ensured no more threats existed, she motioned for a cab to get away from the away. Inside the cab, she telephoned Tel Aviv and spoke in her native tongue. Francesca ordered a missile strike on the Ashbal camp.

Russell paced back and forth, slowly at first and then faster. He did not know how to approach the delicate situation he found himself in. He concluded after another minute to take it head on. "Elsie, we need to make some quick decisions." Russell watched her as she dusted some old china cups, a ritual he suspected she did regularly. She hummed a tune and kept dusting. "Those GROM thugs will be back in force." More humming sounds emerged. "You know that they will back...don't you?"

"Schultz knows our standing orders to torch the house if we are captured." Elise replied in a polite voice. "Don't worry about us dear. We'll be fine."

"Harry's injured and could be a liability if we need to move fast."

"Don't be silly. I remember back in East Berlin he had several bullet holes in him and we still managed to outpace the KGB. Believe me, we will be fine." Elsie kept humming along. Russell felt like he hit a stone wall with the two retired agents. Harry sat in his study reading a novel. He puffed on a cigar and sent plumes of circled smoke in the air. Russell knew the situation had changed as Elsie never allowed Harry to smoke inside. Something had changed and Russell sensed the couple made a decision to remain for a final stand – life or death. Russell became frustrated at the two aging adults.

"Can you talk sense into them?" Russell asked Kitson who sat cleaning his Walther PPK pistol.

"It's not our fight."

"I know that, but they'll be slaughtered here." Russell said. He was concerned.

"You speculate that they would not survive." Kitson looked at his mentee and inquired. "Why do you underestimate them?"

"It's not them. It's the horde of former Polish Special Forces that are rumored to be on their way. They will want revenge for killing four of their own."

"We all had a hand in taking them out." Kitson pointed out.

"True. More than likely they will hit this compound."

"I agree. Don't get me wrong. I think the threat is viable and lethal. These GROM thugs are some of the most toxic mercenaries in the world." Kitson knew their legendary brutality too well.

"What do we do?" inquired Russell.

"Take the fight to them. You have a satellite phone?" Kitson dialed a number that he retrieved from his notebook.

"Hello." Gertz answered the other line.

"You cannot trace this call so do not bother." Kitson replied in an official tone.

"Who is this?" Gertz asked.

"That will come in time. I have something you need."

"I have plenty. There is nothing that I need. I have been very fortunate in my business deals."

"You are corrupt and will pay for your deeds." Kitson blasted.

"Don't be absurd. I am a simple businessman."

"And the Minister of Information is a sound voice of reason?" The other end of the line was quiet. Gertz knew within moments after the Minister of Information was arrested. The UN held him in a secure location within its headquarters.

"What do you have?"

"A tape. Names, dates, payouts. He was quite open in his discussions." Gertz paused for a moment to assess the situation. He had been blackmailed two times before and, in both occasions, Braum eliminated them.

"How much do you want?"

"Two hundred thousand. No diamonds. All cash." Kitson offered.

"Absurd. How do I know what you have?"

Kitson started a tape player. The sound was muffled and noticeably under duress. "Gertz. It was Gertz. He was the one." Kitson recalled fondly how he had his knee pressured in the middle of the Minister's back to help him remember. "There are two containers." Kitson stopped the recorder before the next words resonated.

"Where do we meet?"

"Tomorrow." Kitson paused as he thought for a moment. "At the Kinshasa port." He hung up the phone. Before Russell could ask what else was on the tape, Kitson went to see Harry. He closed the door and would not allow Russell's entrance. Within a moment, Kitson opened the door.

"We're all going to Kinshasa."

The flurry of activities in the house would astonish any crime scene investigator as everyone pitched in and cleaned out everything. Elsie burned papers in the sink. Smoke filtered throughout the house. Russell saw that she removed the photos on the wall and burned them as well. In the front room, she placed four large suitcases and filled them in five minutes. Francesca helped her go through the drawers and tightly pack everything that the two aged, retired CIA agents owned. Jabes and Kitson went room by room to sanitize all fingerprints. Russell needed to find Harry. He walked outside. Harry was silent as he sat on the patio that overlooked the plush flower garden. Harry seemed to be in a daze.

"No one knew where Patrice Lumumba's remains were buried." Harry started. "Rumors circulated that the Belgians spread his remains to the four edges of the Congo. But the truth is we got his corpse from Colonel Mobutu in exchange for information on the Soviet spies wondering around his country. There was a Christian church that Elsie and I moved his body to."

"Why have you not told anyone?"

"It was a promise that I made to Mobutu. I really thought he wanted his country to heal, but in the end he stripped the Congo of wealth just like the Belgians."

"Does Kimba know where his grandfather is buried?"

"He does now." Harry paused for a moment and looked at the old pictures on the desk of Mobutu and himself. A lot had changed from that early photo. "There is so much generational hatred here that it clouds everything. Congolese do not trust foreigners and why should they. For over a hundred years, the Belgians brutalized these people. The French, Germans, Portuguese, Russians, Chinese, and even Americans were no better. No one cares about the Congolese. They only care about the diamonds, gold, uranium, cobalt, and tritium. You name the rare mineral and it is here in the Congo for the taking."

"You never told me what happened when the Belgians came in."

"You wouldn't believe me. No one did."

"Try me."

"At the time, I volunteered to teach at a Christian school. Belgian paratroopers showed up in trucks. There must have been fifteen of them. The local headmaster went out to meet them. But by the time he walked outside, the Belgian officer opened fire and killed him. The others shot into classrooms. Many of the children were killed. I covered as many as I could with my body. I remember looking up at the Belgian officer as he pointed a pistol at my head. He just smiled and walked out."

"Did you ever find him?"

Harry hesitated for a moment. "I did find him, but it took several years." Russell did not need to ask about the outcome as he instinctively knew Harry found his own justice.

"Will you miss your home?"

"Elsie is my home. Wherever she is that is my home." Harry was very direct. "We've been through a great deal and survived. I'm truly astonished that we lived so long. The KGB had standing orders to shoot Elsie on the spot. But now they are our friends. Sometimes I drink with General Tretiak and reminisce about the old days."

"Seems like things went to hell after the Cold War."

"There's a lot to be said about that. Between us and the Soviets, we kept a lot of the African dictators in line. We kept some bad men in power. Some were homicidal maniacs. Some played both sides and gave our secrets to the Russians just as fast as they informed on them." Harry sighed. "Those days were chaotic...fun, but damn chaotic." Russell thought about what he found in the Congo and concluded not much had changed. Chaos still ruled.

The plane ride back to Kinshasa was quiet for everyone. The white C-130 transport plane had four propellers and moved rather quickly. Shortly after liftoff, Russell looked out of the copilot's window as they passed the gorilla habitat. Russell wondered if Doctor Eddy was doing fine with his baby gorillas. It was only three weeks ago that Russell helped him, but it seem like an eternity. Russell had accomplished a great deal. He had one more mission to find a loose nuke. Russell considered if somehow it made it to the black market, especially with Iran and North Korea chumming at the bit to get a hold of a workable atomic weapon. Let alone Al Qaeda, Hezbollah, or some other fanatic group that had an unresolved grievance or just pissed off against America. Russell knew he could not risk a terrorist group getting their hands on the weapon. It was small enough to fit in a shipping container box and could be readily flown anywhere around the globe. Within a day, it could be over top of New York City or Washington, DC in the cargo hold of a transport commercial jetliner and detonated as an air burst radiological weapon. The radiation debris cloud would cover a hundred miles. The sheer panic would decimate economic activity. Terrorists would be able to coincide the airburst and another coinciding attack that would bring America to its knees. Russell knew he could not allow that to happen. He had to get his hands on the loose atomic bomb at all costs.

As Schultz eagerly awaited the return of Russell to Kinshasa, he poured over mountains of intelligence data sent from Langley. For the last year, he could not pry information out of the large intelligence repositories and teams of analysts. Ever since Schultz gave the code word "*Broken Arrow*" that meant a loose atomic weapon on a classified report, he had more than enough assistance. In fact, a team from Langley went wheels up a few hours ago and they were on their way. Schultz did not ask for the additional CIA operatives, however it was not his choice. A U.S. Navy aircraft carrier that already steamed around the Cape of Good Hope and had arrived off the coast. The floating island settled into a hold pattern over the horizon, about sixty miles from Kinshasa. A team of Navy SEALs would arrive in thirty minutes by helicopter. Schultz knew if he requested an air strike that it would generate a lot of angst at the Pentagon and the UN Headquarters in New York. However at this point, Schultz was prepared to go all out in order to destroy this loose atomic weapon. Schultz was not surprised the classified phone rang. It had been ringing non-stop for the last forty-eight hours. Schultz had moved into his office. The stakes were high and he slept very little.

"Are you certain?" Schultz responded to the caller. "How did you test?" The caller on the other end was silent. "How do you know the dead man was Kamal Abdullah?" He doubted the information provided.

Deep in the Congo bush, Rajik drove all night. He was too paranoid to drive with the headlights and his decision slowed the pace substantially. Over the past two days, he moved the bomb nine times. The constant night driving and few hours of sleep had taken a severe toll in Rajik's senses. He became more and more paranoid that he was being watched. Even worse, Rajik feared the bomb leaked radiation and he kept a far distance. The hangar was cleared of all aircraft. No one was allowed inside. A dozen Ashbals walked around outside carrying AK47s. Rajik looked in the middle of the hangar. He stood forty feet away from the cobalt wrapped atomic bomb that would soon change the world order.

CHAPTER 26

Schultz stood outside of the air traffic control tower as the C-130 parked. Russell gave him a quick glance from the co-pilot seat and waved. Russell concluded that it must not be good if the Chief of Station was coming to meet him. The expression on Schultz's face gave away his unpleasant feeling as he saw the ragtag group depart the aircraft. The female Israeli Mossad agent had several weapons hanging off her. The old retired CIA agent Elsie, who was a Russian defector, had four large suitcases that gave the impression they were moving out. Harry hobbled on a cane. Jabes was out of uniform. And Russell came off the transport carrying several long weapons that looked like former Soviet sniper rifles. The arriving passengers from Lubumbashi looked battered.

It was one of those moments that Schultz thought someone sure had a heck of a lot of explaining to do. But, first Schultz needed to get them out of view and into a secured location. He motioned to the embassy's van driver to snatch them off of the flight line before they entered the airport terminal. Several UN officers from Ghana were not pleased when Schultz showed his UN credentials for clearance. The Ghanaians tried to peer into the back of the van. Schultz leaned his foot from the passenger side and stepped hard on top of the driver's foot that launched the vehicle forward. The Ghanaians pulled their pistols and shouted, but they did not fire. Schultz knew two things about the Ghanaian officers; one, they are always taking orders from someone else and two, they are horrible shots. Schultz knew the flight line was being watched and someone would want to know about the team from Lubumbashi. Schultz directed the van to what looked like an abandoned warehouse. The van beeped the horn and several guards came outside. They scanned up and down the deserted factory row street and opened the large metal door. The van made several turns inside and came to rest in a lighted area. Schultz directed everyone out and to the open door. As they exited, Russell looked at a dozen men dressed in black nondescript uniforms. Russell instinctively knew they were Navy SEALs. Six large wooden containers were broken open and stacks of military gear, a small aperture communication link, several large caliber mounted machineguns, sniper rifles, Uzi sub-machineguns, various pistols, a small stack of knives, and piles of all sorts of ammunition. The men, who were previously busy organizing and checking the gear, took a moment to eye the team that they heard so much about. Russell knew by their look that they were professionals.

Francesca wore a tight fitted safari outfit along with a large brimmed hat. She looked all the part of a tourist as she entered the hangar. Russell turned as he heard the female voice.

"Well hello boys." Francesca said. "Are we having fun yet?" Francesca looked at the Navy SEALs after she caught their attention. She puckered her seductive lips at one of them and blew a kiss with her hand. In her other hand, she carried her Desert Eagle massive pistol. Francesca knew how to make an entrance.

"Does anyone have a clue where the bomb is?" Schultz inquired. Russell sensed he was pissed. Everyone looked towards Russell.

"Rajik has it." Russell looked at Schultz. He pointed to several points on the map. "Rajik moved the bomb several days ago before we could mount an assault. We know an Iranian scientist manufactured some type of trigger for the bomb."

"I took out the Iranian scientist." Francesca said as everyone turned towards her. Russell bit his tight lip to conceal his anger. She never mentioned her escapades to him. "The trigger is for a high altitude aerial burst. The bomb's wrapped in a cobalt sheet to enhance radiological fallout."

"More importantly," Kitson inquired as he looked at the others. "What's it being used for?"

"The sketched altitude maps highlighted an area of Cape Town." Francesca said.

"South Africa?" Schultz asked. Francesca nodded. He continued, "Why there. Why not New York or Tel Aviv?"

"For one thing, too far to get away with stealing an aircraft." Russell jumped in. "The only way to get close enough is by pilot and aircraft authentication. Control measures are very tight since 9/11. Any hijacked plane would be shot out of the air."

"And the area that they marked is in the vicinity of one of the world's largest diamond districts." Francesca offered.

221

"Are you certain?" Kitson inquired.

"The bomb had been programmed to detonate nearly directly over top of the eight buildings in a six block area that comprises the largest diamond district in Africa. Cape Town does possess the fourth largest diamond syndicate in the world." Francesca handed Russell a background sheet that listed Cape Town after London, Brussels, and her beloved Tel Aviv. Russell knew the stakes were extremely high.

"Radiological contamination would collapse the world's diamond market." Russell said. He looked at the map and the prevailing wind directions. "It would take a lot of effort to clean up, perhaps decades."

"And Mugabe is sitting on about twenty billion dollars in rough, untraceable diamonds," chimed Kitson with a level of disgust in his voice. For a second time in his life, he became embroiled in the affairs of Zimbabwe, formerly known as Rhodesia.

"We need to move fast." Schultz asked the SEAL Team commander into the room for the final mission brief.

"Who do we take out first?" Russell asked. "Between Al Qaeda, Rajik, Dietger, Gertz, the GROM thugs, we have a lot to handle."

"What about the North Koreans?" Schultz asked.

"No longer a problem," Russell said, "except for one really pissed off North Korean with me for killing his boss."

"They were probably lovers." Francesca joked. Everyone did not get her bad sense of humor.

"We need to hit them hard with everything we got," Kitson slammed his hand on the table. "We have come too far to let this dangerous weapon get away from us. We have to kill and we have to kill fast." No one had a comment. After a long extended moment, Kitson added, "of course, if they surrender that is fine too."

The scene in Kinshasa remained chaotic as rebels launched another attack. The rebel Colonel, backed by Gertz, was back with more child soldiers. Gertz funneled more money towards the insurgency as more instability meant the UN focused more on the rebels. Gertz believed the UN would become so preoccupied with rebels that he could smuggle several containers of uranium out of the country. Gertz locked his office.

He turned the light back on and went back inside to check the safe again. For the fifth time in a day, he changed the code. He became more paranoid. He started to talk to himself more and more as he isolated himself. None of the foreign staff wanted to be near him. The Congolese maids and cooks that were allowed into his apartment stayed in the corners out of view. They knew his temper, his violent tendencies and did not want to be sacrificed to quell his rage. Gertz would not eat any of the food or drink without one of the cooks testing the meal in front of him. He kept a pistol in his waistband; more for show, as he really did not know how to fire a weapon.

Gertz could not get out of the Nakor Industry compound. Throngs of local protestors marched in the street on their way to the UN mission's headquarters. Kimba Lumumba led the way and was surrounded by thirty personnel bodyguards. The stream of protestors stretched over a mile in length. Thousands of Congolese joined in the march that started peacefully and rapidly became an unruly mob. Store windows were broken and Congolese were stealing from one another. Several daring thieves scaled the Nakor fence and were shot by GROM snipers on the rooftop. A big gap emerged in the protestor's ranks as bodies fell from the fence. Within seconds, the gaps would be filled by even more protesters pushed against the fence. The front gate was blocked. Braum stepped out of the front passenger seat and drew his submachine gun from under his jacket. Braum unscrewed the silencer from the end of the barrel and loaded a full magazine. He fired into the air, which caused far more chaos to an already troubling situation. Dozens tried to run away but could not get out of the way and were subsequently trampled. Braum loaded another magazine and fired into the air. More chaos ensued and the weaker protesters were pushed out of the way with many falling to the ground. A massive crushing wave of bodies pressed outward. Braum thought about firing directly into the crowd, yet he knew the UN would want an investigation if any of the protestors outside of the Nakor compound were shot. Gertz smiled.

Across the street Kitson watched the motorcade of four Nakor SUVs drive through the crowd; at some points running over bodies on the ground. He shook his head in disbelief. Kitson called Kimba and thanked him for the diversion and expressed his sorrow for the injured Congolese in the protest march.

Dietger Laurent looked out across his large estate along the Congo River. He had a gun in his right hand. He never felt so threatened. His Congo had changed. Everything had changed. For the past fifty-two years, he witnessed momentous events. He sat ringside for the Ali versus Frazier 'Rumble in the Jungle' championship boxing match. He drank tea every Sunday afternoon with former President Mobutu after they played croquet. He spat in the face of a beaten Patrice Lumumba and paid three Belgian officers handsomely to execute him. Dietger spied for both the Americans and Soviets. He traded uranium on the black market for decades. And he now had a weapon of mass destruction pointed at five million people over diamonds. Dietger walked back inside and placed the pistol on the desk. He continued his conversation with Galpin.

"You'll never be the same after killing so many."

"Those bastards can die in hell." Galpin spat on the ground.

"Many whites will do as well." Dietger offered. He wanted to ensure that they would carry out the mission.

"So what of it. They had succumbed to Apartheid and relished in the blacks taking power. I would just assume to destroy them all."

"You can take that bag as payment." Galpin pointed to the large sack of forty large, uncut rough diamonds worth over ten million dollars on the black market.

"You can keep your blood diamonds. We're not going to need them." Galpin said. It never occurred to Dietger that the South African brother's idea about parachuting out of the airplane and safely getting away might have been insane. Dietger looked at their facial expressions and knew that Galpin and Krause had signed up for a suicide mission.

"Is there anyone in your family that you want payment to go to?"

"No. All dead." Galpin said pointedly. Galpin was finally getting his revenge.

Around the table in the executive suite of the top floor of the Intercontinental Hotel, General Tretiak looked at his comrades, men who violently supported the KGB and the Soviet doctrine. The large bodyguards were former Spetsnaz, Russian military Special Forces. They showed no emotion. They were lethal killers. The Russian Military Brotherhood existed on paper as the retirement community for former KGB officers. A more sinister organization named Voctrad emerged out of the Russian Military Brotherhood, led by General Tretiak. The men seated around Tretiak's table all previously held senior officer ranks within the KGB. These men were betrayed in their ideology when the Soviet Union collapsed. For each of them, the quest for power and prestige never subsided. In fact, their quest grew larger to prove a point to the Americans and the rest of the world.

"Let the Americans chase after this atomic bomb." Tretiak began. "They'll never see what will hit them. Our new partnership with Al Qaeda goes beyond Islamic fundamentalism. It is of mutual interest." The former Soviet General who commanded over eighty thousand men posed to overrun West Berlin slammed his fist on the table. "Before I die, we will witness the demise of the American capitalistic empire." Tretiak pounded his first again on the table. The men seated close to him clapped loudly. He continued, "We will change the outcome of the Congo election. If Kimba Lumumba is elected, he will eliminate corruption. We cannot allow him to become the next Congo President. Worse, he now has strong ties with the Americans."

"We should take him out before the election," the heavy set former KGB propaganda officer said, "We cannot afford to have a runoff election and some surrogate of Kimba getting enough votes." Tretiak nodded and looked over to his best sniper. The man knew he had another high priority assassination mission. His skills were in high demand in Africa.

"What of the Israeli agent?" One of the KGB Colonels asked. "Should we have her killed?"

"No, not yet." Tretiak said. "We may be able to use her as a pawn with the Israelis war on Hezbollah." Tretiak did not mind questions. It showed him that his men understood the circumstances. Tretiak knew the CIA and MI6 would put a price on his head once word leaked of their mission. Tretiak trusted his men and had their complete loyalty. However, he did not trust Al Qaeda and especially not trust Kamal Abdullah. If Kamal double crossed him, Tretiak wanted to make sure

Voctrad would survive far past his own death. Tretiak was impressed by the loyalty of his men. These men were born out of the Soviet collapse and improved their skills. While many disgruntled former KGB and military officers drank their way into depression, Tretiak and his hand selected group prospered.

"What of the Chinese?" Another inquired. "If they get their hands on Zimbabwe diamonds, they will control a major stake in the black market." Everyone at the table had been briefed on the Chinese named Wun and his meeting in Zambia with President Mugabe. Zimbabwe had more rough diamonds than anywhere in the world, yet they could not bring them to market based upon their restrictions imposed under the Kimberley Process.

"Wun is stupid and careless. He will be easy to destroy. The British have already infiltrated his headquarters in Hong Kong." The men around the table were surprised. Each knew that Tretiak had deeply embedded intelligence sources around the world. Even in his self-imposed exile out of Russia, Tretiak maintained close ties to his brother-in-law Vladimir Putin. Tretiak continued. "The Chinese appetite for diamonds will be their own downfall. They are becoming more and more like the fat, greedy Americans. Once we control the world's diamonds, we will make the Chinese pay premium prices and eliminate all of their blood diamond sources." Tretiak had reliable information that the Chinese were heavily involved in smuggling rough, untraceable diamonds out of Liberia. Tretiak continued his discussion. "The Belgians and Gertz are the only others who pose a threat to Voctrad's control of the diamond market. I have secretly passed information to my former advisory at the CIA. Let the Americans and British destroy them. Voctrad will emerge as the world's most dominant diamond cartel."

"And Mugabe?"

"Our longtime friend has seen his last days in power." Tretiak said. Each of them knew that their boss just provided the authorization to assassinate President Mugabe. "With a new Zimbabwe government, we will have better success selling rough diamonds on the world market. We have already begun preparations building a rebel army to destabilize Mugabe." Tretiak pulled out a map and laid it across the table. He pointed to rebel camp locations along the northern border with Zambia and in close proximity to Victoria Falls. "Once the rebel army is strong enough, we will take out Mugabe with a single bullet. We have the Minister of Defense on payroll and he will make sure the vaults at the Central Bank are looted in the chaos. Our men will take possession of the diamonds and fly them out of Africa to our base of operations in Cuba. Once we corner the both the legal and black market for diamonds, we will see our alliance with Al Qaeda destroy the Americans. Voctrad will emerge out of the ashes as the most powerful syndicate history has ever seen. Voctrad will rule the world!" Tretiak raised his fist in the air and pumped his chest violently. The men who were previously seated jumped to their feet and chanted loudly, "Voctrad, Voctrad, Voctrad!" Each of them pumped their fists as well. Tretiak smiled widely as his sinister plan that had been twenty-two years in the making had finally started to arrive.

Deep within the UN compound in Kinshasa, the Congo Minister of Information enjoyed the plush comfort of his private room. The conditions of the ordinary prisons were deplorable for a man of such stature as the Minister to temporarily reside in. The senior UN general placed him under arrest within UN headquarters building. The Minister remarked to several of the UN soldiers who guarded him how he could get used his new plush surroundings. UN leadership did not know what to do with him. Many within the Congo government wanted to prosecute him and hang him. The UN Secretary General wanted the Minister to receive a fair trial. He knew with the election just days away that the incumbent president would quickly execute one of his own Ministers to highlight how he was cracking down on corruption within his government. The door slowly opened and the Minister assumed it was the evening meal. Braum took a strand of piano wire and pulled it across his throat. The Minister of Information choked violently as he lifted his hand against the wire to no prevail.

Chapter 27

Kitson was easy to spot from across the street with his oversized safari hat. The signal was old fashioned for Russell, yet he obliged and yielded to Kitson's experience. Kitson blended in with the crowd of foreigners. Russell watched for the target. Dietger Laurent walked out into the open and headed towards his car. Francesca watched closely from her spot on top of the adjacent building's fifth floor roof. The trigger device rested next to her. The red button waited for her decision. It had to look real. Francesca pressed the button and the explosion engulfed Dietger's armored vehicle. Windows blasted out of the vehicle and sent a shock wave across the street. The force of the explosion knocked Dietger on his back. His black Mercedes sedan lifted off the ground eight feet and it bounced on the ground in fire. Francesca snapped two rounds into the right leg of Dietger's bodyguard. Dietger looked around and saw his own means of safety was to remain close to the ground. The over-weight Belgian wobbled back and forth using his legs. Russell thought Dietger looked more like a large walrus. Dietger got to the corner of the building and raised his body with all of his strength. Blubber bounced off his mid-section. He started running down an alley. He panted heavily and his face was blistered red in color. Russell had no trouble catching up to him. As he approached Dietger, Russell jumped in the air and stuck both of his feet against the fat man's back. Dietger tumbled over face first into the street.

"Don't shoot." He panted heavily. "I'm just a businessman."

"You're scum." Russell pointed the pistol at Dietger's head.

"You can't shoot me. I am unarmed."

"Wrong." Russell shot Dietger in his right thigh. Blood oozed out and rolled over his blubbery leg. Dietger screamed in agony. Jabes turned the van down the alley and slammed on the brakes. Jabes helped Russell load the fat Belgian into the van. Dietger moaned in pain. Russell was tired of the complaining and smacked him over the head with the butt of his pistol. The force knocked Dietger unconscious. Russell checked the wound he just inflicted. He placed a bandage over Dietger's head and next focused on the gunshot wound. Russell did not have any guilt for inflicting the bodily harm, yet he felt some kind of remorse as this scum was now his prisoner. Right or wrong, he still needed to turn Dietger over to the proper authorities for trial.

News of the attack on a prominent Belgian businessman in Kinshasa quickly spread among the international community. Many of the foreigners had not felt safe for days and many wanted out of the Congo. Rumors circulated at a hastened pace. Word became more and more conflicting as gossip prevailed. Some believed that Dietger was assassinated. Others thought he was kidnapped for ransom. Still others hoped their patriarch escaped. Many of the Belgian businessmen went to the Intercontinental Hotel bar to grieve. As nighttime set in Kinshasa, many foreigners huddled at the bar out of fear. Leaders in the Belgian community were extremely scared. Several initiated their emergency evacuation plans and took everything that they could carry in their arms to waiting speed boats – destination away from the Congo chaos.

In Francesca's safe house, Dietger awoke abruptly after the smelling salts were placed under his nostrils. The instant scent of ammonia shocked his obese body into action. His large arms flailed and legs kicked. Russell thought he looked more like a turtle than the walrus. Dietger could not see as a blindfold covered his eyes. He was in a chair and felt the restraints around his arms and legs.

"Who are you?" Dietger asked. "Where am I?" Dietger waited for a response for more than a minute. He thought about what could be happening and continued, "I have money."

"Save your money. It will do you any good here." Kitson looked at Schultz and nodded. A blast of electric shock vibrated the chair and sent Dietger into convulsions. He screamed in agony. Schultz switched the connection to off. The wire led towards four large truck batteries in the corner that he had Tshambe swiped from a UN construction site.

"Stop...stop. I said that I have money." He screamed in agony; "whatever you want."

"Again, I said your money is no good here." Kitson nodded and Schultz zapped him again. The screams became louder.

"You're British. I can tell from you accent. Are you MI6? SAS? Who are you?"

"Someone who takes the sale of stolen nuclear warheads very seriously?" Kitson motioned to Schultz to help him. They pushed the chair backwards and rested it on the floor.

"What are you doing?"

"Tell me where the bomb is."

"I don't know. I never heard of a bomb. What bomb?"

"You are the main conspirator to detonate an atomic warhead over South Africa."

"Absurd. I want my lawyer."

"You will not face trial, but what you will face is death if you do not tell me." Kitson said as he held the water hose nozzle several inches from Dietger's face. As he gulped in large volumes of water, he tried numerous times to catch his breath. Dietger felt like he was drowning. Kitson was exceptionally trained and experienced in administering a controlled drowning.

"Wait...wait." Dietger had a hard time briefing. His sedentary lifestyle made him gasp for air. "No more...no more."

"Where's the bomb?"

"Hezbollah. It was all Hezbollah. They will bomb Tel Aviv."

"Are you certain?" Kitson asked

"Gertz paid them off. He wants to control the diamond market."

"You're sure the target is Tel Aviv?" Kitson sensed that Dietger lied about the destination target. He tilted the chair backwards and splashed water back into Dietger's face. He turned up the pressure on the hose line and forced the water into his mouth. Dietger panted heavily.

"Where is the bomb?" Kitson asked again. "Tell me and the pain will stop." Kitson tilted the chair back upright. "Do you understand?" Kitson heard the deep and heavy breathes from the overweight man.

"You can't stop them." Dietger softly said. "You can't stop them. No one can stop them. They are committed."

"Who is committed? Who has the bomb?"

"You will never stop them." Dietger rambled on the same sentence again and again for over a minute. Kitson knew the interrogation had extended beyond the limits. He knew that without the answers to his questions, an atomic bomb would be detonated over a city, thereby potentially murdering over a million innocent civilians. Kitson thought back to his extensive interrogation training he had with MI6. Also, he thought of his ethical stance as a career military officer. He remembered the interrogation he conducted in Belfast Northern Ireland so many years before. He was fortunate to obtain the bombers intended target before they attacked on Christmas day 1984. Kitson knew the stakes were high. He looked at his prisoner. Dietger was severely obese and panted heavily. The man was beyond exhaustion. Kitson thought the man was having a heart attack. Kitson needed to keep him alive for a few more minutes.

"You have a chance to do right for all of the wrong you and the other Belgians committed in the Congo." Kitson whispered into Dietger's ear. "If you unleash this weapon on the world, there will be untold repercussions." For a brief moment, Kitson was patient. "Whatever riches and glory you expected, they are all gone now."

"Others. There are others who will benefit." Dietger whispered. He sounded incoherent. Kitson knew that he was dying. "It is not my fault." Dietger pleaded, "I am just a simple businessman."

"Who else is involved?" Kitson added. "Is Voctrad?"

"Yes, the KGB. It must be them." Dietger lied again and Kitson knew instinctively that they only way to complete the interrogation was to become brutal. Kitson sprang into action and violently turned flipped the chair backwards and pushed the water hose into Dietger's face.

"Where is the bomb?" Kitson screamed. "Where is the bomb?" Kitson pulled the hose away from Dietger's face and heard something inaudible. Again Kitson listened. In a very faint voice, he repeated the word "Goma" several times. Within seconds, Dietger choked hard and his body stiffened. Kitson attempted to revive the obese Belgian, but to avail. Dietger Laurent, who was the patriarch of the Belgian community in the Congo, died from a massive heart attack.

In the dark Kinshasa night, Russell and Francesca commenced their attack on Nakor Industry headquarters. The glider was relatively silent and Russell could see the top of the building. He pulled the flaps and cut the small fifteen horsepower engine. The baffles from the exhaust pipe were removed and replaced with an advance technology silencer. Still,

Russell did not want to risk exposure to the guards on the ground. Over three hundred feet in the air, Russell and Francesca silently glided towards the Nakor headquarters. Schultz told him not to expect roof top motion sensors, yet Russell did not want to take a chance and aimed the glider towards the large satellite dish. Francesca looked at him in disbelief. However, she knew it was probably the right decision. At this time of night, Nakor was empty and no one would miss the satellite link. They both lifted their legs up and tried to absorb the impact into the metal dish but it still hurt as the glider's weight added to the force of impact. "Shit that hurt." Russell whispered as he rolled. She smiled at him with her megawatt smile. Even in the darkness, her gorgeous teeth showed bright.

Francesca rappelled off the side of the building while Russell held the other end. She tied off the rope outside the office window and placed the centrifugal glass cutter on the plate glass window. The five inch diameter suction cup rapidly attached to the window and the diamond point cutter quickly cut through the two inch plate glass. She slid through the three foot hole and shot two darts into the ceiling. Francesca fed the rope through grappling hooks attached to her waist belt and pulled her body into the office. She flipped down the infrared goggles on her head and observed multiple crisscrossing laser lines a foot off the floor and horizontally across the wall behind the large mahogany desk. She shot another dart into the left corner of the room and shot another one into the right corner of the room.

As Francesca slowly moved towards the wall by pulling the rope, she kept her body coiled tightly like a snake. From the ceiling she placed four extended tubes and positioned the mirrors to reflect the motion detector lasers. The experienced covert agent knew the painting that Gertz hid the safe behind had a motion detector release alarm installed. Any movement of the picture frame outward would initiate the alarm. She took out the hand laser and cut out the painting from the frame that exposed the safe. The digits on the cipher lock were settled back at zero. The keypad was the size and type she expected. She placed the cipher decoding apparatus over top of the keypad and initiated the gadget. Eight digit numbers blasted by in random formats and it took four minutes to break the code. Francesca found the hard drive enclosed in the protective box. She found several folders, stacks of gold coins, and several hundred thousand dollars in cash. She guessed the added weight would be around thirty pounds and the ropes should hold her. She reached inside of her jacket and she pulled out the German Nazi artifact. She placed it inside. Russell waited patiently. He knew the building had electro-magnetic detection and they would not be able to use voice transmitters. He was pleased to see her pull outside of the window. Within a minute she was on the roof.

"Are we good?" Russell asked.

"Yes, I left him a little present." Russell looked at her with suspicion as he thought presents for Mossad were usually attached to C4 explosive. "A swastika that my ancestors kept after being liberated from the concentration camp." Francesca replied. Russell thought for a moment and then realized that it was better to blame the South Africans. Any amount of deception would be beneficial to them. Once Gertz discovered his exposure, he would rapidly move to search for his stolen computer hard drive.

"We are going to plan B for departure." Russell pointed towards the glider he crashed into the satellite dish. "Are you ok with that?"

"It's a breeze." Francesca said as she turned and ran towards the edge of the roof. Russell followed. They both leaped ten feet outwards to the open nighttime space and fell. As they accelerated, each pulled the metal rings on the chest harness and the rectangle black parachutes opened. The specially designed chutes took in the updraft air and slowed their rapid descent. The pull down toggles helped to move them away from the building's compound and toward the waiting dump truck. Tshambe finished his cigarette and stamped it out with his foot. In doing so gave the all clear signal. Russell landed in the soft sand first. A second later, Francesca crashed on top of him and accidently kneed him in the groin. Russell moaned and rolled over in pain.

"Sorry," Francesca said. Russell could not respond. He was in agonizing pain. Francesca smiled at her old lover's misfortune.

Tshambe accelerated the dump truck down the street. After two hours of driving, they arrived at the safe house. Elsie waited up with a bottle of wine opened and already had a few glasses. Francesca and Elsie sat around talking about the mission and laughing like a couple of school girls. Elsie was quite amazed at all of the new technology the Mossad spy used. Russell went to work on the hard drive and gave up in ten minutes after he could not break the entry code. He reviewed several of the files and knew that they had Gertz for illegal weapons smuggling, selling uranium to terrorists and unauthorized governments, and transporting illicit blood diamonds. Russell did not look up as Francesca passed him and went into the bathroom. He heard the shower and ten minutes later she emerged. Francesca wore a silky black nightgown with a high leg cut on the right side. She twirled around for a quick dance and asked, "Do you like?" Russell nodded.

"I'm glad that you think so," Francesca replied. "Glad you have come to your senses about us."

"What about us?" Russell asked.

"I don't know." Francesca could not look him in the eyes. "I have to leave Africa."

"Do you have another assignment?" Russell thought quickly and followed with, "as if you could tell me."

"No, I need to take care of some health issues."

"Were you injured?" Russell knew that she would never tell him if she got hit by a bullet during the GROM raid. Russell sensed she was not telling him everything. He sensed stillness in the air, a defining point in their relationship. He knew someday it would come that he or she needed to make a decision on how to proceed. Last time in Liberia, she left him with a dear John note saying don't come find me, we can never be type of notice. He had no clue or idea to expect what was going to come out of her mouth. She pushed Russell onto the bed and straddled him with both of her legs. She held both of her hands under his chin; forcibly to get his attention. When she knew that she indeed had his attention, she dropped the hammer.

"No mister CIA man," Francesca looked at Russell with an expressionless face and continued. "I'm pregnant."

CHAPTER 28

Russell paced heavily back and forth. He needed to focus. The task at hand would be difficult. Russell puffed heavily on the fat Cuban cigar Schultz provided. The memento was for the after mission celebration, but Russell needed a quick enjoyment as he prepared to enter yet again another combat mission. He could not get Francesca's last words out of his head. His former lover was pregnant. Russell did not dare ask if he was indeed the father. A question like that could have resulted in a bullet to the back of the head. He cursed Francesca, her dad, and himself for falling under the spell of her seductive ways. Russell looked at the SEALs while they loaded weapons and ammunition crates into the helicopters. One of the SEALs closest to him looked up with a peculiar stare. Russell realized that he mumbled aloud. He stopped and climbed towards the back of the cargo helicopter. The UN did not have any attack helicopters as their mission was humanitarian versus combat. Russell looked inside the wooden crates that possessed all types of missile launchers, machineguns, grenades, and ammunition. Russell looked down at the cigar in his hand and eyed the sizeable amount of explosive material next to him. Quickly, he crushed the cigar with a boot.

The four large UN transport helicopters were on fast approach at tree top level. When Galpin heard the sound, he ran out of the hangar. He could not tell which direction the noise was coming from. He shouted to Krause and pointed towards the attack helicopter resting idle on the launch pad. Krause ran across the flight line towards the Russian built KA50 Black Shark. It was an archaic machine from the Soviet days. It possessed counter-rotating blades. The aircraft was over twenty-five years old and poorly taken care of. Gertz purchased the machine on the black market and Rajik had it shipped into the Congo. Krause could not get the four rocket pods operational but he could fire the guns. Krause began preflight checks and started the engines, which would take almost eight minutes.

From the cockpit, Russell watched Jabes navigate in formation behind the other three helicopters. Russell slapped Jabes on the back and went back into the rear of the helicopter. Russell borrowed a black nondescript uniform to match the SEAL Team. His head raced with thoughts about Francesca's pregnancy. They had not been romantic in three months. He wondered what she thought. However, he knew better not to inquire with a somewhat psychotic, heavily armed, and deadly trained Mossad agent. He remembered the note Francesca left after she departed Liberia, *"Don't try to find me, it cannot be, we cannot be."* Russell had to get his head clear. He looked over at the two SEALs and saw them talking into their microphones. Russell switched on his headset and transmitted sound checks. The raid site was five minutes out.

Galpin ran back towards the hangar and got on the back of a pickup truck that had a fifty caliber machinegun bolted onto the chassis. Galpin yelled to some of the Ashbals to fight. They ran inside to get weapons. The young boys returned and fired indiscriminately into the air at the unseen sound. Rajik emerged and yelled at them to stop shooting. The first two helicopters appeared over top of the trees and Galpin unleashed a barrage of fire from the large caliber machinegun. The helicopters banked to the right.

"We're taking fire. Pull back to the right. Tango 3 and 4 come up towards the left side of the airstrip." The garbled sound in the headset caught Russell's immediate attention. Russell looked at the SEALs as they quickly sprang into action. One of them pulled out a long sniper rifle and clipped on a high powered scope. The fifty caliber sniper rifle was extremely accurate up to two thousand meters and carried a ten round clip. The second SEAL spoke into the microphone and asked Jabes to hover. He held a long range spotting scope to his right eye.

"Eighteen hundred meters." The spotter hollered over the sound of the aircraft engine. "Right two five degrees, wind left fifteen miles, elevation three point five degrees."

"Roger," replied the sniper.

Galpin had pressed the weapon's trigger so hard his entire hand hurt. He felt the vibration of the gun that nearly shook all of the rust off the old pickup. He did not pay attention to the window as it shattered. He kept firing at the two UN white helicopters as they banked away from the airstrip. He lined up the sights and fired more. He saw a puff of black smoke come out of the back of the second one.

"Up half a degree," The spotter yelled. In a split second, the sniper fired his weapon. Galpin collapsed as his entire rib cage exploded.

The small fast attack Russian helicopter that resembled a black spot to Jabes lifted off. The object accelerated faster than Jabes thought any helicopter possibly could. Krause looked down to see his older brother lying flat against the truck. Blood covered his entire torso. He pressed the throttle forward and initiated the weapon's trigger. Jabes knew instantly that it was an attack helicopter and banked the UN helicopter to the right as rounds flew past to the left. Several rounds cut into the metal skin. A warning light illuminated for a fuel leak. He knew several more rounds could ignite the dripping fuel and the helicopter would explode. The two SEALs helped each other patch up their wounds as both were struck by metal from the helicopter's exterior as the rounds blasted the hull apart. Russell ran to the front.

"Jabes, how are you doing?"

"The fuel tank was hit. We're going down." Jabes snapped.

"How long?" Russell asked.

"Don't know, two, maybe three minutes." Jabes said as he jerked the stick as more rounds raced past. More warning lights ignited the counsel. "We are going down." Jabes switched frequencies. "Mayday...mayday."

Russell put the headset back on and ran towards the back. He looked at the weapons in the crates. Immediately, he dismissed the AK47s and submachine guns. The rounds would only bounce off a fast approaching, heavily armored helicopter. Perhaps, he could get a shot into the pilot's windshield but the round would still not penetrate it. He needed something more powerful. The only remaining item that he could use was the anti-tank missile. He picked up one that looked like a relic. The manufacturer date stated 1984 and it was stored in the humid conditions of Africa. He did not have time to think about the shelf life of the weapon. He pulled the red safety tag and opened the retractable sites. He had one chance.

"Jabes," Russell shouted. "When I tell you, bank hard left and keep it steady."

"What are you going to do?"

"Take out the aggressors." Russell said nonchalantly.

"How?" Jabes injected.

"You don't want to know." Jabes looked concerned. Russell continued, "As a warning, you will experience a heat wave coming up towards you, just keep it steady."

"Roger," Jabes replied with suspicion in his voice.
Russell aligned the sites with the fast approaching attack helicopter. Krause fired again and tore into the rear tail section. Krause passed overhead. He pushed the yoke forward and came back around.

"Bank left now." Russell yelled. Jabes twisted the frame into a left turn. The rotors shifted and barely obliged.

As Krause came out of the turn and moved left, Russell lined up the sights for a direct shot. He pressed the red button that ignited the propellant. A large after blast of heat rose up the back of Russell's neck. He kept the weapon straight even with the fireball. He did not want the last split second of shaking rattle his only missile shot. Krause had no time to react. He never thought he would receive fire from the unarmed aircraft. The explosive projectile struck the attack helicopter straight onward. From the distance Russell saw the projectile rip into the windshield. The explosion erupted into a larger one as the fuel tank burst into a fireball. The overhead rotors continued to turn as the attack helicopter started to descend, slowly at first. Within three seconds, it descended more rapidly. Russell smiled widely as he saw the attack helicopter fall out of the sky.

"Jabes," Russell shouted. "You ok?"

"Ok." His response was quick and he followed up with a brief update. "Still losing fuel."

Russell was pleased that the heat from the missile launch did not ignite any of the fuel spilling out from the rear of the aircraft. Fortunately, the fuel splintered into the air randomly away from them.

"Where can we land?" Russell said as he ran into the cockpit.

"Not much here." Jabes said as he glanced out the cockpit.

"How much longer do we have?" Russell inquired again.

"Thirty seconds...tops."

Russell pointed and shouted. "There, bank right. Five hundred feet is a spot." Jabes looked quizzically at the direction of Russell's finger. "That church." Jabes rested the smoking helicopter on the large grass field. Russell assisted the banged up SEALs get on their feet.

In Kinshasa's port complex, Francesca, Schultz, and Kitson spread out and moved across the twenty acre container holding area. Large cranes moved back and forth. Each lifted the oversized forty foot containers. The holding area was vast as more and more commerce grew. Containers were stacked all over. The volume was too immense for even a trained eye to find illegal contraband. Tshambe wore coveralls and easily passed as a dock worker. Tshambe walked back and forth several times checking the numbers on the containers. As he turned the corner inside the maze of large containers stacked three in height, he was apprehended by Rajik's Ashbals. A gun was placed against his head. He grimaced as he made a prayer, but before he was shot, Francesca blew the head off the Ashbal with her high powered sniper rifle. The muffled sound from the sniper's silencer did not reveal her position. The four other Ashbals fired in her general direction. As several bullets from the AK47s ripped all around her, she remained concealed. She fired several more shots and eliminated four Ashbals. Several more came running out of the warehouse and fired randomly in the air. They were surprised by the concussion sound of a truck blast a large hole in the fence. Elsie sped directly at them. As they turned and fired at the truck, Harry unloaded an Uzi sub-machinegun in their direction striking several of them multiple times. Within moments the area was secured. Schultz tested his radiological meter on the container. The needle nearly burst out of the dial from the high level of radiation. Schultz slammed satellite tracking devices on the containers and dialed the number for the UN Secretary General's office in New York. He was done dealing with the local UN leadership who proved incompetent.

Francesca spotted Gertz run towards his vehicle. He was alone, without protection and ran for his life. Like a lioness on the prowl, she jumped from container to container twenty five feet above the ground. She hurled her body across a six foot gap and barely made the distance. She rolled on top of the container and got back on her feet. She had kept pace with Gertz as he ran as hard as he could. She saw the end of the row of containers and did not have an option. With the might of a lioness in final attack, she launched high above and landed on Gertz back. The knife she had in her hand penetrated his chest so hard that she could not retrieve it. She pulled another one from the sheath on her left ankle and sliced Gertz's throat open. He choked on blood for a moment and fell to the ground. She cut off one of his index fingers and sealed it in a plastic forensics bag for transport to Tel Aviv. She wanted to make sure Mossad headquarters knew she got her man. She did not wait to say farewell to the others and bolted for another safe house before UN security arrived.

Back at the embassy, Russell and Schultz sat on the veranda that overlooked Kinshasa. Russell relayed the assault story and how they were rescued. Schultz briefed him that the atomic weapon was already on its way to a US aircraft carrier floating off-shore. The past twenty-four days since Russell arrived had been intense.

"You did one hell of a job here." Schultz said.

"Does the Ambassador want me gone?" Russell inquired.

"Who cares, he is on his way out. So are a majority of the UN's leadership here."

"Good, let's finally get some people in here who want to make a difference instead of getting paid off and plundering the Congo's mineral wealth." Russell remarked.

"Langley discovered the Ambassador and a few others in the White House had connections with the diamond cartels. This is not over yet." Schultz was adamant.

"That would not surprise me."

"You know the mission is not over yet. We need to get Rajik and find out who are his contacts in Beirut, Syria, and Tehran. Someone large was behind this plot." Schultz conjectured.

"Got it." Russell said. "Don't kill him until we get information." Schultz liked the sound of that and smiled.

"War is hell." Kitson said as he walked onto the patio and raised his drink in the air for a toast. Russell and Schultz lifted as well and finished off their gin and tonics

On the television, Russell saw photos from the Minister of Information's arrest. The news station reported that he had been killed while in UN custody. The newscast showed a previous clip of the Minister speaking several months ago. "We know Congo is fertile territory for terrorist recruitment. We have a huge country with huge jungle where people can do anything and we don't know anything about it. So many people bring dirty money to Congo." The reporter shifted towards the Presidential election and Kimba spoke. "Foreigners are stealing our resources and killing those who oppose them. Vote for me as I will stand against them."

Russell walked back outside on the balcony. Tires burned close to the embassy wall. The apocalyptic scene raged throughout the Congo. Russell thought of the Book of Revelation and what appeared to Russell resembled the end of the world. The 30 July presidential election was only days away and in anticipation, violence erupted throughout Kinshasa. Russell had read the CIA reports on the presidential election. No one gave Kimba much of a chance to win the election and worse chances at surviving more assassination attempts. Many more senior Congolese nuclear officials had been arrested for their involvement in illicit uranium exports. According to CIA accounts, the Commissioner General for Atomic Energy and the Head of the Center for Nuclear Studies were involved in Gertz's plot to illegally export uranium ore. Both were arrested and sent to The Hague for trial.

Russell packed his gear and even wrote a letter for Francesca. Part of him was shocked that he was going to be a father and the other part was joyful. He knew once her father found out that he would have a big Mossad target on his chest. Russell carried the letter in a sealed envelope and handed it to Schultz. The outside only had Lieutenant Colonel Francesca Waszey, IDF. Russell had no address. He had no concept of where she lived either in Israeli or anywhere else in the world. He asked Schultz to mail it to Mossad headquarters, Tel Aviv in a diplomatic pouch. He went back onto to the balcony and finished his fourth gin and tonic.

Russell looked at the CIA's file on Patrice Lumumba. In his inauguration speech on 30 June 1960, Lumumba stated, *"We have known that the law was never the same for whites and blacks, for it made special concessions to the former, and was cruel and inhuman to the latter."* Director, CIA expressed, *"the political leader against whom President Eisenhower expressed the liveliest dislike was not Castro but an African named Patrice Lumumba."* Several notes were made in the margins by the 1960 Chief of Station, Larry Devlin. *"Asked to drug and kill Lumumba; refused Dulles request. Awaiting my ticket out of the Congo."* Russell read more of the classified report. The U.S. was extremely interested in denying the Soviets a monopoly control of the world's cobalt supplies. Belgium government sent 1,200 paratroopers to reinforce the 2,500 soldiers already stationed at two bases: Kitona near Leopoldville and Kamina in Katanga. Belgium forces intervened and restored order but at a cost of over ten thousand Congolese dead. UN resolution 143 called upon Belgium to withdraw its troops.

Over the next thirty years, the Congo became mired in an abusive, corrupt dictatorial government after Colonel Mobutu seized power in a second military coup in 1965. Ultimately the Russians were defeated by capitalism, and the Congo was a small blip in the Cold War. Russell read the last reported words spoken by Patrice Lumumba: *"Freedom is the ideal for throughout history...throughout centuries, men have fought and died."* Perhaps the timing of the assassination was coincidental as President Kennedy was inaugurated three days after Lumumba's death. Ironically, the incoming Kennedy administration made hints at diplomatically engaging Lumumba.

Rajik remained far away from his compound along the Congo River. He had stashed four large bags of untraceable diamonds. As he dug up the bags of rough diamonds, he saw a bright flash of light. Half a mile down the river, an Israeli missile destroyed the Ashbal camp and killed the one hundred and sixty Lebanese orphans. Rajik dug faster. He needed to get out of the Congo. He pointed the boat up the Congo River towards Uganda. He knew if he entered Uganda that he could move north and meet up with Joseph Kony and get refuge. Rajik had sold Kony thousands of weapons for their fight against the Uganda government. He also heard Sudan could possibly break into two and that would be grounds for a new war. Wherever war flourished, Rajik had found a bountiful market to traffic his weapons.

CHAPTER 29

The chaos that Russell witnessed the past few months almost drove him insane. Wherever he went, the smell of death overpowered him. Dead bodies were found every morning. Violent crime surged. The rebels infiltrated Kinshasa and murdered many peaceful Congolese. The uptick in the horrific actions conducted by death squads shocked everyone. Russell tried to comprehend the history and current state of affairs. He needed to get some air after spending five hours writing his after action report. Russell took one last drive around Kinshasa. He did not plan to come back again; ever in his lifetime. He stopped at the Kinshasa sports stadium. Decay and vegetation had overtaken the buildings. Russell recalled vividly a documentary about one of the world's greatest boxing matches: Joe Lewis versus Mohammad Ali. Mobutu guaranteed to pay each professional boxer five million dollars from Zaire's treasury to fight in Kinshasa. The 1974 'Rumble in the Jungle' boxing match of Lewis and Ali was momentous for Mobutu. Now, goats lived in the stadium. Russell walked back to his car and was deep in thought. He did not notice the large man who hid behind a large concrete pillar. Braum waited patiently. Russell walked back to his vehicle and closed the door when the assault started.

Braum forced his foot through the driver's side window. The glass shattered and Braum pulled Russell by his shirt collar out of the vehicle. His massive hands were affixed around Russell's neck. Braum lifted Russell ten inches in the air with a choke hold. "Not just yet," Braum said. He launched Russell onto the pavement. "I will kill you slowly and with much pain." The Polish soldier had a thick accent, yet Russell understood clearly that this man wanted him dead.

Russell coughed heavily and spat blood. "That's the best you got?" Russell said. He was on all fours trying to stand when he saw a large boot accelerating towards his midsection. Instinctively, he tried to block the kick. Regardless, the force lifted Russell up into the air and made him roll over. Again, Russell tried to stand. He spat more blood and believed several ribs were broken. Braum pulled out the eight inch serrated knife from a holster and charged at Russell in an overhand motion. Russell put his wrists together in a crisscross fashion and plunged his arms at the overhand swing. He caught Braum's arm underneath the knife and rolled his wrists overtop. Using his weight against Braum, Russell flipped the heavier, beastly man and at the same time cupped his hands over the sharp blade. In the shift of momentum, Russell ripped the knife from the gorilla's grasped hand. Russell's hands bled substantially.

Without contemplating how to beat the monster-sized man nearly twice his size, he threw the razor sharp knife with all of his might. Braum could not react fast enough. The serrated knife pierced Braum's massive chest and entered his right lung. Braum did not dislodge the knife. He closed the ten foot distance from Russell as he swung in a wild motion. Russell blocked head shots as he moved his hands left and right. Russell kicked the attacker's right leg to bring him down closer to his size. As Braum settled on his right knee, Russell crushed his palms against his ears. The concussion forced Braum into a natural reaction to lift his hands to protect his ears, which gave Russell the opening he needed. Russell clenched his right knuckles into a karate punch and he forcibly struck Braum's windpipe. Again, he struck the windpipe. Braum gasped for air as he rolled back and forth on the ground. His full movement was thwarted by the knife sticking out of his chest. Braum's tracheal was crushed. A wheezing sound fizzled out of his mouth. Russell knew no matter how massive the man, he had to breathe. Russell hobbled over to the gargantuan and pulled the knife out of Braum's chest. He saw his face grimace. Braum could not speak. Russell was too hurt to speak. He reached down with the knife and cut off the large Polish Special Forces soldier's ponytail. He did not know why he did it, perhaps to show Francesca he had won.

Schultz put down the New York Times when Russell hobbled into the US Embassy's coffee shop. Russell tossed the ponytail onto the table. At first, Schultz thought it was a dead rat and quickly realized the magnitude. He looked up to Russell who beamed with delight. It did not take long for the seasoned CIA operative to comprehend what happened.

"You've been busy?" Schultz remarked.

"You can say that." He poured the ice out of Schultz's empty scotch drink over his bruised knuckles. "He was one tough bastard."

"Good riddance."

"Yeah...good riddance."

"You might find this interesting." Schultz tossed a report onto the table. An internal UN investigation had found evidence that UN peacekeepers may have engaged in sexual exploitation and abuse in Congo, as stated by the UN Secretary General. African nations and the UN attended the Conference for Peace, Security, and Development in Goma, near the Rwanda border. The debate focused on granting amnesty to militants who are wanted for war crimes and crimes against humanity. Resolving the status of war criminals will continue to divide Africans. The UN pledged to send 5,000 more peacekeepers. The training of the Congo army would expand and those former members who were not war criminals would be allowed to return to former rank. Russell thought of the Congo. However, Russell again considered the historical context. In 1960, the Belgian Congo was thrust onto the world stage as the U.S. and the USSR bargained for political control. Now the Congo was again thrust onto the world stage after Africa's First World War that claimed nearly five million lives in a nine year period. Most of the civilized world missed the historical footnote to one of Africa's largest human tragedies. Russell concluded one conference was not going to do a damn thing to fix the Congo's chaos.

"We didn't accomplish a damn thing here." Russell was furious. "For every corrupt official or bad guy we take out, more will follow."

"I never pegged you as a cynic."

"Getting my head beat in repeatedly and shot at all of the time made me question a lot of this mission. We took out some real bad apples, but somehow I just wonder if this place will get better."

"The Congolese came out of thirty years of a brutal dictatorship under Mobutu and they had been brutalized by the Belgians for a hundred years." Schultz responded. "Change will be hard to bring about."

"It disgusts me how so many became wealthy at the expense of the average Congolese who live in filth." Russell became loud. Several career diplomats looked over to the table. Russell did not care. "What the hell are America's goals in the Congo?" He added. "Do we even have any capable aid organizations here to help these people?"

"We've eliminated a lot of bad people. Everything we have accomplished has been a step in the right direction, sometimes small steps add up." Schultz leaned over close so others would not hear. "Fortunately, my assessment of the Ambassador's capability during this chaos got him fired."

"He's out?" Russell asked.

"Next flight; should be within an hour." Schultz poured himself another stiff drink. "You need to prepare for the next mission." Schultz said and added. "Kitson is waiting for us in the vault. Inside of the CIA's Chief of Station's vault, Schultz put together a top notched analysis. Schultz pointed the set of maps of Uganda, Sudan, and the northern Congo region where Russell would operate. Across the walls were aerial photographs, intelligence summaries, dossiers on corrupt Ugandan government officials, and the location of a suspected Al Qaeda terrorist training compound. "Operations in Uganda will be just as chaotic as what you witnessed here."

"We need to get our hands on Rajik." Russell closed the note and handed it back to Schultz to shred. "If he sold weapons to Kony, he probably took refuge deep in the Congo, close to Uganda."

"Rajik will be hard to get to if he is with Kony." Kitson said. Everyone knew Kony had a very loyal army who would die for him."

"If you follow the flow of blood diamonds, you should be able to find Rajik." Schultz stated. "Rajik's camp was destroyed by the Israelis."

"The Mossad has been busy." Russell said as he looked at the UN photos of the destroyed Ashbal camp.

"Rajik probably has a stash of rough diamonds to bribe his way out to the Congo." Schultz showed Russell several photos of Asian men. "The Chinese are buying up most of the rough diamonds on the black market." Schultz pointed. "Here are the ones you need to watch."

"What about Kamal?" Russell asked. The UN report was corrected to show Kamal had not been killed. Schultz never trusted the validity of the UN report.

"We got a satellite image of a once abandoned terrorist training camp in the rugged mountains along the border of Uganda and Sudan. Facial recognition showed Kamal. Some desk analysts in Langley believe that Kamal resumed operations." Schultz was not pleased Kamal had escaped Kinshasa. Schultz thought for a moment and added. "There must be some cataclysmic terrorist event on the horizon."

"If he is in Uganda, we'll find him." Russell said pointedly.

"It's a big country." Schultz said and added. "And the Sudan is even bigger."

"We'll have to do some recruiting." Russell said. "Let me see if MI6 can send some support as well. The British have just as much interest to capture or kill Rajik."

Later in the day, Russell sat on the back sat on the back ramp of the C-17 U.S. Air Force transport jet. Sunset was thirty minutes away. His mission called for a nighttime insertion. Russell thought for several moments as he watched one of the most beautiful sunsets across the African landscape. Russell thought of his future with the CIA. Russell thought of the two women who loved him and wanted to walk away from both. He looked at the crumpled note from the Director, Central Intelligence Agency. 'All roads in Africa lead to the Congo. Your efforts helped restore faith and belief in the Congo and all Africa'. Russell knew that once he transferred over to the CIA - they had him for life. He still needed to attend the coveted CIA Farm for operative training. However, he had one more mission before he made the leap.

"We'll have to recruit some help." Russell said. "After this next mission, I cannot wait to get back to the Seattle Mountains to climb."

"You call that relaxation?" Kitson injected. "How about cold gin and tonics on a fishing boat?"

"Sorry to burst your bubble," Schultz looked at Russell, "But you still have to go to the farm." By the look on Russell's face, he sensed Russell was not pleased about more training. Schultz continued, "Seriously, you have to go. Everyone does." A vehicle from the airport security detail raced across the tarmac. Elsie jumped out of the front passenger seat while Harry slowly pulled himself out of the back seat with the assistance of a cane.

"I'm glad to catch you before you left." Elsie said. She handed Russell a box of homemade cookies. "I made you a few treats for your journey." Russell looked bewildered as this lady who could be anyone's grandmother, but also deadly can sometimes be the sweetest person. Everyone thanked her.

"I told her not to fuss." Harry said as he slowly approached. "Your flight should only be two hours, but still she wanted to make something as a farewell gesture."

"Hopefully we will see you again."

"Not in Africa," Harry replied. "We received news today that there is a price tag on both our heads. It appears we need to watch Voctrad more closely."

"I heard Voctrad was a bunch of fat KGB men who cannot give up losing the Cold War." Russell replied sarcastically.

"You better watch out or they will make you a mark as well." Elsie warned.

"Don't worry. I can take care of myself."

"Really," replied Kitson. "Francesca is not around anymore to watch your back." Everyone had a good laugh at Russell's expense. He was not amused. Everyone shook hands and bid farewell. Elsie gave Russell a big hug and whispered in his ear, "Welcome to the company."

Russell looked in the back of Harry's vehicle and waved to Kimba Lumumba. The African American bodyguard sat next to Kimba. Russell heard the soldier assigned to protect Kimba was one of the best. Kimba opened the vehicle's door slowly. He did not know if he should be there. Harry brought him along, even after Kimba stated that he should not be there. Kimba wanted to distance himself from the foreigners. However, Kimba knew that he needed the Americans to keep him alive until the Presidential election.

"How are your chances?" Russell asked Kimba as he shook his hands. The Democratic Republic of the Congo's Presidential election was on 30 July 2006 and just three days away.

"Good." Kimba said, "I think we have a good chance to win."

"Everyone will win when you're elected." Russell heard the American embassy's assessment that Kimba was very popular and had a large lead over the incumbent President who was deemed very corrupt. "Your nation needs to heal."

"Our past keeps pulling us back into chaos. We must look to the future." Kimba said. Russell was impressed with how much Kimba had changed his tone. "Our future will be tied to the progress America and others bring."

"And not the Belgians."

"Unfortunately, we will always have to deal with the Belgians. They have a stranglehold on our diamond mines." Kimba said

"At least Dietger Laurent will not be bothering you." Kitson said.

"There will be repercussions from the Belgians." Kimba stated in a bold manner. "There are always repercussions from our former colonial masters. They use brutal tactics and no one is safe."

"If you need us, just send word." Russell offered. "We will come back to help get your nation on track."

"We have already won," Kimba whispered into Russell's ear as he embraced him. Russell and Kitson waved farewell as Harry and Elsie drove away with Kimba, who wanted to be the next leader of the Congo.

Francesca resisted every urge to shoot Russell when she walked towards the aircraft. Russell had repeatedly refused her advances and wanted nothing to do with her. Francesca's instincts told her to forget about Russell; however, she was in love with the American agent. Francesca's father knew something was wrong when she called him. Her father had the natural instinct and perception to identify the inflection in Francesca's voice as she lied to him. Her father was informed by a close friend who had contacts in Liberia that his only daughter had a romantic relationship with an American CIA agent. Francesca knew that the outcome of the relationship would destroy her Mossad career, yet she feared her father's wrath far more.

"I thought you left." Russell said as he saw his old flame walk towards the aircraft.

"Tonight." Francesca said. She looked back towards the runway to watch the EL AL Gulfstream jet land at Kinshasa International Airport. "That should be my plane now."

"I'll miss you." Russell did not know what to say. He was horrible at saying farewell. The moment was awkward and quiet. Russell felt obliged to break the silence. "You did well here. Hopefully, we made a difference."

"Why don't you love me?" Francesca blurted out. "I am carrying your child, yet you still do not love me."

"I barely know you." Russell said. "For the first weeks of our relationship in Liberia you lied to me. I had no idea you were a Mossad agent." Russell had no clue of Francesca's true identity for a long time. Her cover story working with Doctors Without Borders proved solid. It was until Russell found her safe house and a badly beaten Hezbollah operative she had interrogated to death. With Francesca, Russell did not know what to believe. He would not trust her.

"Don't be so melodramatic." Francesca smiled with her bright shining teeth. She tried to seduce him yet again. "When we are together in Tel Aviv with our child, everything will be alright."

"Are you insane?" Russell blurted. "I'm a CIA officer and you're Mossad. It cannot work. Our two governments will make sure that it does not work."

"And what of our child?"

"For the sake of that baby, you should send it far away from either of us." Russell was blunt. "Our advisories will find that baby and use it against both of us." Francesca did not like Russell's opinion. Her smile rapidly turned to a frown and she really wanted to put that bullet in Russell's head. She wanted to keep the baby, regardless. "We're not meant to be. You said that in the note you left Liberia."

"That was before I knew that I was in love with you."

"It will not work. It cannot work." Russell pleaded with her. "You know as well as I do that in our business any leverage someone has on you can jeopardize the mission. This baby, our baby, will be a target."

"Perhaps, but I'm a good teacher." The deadly female Mossad agent responded.

"You're keeping the baby?" Russell was shocked as she totally ignored his advice.

"Yes, I am. And I am keeping you Tom Russell." Francesca said. She was not about to accept no as an answer. She loved him and now she would stalk him across the world if she had to.

"Did you not understand what I said?" Russell replied. He had enough. He had another high priority mission that would start in a few hours. He did not need this distraction.

"You can do whatever you want with your CIA. We will be in Tel Aviv waiting for you." Francesca refused to listen and thought of a blissful future. "We will have a nice small apartment and we can go for nice walks in the evening. Our family vacations along the Red Sea will be wonderful. We will make a very nice family."

Russell sensed that Francesca must have turned more psychotic in the past few days. He thought about how to handle the situation. He knew that she was armed and would readily put a bullet in his head if she was cornered. He needed to get away from her, far away. Perhaps, her hormones were in overdrive with the pregnancy. Perhaps, she really loved him and would not accept no. Perhaps, she did not want to face her father alone. Perhaps, Francesca needed to have the baby as a counter balance to her Mossad lifestyle. Russell concluded that she was by far the most insane former girlfriend that he ever had. Russell needed to get rid of her. He needed to focus on the upcoming mission. He needed to tell her something that would keep her content. The only thing he thought of was lie to her.

"I'll be there for the birth of our child." Russell lied.

"Don't say it unless you mean it." Francesca wanted to hear the words. She was frightened for the child's safety and knew she would be vulnerable to attack.

"Our religions are different, but we can make it work." Russell gave Francesca a strong hug and kissed her farewell. The aircraft engines started.

"Come to Tel Aviv once you are done in Africa." Francesca pleaded as she waved farewell.

"I will." Russell lied again.

CHAPTER 30

After a long absence from his family, Tshambe was finally able to go home. At first, he did not know if anyone was there. He knocked on the sealed aged wooden door. There was no answer. He knocked on the two windows boarded up with scraps of plywood. Shards of glass were still in the empty window frame. Years before, he had a nice view of the street from his home. Maybe someday he thought his neighborhood would be peaceful enough to have glass windows again. As he turned to go ask a neighbor about his family, the door slowly opened. His family had not seen daylight for eight days and shielded their eyes with their hands. His children ran to his waiting arms. Tshambe was finally home.

The street outside Tshambe's home was vibrant with over a five thousand marchers who protested against the wave of violence that brought Kinshasa into chaos. Tshambe's family held off their celebration to join the political rally. In front of the protesting Congolese was Presidential candidate Kimba Lumumba who was flanked by five African American soldiers. These men volunteered for the assignment and were committed to keep Kimba alive. The 2006 Democratic Republic of the Congo Presidential election would be in a few short days. The future of the Congo was at stake. Kimba Lumumba had surged in the polls. Crowds flocked to hear him speak. Kimba's policies frightened many of the current Congo Ministers who enjoyed the plush lifestyle that corruption and bribes helped to generate. Many foreign businessmen were shocked to hear Kimba adopt the policy of his assassinated grandfather, Patrice Lumumba, to get the non-Congolese out of his country. Many in the Belgian community wanted Kimba dead. However, they would not be the ones who pulled the trigger.

In one of the abandoned buildings that littered Kinshasa's landscape, a sniper from the elite Russian Special Forces unit, adjusted the scope on his rifle. His last assassination attempt on Kimba had failed. Previously, the assassin had used an AK47 that had a busted rear site post used for aiming. He would not make the same mistake. Voctrad had a special sniper rifle flown into the Congo. The assassin trained his eye onto Kimba's head and squeezed the trigger. Several hundred feet away, Kimba waved to the crowd as his head blew apart. His hand lingered in the air as his body crumpled underneath him. The American protection service scrambled to the limp body. The bullet had immense impact and blood flowed. No one would be able to save Kimba Lumumba's life. The former Spetsnaz sniper picked up the shell casing and left a beaten up AK47 in the open window. A van waited for the sniper. Inside, General Tretiak smiled as he knew his infamous organized crime syndicate of former KGB agents had just taken control of the Congo.

Francesca stood outside of Kinshasa's International Airport terminal building and waited for the Gulfstream jet marked EL AL to complete refueling. Her weapons were concealed as she bypassed Congo customs like many foreigners who entered the VIP area. Moreover, she knew the UN soldiers on duty would not dare inspect an Israeli officer's bag. It was a rare time she used her rank of Lieutenant Colonel, Israeli Defense Force. Francesca took a moment and ran her fingers over the necklace charm. It meant so much to her. It was her past. It was family. It was her pain. The small photo was the last one taken as a family before her mother was killed by a Hamas bomber. The ominous inscription, 'For lack of guidance a nation falls, but many advisers make victory sure.' tied her to the Mossad life at an early age.

Francesca did not know how she would explain her pregnancy to her father. She did not want to return to Tel Aviv and even thought of staying somewhere in Africa to have the baby. Her values would not allow her to take a life. She would have the child. Francesca knew her father would be at the airport when she landed and he would know instantly something happened with her. Anxiety resonated in her face. What worried her was not her father disowning her. What worried her was her father's belief that her mission in Liberia was compromised by an American and he wanted Tom Russell dead. Since her father was a senior Mossad operative, Francesca had a valid fear for the man she loved. Francesca thought again and again about what Russell had just told her. She punched the glass window and smashed it. She was mad as hell. She let her love of Russell cloud her senses. Russell had lied to her.

If he would not come to Tel Aviv, she would find him, wherever he was in Africa. Francesca watched as Russell's aircraft lifted off.

Francesca boarded the EL AL plane. Right before the pilot moved onto the taxiway, she ventured into the cabin. She placed her Desert Eagle fifty caliber cannon of a pistol against the pilot's head and smiled at the co-pilot. Both of the pilots were undercover Mossad and knew how deadly Francesca was. She reached into both of their airline bags and pulled out small revolvers. She asked if they had any more weapons and both produced knives that were hidden in sheathes attached to their calves underneath their trouser legs.

Francesca watched the pilots enter the new coordinates she had provided. He did not radio the change to the UN tower control, as required. The commercial jet cruised quickly to 20,000 feet. Uganda and the capital city of Entebbe were moments away. The last time an unannounced Israeli aircraft had arrived at Entebbe airport was on 4 July, 1976. After Palestinian terrorists hijacked an Air France jetliner and landed in Uganda, the despot ruler Idi Amin provided the terrorists sanctuary. As negotiations lingered, one hundred Israeli commandos flew over two thousand miles and landed unannounced. The rescue mission was a resounding success. The aftermath highlighted the point to many terrorists not to mess with Israel. As the Americans celebrated its two hundredth year of independence, the kidnapped Israelis held hostage and threatened a certain death celebrated their freedom. Francesca did not care what the Ugandan's or any others thought. She was going after the man she loved.

Russell and Kitson sat quietly in the loud C17 military transport aircraft. The flight path to Uganda took them south over Burundi and Rwanda. Russell thought hard about Francesca during the four hour flight. He wondered if he handled the situation with Francesca well. Russell looked at the maps again. He had memorized the map's coordinates, yet he wanted to look at the map again. He needed to get Francesca out of his mind. As the ramp door of the C17 military transport aircraft opened, Russell looked out to the open black abyss of African night. He stood still. He did not want to move any closer to the air crew. They had headsets on and worked the cargo. He did not and felt he would just get in the way. He moved his hands over the equipment on the front of his body. He felt the D-ring for the emergency parachute. On his right leg was an MP5 sub machine gun. On his chest he carried a 9 millimeter pistol. On his helmet, he wore night vision goggles. Russell waterproofed the equipment inside of the two packs at his feet which added to the weight. Inside the packs he had enough food, ammunition, and communication equipment for the operation, if it only lasted one week as Schultz professed.

Russell did not take any chances and to the front of him was a wooden crate loaded with extra supplies and sealed empty containers to help keep it afloat. Russell estimated the buoyancy needed to keep the two hundred pound crate afloat long enough for him to pull it out of the water. Several green lights ignited the aircraft cargo hold. The air crew pushed the ten foot zodiac boat outside the back of the aircraft. The green lights transitioned to red. In the darkness and from his distance, Russell could not see the three parachutes. He hoped the transmitters would work. The aircrew chief gave him thumbs up and Russell nodded concurrence, the mission was a go. The aircraft banked and the pilots circled back for the next run.

Russell contemplated the intelligence reports Schultz had shared with him on Al Qaeda operations in Africa. In every report, Kamal was at the top of the list. No one knew what he looked like, until now. Schultz searched for several days and found a surveillance camera that had a clear photo of Kamal's face. Russell had studied the face and made sure he memorized every facial feature. At the same meeting, Schultz had shared classified reports on Hezbollah gun running operations and Rajik was at the top of that list. Two men he despised and each awaited him. Russell instinctively knew word of a U.S. military aircraft landing in Kinshasa would quickly get out to the underground terrorist and smuggling networks. It would not take long for those on the CIA's most wanted list to find out where the aircraft was headed and who was onboard. The only possible covert insertion was a nighttime parachute drop near a friendly nation such as Uganda where Russell and Kitson could meet up with prearranged contacts. The only issue was getting into Uganda and Russell chose a wet jump for the operation. Lake Victoria was sizeable enough for a discreet operation to go unnoticed.

More importantly, Kitson had solid MI6 contacts in Uganda since it was a former British colony.

Russell changed the course of his thoughts for a moment. He wondered how his rescue team was doing in the Seattle Mountains. He saw a news report that stated a small plane carrying eight people on board disappeared in the deep wilderness. Even though it was summer in the mountains, most of the mountains were still capped in snow and the temperatures were below freezing at night. If there were survivors from the crash, injuries matched with hypothermia would kill them if his team did not get them in a few hours. He missed his team. He missed his life. Strangely, he missed Francesca, however difficult she made his existence. After all, Francesca would be the mother of his child.

The aircrew chief talked into his headset and the directed Russell and Kitson to pick up their equipment. Russell and Kitson hobbled forward. Each carried two hundred pounds of gear. The aircrew chief motioned for them to stop. He held up large black scuba flippers and pointed to their feet. Russell and Kitson would land in the water and needed the flippers. At thirty to fifty feet above the water, each man would release from the parachute and free fall into the water. If they got tangled in the parachutes, they would be pulled under water and to their deaths. Both had knives attached on their arms and legs, just in case. Russell turned on the night vision goggles. The infrared beacon on the zodiac would help him guide the parachute towards the boat. Kitson loaded up his gear. Russell helped him position the equipment across his chest. Kitson was not familiar with all of the new gear. Russell had explained the newly designed toggle parachute that they would use, yet Kitson longed for the old style he used in Rhodesia.

"I'm getting too old for this." Kitson spurted out. The British Colonel had served across the globe and happened to be one of the most highly decorated officers in her Majesty's Army.

"Never too old." Russell shouted back to his MI6 partner.

"For God and Queen," Kitson yelled as he walked out into the darkness. The green light remained lit and Tom Russell, a newly hired Central Intelligence Agency operative walked out of the back of the military aircraft. The rip cord attached to the parachute pulled the canvas outward and as the night air filled the open chute. The force vaulted Russell twenty feet back into the night's sky. The quietness of the night caught his senses and his mind erupted with potential thoughts of what could not go wrong. He calmed himself and enjoyed the clean moment of the parachute's descent. He was still over a thousand feet above the water. Lake Victoria was not far below as he slowly descended.

Tom Russell had left the chaos in the Congo and was on his way to Uganda. His mission orders were very direct. He had ten days to find the Hezbollah weapons smuggler, Rajik Nabee, and the Al Qaeda terrorist, Kamal Abdullah – two men Russell vowed to bring to justice or kill, preferably the latter. The clock had started. Terrorist cell chatter that originated out of Africa caused many in Langley to believe another terrorist attack on American soil was eminent and Russell had little time.

Read More of Tom Russell's Adventures

1: Madness in Liberia

In a fourteen-year span, one million were displaced and over 400,000 were killed out of a population of three million. Catastrophic civil war ripped apart Liberia, a nation formed by freed American slaves with the dream of a new beginning. The despot ruler, Charles Taylor is tossed out of power, yet his diabolical son attempts to wreak havoc. Rebels who remained loyal to Taylor prepared revenge while Hezbollah and Al Qaida operatives jockeyed for position to control the illicit pipeline flow of narcotics through Africa into Europe and eventually the United States. A small team of Americans joined by their British liaison were sent to collect information on Taylor's war crimes and quickly they became entrapped in a deadly game where there are no rules... only the madness that consumed Liberia.

2: Crisis in the Congo

3: The Ebola Odyssey

With his African expertise, Russell's was sent back to Liberia, a society ravaged by abject poverty and the horrors of a fourteen-year civil war. Where he must stop a plan by Hezbollah operatives to attack Tel Aviv with a weaponized Ebola virus. Russell uncovers a secretive group of former KGB officers, called *Voctrad*, which sold the Soviet Union 1960s-era Ebola weapon technology. With the help of his British liaison from MI6 and the mother of his child, an Israeli Mossad agent, Russell finds himself in a deadly match with *Voctrad*, Hezbollah, and an Al Qaeda terrorist cell intent on releasing the lethal virus. If they can't stop them, the virus will spread across the African content and probably the world, an unstoppable wildfire threatening millions of people. The operation has no room for error and Russell must focus on the mission at hand and forget about his son.

About the Author

WWW.ANTHONYCFABIANO.COM

Rising from the enlisted ranks to graduate from the U.S. Naval Academy, Anthony Fabiano retired from the U.S. Marine Corps as a Lieutenant Colonel after 26 years of distinguished military service. He served two tours in Iraq and traveled extensively throughout the Middle East including multiple trips to Afghanistan and Pakistan while assigned to United States Central Command. In January 2010, he led 54 U.S. military mentors into Liberia; the first ever joint team to do so and it became the premier mentoring program in Africa. They entered a nation brutalized by fourteen years of civil war that left over 400,000 dead and one million displaced out of an overall population of three million.

His real-world experience with counter-insurgency doctrine helped to transition the new Armed Forces of Liberia into a military organization that respects civil authority and the Rule of Law.

He has continued his study of Africa's most recent conflicts and the impact of child soldiers on the future stability of the region.

www.ingramcontent.com/pod-product-compliance
Lightning Source LLC
Chambersburg PA
CBHW070749280626
47162CB00018B/2800